DESPERATE
HIGHWAYS

Other Gabe Treloar Mystery Novels by John Maddox Roberts

The Ghosts of Saigon
A Typical American Town

DESPERATE HIGHWAYS

John Maddox Roberts

ST. MARTIN'S PRESS
New York

A THOMAS DUNNE BOOK.
An imprint of St. Martin's Press.

DESPERATE HIGHWAYS. Copyright © 1997 by John Maddox
Roberts. All rights reserved. Printed in the United States of
America. No part of this book may be used or reproduced
in any manner whatsoever without written permission except in the case of brief quotations embodied in critical articles or reviews. For information, address St. Martin's
Press, 175 Fifth Avenue, New York, N.Y. 10010.

Library of Congress Cataloging-in-Publication Data

Roberts, John Maddox.
    Desperate highways / John Maddox Roberts.—1st ed.
        p.   cm.
    "A Thomas Dunne book."
    ISBN 0-312-17176-5 (hardcover)
    I. Title.
PS3568.023874D4   1997
813'.54—dc21   97-18897   CIP

First Edition: November 1997

10 9 8 7 6 5 4 3 2 1

For my parents
Dotsey Scarborough Roberts
and
Charles Francis Roberts,
who set me on my first highway

And for my brother
Frank Roberts,
another Knight of the Road

One

I looked out the office window onto the grayness of Union Street, where a gust of wind blew dust and a few crumpled burger wrappers toward the pedestrian mall. Summer was winding down, autumn was coming on. Soon the leaves would be changing color. I was looking forward to it.

Brighton came in at 9:00 A.M. "What is it this morning?" He walked straight to the Mr. Coffee and poured himself a cup.

"Jamaican Blue Mountain." My major recreation these days was trying out new types of coffee.

"It's good. Don't get any more of that Hawaiian stuff with the macadamia nuts in it. Tastes like crap." Brighton is a retired Knoxville Police Department detective with a net of contacts built up over thirty years. Taking him on had been a major coup and made my work a whole lot easier.

"I like the Hawaiian stuff," Lorene yelled from her little reception office out front. She'd been another find; secretary and accountant for her husband's one-man insurance firm until he died and she sold the company, she was worth far more than I was paying her.

1

We spent the morning going over expense accounts before submitting them to the main office in Cleveland. Dull work, but unavoidable.

"Jesus, Gabe," Brighton said, yawning despite his third cup of coffee, "I thought PI work was supposed to mean gorgeous babes and action and suspense. When are the gorgeous babes gonna show up?"

"They come in at night," Lorene told him. "Gabe gets them all. If you worked later hours, maybe you'd get some of them, too."

For months we'd been handling routine work: divorce, employee pilferage, missing persons and runaways, all the stuff that takes up 90 percent of a PI's time. It was bread-and-butter work, it paid the bills, but more and more lately, I'd been sleepwalking through it. I was bored. I missed the street realities, the excitement and danger of real police work.

By noon we were debating where to go for lunch. Brighton and I were for Darryl's and some ribs; Lorene wanted to try a new Chinese place on Papermill Road. It was shaping up into the major controversy of the day when the phone rang and Lorene went to answer it.

"Gabe, Cleveland on the line."

I took it at my desk. "Treloar here."

"Gabe, it's Delilah. Something's come up and the boss-man is on his way down there. He wants you to meet him at the airport. Just you."

"Well—sure. I'll book him a room—"

"No, he's flying back tonight. He'll only be with you for about three hours."

What the hell? Randall Carson had visited the Knoxville office only a couple of times, announcing his visits weeks in advance and staying at least a couple of days each time.

"What's this all about?"

"I'm telling you all I can. Trust me, it's important."

"I guess it has to be. All right, I'll be there." I wrote down the flight info. Then I told the other two I wouldn't be having lunch with them and might not be back to the office that day.

"What's going on?" Brighton asked. Lorene was trying hard not to look curious.

"Damned if I know."

I still had a couple of hours before the flight arrived. I drove out to a little restaurant near the airport, and while I lingered over a salad and a club sandwich, I thought about my boss, Randall "Kit" Carson.

When I separated from the army in '70 and joined the LAPD, Kit was a veteran cop and a close friend of my partner, Murray. The two of them had taught me how to be a cop, watched out for me and made sure that I never had to learn the same lesson twice. Kit had retired from the department shortly after my wife died and I began the long, slow, ugly slide into alcoholism that ended with Murray's death and my hushed-up expulsion. Kit knew the whole story and offered me a job anyway, giving me plenty of time and leeway to put my life back together. I owed him big.

There was no mistaking Randall Carson when he came out of the boarding tunnel. He'd been recruited in the days after the Korean War, when the LAPD wanted them big and bulky. He'd been the Marine Corps heavyweight champion for two years, good enough to have made a top professional, but too smart to risk his quick mind in pro boxing's brain-damage factory. His suits were always rumpled two minutes after pressing and he always wore a hat, indoors or out. His face was like an old catcher's mitt and as he entered the concourse it wore, instead of the customary grin or scowl, an expression I'd never seen on it before: a deep, painful worry.

"Welcome to Knoxville, Kit," I said, sticking out my hand.

3

He took it and jerked his head in a perfunctory nod. "Gabe. This place got a bar?"

"It's an airport. Sure it has a bar."

"Show me where it is." He was carrying a beat-up old briefcase, the top-opening kind you don't see much anymore.

We went into the bar and he fidgeted while the waitress brought him his beer. Fidgeting was as alien to Randall Carson as his unaccustomed facial expression. When she was gone he drank half the beer and sat back, wiping foam off his upper lip. It seemed to settle him a little. I didn't try to urge him on. Finally he spoke. He didn't hedge, hint or beat around the bush.

"Gabe, Sibyl's disappeared."

Sibyl was his youngest child, a good fifteen years younger than the youngest of his three boys. I remembered her as a bright-eyed, lively little girl, a great favorite of my wife's. Rose and I never had children. I did some quick mental arithmetic. Sibyl would be about twenty-three now. Her mother had been dead for three or four years.

"Tell me what happened."

"Jeez, Gabe, what do I— Look, lemme give you a little background first. You last saw Sibyl she was, what, maybe twelve, thirteen?"

"Around there." She was already away at college when I went to work for Carson.

"Well, she was always a great student, got top marks in high school, National Merit scholarship, the works. She got her BA in sociology this spring, planning to go for an advanced degree in criminology. She's been taking summer courses, plus she had a part-time job at a blood lab that does AIDS research. This is a serious kid, Gabe. She's not some airhead who'd chuck four years of hard work for nothing."

4

"When did she disappear?"

"Four days ago. She didn't show up for class at Virginia Tech or for her job. It was my birthday, Gabe, and she didn't call. Sibyl always calls on my birthday. I phoned one of her friends, asked her to go check on Sibyl, see if she's okay. Soon as I learned she hadn't been seen in class, at work or at her apartment, I was on the first plane out.

"It was Friday morning when I got to Blacksburg. Her landlord let me into her apartment. It looked like she should be back any minute. Her papers were there, her makeup; she didn't even take her toothbrush. Her birth control pills were in the medicine chest, for chrissake! I ran the tape on her phone machine and she hadn't picked up any of her messages since Wednesday afternoon.

"I spent the day talking to her teachers and some friends and her supervisor where she works. Nobody could figure out why she took off. Didn't say a word to anybody."

There was something I hated to say, but I said it. "Kit, are you sure she took off?"

He glared at me bleakly. "You mean she might have been kidnapped, maybe snuffed?" He shook his head. "No, she ran, all right. I got a name from a couple of her friends, a guy she's been seeing. I checked up on him. He had a job selling used cars. His boss hadn't seen him since Tuesday afternoon. Friday was payday and he didn't show to collect his commissions. The owner was sorry to lose him, said he was the best salesman he'd ever had."

"You mean you think she *eloped?*"

"Shit, no! That'd piss me off, but it wouldn't scare me like this. It's who she ran off *with!*" He reached into the briefcase and pulled out a manila folder. I took it and opened it. Inside was a fairly thick file, including mug shots and rap sheet. This guy was not a model citizen.

"Nick Switzer," Carson said. "Scam artist, fence, B&E man, done hard time and spent his early days in juvie institutions."

"Jesus, no wonder he's good at selling used cars. How'd Sibyl get mixed up with a sleazeball like this?"

He closed his eyes and shook his head. "No idea. I found these in her apartment." He took out a pair of hardcover journals and put them on the table between us. "It's her diaries. Damnedest writing I ever saw. I can't make head nor tails of it. You were always the intellectual type, Gabe; maybe you can figure it out. But our boy Nick's name is in there a lot on the last pages." He wiped a big, meaty hand down his face.

"I'm asking you, Gabe: What makes a young woman with a great life ahead of her leave everything, even leave behind her diaries and her toothbrush and her birth control pills, and run like that?"

That much was easy. "Trouble. Big trouble."

"No shit. This fucker Nick Switzer's got my little girl into something awful. If I can't get her away from him quick, the best she's got to look forward to is a stretch of hard time and a ruined life." Now the tears leaked from the corners of his eyes. "She's my baby, Gabe. We had her years after we'd thought Marge couldn't have any more kids."

"You want me to find her." It wasn't a question.

"Everything I could find is in this satchel. There's also ten grand in cash for expense money."

"You don't want me using the company credit card?" Between us, there wasn't even a question that I wouldn't do it.

"This isn't a company investigation. This is personal. You need more money, just call me. If you have to get rough, there are some top lawyers who owe me big. I'm not fooling myself, Gabe. I know I'm too old for the kind of work this will take. You'll do what needs to be done." I knew what he meant. The ten thousand wasn't just for food, shelter and gas. It was for bribes, maybe hiring local muscle.

"I'll get right on it," I told him.

"I'll send someone down to cover for you at the office."

"Don't bother. Brighton and Lorene can handle it for the next few days. I'll tell them I'm called away by a family emergency. They won't believe it, but they're too smart to ask."

"Her car's nowhere to be found, so that's probably what they're driving. It's a white Grand Am, ninety-two, and the license number's with the stuff I'm giving you, but Switzer's probably got new plates on it by now."

He gave me several recent photos of Sibyl. "There's some credit card receipts in here," he said, patting the side of the briefcase. "I had to use some heavy leverage to get those as quick as I did. The last one's from day before yesterday, in Nashville. If any more come in, I'll fax them to you, but I'll be surprised if any do. Switzer must know better than to lay a paper trail."

"Unless he doesn't know she's using her card. Or maybe he figures by the time the receipts show up in her mailbox at the end of the month, the trail will be too cold to do anyone any good." I pondered for a minute. "No idea what it was that spooked Switzer? A guy with this record isn't likely to panic if the local cops come knocking on his door for some routine questioning."

"I ran a check on the area for a hundred-mile radius. In the seventy-two hours prior to their disappearance, there wasn't a major robbery or a serious crime of violence reported. Not so much as a convenience store stickup. Even for that area, it was an unusually quiet few days. I've hired a couple of local guys, top investigators. They're checking every lead they can find on Switzer, spreading word and money around. They'll find out what he's been into lately. As soon as I know, I'll pass it on to you."

If Switzer wasn't running from the police, he was probably running from somebody a whole lot worse, somebody who wouldn't read him his rights or see to it that he got a lawyer.

For the next hour or so we discussed the details of communications, mail drops, private phone numbers and so forth. There was no question that I would be skating close to the rim of illegality on this and I wanted to be covered from as many angles as possible. Carson had contacts and agreements with detective agencies all over the country. If I got busted I'd have a lawyer and a bondsman within the hour.

As I saw him onto his flight out, Carson took my hand for one last time. "Bring her back safe, Gabe." No promises of reward and eternal gratitude. None needed.

By the time I got back to the office, Brighton and Lorene had left for the evening. I fired up the computer and called up the clipping service. That is to say, I tapped the keys and cursed and fretted and got the service after a half hour of getting myself into blank, inescapable screens and turning the damned thing off and rebooting endlessly, if that's the correct term. Lorene could have done it in two minutes. My mind won't retain computer routines.

Eventually, I got the service on-line. It's like the old newspaper clipping services, collecting articles and reports from around the country, even worldwide, relevant to the subscriber's interests. I asked for reports of major crime—crimes of violence or those involving big money—for the entire Eastern United States for the week prior to Sibyl's disappearance. This particular service is used by a lot of police and detective agencies, and the data began appearing on the screen almost immediately. I spent ten minutes figuring out how to get the thing to print out hard copy, because I like to read at leisure, preferably in bed.

While the printer buzzed and clicked and spat out its product, I opened the office safe and pondered what to take along on this expedition. I ignored the guns. They were for special jobs in my own bailiwick. Guns can be an incredible hassle when you're crossing state lines, and I knew that, in the milieu where I'd be moving, I could count on being detained and questioned by local police. If the need should be pressing, Randall could get me one through one of his contacts. Or I could just stop at a local flea market, where guns are usually available, no questions asked. It's not as if guns are terribly hard to come by in America.

I took a nifty little weapon/tool called an Asp. It's a telescoping steel rod of extremely rugged construction. Closed, it's about eight inches long, compact enough to tuck into a pocket or beneath a belt. It flicks out to an extended length of twenty-one inches. It's not what you'd take to a gunfight, but man's first weapon was a stick and it can still be damned useful. As far as I knew it was still legal everywhere, despite its notoriety from having been employed on the knee of a prominent figure skater.

I took the keys for the car we used for stakeouts in the less prosperous parts of town. It was my old Pontiac, which I maintained in perfect mechanical condition, letting time have its way with the exterior. Its paint was faded and flaked, rusty around the edges, sporting innumerable dents and dings. Where I was headed it would be anonymous. Somehow, I didn't think I'd be parking it in the lots of any four-star restaurants.

I typed up a memo for Lorene, explaining that I had to take a couple of weeks off, that she and Brighton could take care of the office and I'd be in touch. She'd know perfectly well that Randall had me doing something questionable, but she'd go along with it.

I glanced at my watch. It was three hours earlier in L.A. I might still catch Connie in her office. I dialed, listened to the ring on the other end. "McInery Detective Agency. How may I help you?" McInery's is an all-woman agency, with an all-female clientele.

"This is Gabe Treloar calling from Knoxville. May I speak to Connie Armijo?"

"Oh, hello, Mr. Treloar. Connie's traveling with a client. She said if you called to tell you she'd get in touch as soon as she gets back. Can I take a message? She'll be checking in here."

"Oh. Yes, please tell her for me that I'm about to go on the road, too. We'll make connections—well, whenever. She can leave a message at my office if I'm not back by then."

"I'll be sure to tell her."

I hung up. Our relationship was like this most of the time: living a continent apart, communicating by messages, getting together every few months. We were both wary, cautious, too much life and experience behind us for easy commitment. That's for television. Connie and I didn't live our lives between the commercials. Nothing was going to be all wrapped up just as the end credits rolled.

By the time I'd made what preparations I was going to, the clipping file had grown depressingly thick. I took the pile of zigzag-folded sheets, turned off the office lights, locked up and headed home.

In my apartment I packed, not bothering to take much more than the bare necessities. I planned on an early start. I put the TV on a news channel, muted. I'd turn on the sound if it looked like something interesting or relevant was on. Then I lay down and looked over the printout. It wasn't nice reading.

Even though I'd requested only reports of criminal activity involving major violence or major money or both, it went on for page after page. The Eastern U.S. could generate an amazing amount of crime in a mere week. I began going over it with several different colors of Highlighter and a fat black felt-tip pen to mark off the items with little to no likelihood of relevancy.

Immediately, I began wielding the black marker liberally. Ghetto crime wouldn't appeal to a man like Switzer. He'd keep his distance from the places where his color would make him stand out. A man who lived on cons and scams would depend upon his plausibility. That alone reduced the list by more than half.

There were crimes listed that were almost certainly mob oriented. These I black-marked as well. Switzer wasn't connected.

There were five or six bank jobs in places as far separated as New York, Atlanta and Tallahassee. These I marked with pink Highlighter as just-barely-possibles. An equal number of jewelry store heists got yellow Highlighter as marginally-more-likelys. These jobs were pulled off by well-organized gangs, and that was what made them seem unlikely venues for Switzer. He usually operated alone, and armed robbers were almost always specialists, rarely straying into the sorts of activities Switzer was into.

One exception was a jewelry job in Washington, DC, that was almost certainly pulled by a single break-in man. Switzer had a history of B&E. I marked that one with green Highlighter as a likely prospect.

Near Virginia Beach a large drug transaction had been ambushed. There were drugs, loose bills and bodies all over the place. It may have involved millions in cash but, once again, this one involved a heavily armed, vicious gang and was probably mob connected to boot. I gave it a pink mark as a very outside possibility.

There were dozens of murders, mostly drug or gang connected. In Florida, five men had been lined up and shot in a back room of a bar. All the victims were Cuban. I marked that one off. In Charleston, South Carolina, four members of a neo-Nazi faction had been gunned down. Rival Nazis were suspected. Another black mark. In Richmond, Virginia, a well-known fence had been murdered and his safe rifled. I gave that one a green mark. Guys like Switzer knew plenty of people like that, and mutual treachery was an ever-present likelihood in their little world. There were a couple more possibles, but nothing that tickled my instincts.

I came to the end of the list all too aware that I was looking at the tip of the proverbial iceberg. These were just the splashiest, most heavily reported crimes. Kidnappings, cons, extortions and blackmailings usually went unreported, and that was the sort of activity that appealed to Nick Switzer.

It was going to mean flying blind, going out into the American vastness in search of a cunning, probably violent sociopath and the intelligent, highly educated woman who had, unaccountably, taken up with him. It was going to be dumb and dangerous and I actually wasted a few seconds questioning whether a man of my age, experience and intelligence had any business stepping off the deep end like this, no matter how big a debt I owed.

Who was I kidding? I hadn't looked forward to anything this much in years.

Two

From Knoxville to Nashville is an easy drive west on I-40, taking less than three hours even if you poke along below the speed limit. I enjoyed the cool of early morning as I pulled out of Knoxville into the rolling hill country that climbs slowly toward the Cumberland plateau. It was still green but fading fast, the abundant leaves bleached and withered by a nearly rainless summer of record-breaking heat.

I put the radio on a news station and gave half an ear to ominous rumblings of yet more war in the Balkans, financial crisis in Mexico, possible trade war with Japan, a hurricane looming off the East Coast, a whole horde of congressmen and political wannabes gibbering about the destruction of America's moral fiber and the imminent collapse of Western culture.

I wasn't paying much attention. I was thinking about Sibyl and women like her, and what makes them give up everything to follow worthless, amoral men.

You hear about them from time to time, when they make headlines: a woman attorney falls in love with a jailed client and smuggles him a gun, helps him escape, sacrifices a promising career and her future prospects, maybe her freedom, for a few weeks of hanging around cheap honky-tonks and dog-racing tracks with a semiliterate lout who's been too dumb to stay out of jail for six consecutive months in his adult life.

Or she's some other professional woman, maybe with a business, home and kids, who one day chucks it all and takes off with some low-level hoodlum, con artist or wanted felon. There had been a recent case near my home in which a highly respected physician lost her licence and barely escaped serious jail time for raiding her hospital's hard-drug supply to feed her lover's habit. He was a high school dropout and petty thief.

They aren't jaded heiresses or spoiled rich kids or the pathetic creatures who propose marriage to prisoners on death row. They're intelligent, highly educated, often extremely successful women. Of all the mysteries of the human heart, why they do it has always been to me one of the most opaque.

Maybe, I thought, it really isn't that much of a mystery. After all, wealthy, powerful men make fools of themselves over cheap bimbos all the time. But I've never equated wealth and power with intelligence, and besides, I *expect* men to act stupid where brain-gonad interaction is concerned. And the consequences are rarely as devastating.

I'd spent a long time the previous night studying the photos. The pictures of Sibyl showed a lovely young woman, her face framed by straight, dark hair, leveling an intent, brown-eyed gaze at the camera. In none of the pictures was she smiling. Words that came immediately to mind were: serious, demure, contained. She had a sheltered look, but there was nothing naive about her expression. She looked like a woman who knew her mind and held the world at arm's length.

The mug shots of Switzer didn't tell me much, not that I expected them to. Mug shots of Mother Teresa would make her look like a bull dyke concentration camp commandant. In the full-face shot he had the dead, marble-eyed gaze of the experienced con. The side shot revealed an unexpectedly fine profile, almost classical in its combination of high forehead and straight nose forming a single, sweeping line, delicately molded lips and firm chin. Carson had turned up some more casual pictures, possibly taken at parties.

It almost made me wish I'd been a Victorian. Then I could have seen "a face that bore the indelible stamp of base passions" or "the unmistakable lineaments of congenital villainy." They always seemed to be able to see such things back then. Instead, I just saw some pictures of a good-looking young guy.

One picture was different from the others. It was one that showed Sibyl and Switzer together, and it was an odd one. They stood side by side, looking straight at the camera, with no more interaction between them than Grant Wood's farm couple in "American Gothic." They were posed in front of an institutional-looking building, both wearing white lab coats, Sibyl holding a clipboard, Switzer's hands casually in his coat pockets, resembling a confident young doctor. His hair looked lighter than in the other pictures and a short, fair beard framed his jaw. Sibyl looked even more serious than usual, her eyes steady behind big-framed glasses. Most startling was the wig. It was blond, wavy and little more than shoulder-length. An expensive wig, too. I would never have spotted it as fake if I hadn't known what her real hair looked like. I took a magnifying glass to the photo and saw that she was wearing blue contacts.

Carson had clipped a note to the photo: *I have no idea what the wig and glasses are for. Sibyl's never worn glasses. Maybe they took this as a joke.* Yeah, maybe. I made a note to send back to Carson: *Check her credit card records for the wig and the contacts.*

Then I'd had a look at Sibyl's diaries. They were in

nice little leather-bound books with gold-leaf page edges and lined, off-white paper. She had beautifully legible handwriting and the earliest entries were typical schoolgirl stuff: the everyday trivia of classes and teachers, friends, dating, studies. I glanced over these and saw that, like most freshmen, she'd been awed by professors, thrilled at living on her own for the first time, smitten by various boys, whom she determinedly referred to as "men," at least until their immaturity showed through their cocky facades and she lost interest.

By her second year the novelty, predictably, had worn off and she realized that many of her professors were jerks, living on her own was lonely and college boys were boys. She settled in for the long, hard haul of getting an education. She landed a part-time job at the blood lab. The pay wasn't much as a lab assistant, but she took it very seriously, happy to be doing important work that could lead to a cure for AIDS.

By the third year an odd, detached tone began to dominate her diaries. The simple, declarative sentences, nearjournalistic reporting of daily events and naive, girlish introspection gave way to disoriented questionings of herself and her world. She lost precision and wandered from her previously solid grounding in reality, growing impressionistic, vague, almost unworldly. The entries from recent months approached a sort of free-floating blank verse.

I could see what had bothered Carson about this stuff. He probably suspected drugs at work. I had more education than my boss and I was pretty sure I detected the influence of twentieth-century poets and philosophers. If her philosophy classes had reached the existentialist-deconstructionist phase, it could explain a lot. College-level philosophy studies can be an intellectual minefield for a certain type of highly intelligent but unworldly stu-

16

dent. It's been that way since the Athenians made Socrates drink hemlock.

About three months before she bolted, Sibyl slid off onto an identity-crisis tangent:

> *I work in the school world, in the lab world, performing as precisely and as silently as a clock inside a glass dome. Daily, hour by hour my hands rotate, performing their functions, and all around me the drones of my life go through their quiet, repetitive motions.*
>
> *But dimly, distorted by the curvature of the glass, I can just see the vivid colors and the hard, purposeful motion of another world. Can the hands of a clock break its own glass?*

What I really need, I thought as I closed the last book, too tired to read further, is to go over this with a really good shrink.

It was still only late morning when I arrived on the outskirts of Nashville. As I reached the city limits I saw one of the most common yet most poignant sights of that city: sad-faced men and women standing beside cased guitars with their thumbs out, hitching a ride out of town. They'd had their try at country music fame and they were leaving, penniless and defeated. At least they hadn't pawned their instruments. Maybe they'd have another try after scuffling around in the local clubs for a few months, refining that surefire hit song until it was even better.

The credit card receipt was from a shop a couple of blocks off the interstate near the old town center, across from a vast old train station of baroque design, recently renovated to house offices and trendy restaurants. Gentrification strikes again.

The place was a fashion boutique for the C&W crowd,

featuring blue jeans in astounding variety, oddly striped shirts, belt buckles that would never make it through an airport metal detector, designer cowboy boots and wide-brimmed hats in several varieties, most of them very large and black. Women's outfits ran to a great deal of fringe. How the once-functional clothing of nineteenth-century gold miners and cattle herders became a fashion statement of the late twentieth century must constitute one of the strangest developments in the history of popular culture.

The saleslady who came to greet me wore white majorette boots and blue jeans tight enough to define her labia. "May I help you find something, sir?"

"I hope you can. I'm looking for a young woman who came in here a few days ago and bought some clothes."

She blinked, her eyelids flashing electric blue. "Oh, my. We get an awful lot of customers through here every day—" I held up one of the head-and-shoulders shots and she blinked blue flames again. "Oh, I remember her! She was just so pretty and had the sweetest voice. She wasn't like the customers we usually get."

"Most of your customers are local?"

"Oh, my God, no! We get tourists from all over the world. It's just that she was more . . . " She waved a scarlet-nailed hand, searching for a word.

"Cultured?" I hazarded.

"I guess that's what it was. You could tell how well educated she was, real soft-spoken, too."

"Was she alone?"

"No, she was with a man. He was helping her pick out clothes."

"This man?" I held up one of the party pictures.

She squinted at it. "I think that's him. Now, he was more like our usual customers. He knew just what he was looking for, picked out everything for her. Are they in some sort of trouble?"

"The young lady dropped out of school suddenly and disappeared. Her family is worried about her."

"Oh. Well, those two probably just took off together. I sort of took them for newlyweds. I mean, it's not like they couldn't keep their hands off each other, just . . . well, you know, lots of little touches and looks back and forth, that kind of thing."

"I know what you mean," I assured her. It didn't sound like she was under coercion, anyway. "What sort of clothes did they buy?"

"Nice things, nothing flashy like the tourists buy. Casual, but top quality."

"Did they say anything to indicate where they might be headed?"

"Oh, I don't think so. They talked about the outfits they were looking at, as I recall. It's not like I was eavesdropping or anything. You just have to pay attention to your customers." She gave it a moment's thought. "I guess they were headed somewhere cold."

"How's that?"

"They bought some real nice winter coats."

"Can you show me?" She guided me to a rack of overcoats, linen dusters and Aussie drover coats, most of them in the currently fashionable spaghetti-Western length, down to the ankles, some with half capes attached.

"These come in all weights," she explained. "I mean, people buy them just to go out line dancing, so they get the linen dusters, those hardly weigh anything, but the man bought one of these." She pulled out a drover's coat. "I forget which color, but it was one with the heavy lining. The lady got one of these." She took a long, ornate sheepskin coat from a rack. It had floral patterns embroidered on it in bright thread. "They're big sellers in places like Aspen and Santa Fe, but we don't sell many here because they're so warm." I took a look at the label: MADE IN CHINA.

The saleslady couldn't think of anything else that

might be useful. So I thanked her and walked out. On the sidewalk I studied the facade of the old train station and tried to plan my next move. A dark-brown Bronco pulled up by me, the driver a man in a pearl-gray Stetson, the passenger a thirtyish woman with short black hair and a fine-boned face. Her eyes were startling—brilliant green with black rims—and they studied me with the easy evaluation of a cobra sizing up lunch. She would have been strikingly pretty, but the levelness of her gaze and the straight set of her mouth were as cold and hard as porcelain. If you were the sort who picked up women in bars and you saw her sitting alone on a barstool, you might go for an approach, but you'd back off the second she turned and looked at you.

When she got out I saw that she was petite—barely five feet tall even in her high-heeled boots, dressed in black jeans and a short jacket with fringe down the sleeves and across the back. In studying her I almost didn't notice the man. He was wearing a hokey Western suit with a yoke over the shoulders. I judged him to be around fifty-five, once boxer-hard but gone a little jowly and paunchy. His face was nondescript but it tickled something in my memory banks. I got into my car as the two of them disappeared into the store I had just left.

As I pulled back onto the interstate, headed west, I remembered where I had seen him before and who he was. Abruptly, I went cold all over.

That evening, from my motel room in Memphis, I called Carson.

"You learn anything yet?" he asked without preamble.

"I'm going to take this in order. First, that picture of Sibyl and Switzer in lab coats—she's wearing blue contacts. See if you can find when she got the contacts and the wig."

"I'll get on it."

"Second, Switzer knows she used the credit card. He

20

was with her and they bought clothes for the two of them. It's protective coloration for the most part—C&W drag, invisible in truck stops and honky-tonks. And they're headed for someplace cold." I described the coats.

"That doesn't tell us much," he said. "Winter's on the way. It may mean we can rule out Mexico and southern California. And Switzer's a dickhead sociopath. You know how impulsive those guys are. The drover's coats are fashionable and it may've just caught his eye."

"Sibyl isn't and she got the sheepskin. They're headed west. Maybe it's the mountains or the high desert; that covers a lot of territory. But it suggests that they have a destination, they're not just wandering aimlessly."

"Yeah, maybe. Okay, give me the bad news." He'd known me a long time.

"Jasper Holt is after them, too."

There was silence on the other end. "Jasper Holt! Jesus Christ! Are you sure it's him?"

"I've seen him before. He went into the Western-wear place just a minute after I left it." I described the incident for him.

"Holt's a bounty hunter. There are no warrants out for Switzer; he hasn't skipped out on a bond lately. Who the hell's Holt working for?"

"Good question."

"This is not good, Gabe. Now he knows you're both after the same guy. That saleswoman must've told him you were just in asking. Do you think he made you?"

"He never glanced my way. But the woman might as well have taken my picture."

"Shit, shit, this isn't something I wanted to hear," he muttered. Then, "Holt's always been a lone wolf. Who's the woman?"

"No idea, but she's one hard-looking piece of work. Find out what Holt's been up to lately, if he's picked up a partner, anything you can get. I have a bad feeling about this."

"So do I. What's your next move?"

"Your pair have been heading west on I-40. According to Switzer's rap sheet, he was busted twice in Memphis. I'm going to check the place out, see if he's looked up any old friends. It was for guys like Switzer that the term 'known haunt' was coined. It's vague, but it's about all we have to go on at the moment."

"Get on it. Holt can have his scalp for all I care, but I want Sibyl out of it first."

"So much for what I've learned. You pick up anything new?"

"One of my guys is real good at getting into places without things like warrants and keys. He scoped out Switzer's pad and he says it's been tossed by an expert. No sign of what the tosser was looking for, but he says it looks like there was nothing there to begin with. You know what I mean—basic furniture, a TV, a stereo, some clothes on hangers and some in drawers—but nothing personal, no pictures or books, souvenirs, keepsakes, nothing like that. He says it was almost spooky, like nobody'd ever lived there. I'm thinking this guy could be a hard-core psycho."

"We've both seen places like that. Ex-cons and people who've been raised in institutions usually aren't strong on what you'd term nesting instincts. They don't put up lace curtains and vases of fresh flowers or try to match the bed linen with the wallpaper design. They live on the street and in their hangouts. Home's just a place to sleep and take a shower. I'd worry more if he'd turned up a lot of drug paraphernalia, or five hundred naked pictures of Madonna with Charles Manson's face glued over her navel or something like that."

"Yeah, well, we can always hope." He wasn't voicing what we were both thinking, so I helped him out.

"Kit, we both know what it means, Holt being on the case."

"Yeah," he said disgustedly. "It means there's money involved. Big money. And people kill for big money, do it all the time. Find her, Gabe."

After hanging up I lay back on my bed and stared at the ceiling and thought about Jasper Holt.

Bounty hunter. It's a term out of the last century and it always conjures up scenes from old Western movies and TV shows, Steve McQueen bringing them back dead or alive. But they still exist. These days, they work mostly for bail bondsmen, going after bail jumpers for a percentage of the bond that would be forfeited if the client failed to show in court. It's quasi-legitimate work, if not exactly the height of respectability. But then, private investigators aren't highly regarded in some quarters, either.

Businesses and individuals can no longer post wanted notices as they used to. All they can do is offer rewards for information leading to arrest and conviction. But there are still moneyed interests with a need to locate people. They were the ones who hired the services of Jasper Holt.

It had been fifteen years before, in L.A. I was a shiny-new detective working fugitive warrants when he showed up at division headquarters, looking for some people. Nobody could believe this guy, with his cornball patter and his hick suit and string tie, showing around these pictures. They'd kidnapped the ten-year-old son of a Houston oilman, he explained. He had reason to believe they were holing up near the USC campus. The ransom had been paid and the boy had turned up strangled and sodomized in a Houston canal. He wasn't there to make them pay for their sins, he said, but he felt that they really should return the money, a large but undisclosed sum.

We tried to blow him off but he walked into the chief's office and gave him a couple of numbers to call. The chief came out a few minutes later looking like his shorts were full of sand burrs. We were to extend Mr. Jasper Holt every aid, he told us. We were not to interfere with his activities, nor were we to bother him about the .357 on his belt beneath the stupid jacket, on the left side for a cross draw. The chief would never afterward tell us who he had called, but California is a big oil state, too, and when oil talks to oil, governors pay attention and kowtow.

The rest I only heard about. The suspects were two men and a woman, all of them veterans of the radical fringe movements of the early seventies. Holt found one of the men in a Korean bar near the USC campus. The guy made a move and Holt shot him through the head.

Next he located the woman in an apartment not far from the shooting scene. She ratted on the second man. Nobody ever found out what went on between them during their interview in the apartment. She never said a word when he brought her in and turned her over to the feds. Nor did she speak during her subsequent trial, not even to her lawyer. For all I know she hasn't said a word to this day. Man number two turned up dead in a car in Encino. That was the last of it. Expert opinion was that the oilman had his money back, or most of it.

I checked into Holt and found what little there was to know. He'd been a Texas Ranger as a young man. He'd accompanied the Johnson administration to Washington and become a federal marshal, the one they assigned to escort the really bad prisoners and serve papers on people who usually laughed at the feds. When the Nixon administration came in, Holt went into business on his own. I'd heard of him from time to time, over the years. He specialized in finding people's money for a percentage, and he wasn't picky about who he worked for. He'd tracked down embezzling bankers, skimming mob dealers, computer scammers, you name it.

Because of the level at which he worked and his network of incredibly influential contacts, he could operate and pack a gun pretty much wherever he pleased. He could secure cooperation from high-placed people because they knew, even if they had no stake this time, they might very well want his services someday.

He was, perhaps, not quite so quick on the trigger as in the old days, but he was one ruthless bastard and he had to be working for someone bad. Why the hell was he after a penny-ante crook like Nick Switzer? Just who had been ripped off?

I decided to have another shot at Sibyl's diary and located the entry where the fateful name first turned up. Carson had folded the corner of the page down.

Respectful as suppliants before the tomb of a saint we fill the classroom with our silence as a gray detective speaks of laws broken and lawbreakers brought to justice, his face a pallid mass of dough in a state of vague animation, lips writhing around jagged teeth as they form words of rape, murder, drugs, unclean greed and all the squalid sorrow of poverty.

Then he speaks a name: Nick Switzer. Even coming from his indistinct, word-numbed mouth syllables of the name click themselves into a hollow of my soul contoured specially for them and there, like a lovely virus, begin to replicate themselves until I am filled to my extremities with their energy. I must find this Nick Switzer.

Three

At one time in America, the highways had unique personalities. They wound among the hills, followed river courses or the old wagon trails, which themselves were laid atop ancient Indian trails and millennia-old game paths. In west Texas and the prairie states they ran flat and straight as a chalkline for hundreds of miles, numbing the brain with their featureless monotony. In the low country they put you right in the swamps. In the mountains they hung over sheer drops that jammed your heart into your mouth at every turn.

You went through every little town in the district on those highways. You bought gas at stations that sold little but the necessities for keeping a car rolling. You ate at roadside diners, you slept in downtown hotels or tourist courts on the fringes. Before crossing the Southwestern deserts you got a canvas water bag to hang off your hood ornament and maybe an odd-looking little swamp cooler that hung outside one window to lower the temperature inside. You dropped it off on the other side of the desert and got your deposit back.

The interstates are different. They're all four-lane, divided highway and they mark the shortest path between major cities, bypassing the smaller communities. At the exits are facilities that peddle everything from lottery tickets to condoms, as well as gas and oil. The fast-food franchises are all the same no matter where you go. Today's highways yield unprecedentedly convenient and quick access to everywhere in the country, and it takes an act of volition to run out of gas, but they give you the paradoxical sensation of traveling vast distances without going anywhere.

It's easy to over-romanticize the old highways. The diners sometimes gave you ptomaine along with Mom's home cooking. It could be a couple hundred miles between filling stations, and roadside ripoff artists abounded. The speed traps were legendary and the local lockups could be the stuff of nightmares. But at the end of a long trip you knew you'd covered some country.

The great postwar highway system is too impersonal. I suspect that the old wagon teamsters and stage drivers said the same thing about the newfangled, paved roads designed for automobiles. They were probably right, too.

Memphis was a long shot, but not as long as it might seem. Not if I was reading Nick Switzer right. The sociopaths are charmers who have something missing in their brains, and it's not just a conscience. Their concept of reality differs from the norm. Their perception of time is skewed and they are unable to plan for more than the immediate future. That's why so many of them, after pulling a caper that required skills and ingenuity that Napoleon would envy, get caught because they overlook some blatantly obvious factor, or because they can't understand how a detective can study their habits and anticipate their actions, or else they just piss away their takings on a childish spending spree, paying cash for a garish car, buying drinks for the house every night, stuffing hundreds down the G-strings of strippers, tossing waitresses fifty-dollar tips. It's the sort of behavior that attracts the attention of even the densest cops.

They have little concept of cause and effect, and they never learn, no matter how many times it is demonstrated to them. They can't understand that what they do has inevitable consequences. Instead, life to them is a chain of random, inexplicable events, coincidences and the actions of alien beings, their fellow humans, whom they can't begin to understand.

However faulty their sense of the present and future, their memories work fine. Confronted with danger, in circumstances they can't control or in a panic, they tend to return to familiar places and reestablish contact with old associates. They're always a little puzzled when they discover things have changed, that the old friends are gone or dead or have gotten older, that the places are no longer recognizable, that other people have been there and done things in the interim. They expect everything to be just as they left it.

So there were sound reasons to believe that Switzer might have looked up an old pal of his named Pat Jennings. Assuming, of course, that Jennings was still in Memphis and neither dead nor in jail, always likely circumstances in the world of Nick, Pat and their ilk.

If Nashville is the city of living country music, Memphis is the mausoleum of dead rock. Monuments to the King crop up everyplace you look, as numerous as monuments to Ramses the Second in the original Memphis. There are Elvis streets, squares and commercial establishments of every sort. You can buy the likeness of the King in the form of liquor bottles, cement lawn statues, paintings on black velvet and grave monuments of Carrara marble. And then, of course, there is Graceland, the hillbilly shack on steroids.

There's also the motel where Martin Luther King was assassinated, but it was slated for demolition.

According to his file, Switzer and Jennings were arrested for illegal withdrawals of cash from teller machines. The bank had dropped charges when they agreed to demonstrate how they had pulled it off. This was not an uncommon arrangement in the early days of ATMs.

I figured Jennings wouldn't be easy to find even if he was alive, free and living in Memphis, but I was wrong. I found him right in the morning paper.

I'd arrived in Memphis late in the evening and established myself in a motel near the city center. After checking in with Carson, I'd tried to immerse myself in the banalities of television but couldn't find anything worth putting me to sleep. Eventually I'd given up and just allowed the disconnected thoughts to swirl through my head, hoping for that seemingly random but subconsciously rigorous connection to surface and give me an answer, or at least a glimmer of understanding. I came up with nothing. Two questions remained as elusive as ever: What happened back there? What makes a woman do such a thing? Eventually, I slept.

I woke early and went out for a run through the still-dark streets of the old river city. I added an extra mile or two to the run as a gesture to my conscience, because I'd spotted a Waffle House near the motel and decided to have breakfast there. Showered and shaved, I bought a local newspaper at a vending machine in front of the little diner and went inside.

The Waffle House chain is a great Southern institution, a monument to the belief that cholesterol is the key to immortality. Early though it was, all the booths were jammed and I had to wait a few minutes for an open stool at the counter. A waitress had a cup of coffee in front of me even as she cleared away the former customer's plates. I studied the relentlessly plebeian menu and ordered steak and eggs with hash browns and a side of blueberry waffles. Since there was no room to spread out my paper, I decided to let it wait.

At a Waffle House all the cooks and waitresses work in a tiny space behind the counter, about six by fifteen feet, from which they provide service with almost magical speed and efficiency. Plus, you get to share their social life, which goes on nonstop. With my second cup of coffee I got the news about Belva's impending divorce, advised Ben the fry cook that quitting night school would be a bad mistake and learned that nobody there had heard of Nick Switzer, or Pat Jennings. Well, it was worth a shot. At a Waffle House you just get back into the same conversation you left at the last Waffle House.

With breakfast under my belt and my plates cleared away, I had room to open my paper. The waitress topped up my cup and I raised it, almost doing a classic sitcom spit-take when I saw the headline and photo on the lower right of page one: LOCAL MAN SLAIN IN BIZARRE TORTURE-MURDER. But it wasn't the headline that choked me. It was the photo of a dull-eyed, thin-bearded young man and the name beneath it: Patrick Alan Jennings.

"You all right, hon?" The questioner was my waitress, Norma, whose dog, Buffy, had given birth to eleven puppies, for which she needed to find good homes.

"I'm fine," I said. "Too much coffee, I guess."

"It can make you jittery," she agreed.

I read the article, my heart sinking further with every line.

The nude, mutilated body of a man identified by police as Patrick Alan Jennings, 28, was discovered Tuesday by his landlady, Mrs. Althea Bryan, in the house he has rented for the past year at 2665 Calhoun Road. "He was a real nice, quiet young man," said Mrs. Bryan, visibly shaken. "I just can't imagine why anyone would do such a thing to him. He never seemed to have no enemies that I know of, and he always paid his rent on time." Police, however, know Jennings as a habitual criminal with a long record of offenses including auto theft, possession of narcotics with intent to sell and check fraud.

The body was found by Mrs. Bryan when she stopped by to remind Jennings that his rent was due. "It came due yesterday," Mrs. Bryan states, "and he was always on time before, so I came by to see if anything was wrong. I heard his alarm clock buzzing away so I called out and I opened the door. He wasn't in front, but there was a terrible smell in the house and I looked in back and found him. I never seen anything so awful in my life. I went right to the phone and dialed 911."

Police at the scene report that Jennings appeared to have been dead since at least the previous night, and that the corpse displayed marks of torture, including cuts in the form of "cult-like" symbols. Detective Sherman Abshire of Memphis PD Homicide states that the nature of the symbols is being kept secret in order to screen out false confessors and prevent copycatting. Police are questioning known associates of Jennings for possible leads in the baffling case.

I left the diner, my head buzzing with caffeine and a whole squirming bucketful of god-awful thoughts. One thing floated to the surface of the mess: I'd seen Pat Jennings's face before.

Back at my motel room I debated extending my stay another night, but decided I might have to head out of town before the day was over. It wasn't as if there were any shortage of motel rooms in Memphis should I have to stay an extra night. I tossed my shaving kit into my bag and zipped it. Then I sat at the tiny table by the front window in the full morning sunlight and took the little stack of photos from my briefcase. I took one of the party shots and laid it next to the front page of the paper. In this one, Switzer and Sibyl sat on a couch, Switzer's arm around her shoulders. Switzer was grinning, a can of beer in his free hand. Sibyl looked less tightly laced than usual, holding a plastic cup of what looked to be red wine. The couch was shabby, the bookshelves against the rear wall made of planks laid across cinder blocks. Some of the books on the shelves had spines marked with the college library system: a typical student party in typical student digs. Just behind the couple a man stood, his face in profile, talking to someone out of the frame.

The face looked less oafish in profile, without the skimpy beard, and the hair was almost military short, but it was Jennings, all right. He looked three or four years older than in the mug shot, a little harder, a little more self-possessed.

I sat back and wondered how Carson was going to take this. Whatever happened back East, Sibyl and her boyfriend were involved in a murder now. Of course, it could just be coincidence, but I didn't believe in coincidence. Did Nick and his old buddy have a little falling out? Torture complete with "cult-like" symbols didn't sound like Switzer's style, but you never knew. Sometimes, people displayed unexpected depths. And if Switzer had done it, Sibyl was involved, no help for it.

It occurred to me that someplace, in some other part of town, Jasper Holt was looking at the same article. For a moment I entertained the thought that he might have got to Jennings a little ahead of me, perhaps interrogated the poor bastard a bit too rigorously trying to locate Nick. The "cult-like" markings could be simple misdirection.

But that was letting hope cloud logic. Holt might have reached Memphis ahead of me the day before, but if the local medical examiner was right, Jennings had died the night before I saw Holt in Nashville. Of course, I had no idea what direction Holt had been traveling.

I shelved the thought, determined not to jump to conclusions. I didn't know enough yet. Hell, I didn't know *anything* yet. And how was I going to find anything out?

I had the name of the detective in charge of the investigation, but somehow I couldn't picture myself going up to him and saying, *Excuse me, Detective Abshire, but I'd like to have a look at Pat Jennings's body, and could you tell me what you've learned so far? Just curious, you know.* It was a cinch he'd blow off an out-of-town private investigator, but he'd sure find out who I worked for and want to know why I was snooping. That was no way to keep Sibyl out of this increasingly dangerous mess.

Well, Carson hadn't laid all that money on me for nothing. Time to spend some of it.

I looked through the Memphis phone book from the bedside table, wrote down a few numbers and addresses, and went out to my car. At a nearby gas station I filled up and bought a Memphis map. My first stop was a small printing firm, where I ordered some business cards and paid a hefty extra charge to have them ready by afternoon. Then I went to call on Mrs. Althea Bryan.

Her house was in a pleasant, middle-class neighborhood near Rhodes College. It was one story with clapboard sides, probably dating from the twenties, when there had been streetcar tracks down the middle of the street and a few ancient Civil War vets still sat on the porches telling anyone who would listen how it had been shelling the Yankee gunboats from the batteries down by Mud Island. Those might have been good times in these parts, when life wasn't so hurried and guys like Louis Armstrong and Fats Waller were starting to show their stuff in the darktown clubs, when a few molecules of methanol in the bootleg hootch was the major worry and you hardly ever came across a mutilated corpse with cult markings carved on it.

I discarded the brief, romantic musing. Those times were undoubtedly just as screwed up in their own way.

The woman who answered the doorbell restored my faith in the immutability of certain basic truths. She wore an old bathrobe and had curlers in her hair, right out of central casting.

"Yes?" She blinked behind thick glasses.

"Mrs. Bryan?" I played it eager and friendly. "Mrs. Althea Bryan?"

"That's me. What can I do for you?" She wasn't unfriendly, but she was plainly tired of callers.

"My name is Gabe Treloar. I'm a writer, and I was wondering if I could speak with you about the murder of your tenant, Pat Jennings."

"Another reporter? I think I've said about all I can about that. You need to talk to the police."

"Actually, I'm not a journalist. I'm writing a book about cult murders, and according to this morning's paper, there seem to be cult overtones to this case. Can you confirm that?"

"Oh. A book? Well, why don't you come on in? I guess I can tell it one more time." Bingo. A few minutes of fame in the local press was one thing. Immortality in a book was another. She showed me to a genteelly shabby living room inhabited by an elderly striped cat. "Can I bring you some coffee?"

"Please, don't go to any trouble."

"I just made a pot."

"Well, if it's already fixed, that sounds wonderful." Besides putting her at ease with a little domestic ritual, my early morning caffeine had worn off and I was in need of a transfusion. While she was in the kitchen I tried to make friends with the cat, but it ignored me. She returned in a few minutes with cups and saucers. She waited until I'd taken a sip and nodded appreciatively.

"Have you published many books, Mr. Treloar?" she asked, hair curlers being no impediment to good sense. I was ready, having planned my persona while making the day's preparations.

"Up till now I've just published in academic journals; the *Journal of American Criminology, Police Science Quarterly,* some others like that. I teach criminology." I was pretty sure those were the names of some real publications. I knew there were some with similar names, anyway. "You know how it is in academia. Publish or perish. People are interested these days in the recent rash of cult murders and I've been researching incidents in the South. The Jennings murder looks like the latest." I projected an eager interest without being creepily morbid.

"I see." This time she favored me with a smile. People have come to distrust journalists, but academics are eminently respectable, even if most people have no idea what they do. "Well, I hope you won't be disappointed. I believe that police spokesman got a little carried away with the cult thing, then the newspapers took that ball and ran with it."

"You mean there weren't any cult markings on the body?"

"Well, I'm just not so sure. I didn't go real close and look him all over, you know. As soon as I seen that poor boy dead like that, I ran and called 911. There wasn't writing in blood on the walls or nothing like that." She gave a little shudder. "It was awful enough as it was."

"Why don't you just tell me what happened?" I took out a pad and pen, but that was mainly to look more in character. I turned on the little recorder in my pocket for the real record. "I'll take a few notes. I may interrupt to clear up something. I hope you don't mind."

"No, that's all right. Where do you want me to start?"

"To begin with, when did you rent the house to Jennings?"

"He took the house last September, just over a year ago. Answered an ad I put in the paper."

"Did he have any recommendations? Did you speak with anyone that knew him or check his credit references?"

"No—usually I do that, but he seemed like such a nice, well-spoken young man, and he paid down first and last months' rent and the damage deposit, cash, no argument. And he never give me a bit of trouble or worry. I was just so surprised when the police said he had such a bad record."

"So he didn't have visitors you thought might be suspicious?"

"Well, I didn't snoop," she assured me, then added, "Now, I own the house next door, 2667 Calhoun. Mildred Rutherford's rented that house from me for more than ten years, and she's never been slow to tell me if the renters next door didn't suit her. She never had a word to say about poor Mr. Jennings. No loud parties, no lowlifes hanging around. If Mildred sees so much as a motorcycle and a tattoo she thinks she'll be robbed and murdered."

"Some people spook easily."

"But he always paid on time, always polite, smiling— of course, I know it makes sense to be suspicious of someone who's *too* nice and smiles a little too much, but he never gave me any reason to be distrustful."

"Did he tell you what he did for a living?"

She nodded. "He said he was a computer consultant, a freelance troubleshooter. He said that he fixed crashed systems and got rid of those computer viruses, things like that."

A good, amorphous cover, like academic author. I knew from his record that he had a certain degree of skill with computers, and a cover like that was just the thing to snow someone of the pre-computer generation like Mrs. Bryan or, for that matter, me.

"Was he ever away for extended periods?"

"If he was going to be away for more than two or three days he always told me, and I'd go by to take his papers inside and feed his fish."

"Did he do that often?"

"Oh, maybe three or four times since he rented the house."

"Was he away for any length of time recently?"

"He went out of town for almost two weeks just a little while ago. He was only back about two days before he got—well, before he was killed." She frowned a little. "Why do you ask about that?"

Suddenly I remembered who I was supposed to be. "I was just wondering, when you went into the house to take care of the fish, did you see any sign that he might have been involved in a cult? I know you didn't snoop, but was there anything that looked really odd?"

"No, he really didn't have much in the house—of course, I was only in the living room, where he had that little aquarium. He had a computer with all those things they stick on them, a printer and one of those faxes or modems or whatever they call them."

"I see. Did he get his mail delivered there?"

"No, he had a post office box, but I think he really did everything over that computer. So many people do these days." This last said wistfully—another poor soul left behind by the new age. Sometimes, I felt the same way.

"So, no occult paraphernalia was in evidence?" I was careful to sound disappointed.

"Not a thing. I mean, I don't know a whole lot about that sort of thing, I'm a Christian woman, but I've seen shows on TV about devil worship. I didn't see any of those pentagons or pentagrams or whatever, the stars and

37

the upside-down crosses. No black candles or goat heads or things like that. Anyway," she added, "it seems to me that it was whoever killed him was the devil worshiper, not Mr. Jennings."

"That's an excellent point," I agreed. "But often the victims in these cases are in one way or another connected with the group, maybe backsliders, former members who've tried to leave, that sort of thing."

"I see," she said doubtfully.

"Why don't you tell me just what you *did* see, when you found the body."

"Well, like I said, I didn't see much. Mr. Jennings didn't pay the rent on the date due, the way he always did, then he didn't call me the next morning and I didn't get any answer when I called him, so a little after noon I went over to see if anything was wrong. He didn't answer to the doorbell, and I could hear his alarm clock buzzing away inside, so I went in and called his name. There wasn't no answer, but I knew right away something was awful wrong because there was this . . . this terrible smell in the house." Her face twisted at the memory. I was about to tell her that I knew exactly what she meant, that I'd encountered that revolting smell many times before. Then I remembered who I was supposed to be and kept my mouth shut.

"I went into the back of the house, and it wasn't easy to make myself do that."

"It must have been frightening," I said.

"It was. I'm not what you'd call a squeamish woman, but when I found him I come about as close to fainting as I ever did in my life. He was laying there on the floor and there was just blood all over him. Don't ask me if there was anything . . . missing. I didn't go close enough to see." She grimaced and shuddered.

"What were the cult markings the paper mentioned?" I prodded.

"Like I said, I kept my distance, and there was so much blood you'd've had to go close to make out much of anything. The only thing I saw for sure was an arrowlike mark right here." She placed a fingertip to her forehead, just above and between her eyes.

"Arrowlike?"

"Yep. There wasn't much blood from it, that's why I could see what it was. Shaped like an arrow pointing out a direction, like on a map."

We talked for a few more minutes, but she had little to add. I rose and thanked her and she escorted me to the front door.

"When your book's finished," she said, "do you think you could send me a copy?"

"I'll be sure you get one," I said, feeling a twinge of guilt at the petty deception. But something more important occurred to me. "I forgot to ask: You said you found Jennings on the floor. How was he bound?"

"Oh, he wasn't tied up," she said with that now-familiar grimace. "He was nailed there."

My thoughts as I drove away were not pretty ones. I tried to push away the revulsion and dread and concentrate on the essentials. So he'd been nailed to the floor. Not elegant, but efficient. Maybe someone just forgot to bring a rope. Or was it ritualistic—a blasphemous crucifixion parody? Somehow, I didn't think so.

I find the recent fascination with cults and satanism to be a piece of mass hysteria on a par with UFO abductions and Elvis sightings and all the rest of the tabloid arcana. Maybe we just got so used to living with fear that, when the Soviet Union collapsed and the likelihood of nuclear apocalypse receded, we had to come up with something else to terrify us.

Americans have always been prone to fits of wild enthusiasm and unreasoning fear. The most casual reading of history will turn up dozens of examples, from the California Gold Rush to the overnight fear of Martian invasion set off by a single radio broadcast. Fear of Catholic plots and Jewish plots and Red scares have washed over the nation and receded with tidelike regularity decade after decade.

Once, a government propaganda machine was necessary to give these inchoate disturbances any sort of shape or direction. One such program had people calling sauerkraut "liberty cabbage" and made teachers scissor pictures of the Kaiser out of children's history books. A generation later the same machine transformed the Japanese overnight from a quaint, exotic people with exquisite manners into squat, ugly brutes with protruding teeth, slit eyes and thick glasses.

Now, the sensation-starved modern media and popular culture continually pick up the obscure, the arcane and the recondite, and through sheer pervasiveness and repetition blast their weird symbologies into the national consciousness. The looniness of disturbed recluses becomes the craze of the masses.

When I was a boy, even seeing a UFO was the rarest of experiences. During my first three decades I never met anyone who claimed to have spotted one. Now more people have *ridden* in the damned things than travel in cars on an average day. Multiple personality disorder used to be the rarest of all psychological conditions, with maybe three confirmed cases in the entire literature of the field. Now it's more common than the cold, especially in criminal defenses.

It's become the same with occultism. Once, a few professors and historians and the occasional author of lurid novels were familiar with the medieval symbols of demonism, satanism, witchcraft and so forth. The Age of Reason swept them aside as the rubbish of an ignorant past. They were revived from time to time by cranks and frauds and employed to fleece the gullible, most recently in the twenties by characters like Aleister Crowley and Madame Blavatsky.

Then the rock music crowd discovered the colorful, outrageous symbols used by the old guys back when being too antiestablishment could get you burned at the stake. They looked terrific on album covers and T-shirts and they provided a new look in a field that changes design as often as the fashion industry. Above all, they outraged their elders, which has been half the point of rock music since I first heard Elvis when I was eight years old.

People who, a few years back, would have laughed at the sheer ludicrousness of animal sacrifices, black masses and demonic possession now believe that America at the end of the twentieth century is under siege by a five-thousand-year-old Middle Eastern bogeyman. Go figure.

Whatever the reality behind the nuttiness, it all makes a fine cover for more prosaic crime. Untold assaults, murders, kidnappings, rapes and other felonies have been dressed up with a few colorful mutilations, daubed symbols and satanic-sounding slogans to be picked up by the popular media and trumpeted as sinister occultism instead of the same old squalid viciousness.

The demise of the late Mr. Jennings looked to me like just such a gussied-up murder. Whatever he was involved in, it wasn't satanism, and a man like Jennings lives his whole life in the shadow of premature, violent death. Supernatural interference is not required.

I drove back to the printing shop and picked up my new business cards. They identified me as Gabe Treloar, author. The address and phone number were those of my apartment. There is no law against impersonating an author. Anyone can claim to be one. You don't have to have actually published to claim to be one. All sorts of people who intend, someday, to get around to writing that book say that they're writers. So, technically, I wasn't committing fraud.

I wanted a look at Jennings's body. Official channels were pretty much out of the question, but my line of work is made much simpler by the fact that low-level municipal employees are poorly remunerated.

The guy behind the reception desk at the city morgue was white-haired, his eyes big behind thick glasses, probably within a year or two of retirement. This was a bad sign. A man with his pension at stake wasn't likely to come cheap, if at all.

"May I help you?" he asked. Behind his desk a hallway stretched, gurney-wide doors opening off it. Near the far end a tall, fat young man dressed in institutional whites listlessly mopped the floor.

I handed the desk man one of my new cards. "I hope you can. I'm compiling a book on cult murders. Yesterday, you received the body of a man named Patrick Alan Jennings. According to this morning's news, the murder may be cult related. Would it be possible for me to view the body?"

He handed back the card as if it might contaminate him. "You have a court order?"

"No, I'm afraid not. I just need a brief look to confirm whether marks said to be carved on it correspond with some found on other victims whose cases I've studied."

"That particular body is the subject of an ongoing homicide investigation. You can apply for a copy of the medical examiner's report. You should be able to get it in five or six months, if the case is closed by then."

I smiled and pitched my voice a little higher than necessary. "I'm working under a deadline here. But my publisher can be pretty generous if it's important to the book."

He blinked behind the glasses, his face about as expressive as those of his charges. "Then ask your publisher to buy you a court order. Otherwise, wait for the report. Will there be anything else?"

"I guess not," I said, giving him a slow-burn look. It seemed to have no effect, but it wasn't meant for him anyway.

I went out to the parking lot beside the building and got into my car. I didn't have long to wait. The orderly came out a side door a few minutes later and lit up a cigarette. Just another employee taking a smoke break outdoors, the way they all have to these days. He scanned the parking lot casually, spotted me and sauntered over. The meaty, hairy forearm he leaned on the driver's-door window was biker tattooed.

"Hey, buddy, how bad do you want a look at that stiff?"

"A hundred dollars' worth."

He snorted, a smoky, grunting laugh through his nostrils. "This job ain't much, but it's worth more'n that. Tell you what: Old Perkins is gonna be suspicious now, but he goes off shift at nine. You be at that door I just come out of at eleven-thirty tonight and I'll give you five minutes with that stiff for five hundred."

"That's a little steep," I said for the sake of form.

He shrugged his fat shoulders. "It's your book, man." His hair was buzz cut, his chin beard and mustache neatly trimmed. The younger generation of bikers don't go in much for the luxuriant locks and full beards of the older ones. Bikers are a conservative lot, but change comes even to their tradition-bound little world.

"Okay, it's a deal."

"Gimme fifty now. I'll slip it to the night man and he'll let me take his shift." What he would probably slip to the night man would be a short dog of red, but he had his own little scams and deceptions, just as I had mine. I took out my money clip, peeled off a bill and contemplated the

43

stern face of Ulysses S. Grant for a moment before handing him over.

The orderly pocketed the bill. "See you tonight," he said, turning away to give me a view of the stubbled roll of flesh that bulged over the back of his collar. Sometimes there is much to be said for long hair.

I arranged for an extra night at the same motel, even got the same room, and made a call to Carson. I tried not to sound too despairing as I gave him a brief rundown on the Jennings situation.

"Oh, God, Gabe," he said, his voice sounding truly sick and about a hundred years old. "What's he got my little girl into?"

"Let's not jump to conclusions," I said, taking the stern line that he used to take with me when I was a rookie. "This may have nothing at all to do with Switzer. It's just something we have to check into. People like this kill each other off every day for no reason that makes any sense to us. So far, we have no evidence that that they even stopped in Memphis."

"Yeah, sure," he said, totally unconvinced. He gathered his resources and went on, sounding something like the old Carson. "Listen, here's something that just came in: One of my guys turned up a bill of sale in Switzer's apartment. Two months ago he bought a bunch of lumber: some sheets of plywood, two-by-fours, screws, paint and about two dozen hinges."

"Maybe he was building a doghouse."

"No dog, and what kind of doghouse needs that many hinges, anyway? Nobody describes him as any sort of handyman. It seems a little out of character. Anyway, I'll set my people to finding out if anyone remembers this Jennings character. You call me back tonight after you've had a look at the stiff."

I assured him I'd do exactly that. I had several hours before my appointment with Jennings, so I turned the TV on to a news channel and watched long enough to satisfy myself that there was no cross-country crime spree being perpetrated by a couple answering Sibyl and Nick's description.

I turned off the set and pondered. First frantic flight, then possible involvement in torture-murder, now, of all things, carpentry. Maybe it would all make sense, someday.

I had no appetite and not the slightest inclination to try out the tourist attractions of Memphis, so I took out Sibyl's journals for another try at her cryptic musings.

The bar is a dark place on a dark street. My mind tries to transform the huddled, scuttling shapes on the sidewalk into the menacing demons of drama, but they are only the defeated and discouraged, rendered first colorless, then nearly transparent and weightless by the pointless suffering of their lives. I go inside. The air here bears a charge, a slight tingle, as if life is sometimes lived here in such a way that unscheduled, unpredictable things can happen. This may be a place where, under the right convergence of circumstances, two plus two can sometimes equal green.

I ask the bartender if Nick Switzer is there and he nods toward a rear table but I have already seen him, needing no more identification than the neon aura that shimmers around him. His hard-planed, solid thereness draws me like gravity. He smiles as I ask to join him, speak the inane words I have prepared, of my scholarly study in need of a subject, of a genuine criminal to raise my insubstantial thoughts to the level of genuine mediocrity.

Still he smiles and pays no attention to what I have said, but instead reaches to my breast and peels away the envelope of skin, the cushion of fat, the hard, bony armor, lays bare my heart and reads the truth there.

Well, so much for meeting cute. I still knew nothing about Nick Switzer. Was he really some kind of psycho Svengali? Or was he just a commonplace sociopathic twit and the outlaw demon merely a construction of Sibyl's imagination?

Four

The lot was nearly deserted when I parked there at 11:25 P.M. The only light came from a bulb over the side doorway. Besides my car there was only a battered pickup and a Harley hog. At 11:29 P.M. I got out of my car and crossed to the door. It opened seconds later and the orderly already had his hand out.

"You bring it?" I handed over the four folded hundreds and the fifty and he riffled, then pocketed them. "Come on. You got five minutes."

I followed him through a maintenance hall and into a room where empty autopsy tables awaited their clients. Everything had that antiseptic smell common to hospitals, morgues and the working areas of funeral homes. We went to another room, where the slab drawers were ranked like filing cabinets, their anonymous dead stored like documents. The orderly walked to one and pulled it open. He peeled down the sheet and stood back.

"Knock yourself out, buddy," he said. "This one's got some real entertainment value."

I stepped closer. "For a hundred bucks a minute, I hope so."

He cut a glance at me, one eyebrow cocked. "You're a book writer, huh?"

"I'll be collecting my Nobel prize for literature any day now."

Pat Jennings was still recognizable as the man in the photo with Sibyl and Switzer, still cropped-haired and clean-shaven. I was relieved to see that the body hadn't yet been autopsied, a radical procedure likely to obliterate lesser desecrations. It wasn't difficult to read what had happened to Pat Jennings.

Torture isn't a terribly complicated art. If what you want is information and you don't especially care whether your subject survives or looks good afterward, no exotic gear is required. Jennings had been worked over with the old, reliable pliers-and-blowtorch combination. The fact is, there is only so much physical pain you can inflict, and on a male subject these simple tools, available at any hardware store, will do the max. Anything more complicated is pure melodrama and fetishism.

When you hear about the CIA running torture schools for the secret police of our pet dictators, they aren't teaching them how to inflict pain. That's a task understood perfectly by even the most backward Third World political thugs. What they are teaching is how to torture and leave no marks on the body, how to leave the victim looking perfectly sound to the international press, able to speak coherently, and unable, ever, to prove that any torture had taken place. The scars are there, of course, but they're down inside the brain where they don't show.

Whoever did the job on Jennings hadn't been worrying about the press. There were livid ligature marks beside the mouth, and a massive bruise covering the left side of the jaw, cheek and temple. The ligature mark was caused by the gag, which had performed the double service of muffling his screams and preventing him from biting his tongue. The bruise was caused by the knot. Obviously, the torturer had used a stick through the knot to tighten the gag, then loosen it periodically to give Jennings a chance to talk. It was grisly, but I'd seen the marks many times before, as an MP in Saigon and as a police officer in L.A.

The crucifixion marks were another thing entirely.

There were holes an inch or two above the wrists, between the bones of the forearm. They might have been mistaken for bullet wounds, but they were a bit ragged and distorted by Jennings's futile struggles against the unyielding nails. Other nails had been driven through the ankles, or else one ankle had been placed atop the other and a single nail driven through both. Like most men in macho professions I pride myself on a strong stomach, but the thought of what that must have felt like put a knot in my gut.

"Were the nails still in him when he was brought in?" I asked.

"It wasn't my shift when he came in. I heard there was a twenty-penny spike through both his ankles, but I can't swear to it." He shrugged. "Whatever it was, somebody didn't want him going no place."

The "cult-like" marks weren't impressive, compared with the rest. On his chest had been carved the letters *DTT.* On his forehead was a stylized, broad-headed arrow: ↑. They didn't look like any cult marks I had ever run across, but there is a whole heraldry of gang logos, a minor art form of our age. When you see them, you're looking at something far more relevant and dangerous than minions of Satan gearing up for Armageddon.

"You ever done time?" I asked.

"Naw. I'm just pullin' this shit job 'cause I got laid off at NASA. That downsizin's a bitch. You got two more minutes." He'd regarded my crack about the Nobel prize as a challenge and wanted me to know that he had a gift for sarcasm, too.

I pointed to the letters and the arrow. "You ever see those marks inside? Or anywhere else?"

"Never seen nothin' like 'em," he deadpanned. I made a move toward my wallet. "Keep your money," he said, drawing up the sheet. "Time's up. Let's go." I still had half a minute but there was no more to see and I wasn't going to learn any more from the orderly. But as he saw me out the door some spirit of beneficence moved him to say, "I was you, I'd find me another book to write. There's some people it don't pay to fuck with." He scanned the parking lot with nervous eyes and shut the door.

I walked out of the pool of light and got into my car. It was late, but I still had a lot to do before returning to my motel and reporting to Carson.

While I drove, I tried to shove aside the impedimenta of personal involvement and put together what I knew, dispassionately. Whether it's police work or pure science, nothing clouds the rigor of logic like the will to believe. It makes you overlook the obvious and stress the unlikely in order to make things add up the way you want them to.

Pat Jennings had been no bodybuilder, but he'd been a reasonably strong young man. Someone wielding a hammer and nail would have needed a lot of help holding Jennings down while he accomplished his task. Sibyl couldn't have resisted what must have been violent struggling.

Holt? He was getting on in years but he'd been a powerful man once. His woman friend was tiny, but it would be no problem for him to hire all the muscle he needed. I made this as a job for at least three strong men.

Unless, of course, Jennings was unconscious when it happened. But I doubted that. To render a man unconscious, which is never as easy as it looks in the movies, then to pound nails through his arms and ankles before he revived, was to risk death by shock before he could talk.

And whoever had tortured Jennings had urgently wanted him to talk.

Although the marks signified something frightening enough that the morgue orderly wouldn't accept money to talk about them, they might also have been fakes intended to mislead investigation. It's done all the time. With an effort of will, I forced myself to envision Sibyl and Switzer doing it.

Had Jennings betrayed his old buddy? That wasn't too hard to picture. Sociopaths don't have real friends, just associates. They may be surprised by treachery, but the result isn't hurt and a broken heart. The result is rage. Switzer's record of nonviolent offenses didn't mean he was incapable of sadistic brutality. The right provocation could reveal a different Nick Switzer entirely.

Sibyl? She might not have been present. Or she might have been not only present but participating. I had to face the fact that I hadn't seen her in many years and I had no idea what sort of twisted psyche might dwell behind that demure face. After all, she had done one utterly unexpected thing in running off with the little bastard. Maybe to her own surprise she'd found that she liked the amoral life of the outlaw.

In a strange fashion I found a little reassurance in the forthright, professional methods used by the torturer. It's when torture is done for sick, sexual thrills that you see the exotic trappings, the bondage gear, the flaying, the mutilation, the obsessive concentration on genitals and orifices.

A hardened old L.A. cop had once summed it up for me with brutal succinctness: "When they work on a guy's balls they want to make him talk. When they work on his dick they're just having fun."

Jennings's house was in a shabby residential block not far from the river. It was a one-story clapboard cottage, as were most of the other nearby dwellings. A dirt driveway led to a carport tacked onto one side of the house. No garage, no sheds. The nearest streetlight was at the corner, four houses away. Yellow crime-scene tape x-ed the front door and the side door beneath the carport.

I drove by slowly, then cruised the adjacent blocks, looking for signs of surveillance. I saw none, and I wasn't surprised. The death of Pat Jennings hadn't sent the Memphis police into a tizzy. The fact that the ME hadn't gotten around to his autopsy had already told me that.

On the other hand, the local police weren't the only ones with an interest in the late Mr. Jennings, and I'd rather take my chances with the toughest homicide detective in America than with a loony who uses twenty-penny nails for handcuffs.

I wore dark clothes but no commando drag. There's nothing like a black turtleneck, pulled-down watch cap and camouflage paint to tip off a passing prowl car that you're up to no good. I had my collapsing baton, a penlight, a pair of surgical gloves and a couple of compact tools, but nothing as distinctive as real burglar tools. Besides those being difficult to explain, I doubted that this crib would be that hard to get into.

I spotted no signs, but if the watcher was a real pro, I wouldn't. I parked the car on a side street and walked back to the house, trying not to think, just observing. A few belated crickets still chirped, there were distant traffic noises, but the neighborhood was otherwise about as silent as an urban neighborhood ever gets. Chances were everyone was asleep, but I knew from the landlady that at least one neighbor kept an eye on the house. Just my luck if the old bat was an insomniac.

When I reached the house I cut into the driveway, not running but not wasting any time either. I expended a lot of nervous energy worrying about headlights, barking dogs and so forth. If you don't have the peculiar mentality of the pro burglar, B&E is rough on the nerves. Your stomach is jumpy and you're embarrassed by an urge to defecate. Real burglars had described to me the near-sexual rush they got from entering a locked home. I knew that I was never going to enjoy that particular sensation.

I went around the house and found the back door also x-ed with tape. The yard was surrounded by a six-foot board fence, providing me with a minimum of cover. A quick try at the rear windows let me know they were locked. I pulled the lower ends of the tape away from the door frame and tried the knob. It was locked, naturally, but I felt the door wobble. The frame was warped and the hinges were loose. With that much play, I didn't have much difficulty getting a strip of stiff plastic between the lock and the jamb. The door opened almost silently.

I stepped in and closed the door behind me. For a while I just stood there, listening. There were the inevitable noises made by a frame house, but nothing to indicate the presence of another human being. I breathed slowly through my nostrils, willing my heart to slow down. Gradually, my nervousness subsided. I was ready to get to work.

I was standing in a utility alcove that opened off the kitchen. To one side were a washer and dryer, both of them old. On the other side stood a water heater and an old-fashioned coatrack. I stepped into the kitchen and made a quick scan. I detected no cooking smells and the pantry held little except instant coffee, sugar and a few cereal boxes. The refrigerator held a quart of milk, some jars of condiments and a few microwaveable meals in the freezer box. Jennings had done most of his eating out.

I passed a door that led to the bedroom, leaving that for last. In the small living room I found what looked like a fairly advanced computer setup, some magazines mostly devoted to computers, and a tank of somnolent fish. A telephone stood on a little stand next to the computer. I pulled out a drawer beneath the phone and found a pen and pad. The top sheet was blank but I tucked the pad into a pocket anyway. All the wastebaskets were empty, their contents probably appropriated by the police.

I glanced at my watch. Five minutes had elapsed since I entered the house. Now for the main event. I went to the bedroom.

The chalked outline on the floor was one of the most unusual of the many, many such I had seen. As I played the beam of the penlight over it, I saw that it was in the classical Jesus pose, arms at full extension, feet together. To the landlady's eyes there had been a great deal of blood, but in fact, the nails had nearly sealed the crucifixion wounds, the torch and pliers had caused little bleeding and Jennings had probably died of shock or asphyxiation.

I knelt by the outline of the feet and played the light over the area. There was only one nail hole, so both ankles had been transfixed by a single nail. Then I noticed something on the floor three or four inches away from the mark made by the nail. It was almost obscured by the splotch of blood beneath where the ankles had been, so I fished my magnifying glass from a pocket and bent over. It's not like Sherlock Holmes's big glass. It's a folding model, the kind geologists use, compact and very powerful.

Magnified, I saw a conical hole in the wood about a quarter inch across and as deep, its edges blurred by blood-clogged sawdust. I snapped off the light and sat back on my heels. I was sweating, and not just from holding my strained pose. Something had been bothering me about the single-nail idea, and now I had the answer. It wasn't a nice one.

It had occurred to me that the guy with the hammer had a difficult task, even with a couple of friends to sit on Jennings and hold him still. The human ankle is a bundle of tiny bones bound by tendon. Driving a nail straight through such a mass without it turning would be awkward at best. Stacking one ankle on top of the other would make it damn near impossible. The shallow hole told me how he'd done it. Like any carpenter needing to nail a difficult piece of wood without splitting it, he'd bored himself a guide hole with an electric drill.

After that, my search of the bedroom was anticlimactic. It had been thoroughly searched and everything that might have been of interest carted off by the police. There was fingerprint dust everywhere, but someone with the foresight to bring along his power drill isn't going to forget his gloves.

The closet held nondescript clothes, mostly casual, along with some out-of-date disco threads. There was a security guard's uniform, more expensive and classy than most, but anybody can get a security guard's job these days. There was even a pair of spit-shined oxfords, now dulled by fingerprint powder, to go with the uniform.

I let myself out of the house and carefully replaced the crime-scene tape. As I walked back to my car the jitters returned full force. They didn't stop until I was back in my motel room.

I picked up the phone and dialed. "Carson here." It was past 2:00 A.M. where he was, but his voice didn't sound sleep-fogged. I gave him a rundown of what I'd learned that evening. "Sibyl had no part of that," he asserted flatly. I didn't bother to contradict him.

"What about the marks?" I asked him. "Have you run across any like them?"

"No, but there's so damn many gang trademarks it's like trying to memorize every cattle brand in the West. Thing is, Switzer and Jennings have no record as gang guys."

"If they operated on the street they had dealings with the gangs. Stiffing a gang is a good way to end up dead.

And they both pulled hard time. Jailhouse gangs are a lot smaller than street gangs, but they're even meaner."

"Or it could just be a dodge."

"There's that, too. What have you found out?"

"Okay, first, the wig. She bought it six months ago. It's a top-of-the-line model, cost twelve hundred bucks. She got the blue contacts at the same time."

"Were the wigs or the contacts in her apartment when you searched it?"

"Nope."

"What about Holt? Have you turned up anything to tie him to all this?"

"Nothing useful so far. He's a man who values his privacy, even when he's doing legitimate work. The last few years it looks like he's been doing his usual work, chasing down skimmers, retrieving ransom money and so forth. Still works alone. Nobody seems to've seen this woman you saw with him. Last report I have of him's two months old. He was doing something for somebody in Honolulu."

I tried to imagine Jasper Holt with his Western suit and Stetson hat in Honolulu, but it was just too surreal. "Any more credit card purchases?"

"Not yet. I may know more in the morning. What's your next move?"

"Good question. I'm at a dead end here. Jennings was the only known associate I had here in Memphis and I can't go talking to the Memphis police about Switzer without putting Sibyl's neck in a noose. They may still be here but I doubt it. Even if they had nothing to do with what happened to Jennings, they know about it now. Would you hang around knowing what just happened to your old buddy?"

"Yeah, but what direction? We're figuring west, but we could be wrong. No sense heading out on I-40 if they've gone to New Orleans. Sit tight there for a while.

I'll get back to you as soon as I find something. You do the same if you turn anything up."

I hung up and lay back on the bed, tired but still a little keyed up from the long day's events. Time to think like a detective.

Jennings: Somebody wanted him to talk and had worked him over for a long time. Let's presume that the torturing was done by a third party who wanted Jennings to tell where Nick and Sibyl were. There are very few people who can withstand prolonged torture even when the lives of loved ones or the good of their country are at stake. A petty crook like Pat Jennings? Hell, Butch would rat on Sundance at the first squeeze of the pliers. Whatever they wanted from Jennings he probably didn't know.

The wig and contacts: Sibyl bought them six months ago. She spent a lot of money to get the best quality. But they weren't in her apartment when she bolted. Either she had them with her when she ran, or she'd already gotten rid of them. Why throw away a twelve-hundred-dollar wig that was practically new? Because it and the contacts were evidence. They tied her to something she wanted to escape.

The next morning I took the pad I'd found in the telephone stand at Jennings's house and sat with it at the little table in front of the motel room's window.

There are a couple of good, low-tech ways of taking an impression from a second sheet. The old, familiar one is to run a pencil point back and forth across it, getting a negative picture of the upper sheet that has been written on. But that one is a little rough so I used the more laborious but delicate method. With a penknife blade I scraped the tip of a number-two pencil, depositing little piles of fine graphite powder all over the sheet. When I had enough powder I gently shook the pad back and forth, distributing it evenly over the entire surface. When that was done

I rubbed the powder with my fingertips, using the lightest pressure I could.

Immediately, faint impressions showed up. I got some very faint phone or fax numbers, some of them overlapping, none quite legible. They had been written on successive sheets. One set of figures was much clearer than the others, written larger and overlapping several of them. It must have been written on the last sheet and it was something important enough that Jennings had written larger and used extra pressure. It's something that most people do unconsciously.

Two letters and four figures: GL1505. Not a phone or fax, not a safe combination. So many things in modern life are named, classified and regulated by letter-number combinations that speculation was a needle- in-haystack proposition, but something about this combination seemed faintly familiar. Like most people, I use private mailing systems a lot, especially for parcels and for express deliveries. This looked like the tracking numbers those services use. I reached for the phone book.

My first try was the biggest: FedEx. When I got through to an actual person, I said, "My name is Patrick Jennings and I'm calling from Memphis, Tennessee. I've been expecting a parcel to be delivered by FedEx for the last few days and it hasn't arrived. I'd like to know what's holding it."

"I see. Do you have a tracking number for that shipment, Mr. Jennings?"

"Yes, I have: GL1505."

"I'm sorry, but that isn't a Federal Express tracking number. Perhaps the sender employed a different service."

I thanked her and hung up. Next I tried UPS, then a couple of others. I drew a blank each time. The last express service listed in the yellow pages was Zodiac Air. I gave them a buzz.

"Zodiac Air. How may I help you?" I gave him the usual spiel, ending with the call numbers. "Let me see . . ." From the other end came the click of computer keys. "Mr. Jennings, according to our records, you signed for that parcel on Monday at eleven-thirty A.M."

"Oh. My son must have signed for it and forgot to tell me. You know how teenagers are. Sorry to have bothered you."

"Happy to be of service."

I replaced the phone and it buzzed the moment it touched the cradle. I snatched it up. "Gabe here."

"Gabe, I got something for you. Sibyl's car turned up in Oklahoma City yesterday morning. Tags are gone, but it was ID'd by the engine number. It was never reported stolen, so they called her and left a message on her answering machine. I called, gave 'em a story about how she's here with me, it must've been swiped from in front of her apartment and she never knew about it. Told 'em I'm sending somebody to take care of it. I'm gonna fly a guy down there with temporary tags to bring it back, but I want you to look at it first."

"Damn. They know someone's after them so they've ditched their vehicle. They probably drove while it was still dark and got rid of it before daylight. Less chance of being spotted that way. Let me tell you what I just learned." I gave him the story on the express mail shipment.

"Nice work, Gabe. It's gotta be connected, same day he was killed and all. So maybe Switzer sent something on ahead to Jennings, picked it up when he got to Memphis, then split."

"It's a scenario that works," I agreed, not pointing out that it was the best one as far as Sibyl was concerned. "If

59

that's the case, then whoever worked over Jennings may have been after the parcel."

"Yeah, and Jennings couldn't squeal about it because he didn't know where Switzer went with it." I could tell he liked the idea a little too much, letting hope cloud his judgment. "You think the Memphis PD got the top sheet from that pad?"

"Maybe, but I doubt it. They'd've probably taken the whole pad, not just the sheets with writing on them. I figure it was wadded up in a wastebasket. They emptied those, but who knows when they'll bother to look, if ever. They're not giving the case high priority."

"Your next stop's Oklahoma City, Gabe." He gave me the names and numbers of people to talk to about the car and we went over the details of the story to give if anybody should bother to ask. Every big city has a lot more to concern itself with than the odd abandoned, out-of-state car.

"I'm on my way."

Five .

A t Memphis you cross the Mississippi River, the nation's great divide, an immense, vertical stripe that separates East from West far more decisively than the invisible Mason-Dixon line ever divided North from South. Next to the highway near the river stands a big, shiny pyramid, witness to the fact that, by the time settlement reached the river, America had run out of Greek and Roman city names and had started on Egypt. A way north, at the Mississippi-Ohio river junction, stands Cairo, Illinois.

I drove slowly across the bridge, savoring the sight of the river in the morning light. It always calls to mind the image of palatial paddleboats with their tall stacks belching smoke and cinders, of Mike Fink and the keelboatmen, of Huck and Jim on their little raft. Once the States had ended here. Beyond lay the Great West, mysterious, full of hidden riches and sudden death. Out there were Mexican armies, bands of warlike Indians, all the outlaws and malcontents who had rejected or been rejected by the civilized East. You crossed that river to go out to the California gold fields or to settle the promised land of Oregon, and you knew that, if you lived to see the end of the

61

journey, you would almost certainly never see home again. The journey was too long and dangerous and full of hardship. Now it's about three hours by airplane, but you miss an awful lot that way.

On the other side of the river the bridge carried me over the broad mudflats of the western floodplain, then dropped me onto the relatively dry ground of the town of West Memphis, Arkansas. For most of the morning I drove across the swampy flatness of Arkansas, passed Little Rock, and by late afternoon was driving into Oklahoma City. I was still quite a way from my destination, because you pass the city limits long before you can actually see the city. The city fathers didn't believe in letting anyone escape paying city taxes, presumably.

When I reached the downtown area, I drove around for a while looking for one of the addresses Carson had given me, but mostly familiarizing myself with the town's layout. It's something I do habitually. Knowledge like that can come in handy when you least expect it.

At one point I pulled up by a vacant lot and felt insect feet running up my spine when I realized what it was. Not long ago, a big federal building had stood on that spot. Lunatics with some fertilizer, diesel fuel, a load of hate and a weird agenda had blown it out of existence along with a lot of unsuspecting human beings. It's how you make a point these days.

There's a great deal of nuttiness abroad in the land, of late. People are shutting themselves up in armed compounds, terrified of mysterious black helicopters and conquest by, of all things, the United Nations. I suspect it all has something to do with the approaching millennium. Premillennial jitters are beginning to run rampant. I shudder to think that A.D. 2000 will be a presidential election year.

The impound lot was surrounded by a chain-link

fence topped with barbed wire. The old guy at the guard booth looked like a retired cop.

"So you're here to pick up the Grand Am?" He peered through his glasses at a clipboard.

"No, I just need to look it over. Someone will be along later to take it back."

"It's right down here." I followed him past forlorn tow-ins and a few prizes, including a sleek, black limo that looked like something a Saudi prince would own. I paused by that one.

"Drug dealer?" I asked.

"Yep. They brought it in from the airport lot. It was a hot spell and somebody complained about the smell. Dealer was in the trunk."

"That'll make it hard to get rid of." I'd run into a number of those in my years with the LAPD.

"Yeah, you can never get that smell out. Nice limo, otherwise."

We reached the Grand Am and the old guy unlocked the driver's-side door. "Usually, they get boosted and drove halfway across the country, they're in a lot worse shape than this one," he said.

The car showed the effects of a cross-country drive, but that was nothing a self-service car wash wouldn't fix. The car had been well cared for and the interior was clean, without the usual litter of burger wrappers, bank cash envelopes and so forth. Sibyl was as fastidious about her car as she was about everything else in her life, except maybe her taste in men.

"Would you open the trunk for me?" He popped the lid. There was a spare tire, a jack, a tire iron and a couple of flares. No luggage. The carpeted interior looked as if it had been recently vacuumed.

"Just lock it up when you're done," the old guy said, already walking back toward his booth. A tow truck was coming in with a Buick that was pocked with bullet holes.

Either they'd sanitized the car before abandoning it, or there hadn't been anything in it when they lammed. I sat behind the steering wheel to think about that.

They'd run without stopping to pick up their belongings, bought clothes in Nashville, but probably no more than would fit into a suitcase. That left the parcel, size and contents unknown.

I leaned over and opened the glove compartment. It had been cleaned out, too. Title, registration and insurance papers were gone. It would have made no sense to take off the plates but leave the paperwork in the car. The serial numbers? Those aren't easy to remove. From all appearances the two weren't making an effort to wipe out all traces of their existence. They seemed to think a few days' head start would see them clear. But clear of what?

I got out and pushed the seats forward. Not even a lost quarter to be seen.

"I don't expect you're likely to find anything."

I straightened up and turned around to face Jasper Holt. Just behind and to one side of him, the small, dark-haired woman was looking me over with her cool, unnerving evaluation.

"You get around pretty quietly for a man in cowboy boots," I said to him.

He grinned. "Could be your hearing ain't what it used to be." He turned slightly. "Tina, this is Mr. Gabriel Treloar, late of the Los Angeles Police Department, currently in the employ of Randall Carson. Treloar, this is my assistant, Tina."

"Pleased to meet you," said Tina, who apparently didn't have a last name. Her tiny hand was surprisingly strong. Her inch-long hair was fine as kitten fur.

"Pretty good, Holt," I acknowledged. "I'm sure you don't remember me from fifteen years ago. Did you run my plates?"

"Did we meet on one of my visits out there? I confess I don't recall. Yes, Tina noticed you back in Nashville and memorized your plate number."

"Not bad. What tipped you?"

"Ain't hard to spot a cop," she said.

Holt grinned again. "Ain't she something? I let you walk right past me, but Tina read you like a neon sign."

I caught her flicker of annoyance at his patronizing tone. "We won't learn nothin' here," she said.

"Right you are. Treloar, it's gettin' 'long about suppertime. What do you say we grab us a bite and talk?"

The restaurant was about five blocks away. I used the short drive to get my thoughts in order, all too conscious that this might be a man who had taken a power drill to a fellow human being's anklebones. I didn't think so, but what did I know about him except his reputation? This could be a terrific break or awful danger.

They were already seated and looking over menus when I joined them.

"I stop by here pretty often when I'm travelin'," Holt told me. "They have real down-home cookin' and I recommend the chicken-fried steak and biscuits."

"Holt, can we come to an agreement here? I won't be Sam Spade if you won't be Andy Griffith."

"I know about Andy Griffith," Tina said. "Who the hell's Sam Spade?"

"Before your time," Holt said. "A man can't escape his upbringing, Treloar. But if it'll please you, I'll dispense with the regional pleasantries."

The waitress took our orders and I threw out an opener. "Who are you working for, Holt?"

"I hope you'll understand if I can't answer that. My client requires complete confidentiality."

"Then you have the advantage, because you know who I'm working for."

"Naturally. Your client is your boss and you want to find Miss Carson. We're not in competition there, Treloar. It's young Mr. Switzer I'm looking for."

"More specifically, you're after something Switzer has in his possession."

His eyes narrowed. "Correct. How do you know about that?"

"Switzer hasn't jumped bond and there are no warrants out against him. Last I heard you hadn't taken up scalp hunting. You recover things for people."

He sat back. "Fair enough. I'll be honest with you, Treloar: Under other circumstances I'd be more than happy to work together with you on this, but I'm bound by my client's wishes. I repeat, though, we are *not* in competition here. If one or the other of us doesn't find them soon, Miss Carson is going to be in terrible danger. Hell, she's in danger now."

"And Switzer?"

"No matter what we do, Switzer's a dead man. I won't drop the hammer on him 'long as he don't throw down on me, but he's finished anyway."

Our orders arrived and I worked on a Caesar salad while Holt plowed into a chicken-fried steak and pan gravy. Tina had ordered a double bacon cheeseburger with fries. She had an amazing appetite for such a small woman. She shook ketchup over her fries and abruptly her eyes cut up at me with that rabbit-freezing stare.

"This the way you old pros operate? You swap these little jabs back and forth, try to act like you know it all and find out what the other one knows? Coupla grown men oughta have more sense."

"Now, Tina." Holt gave me a tight-lipped smile, seeming almost embarrassed.

"Treloar," Tina said, ignoring him, "I saw you go into that Jennings boy's house. Why don't you tell us what you found there and we'll tell you a few things and we can get on with this 'stead of sittin' here playin' grabass like punks on a street corner?" She took a ferocious bite of cholesterol, coronary occlusion apparently being among her less urgent worries.

"The lady has a point," I allowed. "All I want is Sibyl Carson alive, safe and away from the law's notice."

"And all I want's my client's property," Holt said, casting a seething look at Tina. "You'll have noticed from the late Pat Jennings's condition not everyone involved in this has such delicate sensibilities. You go first."

So I told them about my late-night foray into Jennings's house. Tina's eyes didn't flicker when I came to the part about the power-drill crucifixion. Holt nodded appreciatively when I told them how I'd found the parcel tracking number. At the end of it I turned to Tina.

"My compliments. Before I went in I checked the neighborhood for a stakeout. I never spotted you." She just shrugged, as if avoiding the notice of fools was no big feat.

"It's about what I figured," Holt said, nodding. "So Switzer shipped my client's property off to Jennings and then picked it up just before our third party came calling. I must admit that Black & Decker questioning indicates we're dealing with some hard cases."

"Did you get a look at Jennings's body?" I asked him.

He shook his head. "Didn't need to. I got a look at the crime scene photos."

"Must be nice to have contacts like yours. What did you make of the marks carved on him?"

"The *DTT* fails to ring a bell. The arrow item carved on his forehead, that could be a number of things." He took a pen from inside his coat and sketched the mark on a napkin. "It could be a directional arrow, but that doesn't make much sense. I faxed it to a fella I know at Cambridge, professor of semiotics. You know, the study of signs and symbols and such? He came up with a couple of possibilities. One's something called the Broad Arrow. It was used for a number of centuries to mark British government property; ordnance and the like. They used to stamp it all over convicts' uniforms, the way we used to use striped overalls here."

"Somehow I don't see a crazed British bureaucrat figuring in this," I said.

"Neither do I. The other thing he came up with is a runic symbol called Tyr." He spelled it for clarity.

"Runic?"

"Yep. Viking and Anglo-Saxon alphabet, before they started using the Roman system. It was based on the Roman letters, but simplified, and with some new symbols for sounds that didn't occur in Latin. The symbols themselves were made up of straight lines to make them easier to carve in wood, paper being in short supply up north."

"So what does Tyr mean?"

"First off, it's just the sound for *T*. But each rune also had a religious meaning. Tyr was the name of the war god, so the sign could stand for war, or for death."

"*DTT,*" I mused. "One of those *T*'s could stand for 'Tyr.' We're back to that cult stuff and I think it's crap."

"Lots of little hairball groups these days devoted to things other than sacrificing goats to Satan," he pointed out.

I looked at Tina. "Did it look familiar to you?"

"My husband had a bunch of jailhouse tattoos, but nothing like that. Could be someone faking us out."

"That occurred to me," I said. "So why is this so complicated, Holt? Switzer scammed your client out of something, probably money or something worth a lot of money. Your client wants it back, that's reasonable enough, no reason to be cagey."

"I never said he scammed my client for anything."

Tina rolled her eyes ceilingward in disgust, but he cut a glare at her and this time she kept her mouth shut.

"You're not holding up your end, Holt. I'm telling you what I know and you're holding out."

He leaned forward on his elbows and dropped the affable act. "You're a hell of a lot more desperate than I am, Treloar. You want to save that little girl's ass from the law and I'm here to tell you that's the least of her worries. You know the kind of pull I have. You screw with me and I can have you picked up and held on any number of charges. Maybe nobody'd hold you for long, but I'd be way ahead of you. You just be grateful I'm playing ball with you at all."

I had to swallow that one because it was true. "In that case, I have work to do. I need to talk to the officer who found Sibyl's car."

He smiled again, friendly as a fairy-tale wolf. "I can save you that little chore. It was abandoned at a rest area just west of town and towed back here. Looks like they've jumped off the map."

"Damn," I said, disgusted. "They're hitching."

"Exactly. No car to trace and I don't imagine they'll be using her credit cards from here on. It's been sorta easy up till now. The next part's gonna be downright challengin'."

We finished eating and Tina excused herself. She clicked off on her little, silver-plated heels toward the ladies' room and I watched her go, the fringe along the back of her jacket swaying like a line of diminutive whips. She dressed and talked pure trailer trash, but there was a fierce, sharp intelligence in her eyes, along with a lot of close-reined anger.

"How did a solitary operator like you end up with a partner?" I asked.

"Assistant," he corrected me. "Tina's still learning the business. We met a while back when I was trackin' one Dodge McKay. Remind me to tell you his sad tale sometime. She was at loose ends and you might say unsuited for conventional employment. I'm gettin' along in years, no longer up to all the legwork my vocation entails, even in this age of computers. We arrived at an understanding."

"What's your next move? They could be in L.A. by now, depending on the rides. No credit card purchases to chase, no known associates this far west; there's not much to go on."

"Very true. I'll have to fall back on my many years of experience with Switzer's kind. They can throw you short-term surprises, but overall their thinking and behavior patterns are predictable. Plus, I have a resource you don't. I can tap my police contacts, have 'em on the lookout for our two little lovebirds. And you have a resource I lack." He sipped at a cup of black coffee.

"What's that?"

"That little girl might call her daddy. You'll let me know if she does that, won't you?" He handed me a card. It just had his name and a call-forwarding number.

I took it. "If you find them first, you'll contact me?"

"Right. I'll do what I can to keep that silly little girl safe, but I can't make any promises. She's hooked herself up with a prize loser this time. Women who do that usually suffer the consequences."

"All too true." I knew well what he meant. The big score is the great, immemorial losers' fantasy. They're unsuited for any sort of steady work; they lack foresight and creativity. So they dream about the big score. For the typical schmuck, the law-abiding loser, it's hitting the lottery, finding buried treasure, the unexpected death of that previously unknown rich uncle—pure, gratuitous wish fulfillment.

For the sociopathic criminal loser it's that once-in-a-lifetime job, the fabulous sucker, the ultimate scam that will net millions and let him retire to a life of luxury safe from the law and from the wrath of his victims. These losers sometimes act on their fantasies. But they always screw up because it's in their nature to. What they never seem to take into account is the fact upon which Jasper Holt had made his career: People with millions to lose can pay to get that money back and punish the transgressor.

It looked as if Nick Switzer had pulled off his big score. Now he faced the difficult task of living to enjoy it.

"They've disappeared into the West, Gabe," Holt said. "It's a big area, and it has a floating population that's never been tallied by any census."

I nodded. "It's the American thing to do. Been that way since boys in trouble back East took the Natchez Trace and headed into the unknown. Sheriffs used to write *GTT* after names on their wanted lists, for 'Gone To Texas.' "

He smiled with genuine delight. "I just knew you had the feel and insight for this sort of thing. Do you think Switzer's a romantical sort like us? Think he's decided to do the classic thing and go west to be an outlaw?"

"Maybe. I was thinking the outfit he bought in Nashville was C&W camouflage, but it's also gunslinger drag. He could be pretty far out of touch with reality."

"But I'd have thought young Miss Carson would have been more firmly grounded," Holt said.

I told him a little of what I'd gleaned from Sibyl's diaries, few specifics but the general tenor, and he shook his head with dismay.

"Oh, my, this could be bad. Might I have a look at those books?"

"Uh-uh. If you're going to be coy about your client's identity and the nature of his loss, I can guard the privacy of my client's daughter." By this time Tina had rejoined us.

71

"Then, do you think you could check into her course load?" he asked. "I'd like to know what philosophical writings she was into that last couple of semesters."

"Why?"

"Specifically, I'd like to know if Nietzsche was on the list. I can just imagine our girl reading Nick a few chapters of an evening, bedtime stories, so to speak. 'Specially certain passages from *Beyond Good and Evil,* lauding the criminal as a superior being. It's been the downfall of many a half-educated fool."

"A little philosophy is a dangerous thing," I said, amazed. There was more going on under that Stetson than cornpone patter and pit-bull menace.

"Don't let him get started on that Neechee guy," Tina warned me. "He'll talk long enough to raise warts on a bowling ball."

"Tina doesn't share my enthusiasm for nineteenth-century German philosophers," Holt said.

"It's a rarefied taste," I told her. "Jasper, are you serious or just blowing smoke?"

"Look into it," he advised.

"All right. What's your next move?"

"I got my feelers out. He could pull a fast one and double back on us, but I expect his general trend to be westward. Keep goin' west and we'll be gettin' closer to them."

"Same here. I'm figuring the high plains or the Rockies, from the clothes they bought, but it doesn't mean they won't go to ground and hole up for a while between here and there. I'll take it slow. Do you think he still has your client's goods in his possession?"

"I doubt it. Now I know he shipped it to Jennings, I figure he's sent it on ahead again, knowing there's pursuit close behind him. They repeat patterns, remember."

"It's why we call them patterns. That means a destination, another former associate, unless he's willing to risk the post office and the general delivery box in some town out there."

"Awfully risky," Holt said. "I'm more inclined to expect another known associate. I'm looking for records of any previous activities on his part out there, but he'd've been using an alias and small-town police departments tend to be sloppy about things like fingerprints and close ID checks."

"I guess we might get lucky," I said. "Maybe we'll see them standing by the side of the road with their thumbs out."

"If them two've gone out in the wind we ain't gonna catch 'em by lookin'," Tina said. "We're gonna have to wait for Switzer to screw up."

"Suppose he doesn't?" I said.

"That boy'll screw up because it's what he was born to do," she said. "He'll join NASA and fly to the moon before he gets over that little disadvantage."

We broke up our little confab and went out to our vehicles. Evening was fast drawing on. We bid one another good-bye and good hunting and drove away.

It was conceivable that Nick and Sibyl had doubled back and found themselves a crib in Oklahoma City. It was a good place to disappear into, but I didn't think so. They had set out west and, like Newton's objects in motion, they were going to keep going that way until acted upon by an outside force.

As I headed out toward the edge of town I wondered whether I was going to tell Carson that I'd linked up with Jasper Holt and, in a strange fashion, was cooperating with him. It might be a bad move. Just mentioning Holt's name had scared him badly. He was too personally involved and saw Holt as a hired killer. Of course, he might be right. Holt might be snowing me. I didn't doubt he could run a con that would make Nick Switzer look like an amateur. I might be signing Nick and Sibyl's death warrants, not that Nick's demise would make me lose much sleep.

The sad fact was, Holt was right about how desperate I was. Without his sources to tap, my chances of finding the two were greatly reduced. I had to go on instinct, and mine told me Holt wasn't a contract killer. That he was one ruthless son of a bitch I had good reason to know, but I thought pride if nothing else would keep him from taking a hit contract. He was a top manhunter, and that's a professional category far rarer and more valuable than common assassin.

A few miles out of town I found the rest area where Nick and Sibyl had abandoned their car. It was like hundreds of others along the interstates: a parking area for cars and one for trucks, a central building that housed rest rooms, a smaller one for vending machines, a big map under Plexiglas attached to a wall.

I got a can of apple juice and went to one of the concrete picnic tables in the little parklike area between the parking lots. I sat on the table's corner and put my feet on the bench, and with my elbows on my knees I faced the pink glow in the western sky. The place was almost deserted, and traffic on the highway was infrequent, so I could hear the wind in the long prairie grass that grew on both sides of the highway to the limit of visibility. The landscape was flat as still water.

From here that young woman, full of beauty, intelligence and promise, had disappeared into the vast American emptiness with her hope-to-die-and-go-to-hell boyfriend. They were out there somewhere, among the floating population Holt had mentioned. Finding them was going to be like trying to locate a puff of smoke in a heavy coastal fog.

Six

Up North, down South, back East, out West. Our expressions of geographic orientation say a lot about our perceptions and our history. For hundreds of years, maps have made us think of the north-south axis in terms of up and down. National expansion made the East the place of origin and return, the West an open-ended destiny. Geographical America is roughly flat and horizontal, its boundaries mostly invisible; state lines you can step across without noticing, lesser subdivisions marked nowhere except on a map.

Social America is vertical and multilayered. Its boundaries, while porous, are fairly rigid. Your place in it is determined by a great many things: money, education, dialect, just plain disposition are among them. We're all familiar with most of the gradations. There are the privileged old families with their estates, Ivy League schools, old money; the white-collar middle class of the 'burbs and the better neighborhoods of the cities; the blue-collar, lower middle class of the industrial sprawl; the military; the ethnic enclaves; the ghetto poor. At the bottom are the homeless, the deranged and the chemical dependents of all races so outcast nobody will claim them.

I was headed into one of the strangest and least known of the social and geographical strata. It is what Holt referred to as the floating population. They are the fringe dwellers, the drifters, the losers, the down-and-out, the gypsies, living on schemes and scams and often as not on nothing at all, united in their inability to function in the everyday, nine-to-five world. What distinguishes them from the others is their mobility. They hitchhike or travel in broken-down cars, pickups and vans, and often as not they sleep in them, or they live in the cheapest motels, the ones well back from the interstates, which rent out rooms by the month.

They pick up a living here and there, selling crafts or junk in parking-lot flea markets, doing odd jobs, working for wetback pay, maybe picking fruit in season or following the grain harvest north. Some of them are pretty good at milking the welfare system and the charities. If they have any musical skill they knock around the clubs, their combos forming and dissolving like amoebas under innumerable names. They travel singly and by twos and in whole families, their lives spent amid noisy truck stops, seedy carnivals and long stretches of lonely highway, buying their clothes in secondhand thrift shops, food from day-old-bread places and roadside stands. They are the ones who hear a whole orchestra of different drummers.

Nobody knows how many of them there are. They don't fill out census forms, they don't register to vote, they don't stay in one place long enough to establish residency or attract notice, unless they get into trouble. There may be millions of them, sleeping in their cars or under bridges, in paint-flaking, neon-flickering motel rooms when they're flush, and in the open air when they're broke.

I call them the motorized homeless. If you want to disappear in this country, there is no better place to do it than by fading into this half-world of the terminally alienated.

I decided that some protective coloration was in order.

Tina had spotted me a little too easily. I was already driving a car that would pass muster in the roadside demimonde. Just to get that properly rumpled, seedy look, I slept in it at the rest area, then drove on in the early morning without shaving. This called for treading a fine line. If you look too much like a bum, the police stop and question you as a matter of course.

I reached the outskirts of Amarillo just after noon, taking my time and keeping my eyes peeled. Hell, I thought, I really might see them with their thumbs out. Anything can happen. I left the interstate and followed a series of signs to an open-air flea market. It was held in an abandoned drive-in movie theater, a dying American institution being replaced by a flourishing one, like those Western ghost towns transformed into theme parks.

I left the car in a grassy field and walked among the bargain hunters. Folding tables were set among the forlorn stumps of speaker stands, the huge, looming screen providing shade for a few tables whose proprietors had been energetic enough to stake out their claims early. The wares on display ran the gamut from home-canned fruit to firearms, from beautifully crafted quilts to chrome-plated tools from Asia that I knew, from bitter experience, would snap or strip out the second or third time they were used.

The merchants were mostly professionals who carried their wares and their tables in trucks, traveling a regular flea-market circuit. Here and there I heard vendors conversing among themselves in Romany, the ancient Gypsy language. This was yet another of America's invisible populations, engaged in the true underground economy, selling and trading and never, never bothering anyone with extraneous concerns like licensing and interstate commerce regulations. If you were delicate about things like your tax money being used for war or welfare, this was one place you could shop with full assurance that not one nickel was going to be passed on to any government agency.

I located a bin of footwear and pulled out a pair of worn but serviceable huaraches, Mexican sandals with woven leather tops and tire-tread soles with a few miles still left on them, and a pair of steel-toed engineer boots for colder weather. I further enhanced my wardrobe with a fleece-lined leather bomber jacket, once very expensive but now looking like it had flown too many missions. Flea market chic comes and goes in the world of high fashion, but I was going where it was a permanent condition.

I wandered about for a while, trying to get a handle on this separate world with its understood if unwritten laws, its specialized jargon, always keeping in mind that, like the society at large, that of the motorized homeless contained smaller subcultures, each with its own customs and cant.

Tina, for instance, had said that Nick and Sibyl were "in the wind." That's biker terminology and, along with her ex-husband's jailhouse tattoos, said much about the life she had come from. Here, even the body language differed subtly from one group to the next. If the subculture was a clannish one, like the Gypsies or the outlaw bikers, the special arcana of the group served as protection against infiltration by outsiders.

I stopped by a table where a young woman displayed a variety of silver jewelry and leather crafts, most of it decorated with designs dear to the hearts of everyone from metalheads to Nazis to New Age crystal freaks. There were dragons, skulls, SS lightning insignia, little wands decorated with colorful quartz, rings formed from tiny figures of couples performing acrobatic sex acts, incense burners decorated with gods from about twenty different mythologies and so on.

"See anything you like?" She wore a silk head scarf, a long-sleeved gray leotard with an ankle-length skirt of dazzling Indian cotton, and generally looked like a refugee from Haight-Ashbury of 1967, a time about ten years before she was born. She had a nice smile and, mercifully, lacked the vacant-eyed airhead look of the transcendentally blissed New Ager.

"Actually," I said, "I was looking for something with this design." I took out a pocket pad and sketched the arrow design with my pen.

Her smile grew brighter. "Tyr!"

"Uh, yeah," I said, astonished.

"I'm afraid I don't have anything with Tyr on it," she admitted. "Are you into rune lore?" She rummaged around in a big satchel beside her folding chair and emerged with a small drawstring bag of green velvet. Tugging the string open, she spilled a couple dozen irregular-shaped tiles onto the tablecloth before her. Each tile bore a single, angular character. The characters looked vaguely familiar, from pictures I'd seen of old Viking monuments.

"I can cast the runes for you," she offered. "I charge ten dollars for a reading, and I've always had good results. Personally, I think the runes are superior to the cards for an accurate reading." She shuffled her fingers among the little tiles and came up with one, the now-familiar arrow symbol. "Is Tyr your personal sign?"

I took it from her magenta-stained nails. The tile was roughly teardrop shaped, an inch long and maybe three quarters that at the widest point, made of unglazed, salmon-colored ceramic with the character crudely incised and colored with black pigment.

"No, it's just that I know some guys who use this as their logo—kind of like gang colors, you know? I thought I'd pick up something with that design as a present for one of them."

She shrugged and spread her hands. "Sorry. I could make you something, but I'd have to have an address to send it to, and it'd be quite a while. Me and my old man won't be getting home for another month."

"Never mind," I said, then, "Do you know of these guys, the ones who use Tyr as their logo?"

She frowned. "I don't know of anyone who uses that one. Now, there's a bunch that use this one." She picked up another of the little tiles, this one roughly rectangular. The symbol in its center consisted of a straight, vertical line with two branches slanting upward from either side, like a cross with its arms directed upward or an old-fashioned peace symbol from the sixties turned upside down and without the circle: ⅄. "But you don't want anything to do with that bunch. They're nasty. Really evil." She gave an exaggerated shudder and grimace.

I felt that old tingle. "Who are these guys? I don't think I've heard of them."

"You wouldn't want to. It's the White Front. You've never heard them on the radio?"

"I listen to NPR, mostly."

"Well, you wouldn't believe what you pull in driving around in a van in the middle of the night. There's this guy, name's Douglas Tyler, runs the White Front from someplace in West Virginia. Talks all the time about how Jews control the world and blacks are their subhuman stooges and like that. But he doesn't rave, he's real smooth, and he could almost get you to believing it if your head was in the right place. He's always calling for race war to purge the world of evil, and that kind of thing really scares me, you know? I mean, personally, I follow the Goddess, but I was born Jewish, and my old man's of the African persuasion, and we'd be number one on that freak's hit list."

I held up the little tile. "What's it mean?"

"That one is *eolh*. It's Old Norse for 'yew tree.' Phonetically it's the symbol for *X*, but it's used to mean life, happiness, all the positive things. Pretty creepy that the White Front would use it, huh?"

"Yeah," I said. "Sounds like the opposite of Tyr." Something occurred to me. "You can't see a logo like this on a radio broadcast. How'd you learn the White Front uses it?"

"Those guys pass out fliers just like the evangelists. I wouldn't be surprised if some of that garbage was floating around here. I mean, you always see neo-Nazi stuff around, but most of it's harmless." She gestured to some of the items on her table. "This stuff I mostly sell to punks and metalheads. They don't know what it means. It just shocks their parents, and that's enough for them. Even the White Power people and the Klan and most of them aren't much to worry about. They're mostly just stupid losers. Tyler and his guys are different."

"How's that?"

"If anybody could get that Nazi stuff going again, it's him. That vicious fucker's smart."

On a hunch I bought a bag of the rune tiles, along with a booklet explaining their meanings and instructions on how to use them to read the future or solve personal problems. The hippie-type lady pointed out to me, apologetically, that this probably wouldn't do me much good. She explained that things like crystal balls, tea leaves, tarot cards, runes, palm lines and so forth were only as good as the talent of the reader. If you didn't have the talent, you might as well go by a newspaper horoscope. That was okay with me. I wasn't planning a career based on reading the runes.

Now I had something to look for. I paid special attention to the tables featuring the sort of subculture paraphernalia my agreeable hippie lady sold. It didn't take me long to find a table catering to bikers: lots of black leather and chrome, hats and belts, chaps, boots and miscellaneous gear. One corner of the table featured a few stacks of printed material. Most of them were pamphlets run off on antiquated mimeograph presses, the paper the cheapest obtainable, the print fuzzy and all but unreadable. But one stack was different. The thin pamphlets were nicely printed on slick paper, neatly bound and stapled. The cover showed a beautiful blond child, her face glowing with happiness and health. Above her head was the title *Endangered Species?* In the upper-left-hand corner was the *eolh* symbol, in this case drawn to resemble a leafy tree.

I picked up a copy and caught the eye of the guy behind the table, a fat, bearded man who looked as if his hemorrhoids wouldn't allow much biking these days.

"How much are these?" I asked.

"Them's free, brother," he said, his eyes twinkling incongruously above cheeks laced with ruptured veins.

I flipped quickly through the pamphlet, seeing that it was well laid out by someone who knew a bit about magazine format. "That's amazing," I said admiringly. "I'll never understand how Mr. Tyler can just give away material like this. I mean, I've worked on a few magazines—*Iron Horse* and *Easy Rider* and a couple of others—and I know how much it costs to put out even a little one like this." I shook my head in wonder.

"You're right on there, brother," my new friend told me. "He's the only man in this country who really knows what's going on. He knows what it'll take to save the white folks of the world." He leaned back in his chair and took off his steel-rimmed glasses, polishing them with his shirttail. "I mean, it ain't like I hate anybody." With a gesture of his shaggy, blond-and-gray head he indicated the rest of the flea market. "These folks, some of 'em are niggers and Mexes and Gypsies; they're mostly pretty decent and we get along okay, but we all know the score, don't we? Sooner or later it's gonna come down to a question of us or them, and it's gonna have to be us, right?"

I nodded. "Mr. Tyler knows, huh?"

"Right." He tapped the stacks of printed material. "Now the media," he pronounced it *meedja*, "is all owned and run by Jews. You can't run no printed matter past 'em into the regular places that sells books and magazines. Same with TV and radio. But here we got a way to get out the word that they don't control."

"Well, thank God for that."

"Amen."

I flipped through the pages again. "Still, it kind of makes you wonder. It must take some real money to put this out. Do you think it all comes from membership dues?"

This time he smiled, showing stained teeth. "I guess you ain't really too familiar with the movement."

"No," I admitted sheepishly. "I've never been very political. But lately I've seen the way this society is headed and it scares me; I mean, you know—the way people are flooding across the border and the cities—hell, you can wander around for days trying to find someone who can speak English. And you can't trust what the newspapers and the TV say about it."

He nodded solemnly. "It ain't America anymore, is it? Naw, the Front don't use membership cards and nobody pays dues. That's the way they keep track of us, you see? Best not to leave any kind of paper trail, make it easy for them to track us down. Membership's here." He tapped the layer of fat somewhere near his heart.

"That's the smart way to do it," I agreed.

"Lemme see, I think I've got some copies of the book list here somewheres." He got up and shambled to the open rear door of a beat-up Dodge van, picked up a crate of printed material and carried it back to his chair. "Yeah, here it is. It's the latest one, come out about a month ago."

He handed me a copy. It was in magazine format, about sixty pages of it. Besides the runic logo, the cover featured an old photo of a sculptural group, an idealized couple with two children, all portrayed conventionally nude in white marble. A blurb inside the cover identified it as the work of Arno Breker, Hitler's favorite artist, and went on to say that the monument was "destroyed by Jewish Bolsheviks at the end of the War."

"I didn't know he sold books, too."

"Yep. You'll find publications in there you won't find anyplace else. Lately he's added a line of videotapes, too. You buy your books and tapes from there, and you'll be helping finance the movement. And it's all perfectly legitimate, protected by the First Amendment. Even the liberals ain't repealed that yet. And I'll tell you something else: A few years ago, that catalog wasn't ten pages long. The movement's growing, brother."

"Well, that's good news," I said, grinning.

"Back page of the catalog's got the map and the call numbers of the local radio stations. 'Bout anywheres in the country you can tune in to one of 'em. Only place you'll hear the truth broadcast. There's Internet sites, too, but I keep on the move so I never get a chance to check on them. This'll give you a pretty good idea of what the Front's all about and what we're up against."

"Well, I'm sure grateful for your help. I'd just run across a couple of issues of the magazine before. I didn't realize the movement was so big or so well organized."

"It's big and growing, and it's the only hope for us. Keep the faith, brother."

I walked away with a lot to think about. It had been kind of fun, falling into character to ingratiate myself with an informant. Then I thought about why it had been so easy: About half of my former colleagues on the LAPD had talked just like that.

I bought a bag of tamales from a vendor, picked up a can of soda and carried them, along with my purchases, back to my car. I tossed the clothes and footwear into the

trunk, then sat on the fender to eat and peruse the literature. For a while I busied myself with the complexities of
eating tamales. There is an art to getting them out of their
cornhusk wrappings without getting the sauce all over
you. If they're made properly, the result is worth the effort.
This being Texas, they were made right.

While I licked sauce off my fingertips and cooled my
mouth with soda, I flipped through the pages of the book
catalog with my less greasy hand. Douglas Tyler, neo-Nazi
guru and bookseller, offered an astounding assortment of
literature. About half of it was perfectly legitimate: scholarly histories of Greece, Rome and the Celtic and Teutonic
peoples; Penguin Classic editions of Homer and Virgil;
the Norse sagas; medieval romances and so forth; books
on European history and archaeology, art and mythology.
There were even recordings and videotapes of Wagner-
ian operas.

The rest of it was crackpot propaganda of the wildest
sort, almost all of it touting Aryan racial superiority and
a worldwide, history-long conspiracy by Jews to destroy
Western culture and establish themselves as the master
race. There were written and photographic histories of
World War Two as seen from the German side, recordings
of Nazi marching songs and a number of works claiming
that the Holocaust was a myth created by Jews to inflict
guilt on Aryans and gain sympathy. These works took the
odd position that, while the Holocaust never happened, it
would be a good idea, anyway.

Reading the copy, I began to see what my hippie lady
had been getting at. Tyler's written style was neither shrill
nor ranting. He presented his arguments as perfectly reasonable, advanced them in scholarly fashion and even
displayed a certain dry wit when discussing current
political policies and attacks by his numerous critics. He
even, by way of "balance and fairness," offered books by

Jewish scholars critical of Jewish religious practice or Israeli policies.

It occurred to me that, to the uncritical and ill-educated, this stuff might look like genuine scholarship from a prestigious source. Tyler wasn't shy about putting the Ph.D. after his name. It seemed that he held a doctorate in mathematics. How this qualified him as an expert on history and conspiracies, he didn't explain, but he certainly wouldn't be the first crank to use his degree in one subject to lend authority to his opinions in a totally unrelated field.

Unfortunately, this did little to help me with my central problem: Where the hell were Nick and Sibyl, and what in the world did this stuff have to do with them? For all I could tell, the White Front was a one-man operation located on a West Virginia farm, its only connection to my case being the use of a runic symbol, which might well be purely coincidental.

Still, I had that tingle that told me I was on to something. Over the years, I'd learned to pay attention to feelings like that.

Seven

The stretch of Amarillo that rambles along I-40 is a brain-numbing lineup of motels and eating establishments that seem, at a glance, to be capable of feeding and lodging a medium-sized nation. Amarillo lies at the intersection of two interstate highways and it is the only major city for a long, long way in any direction. From the highway, there was virtually nothing to distinguish it from any other such stretch of road except for its inordinate length. I couldn't see a single business that wasn't a part of a chain, from Wal-Mart to Taco Bell to Holiday Inn. Texans pride themselves on the unique quality of their state, but nothing of the sort was apparent from where I was sitting.

I drove on toward the western end of town and got off the interstate once again. A few minutes of driving took me to a seedy district of thrift shops, boarded-up storefronts and pawnshops with metal grilles pulled across their front windows. It had probably been a respectable, working-class neighborhood once, before the interstates and the malls leached away the traffic and business and property values plummeted.

It was late afternoon, I'd run out of leads and I had

some calls to make, so I looked around for lodgings befitting my new status. It didn't take me long to find just the place.

The sign was a big one, announcing that this was the North Texan Motor Court. The lettering had been touched up, but a painting of a buckaroo riding a bronc while improbably twirling a lasso with one hand and firing a six-shooter with the other had been allowed to flake away, faded by the fierce prairie sun until it was as faint as a badly executed fresco on the wall of a medieval monastery. The lettering and figure were outlined with delicate neon tubing and I was curious to know whether it still worked, or had been allowed to go the way of other remnants of a better time.

I opened the office door and the smell of curry hit me like a blow in the face. The woman who came through a door in the rear of the office wore a sari and had a single, blood-red dot in the center of her forehead. Through the door I could see three small children enthralled by a television cartoon show, overseen by a much older woman, also wearing a sari. They never even glanced my way.

"Yes?" the younger woman said through a smile of hallucinatory whiteness, the single, lilting syllable both greeting and question.

"I need a room for the night," I told her.

"You will be staying only the one night?" A tiny diamond winked from one nostril.

"I may be staying longer; it depends."

"A single for one night is seventeen dollars. If you want to stay for one week it is eighty-five dollars. For one month, one hundred ninety dollars." I was willing to bet they had yearly rates, too.

"I'll just take one for tonight. By tomorrow I'll know whether I'll be staying longer."

"Very good. If you want to extend for a week, we will refund the extra you pay for the first night. Your room is on that end." She pointed toward the southern end of the building, her slender wrist circled by a dozen bangles.

I took my key outside and drove down to the last room. The motel was single story, shaped like a shallow V with the office in the middle behind a shingled canopy, a poor man's porte cochere if ever there was one. The parking lot that separated it from the road was barely big enough to accommodate one car for each unit, and it was already overcrowded since at least half of the vehicles there were pulling freight trailers. One was even towing a two-horse trailer, mercifully free of occupants.

I parked and unlocked the door to my room, letting it swing wide and giving the interior a quick scan before setting foot across the threshold. It was an old habit from my cop days, and I figured it was one I'd better cultivate from here on. This time the room beyond held no visible menace, but it always pays to be sure. I went on in and wrinkled my nose at the musty smell, something I knew I'd just have to get used to.

It contained a single, narrow bed, an elderly television atop a dresser, a hot plate on a corner table, an alcove with a sink and next to that a closet-sized bathroom with a toilet and a shower stall. Next to the bed was a stand with a lamp and a telephone. It was reasonably clean, except for the ineradicable dinginess and grime of age. The wallpaper was mottled and peeling, the carpet all but nap free and worn almost through to the floorboards in the heavy-traffic spots. I tossed back the grayish, often-patched bed linens to surprise any lurking, six-legged inhabitants, but it looked as if I was to be spared that particular unpleasantness.

It was typical spartan Third World accommodations, depressing but livable. I went out and brought in my luggage, glanced at my watch, saw it was time for the evening news and turned on the television. The picture was fuzzy, the colors uncertain, but from the distance of the bed it was clear enough and the sound was all right. In all, this probably passed for near-luxurious digs among us, the motorized homeless. I learned that I had barely missed intersecting the path of a tornado earlier in the day. It had torn up a chunk of grazing land east of the city about an hour after I'd passed through that stretch. My luck was holding.

Aside from the usual local, national and international awfulness, nothing I saw in an hour of news watching seemed to have any relevance to my forlorn quest, so I snapped the TV off. No remote, of course.

It was getting about time to report in to Carson, and I considered my words carefully. I had to keep him informed, but I didn't want to alarm him. He picked up on the second ring and I told him where I was and that Nick and Sibyl were probably hitching, but I left out my interview with Holt and Tina. He was a little surprised that I wanted a copy of Sibyl's course load, but I said that it might help me interpret her enigmatic diaries and he agreed to fax me the information.

I brought up the possibility that the mark carved on Jennings could be a runic symbol, and that I'd found a possible link to the White Front, but stressed that it was a long shot. He didn't think a connection was likely, but he'd look into it.

"I'm sorry I don't have more to report," I said, "but without the car or more credit card purchases, there isn't much to follow."

"Hell, you're the only one's getting anything accomplished, Gabe. You've followed 'em halfway across the country already. They'll turn up someplace."

"I'm going to check out the dives and honky-tonks tonight. Albuquerque's the next big city on I-40, and if I haven't found anything to make me want to hang around here, I'll head that way tomorrow as soon as I pick up your faxes." I looked through the yellow pages and located a fax service not far from where I was staying, gave Carson its number and signed off.

For a while I lay back against the pillow, staring at the ceiling, then I reached for my White Front literature once more. This time I went through the newsletter with the picture of the Aryan child on the cover. The title of the publication was "National Guardian," and the masthead claimed that this was volume 25, issue 6. Owner and editor was Douglas Tyler, with a few contributing editors and writers credited. Articles in this issue had titles like "The Big Lie: How Our Enemy Duped America Into Taking the Side of Evil in WWII," and "Why Our Schools Are Racial Jungles." One drew my attention immediately: "AIDS: A Disease With Real Promise." Sibyl had worked in an AIDS lab. It wasn't much of a connection, but what else did I have except a runic symbol?

The AIDS article was one with Tyler's name on it. It began with a brief history of the disease from its first known appearance in the U.S. until the present, then went on to pontificate about it. Tyler seemed to think that AIDS was one of the better developments of recent decades. First, it attacked the "perverts foisted upon us by the Enemy as role models for the young." Second, he noted its predilection for drug users. Third, and perhaps best of all, he gleefully pointed out, was its far higher incidence among nonwhite populations, especially the catastrophic proliferation of HIV infection in Africa, which, he said, "bids fair by the first decade of the 21st century to reduce the population of that continent to the far healthier level of the mid-19th."

It still didn't tell me much but I felt that a connection was there, however tenuous. It might have been too tenuous had it not been for the picture of Nick and Sibyl, the pair of them looking like models for those Aryan statues with their clothes on, posing for an SS medical corps recruiting poster.

It was almost dark by the time my stomach told me it was far too long since those tamales. I checked myself in the cracked, cloudy mirror over the sink before stepping out and saw that my silvery stubble was coming along nicely. Dressed in thrift shop clothes, I was acquiring the proper look all too easily. It occurred to me that no middle-aged American male is more than a couple of shaves and a few missed meals away from being a derelict.

I closed the door behind me and the parking lot gravel crunched beneath my surprisingly comfortable huaraches. I got into the car and began to cruise aimlessly, not looking for anyplace in particular, just soaking up the ambience. Most of the people on the sidewalks looked defeated, and there were the usual kids hanging around, doing nothing. I saw a couple of desultory drug deals being transacted, probably too commonplace to attract the attention of a beat cop, not that there were any cops around. I stopped at a noisy taco stand and sat at one of its outdoor, concrete tables to wolf down the specialty of the house while lowriders cruised by, emitting seismic bass notes, pot smoke drifting from their slightly opened black windows.

Fortified and ready to face the night, I went out to prowl the bars, marking the joints that had pickups and motorcycles in their lots, passing on the ones where the cars were too new or too clean. Inside, they were much alike, with poor lighting, gaudy signs advertising brands of beer, noisy jukeboxes and pool tables, where the patrons were at their most serious.

At each one I bought a beer and pretended to drink it, looking things over, getting in conversations with whoever was sitting next to me but not attracting much attention otherwise. By the third place I could see that this was a bust, a long shot that wouldn't pay off. There was nothing to make my antennae stand up and quiver, nothing that said my two errant young lovers might have passed this way.

I decided to give it one more try before calling it a night, and in the fourth place a woman slid onto the stool next to me.

"You're gonna have to do better than that," Tina said.

"Better than what?" She was attracting a lot of longing looks from the male patrons and envious ones from the females, but she ignored all of them.

"Buy me a beer and I'll tell you." I signaled the bartender and she picked up the schooner when it arrived, took a sip, set it down. "It ain't enough to just not shave and wear funky old clothes. You walk too confident to blend in. You step right out and keep your head up and your shoulders back like some goddamn drill sergeant. You want to look down and out, you got to slump some, maybe shuffle a little. Keep your hands in your pockets and your head low. Look at people sideways, not straight on."

"I'm just trying not to stand out, not look like some wino." Her remarks stung a little. I'd thought I was doing a good job of transforming myself. I'd never worked undercover during my police days. It seemed there was more to this than I'd thought. "Where's Jasper tonight?"

"Off conferrin' with his old cronies. He didn't invite me along. Told me to cruise around the less respectable parts of town, check out the drifter hangouts, keep an eye out for you. I seen—saw your car a while back and thought I'd see what you was up to."

I figured Holt had sent her to spy on me, but didn't think the point was worth arguing about. "Does he ditch you often?"

Her eyes shifted away from mine for once. "Sometimes I don't think he trusts me like he should, acts like maybe I ain—I'm not up to the more demandin' aspects of our line of work. I figure it's one of them male things. He treats me like I don't have good sense."

She took a pack of cigarettes from her purse and tapped one out.

"Like the way he keeps correcting your grammar?" I said helpfully.

She lit up and took a drag. "It ain't like he's one of them—those professors he's always readin'. He don't come from no—" She paused and grimaced. "Aw, shit, now you're gonna have me doin' this all evenin'."

"Just take it easy. I'm not going to jump on you. I'm not your eighth-grade English teacher." Inwardly I winced, thinking too late that she might not have made it that far. "Look," I said hastily, "let me tell you a little story."

So I told her one about a movie star I'd arrested once, a glamor queen world-famous for her portrayals of beautiful, sophisticated ladies of finishing-school elegance. When Murray and I arrested her for drunk and disorderly, not only had her language been foul, but she'd delivered it in a grammarless South Philly dialect so raw she'd made Tina sound like a Vassar girl by comparision.

Tina puffed on her cigarette and nodded. "I always took that woman for a slut. Well, has our little coed checked in with her papa yet?"

"Not as of a couple of hours ago. You two learn anything?"

"I don't think Jasper's bein' completely open with me, but I heard him callin' his contacts west of here. 'Course he had 'em lookin' for that Grand Am and now he wants 'em to be on the lookout for two hitchers."

"Has he been circulating Sibyl's picture?"

"Uh-uh, just Switzer's. Told 'em he was most likely travelin' with a woman, that's all."

"Any response?"

"Nothin' definite. You know how it is. Coupla possibles in New Mexico and Arizona, but nothin' clear enough to go tearin' out that way just yet. They serve food here? I'm about ready to starve. I missed dinner." She signaled the bartender and conferred with him for a while.

I held a little debate with myself, whether I should talk about my White Front hunch. I nixed the thought. I didn't have anything real and there was a good chance that Holt would take the opportunity and run with it, if he was still holding out on me, as I strongly suspected. Our powerful and justified mutual distrust was standing in the way of what might have been an efficient partnership.

"You headin' out in the morning?" Tina asked, lighting up another cigarette. "If I knew, it'd save me the trouble of looking around for you."

"I don't know yet. I'm waiting on some information from my boss, that college course load Jasper was talking about, some other things. You?"

"I'll know when he tells me."

"It's hell being the junior partner," I said.

When her food arrived I got up. "I'm getting too old for these late nights."

"Sleep tight," she said, reaching for the ketchup. In front of her was a huge, sloppy barbecue sandwich and a pile of french fries, along with another beer. I hesitated, fighting the urge, but I couldn't help it. It was the Californian in me.

I nodded toward the greasy platter, the beer and the half-smoked cigarette. "You keep that up, you're going to die young."

She looked at me and blew smoke. "Too late for that."

When I got back to my motel it was transformed. The sign out front had burst into glorious, neon brilliance. Parallel tubes beneath the eaves made horizontal stripes of orange and green and crickets sang a chorus from the weed-grown lot behind the building. A few patrons sat in painted steel chairs outside their rooms, talking and passing around cans of beer. Cigarette ends made firefly winks in the darkness. It was almost seductive, if you didn't know what it looked like in daylight.

I got out of my car and the illusion faded. The neon flickered and the old tubes buzzed, drowning the music of the crickets when you got close to them. The sparkle from the parking lot was from the shattered fragments of long-perished liquor and wine bottles. The air was still and the smoke from tobacco and pot hung around too long. As I opened the door to my room, I could hear voices raised in argument next door. I was glad mine was an end room. At least it would have one quiet side.

I reached in to flip on the lights and did the usual scan before I stepped inside. Everything seemed to be as I'd left it. It wasn't all that likely anyone would be taking an interest in me, but paranoia had to be a bedrock quality of my new life. Besides, I still thought it was a little too neat, Tina showing up next to me the way she had. She might have been engaging my attention while Holt tossed my room. But then, if Holt had been in, I'd never know it.

No sense worrying about it. I locked the door and set the chain, more as a gesture than any practical security precaution. The flimsy door would fly to splinters at the kick of a halfway determined foot.

I watched the late news but there was nothing of interest and I shut it off. Stretched out on the bed in shorts and T-shirt, I was tired but still too wired to nod off. It had been a long day with more mental activity than most. I pored over the White Front literature until my brain was numbed by its relentless if poorly thought out propaganda. Then I had another shot at the last volume of Sibyl's diaries. If that couldn't put me to sleep, nothing could.

Nick and I swim in the free-form amorality of his world. With my protective coloration he cruises my academic

*world, a barracuda among minnows. He will transform
my world to his reality. My workplace of common, plod-
ding science becomes his baroque alchemist's den, his
wizard's sanctuary where from illusion and perverted
desire he will conjure the evil miracle, bait the trap to
snare demented trolls.*

That did it.

I jerked awake in an instant, eyes staring, heart ham-
mering, panicked and unaware of where I was. The room
was washed with strobing red and blue, the air crackling
with static, mechanical screeches and shouting voices.

"Police! Open up now!" Shoe soles crunched on gravel
and pounded on pavement. "Open up! Open up!" Then,
"Break it down!" There was a deafening crash, male and
female voices shrieking, and my nerves jangled beneath
my skin and primitive, vestigial muscles contracted to
make the hair stand up, make me appear larger and more
menacing to the predatory beast invading my den.

After a few seconds my heart began to slow, the adrenaline to dissipate. My door was intact. They were raiding
the room next door. I got out of bed, pulled on my pants
and opened the door cautiously. A woman in uniform and
black leather harness glanced my way for a moment, then
dismissed me. I stuck my head out and saw five patrol
cars crowding the already jammed lot, their lights gyrat-
ing wildly and their radios blaring to the black skies of the
Texas night.

The cops already had one man belly-down on the
sidewalk, his fingers laced at the back of his head, a shotgun muzzle jammed into the cleft of his buttocks just to let
him know that resistance would be a really bad idea. Two
more men were hustled from the room and thrown face-
down, then a woman in a slip, crying and babbling. Her
hands were cuffed behind her but she was spared the
rougher treatment.

Other patrons had come out of their rooms to see the spectacle, some of them in bathrobes or pajamas, men and women looking disgruntled at being roused from sleep but not at all surprised or shocked at the colorful scene outside. Late-night motel-room rousts had to be a fairly frequent occurrence in their lives.

A cop emerged from the raided room with a cardboard box from which protruded the muzzles of a couple of sawed-off shotguns. Another carried three pistols dangling from a loop of plastic cord strung through their trigger guards. In his other hand was a transparent plastic bag full of smaller bags. Some seemed to contain white powder, others money.

It occurred to me that I had heard arguing voices from that room earlier in the evening. I was glad things hadn't gotten really heated. The walls were too thin to slow down a BB, much less the sort of firepower those people had. I didn't see any familiar faces among the arrestees, who were being hustled into the backseats of cars while another uniformed woman droned them their rights.

A mustached officer turned my way and barked, "Get back inside. This ain't your fuckin' TV!" All along the motel sidewalk, cops were ordering the other bystanders to do likewise. I knew better than to take it personally. I was now at a level of society where the relationship between cop and civilian was not that of civil servant and taxpaying employer. From here on my freedom to move was purely a matter of tolerance, subject to cancellation without notice by anyone with a uniform and a suspicious mind. Good lawyers were for people who could afford them.

I watched through the front window as the suspects and the evidence were driven away. For a while some of the cops sat in their units writing on clipboards while a couple of plainclothesmen questioned an Indian man, probably the owner, beneath the canopy. Then the last of them drove away and the outside was peaceful again in the flickering, buzzing neon glow. What went on behind the drawn curtains of the other rooms I couldn't even guess.

It took me a long time to get back to sleep.

Eight

The fax place turned out to be a private mailing service that offered letter and parcel delivery, as well as mailbox locations for people on the move. There were no posters proclaiming that disgruntled employees would never arrive to shoot up the place, but the implication was there. It made me feel old. I could remember when there were few options other than the post office for delivering things. Hell, I could remember when you could send a first-class letter with a purple three-cent liberty stamp.

The business was located in a small, open shopping mall a few blocks off the interstate, the kind that features a supermarket, a liquor store and a few other businesses of the sort that usually don't locate in the enclosed malls. There are gradations to this phenomenon that I've never figured out.

Before checking on my faxes I stopped at a McDonald's and got a large cup of their infamously hot coffee to get my heart started, passed on the high-fat eatables and ambled slowly over to the mailing service, sipping gingerly.

The clerk, a pretty high school girl, brought my faxes and had me sign for them. There were a number of sheets, most of them involving Sibyl's studies. Additional sheets had some White Front info, and I took the little stack out to my car to drink coffee and look it over, bracing myself for another long day of cruising I-40.

Sibyl's freshman year and a good deal of her sophomore year had been spent getting her requirements out of the way, all those English 101 and History 101 classes that are the bane of student life. Beyond that, she concentrated on sociology, criminology, psychology and philosophy. Checking on the latter I found, sure enough, "Kant, Schopenhauer and Nietzsche" and, the next semester, "Introduction to Nietzsche." So she'd been intrigued enough to study the old coot in more depth.

So Holt had been right. Or maybe he'd just been showing off. For all I knew he already had a copy of Sibyl's course list and was just trying to seem more astute than he was. The more pertinent question was, was this relevant? If so, I couldn't figure out why, except that a half-assed study of almost anything can get you into trouble.

I set that aside and looked at the pages on the White Front. It looked as if Carson had gotten hold of one of his contacts, who sent him this summary in the middle of the night. Computers and faxes really are wondrous things. The first paragraph was a bare-bones overview of a whole movement.

The White Power movement in America has no central organization, no unified leadership and no fully articulated ideology. In this it differs radically from Italian Fascism and German National Socialism. This is in part because of the intransigent and exclusionist attitudes of the various splinter groups, which are forever fragmenting over minor differences, and in part a deliberate policy designed to frustrate the activities of watchdog agencies. As a result, numbers can only be guessed at.

Some members of any group are sure to belong to one or more of the other far-right organizations."

That was clear enough. The next part was about Tyler and his organization.

Douglas Tyler (b. 1943) is the founder of the White Front and publisher of its newsletter, "National Guardian." He lived most of his early years in Illinois, received a Ph.D. in mathematics from Rutgers and taught mathematics at the University of Oregon from 1969 to 1975. He left the university, citing control of the math department by a clique of Jewish professors and favoritism toward Jewish students and "unqualified non-whites." For three years he worked at various magazine publishing houses in New York, and apparently during that time he made contacts among a number of extreme-right-wing organizations.

In 1978 Tyler founded the White Front in Alexandria, Virginia. From the beginning he emphasized the importance of propaganda and the necessity of getting out his race theory. He has forged links with many other white supremacist groups, while doing little to hide his contempt for groups such as the Klan and Christian Identity. He considers Christianity to be a fraud perpetrated by Jews to weaken northern European gentiles. He has little patience with the Klan because of what he perceives to be their obsession with blacks, whom he considers to be too inferior to represent a serious threat. Blacks are a menace, he claims, only because Jews first empower and encourage them, then protect them from white retaliation.

Tyler has built up an impressive book distribution and publishing establishment, featuring an assortment of respectable as well as crackpot literature. Many well-known authors and publishers would be surprised to find their works offered in his catalog. He also lectures and makes regular radio broadcasts, spreading his gospel of white supremacy. He can be an impressive public speaker and is careful to be the soul of reason and affability when speaking to the press or other outsiders.

He has taken great care to keep his distance from violently inclined groups, and often emphasizes the necessity of organizations like his own keeping above terrorist tactics. Nothing, he stresses, must be allowed to give the enemy an excuse to cut off the flow of propaganda. This does not stop him from giving such groups all the covert encouragement he can, and his call for race war is incessant.

In 1991 Tyler moved his operation to a farm outside Beckley, West Virginia. Ostensibly, this was to get away from "the Zionist government and their controlled media" but more likely to take advantage of lower property values and a generally less hostile population.

The conclusion summed up the subject baldly: "Douglas Tyler is by far the most intelligent and best educated leader in the white supremacist movement today. Only the extreme virulence of his positions has prevented him from becoming a far greater menace than he is."

There followed a list of statistics, dates and addresses. It even included his current telephone number. At the very bottom was a note from Carson: *The feds keep a pretty close watch on this guy. I don't think he could get away with much, but maybe you're on to something.*

I set the paperwork aside and finished my coffee.

Amarillo felt as cold as the last few sips. I looked around for a trash can, then thought better of it and tossed the cup over my shoulder onto the floor behind the driver's seat, for that little touch of convincing verisimilitude. I started up the car and headed out for I-40 and points west.

West of Amarillo, the terrain begins to change dramatically. For a while you are on flat, short-grass prairie, where the trees are few and stunted, their foliage flattened out and attenuated, permanently bent away from the direction of the prevailing wind. The most prominent features are occasional grain elevators and at one point I passed an enormous cattle feed lot next to the highway. Its stench was so awful that I could only wonder what it must be like in the hottest part of summer.

Then, just before the New Mexico border, everything changes. The grass thins, then all but disappears. The flatness gives way to deep erosion, and vivid colors leap from the soil—vibrant reds, orange, yellow and every shade of brown from deep umber to palest beige. Instead of high mountains or rolling hills you see steep-sided, flat-topped mesas, their sides horizontally streaked in all those colors, like layer cakes baked by a demented chef. This is where the desert Southwest begins.

The country seems waterless, but you can see the most drastic effects of water everywhere. The ground is cut up with dry washes and riverbeds that look like something you'd see on Mars, as if there had been no water there for millennia, but they can fill to roaring spate in a minute without a single cloud in sight if there's been heavy rain in the nearby mountains. Those mesas are the worn-down nubs of mountains, with their sides torn away and exposed by the relentless action of water against earth that lacks protective vegetation. The water is in no hurry. It has plenty of time to do its work.

It is a hostile, brutal, unforgiving terrain, and for my money it is the most beautiful in America. At first glance it appears to be absolutely unchanging, but it isn't. Aside from the disconcerting way the dry watercourses can fill in an instant, the whole desert can change colors like a chameleon. You'll see rain sweeping in from miles away like a huge, gray curtain. It wets the ground, changes the smell of everything, then moves on. Within a day or two the desert turns a shocking green, starred with wildflowers of hallucinatory color and vividness. Cacti so withered and brown you'd swear they were dead suddenly turn green, swell and bristle with menace and put out absurdly inviting blossoms. In another few days everything is brown again.

This land was the refuge of marauding Apaches and the El Dorado of crazed prospectors and it was never conquered in any meaningful sense of the term. The sun of this land bleached the bones of uncounted thousands of pioneers, along with those of their horses and cattle. The vast drylands that spread across the greater part of six states still feature the lowest population density of the original forty-eight by a considerable margin.

With its uncompromising indifference to humanity, its barren beauty and its harsh light that throws all moving figures into bold relief, it's no wonder that about 90 percent of that quintessential American art form, the Western, is set amid the existential landscape of the desert Southwest.

It's a hell of a place to find anyone at all, but at least the cities are fewer and the population not only thinner but less anonymous than in the East. This was a place where people retained their individuality even in crowds.

I stopped at the first rest area inside the New Mexico state line, a facility beautifully designed to blend into the landscape, with adobe-textured walls and softly rounded corners, its roof jagged with solar collectors. It featured the usual markers and historical plaques giving the names and dates of expeditions that passed that way long ago and defined its position not only geographically but geologically.

I went inside and picked up a handful of maps and brochures featuring the attractions of New Mexico, from Carlsbad Caverns and White Sands to the south to the ski resorts around Taos in the north to the big Indian powwow held yearly in Gallup in the west. There was a reenactment of the Lincoln County War being staged in Fort Sumner just a few miles away, with actors impersonating Pat Garrett and Billy the Kid, featuring the Kid's famous breakout from the Lincoln County jail and culminating with the final confrontation between the famous pair. I wondered how they planned to stage that last one, since it took place in a tiny, pitch-dark bedroom.

Armed with brochures I went back outside and sat on the trunk lid of my car, feet resting on the bumper, to study them. Dry, desert wind swept in from the north, rustling the dry grass of the little oasis. This time of year, with winter coming on, it was mercifully cool. In high summer it would be a ferocious, desiccating blast.

For a while I just gazed out across the desert view to the north and thought, trying to get my ploddingly middle-class mind into the sociopathic weirdness of Nick Switzer's brain. Like turning derelict, I found this all too easy, as well. People used to come west to escape the social strictures of civilization, to a place where, if you could keep your scalp off an Apache's lance and avoid thirst and starvation, you could do pretty much as you pleased. If the fancy struck you, you could be a killer and marauder yourself in one stretch of the vastness, then settle down as a respectable citizen in a community far away. Plenty of them did that.

A disposition that would get you reviled and hanged in the East could earn you the status of local hero and legend in these parts, as in the case of the aforementioned

Billy the Kid. Of course, it could mean a death as early as his, but so what?

This place could be the fantasy world of Nick Switzer brought to vivid, three-dimensional life. He would find it both exciting and reassuring. Here he might feel a little safer, a little more in control. Here, he might slow down a little and enjoy himself. After all, he'd just done something wild and daring, something that had the hounds of vengeance pursuing him. He was on the run like Billy with Pat Garrett on his trail, like Butch Cassidy fleeing the Pinkertons, always a little bit too smart and too brave for them to catch. And he wasn't alone. He had this beautiful, classy, intelligent woman to adore and admire him, to stroke his ego and tell him what a big-time winner he was.

I looked out and saw the low sun of morning striking starlike flashes of light from the desert floor. Here the glints came from mica, not broken bottles. The smells were of sage and creosote, not stale pot smoke and car exhaust. After chasing them blindly for days, I had a feeling that I might just catch up with them around here.

I'd picked up an hour when I crossed the state line, New Mexico being on Rocky Mountain Time. So it was still well shy of noon when I drove into the musically named town of Tucumcari. I dropped off the interstate and took the business route through town. This stretch of I-40 follows the path of old U.S. Highway 66, and everywhere you see signs referring to it, cashing in on the wave of nostalgia for the storied old road. A good proportion of the businesses seem to have "Route 66" in their titles.

The sidewalks were modestly crowded with people, mostly wearing Western-style clothes. A banner across the main street informed me that there was a rodeo at the town's fairgrounds. I pulled in at one of the convenience stores that have just about replaced gas stations and filled up my tank, just another beat-up-looking guy in a beat-up car. A clerk in a glassed-in booth kept a close eye on me, lest I drive off without paying. I set his mind at ease and parked the car out of the way of traffic, got out again and gave my creaky knees some exercise. It seemed my legs cramped more and more easily on long drives, these days, and I hadn't gone for a run since three days before, in Memphis.

If they were hitching, chances were good that they were traveling in short hops, getting out at places like this, where there were good opportunities for catching another ride. The open road was the worst place, where people were most suspicious of hitchhikers, and where they would attract attention from highway patrol cruisers.

The startling sound of hooves made me look around, to see a small group of men and women, mounted on ornate saddles, their beautifully groomed horses serenely oblivious to the street traffic.

Rodeos. Yet another gypsy subculture, this one a display of cowboy skills obsolete for the better part of a century, but wildly popular nonetheless. There were Indians in black hats and moccasins, but whether they were with the rodeo or just locals I couldn't tell.

A flicker of something colorful caught my eye, and my mind did a flashback to the Western-wear shop back in Nashville, to the rack of embroidered sheepskin coats. For an instant I saw a pale oval of face framed in dark hair glancing back over a shoulder, a dark eye bright as a bird's locked on mine, then I was surrounded by a crowd of teenagers, laughing inanely and squirting one another with water pistols. I started pushing my way through them, got squirted for my pains, and by the time I was clear of them my vision had disappeared.

I stalked up and down the street, looking down the side streets, gazing into shop windows, and probably transmitting the impression of a deranged panhandler, not that anyone was paying me much notice. I kept seeing colorful coats, but those were all the rage of late. Dark-haired young women weren't in short supply, either.

I stopped on a corner to collect my wits. Had I really seen anything? This could be a symptom of the dreaded white-line fever, chronic affliction of people who spend too much time staring past their hood ornaments at the road ahead. You go into trances, you hallucinate, you see things that aren't there and hear voices muttering from your carburetor.

I was shaken from my disturbed reverie by the sounds of drums and horns. The sidewalks were thronged now, people crowding the curbs to catch the show. A parade was coming. First a few slow-cruising convertibles floated by, incredibly pretty girls seated atop the backseats, waving at the crowd, local beauty queens in their moment of glory. Then came an honor guard in singing-cowboy getups, mounted on resplendent palominos and Arabians, bearing U.S. flags and the yellow-and-red state flag of New Mexico, and a man on an Appaloosa wearing a huge sombrero and a skintight charro costume holding the eagle-and-serpent flag of Mexico. Next came buckskinned and feathered Indians in Day-Glo colors unknown to Sitting Bull and Cochise.

A high school marching band went by, discordant, out of tune, obeying a tempo invented on another planet, but spirited and harmonious in spite of it all. Then a large mounted group, most of them young men destined to quite literally risk their necks for the entertainment of the spectators. At least half of them were wearing caped Aussie coats like the one Switzer had bought, a design that had crossed an ocean to become the rage of American horsemen.

Then they were gone, leaving behind only a lingering smell of horses, a not-unpleasant scent preferable to most street odors. I went back to my car and cruised the streets for a while, going slow, keeping my eyes open, all too conscious that I was probably wasting my time. They might have passed through here days before. Chances were slight that the woman I'd seen, or thought I'd seen, was Sibyl.

I saw no trace of Holt or Tina, nor of their brown Bronco. Were they ahead of me? I couldn't help the nagging suspicion that one of Holt's sources had tipped him, that Switzer had been seen in Albuquerque or Flagstaff or Denver. The hell with it. This second-guessing could drive me nuts. I drove slowly the whole length of town, seeing nothing more to grab my attention.

With a distinct sense of unease I pulled back out onto the interstate, feeling that I might be letting an opportunity slip. But there was an awful lot ahead of me and it was too early in the day to slow down.

The highway climbed slowly, the increase in altitude almost unnoticeable, ascending to the high plains. It doesn't make your ears pop, but before long you find yourself an impressive number of feet above sea level. By the time I reached Moriarty—altitude 6,000 feet, population 1,399—I was yawning frequently, a sure sign that the air was getting thin. I stopped there for gas and consulted one of my maps. The mountain range straight ahead, I learned, was called the Sandias. To the south were the Manzanos, and the snow-covered peaks I could just make out to the north were the Sangre de Cristos. The names meant, reading from south to north, "Apples," "Watermelons" and "Blood of Christ," a jarring juxtaposition even in this land of stark contrasts.

Something about the name of the place picked at my memory until it came to me. Dean Moriarty was the manic, half-visionary, half-psychopath protagonist of Jack Kerouac's *On the Road*, madly hauling the hapless narrator, Sal Paradise, all over the postwar American landscape, including sizable chunks of this very highway. And here I was, chasing the Sal and Dean of the nineties.

I was going on hunch and gut instinct, and Holt was probably ahead of me. I had a crazy inspiration. Maybe I was seized by the spirit of Kerouac's feckless, long-gone heroes. Maybe it was the altitude, with my brain operating on less than its usual ration of oxygen. Whatever, I got the stat sheet on the White Front out of my satchel and walked over to a pay phone.

They don't put them in glass booths anymore, with folding doors for a little quiet and an illusion of privacy. So I punched in the number I wanted, charging the call to my office phone, then stuck a finger into the ear opposite the one I listened with, to block out some of the traffic noise. Far away, in rural West Virginia, a phone rang.

"National Guardian. How may I help you?" The voice was deep, well measured, the voice of a college professor trained in one of the more old-fashioned schools.

"Am I speaking to Douglas Tyler?"

"I never deny it. What might yours be?"

"It's Treloar. I'm looking for a man named Nick Switzer and I believe he has something that belongs to you."

He paused just a beat too long. "I'm afraid the name means nothing to me, and I haven't lost anything."

"Look, Mr. Tyler, I'm not after what he took. I'm interested in the welfare of the young woman with him. Let's cooperate here. Let me get her away from him, and then you and the guys with the power drill and the Tyr insignia can do whatever you want with Switzer."

Tyler sighed. "Mr.—Treloar, is it? A fine old Cornish name, by the way—I know perfectly well that my telephone is tapped. I will not weary you with the tale of the many, many times the JDL, the Zionists, the Israel lobby and their FBI hatchet men have tried to get me to incriminate myself. It's clear to me that you are referring to

111

something illegal in which you imply that I am involved." No way was this guy going to end a sentence with a preposition. "The Enemy have no respect for the Constitution of the United States, particularly the First and Fifth Amendments. I do not know the man to whom you refer, nor do I know the woman whose welfare concerns you, nor whatever may or may not be in their possession. I am further unaware of any storm troopers who employ Tyr for their insignia and a—did you say a power drill? Whatever government agency you work for, tell them they are wasting their time."

"I didn't say anything about storm troopers. Look, Tyler, I'm not the only one after—"

"Mr. Treloar, I am a busy man. Good luck in your pursuit, but good day to you, sir." The phone clicked decisively.

All right. It was stuff like this that made me, from time to time, feel like a real detective: playing a hunch, feeling that vague, uncertain little itch coalesce into something firm, solid and real. Tyler was lying. Just what he was lying about I still had to learn, but the connection was there. He knew about Switzer, he knew about the—storm troopers?—who had tortured and murdered Pat Jennings.

I felt so good I kept fumbling the dial buttons trying to punch in Carson's number. I got him on the third try.

"Kit? Tyler's our man. Find out everything you can about him. See if he was in Sibyl and Nick's part of the country any time in recent months. Get your guys there to see if he's had anybody investigating there since they disappeared. And we're looking for—get this—storm troopers."

"What? Slow down, Gabe. Tell me what you've found out, but do it slow."

So, trying to be all calm and analytical, which isn't easy when you're going on hunch and instinct, I told him about what I'd done that day.

"Do you think that was really Sibyl you saw?"

"I doubt it. But I've got a feeling they're close and I have to get to them before the guys with the arrow sign do."

"I'll be putting my guys to work on this; in the meantime, speaking of the boys who sign their work with that arrow and who now look like a definite possibility—how far are you from Santa Fe?"

I got my New Mexico map out of the car. "From here to Albuquerque on I-40 it looks like maybe forty-five minutes. I can catch I-25 there and it looks like Santa Fe's maybe another hour."

"Okay. I got a contact there, name's Ray Padilla; he's a PI who spent about thirty years with the New Mexico State PD, a lot of it with the corrections department. He says he's seen that arrow mark before and he'll brief you. I'll let him know you're coming."

"Okay. Tell him I'll be there in a couple of hours." I wrote down the number Kit gave me. My mind was buzzing, hopped up, even, on this little success. Another connection snapped into place and I dug out the clipping service printout I'd run off back in Knoxville five days earlier. "Kit, there was a neo-Nazi snuff in Charleston a few days back, four of them gunned down, rival Nazis suspected. See what you can find out about that." I gave him the bare stats from the clipping service.

"I'm on it. Call me tonight from Santa Fe. And Gabe?"

"Yeah?"

"Cut down on the caffeine, will you?"

"Okay. Kit, you think Jasper Holt's working for Tyler?"

"Well, who the hell else could it be?"

113

Nine

I-40 climbs the eastern slope of the Sandia Mountains gradually, goes over them through a pass called Tijeras Canyon, where the western slope falls away dramatically to reveal the Rio Grande Valley and the city of Albuquerque, which carpets the bottom of the valley for miles to the north and south, and spills over its edges to the east and west for a considerable margin. Like so many of the larger Western cities, it's located at the base of a mountain pass next to a river, making it a natural trading crossroads in the old days. Now it's a typical Sunbelt city, probably 90 percent of it built since World War Two and the invention of air-conditioning. From the overlook at the western end of the pass, it looked roughly X shaped, running east-west along I-40, north-south along I-25 and the river, with large stretches of vacant land between the limbs of the X.

At the bottom of the mountain was an exit for Central Avenue, which marked the old path of Route 66 and cut straight through the city. The interstate looped slightly north, skirting the older part of the city. Midway through Albuquerque, I-40 intersects I-25, which goes south to El Paso, on the western tip of Texas, and north all the way through Colorado and Wyoming, clear to the Montana border.

I turned north onto I-25, feeling a slight wrench at being off the highway I'd followed since Knoxville. The road began to climb again, Albuquerque being a valley town a mere five thousand feet in altitude. As I continued north the sagebrush-studded desert began to sport colorful, softly rounded rock outcroppings and I almost expected to see a jet-powered roadrunner closely pursued by a hapless coyote.

I had a vague memory of Santa Fe. When my family had moved from Ohio to L.A. back in '64, we'd stopped there for an afternoon. I remembered a small, truly unique town little changed since Spanish colonial days, where Indians sat in the shade of a colonnade on the town square selling jewelry displayed on colorful blankets.

What I didn't remember was the cluster of ugly trailer parks spoiling the view of the quaint old town at the base of the beautiful mountain. I got off the highway and checked into a motel on the outskirts of town. "Seems kind of high," I said, forking over the exorbitant rate.

The clerk looked me over disdainfully. "The ski crowd shows up next month. The rates go up then."

I called the number Kit had given me.

"Zia Confidential Investigations, Ray Padilla speaking."

"This is Gabe Treloar."

"Your boss told me to expect you. You had dinner yet?"

"Nope."

"You know Santa Fe?"

"I was here for maybe half a day more than thirty years ago."

"Well, I'll meet you in the dining room at La Fonda.

It's the oldest hotel in town, right on the plaza. 'Bout an hour be okay?"

"Sounds good. Is it dress-up? I'm keeping kind of a lowlife profile on this job."

"Naw, things ain't got that bad yet. Long as you wear shoes they probably won't chuck you out."

"An hour, then."

I got washed up and shaved and put on one of my more respectable outfits. This took only minutes and it was a short distance to the plaza, so I strolled around for a while, taking in the strange feel of the old town. My brochure informed me that it was the state capital, despite its small size. It had been Spanish colonial policy to locate provincial capitals in remote, preferably mountainous areas to keep them from being dominated by merchants or the big landholders. Its Palace of the Governors dated from around 1610, making it respectably old even by European standards, and had housed successive viceroys and governors representing Spain, Mexico and the United States. Among the latter had been Lew Wallace, Civil War general and author of *Ben-Hur,* who, during his tenure, had offered amnesty to the inescapable Billy the Kid.

In my admittedly vague memory, the plaza and the narrow streets that led from it had been lined with funky old shops offering all manner of Indian and colonial pottery, blankets, jewelry and such. Now every building seemed to house an art gallery, a boutique or a shop selling the same old stuff at breathtaking prices. Out of curiosity I went into a shop specializing in leather wear, where I found an embroidered sheepskin coat almost identical to the one Sybil had bought back in Nashville, for three times the price listed on her credit card receipt. Probably made by a higher quality of Chinese slave labor, I figured.

La Fonda turned out to be an old-fashioned hostelry with its own indoor gallery of shops and a handsome, colonial-style dining room. I told the hostess who I was meeting and she guided me among the tables, some of them occupied by obvious tourists but many by locals who looked like they spent a lot of money to seem casually dressed. I even spotted a couple of familiar faces. One was a well-known actress, the other a director I'd busted for possession more than once.

Ray Padilla stood and put his hand out. He was a head shorter than I, and wider through the shoulders, chest and waist. His hair and mustache were silver. He looked like Zorro's dad, except for his well-cut suit. I took a seat across from him.

"I want to thank you for helping me out at such short notice."

"Carson's done favors for me more than once. I'm glad to be of service." He had only the faintest trace of Hispanic accent. "What do you think of our fair city? A lot's changed since you were last through here."

"Looks like Puerto Vallarta Syndrome to me. It was a sleepy little fishing village until Liz and Dick shot a movie there."

"There you go, man. The jet-setters discovered Santa Fe in the seventies and started buying up everything in sight. A 'dobe house that was a slum when I was a kid brings a million bucks now."

"Those trailer parks outside of town—is that where the people who used to live in Santa Fe live now?"

"That's right. They can't afford to live here anymore. Couldn't even afford the taxes on places their families lived in since before the gringos came. They work for the new owners now. And the new owners just love all this Southwestern ambience. They don't want to see it wasted on a bunch of Mexicans."

I nodded in commiseration at this odd turn of fate. The waitress came for our orders and I let Padilla pick out the house specialties for me.

"Carson says you need to know about the arrow-sign boys, and from the way he was talking, I shouldn't ask why."

"I'm tracking a couple of people and Randall has very personal reasons for keeping it confidential. In the course of my investigation, a few days ago in Memphis, I ran across a stiff with the arrow mark carved on it. The stiff was a known associate of one of the people I'm looking for."

"Then your guy may have got in bad with the wrong people."

"They're pretty bad, all right." I described the nature of Pat Jennings's injuries.

Padilla nodded. "That's them, all right."

"Who are they?"

"First, a little background. You know how the white supremacists recruit in the slammers?"

"Sure. Aryan Brotherhood, like that?"

"Those are the wimps. Most of those guys, they're just scared white boys who want protection from the black and Latino cons, who're organized into their own gangs and just meaner'n hell. The AB and most of the others are mainly just fuckups and losers too dumb to stay out of jail and too poor to afford a good lawyer. They don't read those White Power tracts because most of 'em can't read, period. You might say they aren't heavy into ideology."

"Got you so far."

"But naturally there's a few with a little more on the ball, guys who actually believe that stuff. Guys who, with true jailhouse enlightenment, discovered they have a mission. They're a hell of a lot more sincere about it than the ones who find Jesus in the same surroundings. You say your guy in Memphis had *DTT* carved on him?"

"That's right."

He leaned back in his chair and laced his fingers across his substantial paunch. "Stands for 'Death Troop Tyr.'

They're absolutely the meanest sons of bitches you'll run into in or out of jail."

Now we were getting somewhere. "Are they part of something called White Front?"

"You know how it works. Nobody really controls these freaks. They're to White Front and the other all-talk-no-action organizations what Hamas is to the PLO or the IRA to Sinn Fein. But they can quote that Tyler guy by the hour."

"How many of them are there?"

"Depends. Never very many, because they got high standards. Plus, they tend to kill each other over lapses in dedication to the cause. I wouldn't say there's more than twenty of them nationwide, but Geronimo never had more than about twenty guys with him, and look how much hell he raised."

"Do you have any names?"

"Just one for sure, another possible." He took a leather folder from his breast pocket and withdrew a color mug shot. It showed a young man with a square face and short, crisp blond hair, butcher's-boy handsome, with a broken nose, ruddy cheeks and pale blue eyes. "Jess Marsh. He's the founder and leader of DTT. One of the few cons I know of who waited until he was an adult to get busted. Not a good boy gone bad, just smart enough to let patsies take the fall for him."

"What was he in for?"

"Armed robbery. Knocked over a bank in El Paso with three other guys. They got caught almost immediately and one of them ratted him out. He did time in Huntsville. He joined the AB there but decided they were wusses, so he formed the original DTT with two other hardcores. He busted out after two years, went into the underground, spreading the gospel, recruiting. After a while the guy who'd rolled over on him got paroled. The next day he was found dead, tortured and crucified."

"That sounds like my man," I said, "unless it's a copycat."

"I don't think so. You know how you described the guy in Memphis, nailed through the ankles and forearms?"

"That's how it was done."

"Well, this man was done the way you see on crucifixes in church, nailed through the palms and the feet. It was the same way with some other unfortunates who disagreed with Marsh, mostly snitches and backsliding DTT members. But he finally got caught giving the last nail a few licks. This time the dear departed was a Mexican dope dealer who stiffed Marsh, or maybe he pronounced Hitler's name wrong, who knows with a guy like that? Anyway, this one was done through the ankles and forearms. After the trial, a reporter asked Marsh why the change in his crucifixion MO. He said, 'In the interests of historical accuracy.' "

"I have to hear this."

"Seems that he'd read in a copy of *National Geographic* where they'd found the skeleton of a guy who was crucified for real in the old days, in Israel. Turns out the way the Romans did it wasn't like the pictures at all. They nailed 'em through the anklebones and between the bones of the forearm. It makes sense, when you think about it. A man's whole weight hanging on nails through his hands, they'd just tear right through. The authentic way keeps 'em in place."

"Damn. You can't fault his artistic integrity."

"The man has style. Besides, these White Front people say the ancient Romans were true Aryans. It was only later they interbred with Africans or something and became wops. He wanted to do it the good old Aryan Roman way."

Our dinners arrived and we were quiet for a while, working on them. The *carne asada* was impeccable. "So

Mr. Marsh is out amongst us once again?" I said while catching my breath.

"He was never back in, really. He got busted and tried in Corpus Christi. Then he was sent back to Huntsville to serve his new life sentence, along with the rest of his first ten-to-twenty jolt. The bus got ambushed right outside Victoria. Four men, probably DTT guys, took it like clockwork: had an eighteen-wheeler jackknifed across the road, flares out, two of 'em in highway patrol uniforms with a state car, the works. Killed the guards, turned the other cons loose to add to the fun, then disappeared off the map. That was five years ago. To the best of my knowledge, Mr. Marsh hasn't been heard of since."

I sat back. "Quite a story. Now I know a lot more than I did, but I almost wish I didn't."

"I sympathize. When I worked at the state pen a few years back we had a DTT member with the fine old Aryan name of Juan Martinez. He's the other possible I mentioned." He took out another mug shot, this one of a brown-haired young man with a narrow, pockmarked face. "Insisted that he was pure Spanish, of course, not a drop of polluted Mexican blood. Took some balls to make a bullshit claim like that in our fair institution. The Latino contingent there is about three times bigger than the Anglo, black and Indian combined."

"Do you know if the DTT exists outside of the Texas and New Mexico prison systems?"

"Can't be sure. They're pretty secretive. Even in the slammer, just who belongs is mainly a rumor. Some guards'll tell you the DTT don't exist at all, that it's just convict folklore. Most of what I know, I got from Martinez, because the little prick loved to shoot his mouth off. He's the one told me about Marsh, so I looked into it and found out it's all true."

"Is Martinez still in the pen? Could I talk with him?"

He shook his head. "He was released six months ago.

The new governor got elected on a law-and-order ticket, swore he was going to send up jaywalkers for twenty years, demand the death penalty for double parking, stuff like that. Corrections department started looking for excuses to turn cons loose so they'd have room for all the new arrivals."

Since Padilla was supplying the information, I picked up the tab. As we walked out onto the plaza I caught a strange, tangy scent on the air, a smoke that was almost like incense. I asked Padilla about it.

"That's piñon burning. It's what we use for firewood here. Maybe we'll have a freeze tonight." He nodded toward the crest of the mountain that loomed like a huge ghost above the town, its snowy cap silvered by moonlight.

"One more thing," I said.

"Shoot."

"Does the name Jasper Holt mean anything to you?"

He laughed. "Oh, yeah. We know all about Jasper Holt here. When I was with the state police he came through here headhunting half a dozen times. Arrogant bastard, treated us like peons, but he usually went home with a scalp on his belt. Don't tell me he's involved in this."

"We seem to be looking for the same man, and I'm not sure why." I debated with myself for a few moments, then said, "Look, my boss has given me some leeway in how I handle this." I took out two pictures and handed them to him. "The guy is Nick Switzer. He's a two-bit scam artist and I don't know that he's ever operated this far west."

Beneath a streetlight Padilla studied the photos. "I could take you over to the state pen, about fifteen minutes from here, and show you twenty specimens punched out with the same cookie cutter, but this particular guy, no. He the one that got on the wrong side of Jess Marsh?"

"It's looking like it. The guy in Memphis was a known

associate. Looks like Switzer was with him just before he was killed."

"And this woman," he studied Sibyl's likeness, "I've never met Randall Carson. If I had, would I be searching for a family resemblance here?"

"You wouldn't see any, but you'd be looking in the right place. Holt is looking for these two. He can have Switzer for all I care."

"I get your drift. Hard to picture Holt and Jess Marsh working together, though."

"I don't think they are. There's a lot about this I don't understand."

"And ain't life just like that? If I see Holt, I won't give him any help. Wouldn't be tempted, anyway. New Mexicans aren't great admirers of Texans, and that goes double for the Texas Rangers."

"I appreciate it. And I'd appreciate it further if you'll keep in touch with me through Carson."

"I'll do it."

"And if you should see Jess Marsh—"

"If I see Marsh I'll shoot him."

I thanked him again and went back to my car. My breath made little puffs of steam as I fumbled my keys out and turned the ignition. The car rumbled to life, gasping like me, trying to cope with the thin air. But if the air was thin it was also uncommonly clean.

I arrived back at my motel weary to the bone with yet another long, long day, but I still had things to accomplish. I called Carson as ordered. He heard out my report and was silent for a moment.

"Ah, Christ, this gets worse and worse," he said at last.

"At least it's starting to make some sort of sense. It looks like Nick scammed Tyler out of something and Tyler sent his Death Troop Tyr after him."

"Yeah, maybe. Where does Holt come in?"

"Maybe Tyler hired him as a backup. It's not like Holt's picky about who he works for."

"Okay, let it ride for the moment. At least it's a relief to have satanic witch cults out of the picture. Not that these freaks are what you'd call a comforting presence."

"Were you able to find out anything about Tyler's activities?"

"Not much just yet. Right after Nick split there was a county cop named Woolford from the Roanoke sheriff's department asking around about him, but he just determined that Switzer was gone. He may have just been checking up on a known felon on general principles, but he was doing it in a city jurisdiction."

"Or he may be a faithful subscriber to the *National Guardian* doing a favor for his idol, Douglas Tyler."

"Could well be. Jasper Holt wasn't seen in Blacksburg or Roanoke, and he'd be pretty hard to miss. But there was a woman asking about Nick, hanging around his haunts for a day or two, said she was an old girlfriend, he owed her money or something. Description: white, five foot zero, approximately one hundred pounds, short black hair, green eyes, about thirty, wearing jeans and boots and a lot of fringe."

"Tina. Well, that comes as no surprise. Look, Kit, this is sounding nastier than ever, and I can't help thinking there's a third party involved we don't know about."

"Well, there's a real happy thought. Get some sleep and check in with me tomorrow."

"Right. I'm going back into Albuquerque in the morning. It's a big place; I think they may hang around there for a while. Maybe Sybil's about ready to take it easy for a few days."

"Or they could be in California by now. Or Hawaii."

"We have to play it by ear, Kit."

"Don't I know it. Talk to you tomorrow, Gabe."

I lay back on my overpriced pillow and thought about

the latest bad news. The prison gang made sense. I'd spec-
ulated about something of the sort since hearing about
the marks left on Jennings's body. I hadn't been expecting
anything quite so hard-core and bizarre, but you got to
take 'em as you finds 'em. What had me really worried
was that county cop nosing around. It hinted that these
loonies might be able to tap into a network of police officers who were members of, or at least sympathetic with,
the White Front. If so, they could be way ahead of me.

But then, who wasn't?

Ten

I hadn't slept well and woke up way before dawn. After tossing around for twenty minutes or so, I'd given up on going back to sleep, tossed my things into the Pontiac and headed south. The sun was just peeking over Sandia Crest as the city came in sight, and with it an otherworldly vision.

I almost ran off the highway as a vast, silent globe loomed above me, its colors brilliant in the light of morning, its sides vertically segmented like a peeled orange. An instant later my jangled mind identified the apparition as a hot-air balloon, and even as I recognized what it was, another passed above it.

I pulled the Pontiac over to the shoulder, stopped and got out, my heart still racing a bit, and feeling abashed at having been spooked by this commonplace sight, however colorful and unexpected. A quick scan revealed at least twenty of the huge airbags floating south in ghostly quiet, and in a field nearby twenty or thirty more were preparing to go up. It's what the ballooning crowd call a "mass ascension," and it's one of the most spectacular man-made sights in the world. I remembered that one of my brochures mentioned Albuquerque's annual balloon

126

festival, during which there would be mass ascensions of hundreds of balloons at once. That was more than a month away. These were probably locals preparing for the big event.

I got back into the car and drove on into town, where I did my customary familiarization tour. Albuquerque, I found, was pretty much a modern city with little of the colonial charm of Santa Fe. On the other hand, the prices were more reasonable. There is a small colonial and frontier-period district called Old Town, much of it restored from a ruinous state. The rest dates from after the turn of the century.

Like so many cities, it has gone through three distinct phases. The oldest part lies near the river, which once supported a lively traffic. I learned that, before most of its water was tapped off for irrigation, the Rio Grande floated regular steamboats all the way up from the Gulf. In the 1880s the center of town migrated eastward to meet the newly arrived railroad. In this century, with the automotive boom and its attendant highway system, the town sprawled east-west along Route 66. The storied highway's old path was now Central Avenue, cutting straight through Albuquerque, mile after mile of it. River, railroad, highway—the consecutive forces that have shaped American cities for the past two hundred years. I had seen few cities that showed the three stages of development so starkly. Albuquerque appeared to be three different towns slapped down one atop the other.

It's the Sunbelt phenomenon par excellence, 90 percent of growth postwar, made possible by automobiles and air-conditioning. Cities that stretch in a huge crescent across the south and west of the U.S.—Miami, Atlanta, Houston, Dallas, Albuquerque, Phoenix and, king of them all, Los Angeles—were once sleepy, backward towns where nobody lived except the natives. They were too hot and too remote to attract anyone but tourists. The new mobility and climate-controlled housing made all that cheap real estate attractive.

In Albuquerque, not far from where the two interstates crossed, a cluster of malls strove through use of pseudo-adobe architecture to blend with the dramatic desert landscape, with mixed results. On the lower slopes of the mountains to the east, housing developments sprawled right up to the sheer, uninhabitable rock cliffs, like some sort of human high-tide line. Off to the west, the suburbs had boiled up over the valley rim onto the desert beyond, where the flatness of the skyline was broken by a stately line of three conical, long-extinct volcanoes.

I drove slowly through the center of town, which showed the familiar efforts of urban renewers striving to halt the decay of an old downtown area in this age of the mall. Near the river Central Avenue reverted to a stretch of marginal businesses, bars and the inevitable cheap motels. I spotted a few motorcycle-customizing shops, a sure sign that I was in the right neighborhood.

The motel I picked, the Cactus Inn, might have been transported in one piece from Amarillo, except that it was slightly curved instead of angled, it lacked the carport in front of the office, and the big sign next to the sidewalk was shaped like a huge saguaro cactus. I happened to know that saguaros grow in southern Arizona, not in New Mexico. The guy behind the counter looked like Gandhi.

My room was on the side nearer the river, and as I unlocked the door I caught the river's faint, damp scent. Tall cottonwoods grew along its mud banks, amazingly green and lush in this otherwise parched country. In front of the room next to mine a man sat on one of the inevitable steel chairs. Catching my glance he nodded affably and I nodded back. He held a brown-glass bottle of cheap beer even at this early hour and he didn't seem to be doing anything, just waiting. The room on the other side had its curtains drawn. The parking area held an assortment of cars and trucks, most of them even older and more disreputable than mine.

My room was about what I expected by this time. It had a tiny refrigerator, and a faint scent of chili tinged the stale air. I left the door open to air the place out a bit as I settled in. As soon as these minimal preparations were accomplished, I went outside.

"Mornin'," said the man in the chair. His hair and beard were untrimmed, his shirt missing a button or two where his paunch strained it above his belt. He wore patched jeans and scuffed old cowboy boots, their heels worn down to an odd, triangular profile. On his right wrist was a beautiful silver bracelet set with turquoise.

"Good morning. It looks like I'm your new neighbor." I stuck out a hand. "Gabe Treloar."

He took it. "Arnie Schumacher. You just come to town?"

"This morning. Seems like a nice place."

He nodded. "It is. Real laid back. Hotter'n hell in the summer, but this time of year it's perfect." He gestured to the open door of his room. A plastic ice chest stood just inside. "Grab yourself a cold one."

"Thanks, but it's still a little early for me."

He squinted into the eastern sky. "Sun's been up a while."

"I got to go out and look for a job," I told him. "Can't afford to smell like beer."

"Job market's pretty tight," he said, like it didn't bother him much. "My wife got a job waitressing at a truck stop out on 40."

"Nothing much in your line of work?"

"Gotta keep an eye on the twins." I glanced into the room again. A pair of toddlers amused themselves quietly in a playpen.

I got directions to the washing machines, the ice maker and other amenities of the motel and went to take care of some overdue chores. I'd been on the road for almost a week and my stock of clean clothes was getting low.

In the little alcove that contained the coin-operated washer and dryer a pregnant woman was folding her laundry into a basket. She glanced at me uneasily, for which I couldn't really blame her. As I loaded the washer I saw a police car cruising by on Central. As it passed the motel it slowed and the cop behind the wheel scanned the cars parked there, including mine.

It gave me an odd, disquieting sensation. I'd done the same thing a thousand times myself: checking out the license plates and comparing the vehicles against those on the stolen list, looking for wanted felons and ripped-off cars. It was so automatic that the cop probably wasn't even consciously thinking about it. But if he was a good one, that distinctive missing vehicle would jump out at him, that near-anonymous license number would flash like a neon sign.

Being on the other side of the equation made it all different. I could have sworn that his gaze lingered a little longer on my license plate than really necessary. As if Jasper Holt and Death Troop Tyr weren't enough, that deputy back East had me worrying about the police, too. I couldn't remember when I'd last felt so paranoid. Vietnam, probably. At least there people really had been after me. Nothing personal of course, but a whole bunch of strangers had wanted to kill me for wearing that uniform in their country. There were parts of L.A. that had been almost as bad, but when you went off duty you could go home and relax.

Now, for the first time in a long while, I was adrift in an environment where everyone had to be assumed hostile until proven otherwise. And to think, just a week before I'd been bored.

I organized my things and decided it was time to get

back to work. Enough of this lollygagging around. I got myself just marginally respectable looking and pocketed a stack of my "writer" business cards. One of the advantages of the writer persona is that you always have a good reason for asking questions. Another is that you don't have to be respectable, within limits. A writer acquaintance of mine once told me that his favorite perk of a chancy trade was that he could hang around strip joints, S&M bars and the like and claim that he was just researching his next book.

My destination may not have been quite as sleazy, depending on your opinion of journalism. I found the offices of Albuquerque's major newspaper in the old downtown area. The young woman at the receptionist's desk smiled brightly and her look didn't even falter as she took in my shabby appearance.

"May I help you?" She wore approximately fifty pounds of silver jewelry, most of it studded with turquoise. By now I had figured out that New Mexico is the world's largest consumer of silver, with a near-monopoly of turquoise.

"I sure hope so." I handed her one of my cards. "I'm researching a book on the extreme right movement in the American West. I'd like to have a look at your files on the subject."

"I don't think we have a whole lot of that stuff in New Mexico, not like our neighbors to the north," she told me. "But I know there's been some articles on the subject the last few years. Just go down that corridor," she pointed to her right with a beringed finger, "and go through the door on the end. Mr. Chavez will help you find the files you need."

I thanked her and went to the indicated door. Mr. Chavez turned out to be a surprisingly youthful man, earnest and helpful. This guy hadn't been in the newspaper business very long, I figured.

131

"It's all computerized now," he explained patiently, recognizing that I belonged to the generation that still carved messages on rocks. "All the articles are cross-indexed by subject, date, journalist and so forth. For instance, you say you're looking for articles on the extreme right wing in the West. You can search under *politics, New Mexican,* or *fascism in America* or *neo-Nazis* or a number of other headings. They'll all lead you to where you want to go." He scrolled a menu for me to demonstrate.

"I think I can figure it out from here," I told him.

"Please let me know if you need any help."

I nodded him away and got to work. This was no more complicated than a library's computer index: Just type in the subject or key word and hit *Enter* to run a search string. Article titles would appear and you just punched a number key to call one up. Over the article appeared its date of publication, name of reporter and the news service that supplied it, if any. I remembered the dusty tedium of searching through newspaper morgues, spending uncounted hours leafing through musty old papers, sneezing and coughing, trying to find just one article. These devices were good for something after all.

As the young lady out front had thought, there seemed to be relatively little of the wild-eyed, compound-dwelling, Apocalyptic activity in New Mexico compared with, say, in Montana or Wyoming. Most of the articles on the subject came through wire services from elsewhere. There were, inevitably, a number of locally generated stories and on several of them I saw the same byline: Chance Gamble. This, I figured, had to be a pseudonym.

His articles went back more than ten years and they included probes into leagues of tax-protest lulus, white supremacist organizations, violent antiabortion protesters, guns-and-Jesus enthusiasts and others even more arcane. He was one of the paper's staff reporters.

"Mr. Gamble?" said Mr. Chavez, smiling. "Sure, his office is on the fifth floor."

The office door was open, as if Gamble was hoping for company. I rapped on it anyway.

"Come on in!" The voice was loud and it came from a man wearing blue jeans, a brown suede vest worn shiny in spots and cowboy boots propped up on his desk. A black low-crowned gambler's hat shaded him from whatever sunlight might make its way through the drawn blinds. "What can I do for you?" he yelled, as if I were still outside.

"My name is Gabe Treloar," I said, handing him my card. He studied it through thick-lensed glasses. A gray mustache hung over his upper lip.

"Says here you're a writer. Noble trade, is my opinion. What sort of writing do you do?"

"Political. I understand you're the paper's resident expert on the right-wing lunatic fringe. That's what I'm researching, the resurgence of the Nazi movement in America, primarily in the West."

"Then you've come to the right man." He glanced at the digital clock on his desk. "You had lunch?"

"Not yet. If you'll talk, I'll buy."

"Now you're speaking my language. Come on." He got out of his chair, revealing a belt buckle the size of a saucer and made, naturally, of silver and turquoise. Standing, he was two or three inches taller than I and rail-thin. He didn't bother to close his office door as we walked out.

"Who's your publisher for this book?"

"Actually, I don't have one yet. I've sent out a prospectus to several. You know, chapters and outline, that sort of thing. I've had several show some interest, mainly smaller presses, but they want to see more material before they commit."

He nodded as we got into the elevator. "I guess there's

a lot of competition in the field these days. Used to be there was only a few of us paying attention to the weird right-wingers. Everyone else was too preoccupied with the Red menace and the Mafia, I guess."

"Nobody expected the Soviet Union to collapse," I agreed. "We all thought the Nazis were long gone. The American Nazi Party, George Lincoln Rockwell, that was just a joke."

"It's no joke now."

The restaurant was only a block away so we walked through a brilliantly clear midday, the temperature maybe seventy, a light breeze dispersing any smog that the morning traffic might have generated. I decided I might want to retire somewhere around here. A plump waitress in a peasant blouse and colorful, flounced skirt showed us to a table while Gamble exchanged greetings with almost everyone we passed. He was obviously a fixture in this place.

The menu consisted mainly of chili in bewildering variety. I asked Gamble about it and he set me straight on a few things. First off, in New Mexico, the spelling was *chile*, not *chili*. The latter was the way Texans spelled it. New Mexicans, I was learning, considered Texans to be wrong about almost everything. Second, the subject of chile was very nearly a matter of religion in these parts so I accepted his guidance in ordering. My thirty-year experience of California Mexican food, I was informed, was useless in the presence of the genuine article.

"First, let's get some terminology straight," Gamble began as we sipped iced tea with lime. "Most people throw around terms like 'Nazi' and 'Fascist' like they know what they mean, which they don't. The American far-right nuts rarely qualify as either of them. Fascism was an Italian movement started mostly by World War One vets, who figured the old monarchist institutions had no place in the modern world. They were anticlerical because they despised the Catholic Church as an international institution, but they weren't anti-Semitic until they fell under German domination. In fact, the early Fascists, unlike the Germans, didn't consider anti-Semitism to be a racial policy. They thought it was a *Church* policy and therefore outdated and laughable.

" 'Nazi,' properly speaking, refers to German National Socialism, another movement mounted primarily by World War One vets, and sharing some characteristics of Fascism, such as extreme nationalism, militarism, police-state tactics and hatred of communism, but wildly different in others: the centrality of race theory—for instance, anti-Semitism—the passion for scapegoating. More than anything else, their addiction to loopy, wild-eyed mysticism and irrationalism, which the Italians considered comical. They were careful not to laugh, though, because the Germans were about a hundred times more militarily efficient than the Italians."

"Got you so far," I told him.

"Of course, I figure you know this already; I just want to make my meaning clear. What's called the neo-Nazi movement in this country has little to do with old-style Nazism. What the neos have in common with the old Nazis is a fetish for the uniforms and insignia, racism, love of ritual and worship of kick-ass attitude.

"The American far right is wildly disparate in makeup. What virtually none of them want is government in any form, a distinctly un-Fascist, un-Nazi attitude. The old guys despised only *weak* government. They *wanted* to be governed with an iron hand. They understood the importance of discipline to their philosophy and their aims."

"How do the Western organizations differ from the others?" I asked him, remembering what I was supposed to be researching.

"The West is, I need hardly point out, primarily rural and thinly populated. People who came here in the last

135

century thought they were getting away from the government back East, but it followed them. Farming and ranching are the Western lifestyles, and that means constantly skating close to disaster and bankruptcy. Banks have never been popular, and the farm and ranch foreclosures during the Depression made the hatred even worse. That's happening again, and the freaks are stepping in to provide a scapegoat: banks equals international banker's conspiracy equals international Zionist conspiracy.

"If there's one thing that's more hated than banks it's taxes. The loonies have an answer for that one, too: a uniquely personal vision of the U.S. Constitution. Some of them claim that Americans are not constitutionally bound to recognize any authority higher than the county sheriff."

"That's the Posse Comitatus belief, right?"

"They're the ones who came up with it first. Beats me why these people find it so attractive. They usually hate the sheriff, too. But desperate people will snatch at anything, and the loonies are telling them they don't have to pay federal taxes or honor debts to banks, which, they claim, are foreign institutions."

"If only it was that easy." The waitress slid steaming bowls of red chile in front of us, a sort of red-brown gravy with chunks of grilled pork floating in it. Alongside these were rellenos—whole chile pods stuffed with cheese, battered and deep-fried. By way of contrast there was a basket of sopaipillas, which were light, square, hollow pastries like little pillows. You poured honey into them and it cut the fire of the chile. Like the rellenos, they were deep-fried. Apparently the theory was that the chile made it all slide through your digestive system too fast for it to do any harm. By my third bite sweat was pouring from my hairline.

"Pretty soon your endorphins will kick in and the pain starts to feel good," Gamble assured me.

"Is this how masochists feel all the time?" I asked.

136

"Could be. After a while it gets habit-forming. Southwesterners are all chile addicts. We go into withdrawal when we have to travel away from home."

"It must be an acquired taste." I paused to down some tea.

He kept on talking between forkfuls. "Probably the factor that differentiates American right-wing loons from their old European counterparts more than any other is the influence of the oddball Christian fundamentalist sects like Christian Identity. They come in a number of species, but their usual schtik has it that the white race, specifically white Christian Americans, are God's chosen people, are in fact the original Hebrews of the Bible, the folks currently calling themselves Jews being Asian imposters descended from none other than Satan himself. This would've been a little rich even for an audience in Nuremberg to swallow back in thirty-eight, but most of these people haven't been trained in critical thinking. Education in general is seldom their long suit. They're out there on the prairies and in the mountains, pretty much isolated from the rest of the country and ready to believe that almost any sort of weird enemy is just over the horizon, ready to pounce. The heavy-handed tactics of federal agencies haven't helped much."

"Why the mountain and prairie states and not here?"

"It's a pretty racially homogeneous population up there, settled in the 1860s to 1880s by Northern European immigrants belonging to gloomy Protestant faiths, mainly Calvinism and doom-laden versions of Lutheranism, and that's pretty much what's up there now, with the few surviving Indians mostly living off on reservations. The Southwest, by way of contrast, was multicultural before the word entered the American vocabulary. It's an Anglo-Hispanic-Indian mix with a Catholic-Protestant-Shamanist spiritual life. And then there's the great unifying factor."

"Chile?"

"Right. You'll never see a real Nazi, or even a neo, put away a plate of green without breaking a sweat. This is not fertile ground for people with a master race message."

"Do you think they're politically significant?"

"Aside from their ability to generate news stories, no. There really aren't very many of them. Few are trying to take power. On the contrary, they're trying to *escape* political power. The old Nazis and Fascists had plans, not only for their countries but for the whole world. The militias and the compound dwellers and so forth are too influenced by the Apocalyptics. They think the world's going to end within a few years, so why bother with plans? They want to get to heaven before the Jews or somebody drags them off and sacrifices them to Satan."

I sidled toward my real point. "I take it you're familiar with Douglas Tyler and the White Front?"

"Oh, yes. I listen to his broadcasts every chance I get, subscribe to his publications, of which he generates a suspiciously large amount for a one-man operation."

"How do you rate him?"

"Ideologically, the closest thing to a genuine Nazi leader in America today. Unlike the others he's actually knowledgeable about the old party and the war, although he puts his own personal spin on history. He's pretty articulate but his propaganda is wrongheaded for what he's trying to achieve."

"Why's that?"

"His anti-Semitism, for instance. He's infuriated because Americans were so preoccupied with enslaving Africans and exterminating Indians that they never got to be properly anti-Semitic. So he fulminates against the Jews but he's got no sense of proportion. He tries to demonize them but he overdoes it and makes them seem godlike instead. He claims that this tiny minority controls the whole world almost without effort, is all-knowing, all-powerful, that every nation in the world jumps and goes to war at their command. Hell, even if I was inclined to believe him, I wouldn't want to mess with people like that. When Hitler vilified the Jews, he was careful to make them seem contemptible, able to wield power and influence only because the Weimar government was so weak. Hitler proposed to set that to rights.

"Whatever else the old Nazis were, they were geniuses at grabbing power. Tyler and the hard-core neo-Nazis howl that, once they're in power, they're going to kill all the Jews in the world along with everybody else who isn't a true Aryan. Hell, that's something the old Nazis never said *even while they were doing it!* They never talked publicly about killing people, not even during the war. Hitler let anyone into his movement except Jews and communists. The neos allow only true believers and any slight deviation from orthodoxy is enough to get you expelled. Unlike the real thing, these people do virtually everything possible to assure that they'll never have any credible shot at real power in this country."

"Does Tyler have any sort of following around these parts?"

"I don't know of anything organized, no groups with regular meetings and a newsletter and all that. It's hard to tell, though. A lot of people listen to his broadcasts, and these days they contact one another through computer bulletin boards."

"How about the real hardcores, the terrorists and hitters, the convict gangs and so forth? They need safe houses and meeting places just about everywhere in the country. Do you know of any local support group?"

His eyes narrowed. "That sort of information's a little hard to come by. I'd've collected my Pulitzer by now if I'd cracked a story like that. The FBI was all over here a while back, looking for just what you're talking about, right after the Oklahoma City bombing."

"Without success?"

"Some people were pulled in for questioning. Some were local bikers and eccentrics, there were some ex-cons with ties to white supremacist groups in the pens, a few recently discharged servicemen with records of activity in similar groups that recruit among military personnel."

"Where do people like that hang around here in Albuquerque?"

He paused, suspended between suspicion and disbelief. "Why? Do you enjoy dangerous living?"

"I'm a serious researcher."

"You must be." He took my card from his side vest pocket and squinted at it. "Gabe Treloar. Is that your real name?"

"Why shouldn't it be? It's a hell of a lot more believable than yours."

"It's my real name. Chance was my mother's maiden name. I was just wondering. Since you're lying about being a writer, why not about your name?"

Damn. Everybody was seeing through me these days. "Where'd I screw up?"

"If you're going to pose as a writer, you'd better brush up on the terminology and folk customs. A writer sends a publisher a proposal, not a prospectus. And that chapters-and-outline stuff is for novels, not investigative books."

"I'll make a note of it."

"And the last place a real writer goes to for information is a guy who's probably writing a book on the subject himself."

"There are nuances to this I hadn't considered."

"So what are you? A fed? A cop? I worked the police desk for a lot of years and you look like a cop to me."

I took out one of my real cards and handed it to him.

"That's more like it. What's happened, your client's kid got mixed up with one of the nutcase groups and you think he's hiding out here?"

"Something like that."

"Okay, play it close to your vest if you want. Tell you what: I'll give you the locations of a few spots where you might pick up some information. If you learn anything really interesting, anything concerning an active group operating here in Albuquerque, or in New Mexico and the Southwest in general, you'll pass it on to me, agreed?"

"Agreed. And thanks."

"Don't thank me just yet. What I'm going to tell you may just get you killed. Some of these people give whole new meanings to the word *paranoia*. And I don't just mean the skinheads and neos, but all of their fellow travelers in the weirdness underground. If they suspect you aren't what you represent yourself to be, like I just did, they'll probably kill you, just on general principles. You'll notice that I don't go around interviewing these people even though they'd be wonderful informants."

"I'll be careful, and you've got a deal."

"It's your life. Okay, there's a bar called Aces High. It's out on Coors Road just north of I-40. It's pretty much a biker's strip joint and you will see no, I repeat *no* black, Hispanic or Indian faces inside. Looking for informants, I suggest keeping your eyes on tattoos. Insignia on the clothes are affected by nearly everybody, but the tattoos are the mark of the hardcores. You know what to look for?"

"I'm pretty well versed in gang heraldry." I sketched the Tyr sign on the tablecloth in salsa. "You know that one?"

He glanced at it. "Well, shit, I guess I won't be learning much from you. If you're looking for those people you've got the life expectancy of a Western Front fighter pilot in 1917."

"Have you encountered them?"

He shook his head. "Just talk and rumors. But I know they're damn well for real and they're the baddest of the

141

bad. The minute the news came in from Oklahoma City I figured they were at the bottom of it and I'm still not convinced they aren't."

"Anyplace else?"

"There's a motorcycle shop on Central near the river called Hog Heaven. It's a hangout for White Front enthusiasts, where they distribute the literature and hold bull sessions and sit around to drink beer and listen to Tyler's radio broadcasts."

"That one's practically within sight of the motel where I'm staying."

"Which one is it?"

"The Cactus Inn."

He nodded with satisfaction. "I've had some good stories out of that place. At least a dozen murders over the last decade, with numerous nonfatal shootings and stabbings. A few suicides. Some sizable drug busts. Lively little place, good location by the river. It's cooler there in the evenings than most other parts of town."

"A raffish clientele adds charm to any location."

He grinned. "Don't scare easy, huh? Just as well, I guess. I hope I've done you some good. Right-wing nuttiness may prove to be a fad that will fade with the new millennium, but chile is an eternal verity."

"I don't know how to thank you."

"Just pick up the check. And don't forget to leave a decent tip. Juanita has three kids."

Eleven

The proprietor of Hog Heaven was pretty representative of the type: shaved head, handlebar mustache, smashed-in nose, earrings, brief denim vest covering nothing but a few of his many tattoos. A quick scan revealed swastikas, SS lightning marks and Nazi eagles among the American flags, bloody daggers and predatory cats, but no Tyr rune.

"Can I help you?" he said in a surprisingly high-pitched, almost friendly voice.

"Just browsing." I walked over to a rack of magazines and books wedged between a glass case of chrome-plated skull rings, wallet chains and assorted chrome doodads for choppers, and a wall display of bumper stickers proclaiming, HELMET LAWS SUCK, WHITE AMERICAN MALES—THE ENDANGERED SPECIES and antisocial messages such as I SHOULD HAVE KILLED YOU YESTERDAY.

The magazines were mostly devoted to motorcycles, almost all of them American, meaning Harley-Davidson, the only remaining American manufacturer of this form of transportation. The occasional German or British product was covered, but no Japanese motorcycles, known to the cognoscenti as "rice burners," need apply. And overwhelmingly the bikes were choppers—modified machines, low-slung brutes with high handlebars and extended forks so the skinny front wheel was way out in front. Many of these machines were adorned with barebreasted models who draped themselves over the seats and handlebars, and of the two the bikes seemed to be the objects of greater sensual interest.

There were catalogs advertising biker regalia of the sort familiar for the past fifty years: leather jackets and chaps, boots, caps and helmets, goggles, gloves—stuff that had looked really cool on Brando back in the early fifties, fully stylized by the time Fonda and Hopper made *Easy Rider* in '69, and pretty much the same ever since.

Even my long-jaded sensibilities were jangled by the tattoo magazines: *four* slick-paged monthly magazines dedicated solely to tattooing. The mind reeled. Inside, they celebrated the glories of "skin art" and its tribal corollary, piercing. It looked as if the old ships-and-anchors stuff was passé. The people on these pages displayed unbelievably lavish, rainbow-colored designs that covered whole torsos, legs, even entire bodies, including faces. Yet another strange mania carried to its ultimate extreme.

There was some White Front literature, but it was the same stuff I'd found at the flea market back in Amarillo. I turned to the proprietor and gestured to the shelf holding Tyler's publications.

"Do you have any newer stuff? I already have these."

He looked me over carefully. Then, apparently satisfied by what he saw, "Guy that delivers it comes by once a month. He won't be by again till next week."

"Too bad," I said. "I'm needing a propaganda fix."

"I know what you mean," he said. "It's good stuff. The man's maybe a little buggy about Jews, but he lives back East. He prob'ly don't know the spics run everything here."

"Tell me about it. I'm from L.A. Between the wetbacks,

the niggers and the gooks, a white skin's getting to be a death sentence."

"L.A., huh? What brings you to these parts, other'n the highway?"

"There's some people back in California I'd just as soon not talk to. Had to take a little vacation."

"I know how it is, been there myself."

The buzzer at the front door sounded and a pair of specimens walked in and I fought hard to avoid the head-to-toe evaluation that gives away a cop every time, instead pretending to return my interest to the magazines.

The taller was brown-haired and bearded, lanky, with big hands. The other was slight, almost effeminate, clean-shaven with long, fine blond hair. Neither wore biker attire, the taller favoring Wranglers and a brown leather bomber jacket, Blondie an ankle-length linen duster. Both wore dark shades but the blond one took his off as he entered, revealing washed-out, pale blue eyes with the glazed look of the genuine wacko.

"Need to speak with you, brother," the shorter man said to the guy behind the counter.

" 'S'what I'm here for."

"You got a office?" The taller one asked, his prominent Adam's apple bobbing on his thin, sinewy neck. The two of them glanced my way, as if I might be eavesdropping or something.

"Uh, right this way." The bald guy conducted them through a door behind his counter into what looked like a stockroom at the rear of the shop. As they went in the taller was pulling some folded papers from inside his bomber jacket.

The urge to tiptoe over to the door and listen in was almost overpowering, but I fought it back. The creaky old wooden floorboards would give me away for sure. The voices back there were quiet, no arguing or urgency. After no more than three minutes they emerged and I just managed to hear the blond one saying, "Be sure to pass the word along if he comes through here," shutting his mouth after the last word just as he passed through the door. The two didn't even look my way as they left the shop. I glanced out the front window in time to see them get into a dark-blue van, but without rushing to the door I couldn't get the license number.

The proprietor looked just slightly rattled and I decided that this was absolutely the wrong time to inquire. At his glance I just smiled and shrugged my shoulders. "Don't even want to know about it, man," I assured him. "Ain't none of my business."

"Them's spooky dudes," he said. "It prob'ly don't mean nothing, though."

"Say, my man, some brothers out in L.A. told me about a bar here called Aces High, said jungle bunnies and taco benders don't frequent the place. It still in business?"

"Sure. I go there 'most every night." My lack of interest in his recent callers and my knowledge of his watering hole seemed to reassure him. "It's about the only place in town where you can go and just be white without havin' to apologize. The chicks are tasty and the food's not bad, either." He gave me detailed instructions on how to find the place and I gave him a clenched-fist salute as I walked out.

"Keep the faith, brother," I said, hoping that salute was still accepted.

I went back to my rented room, thinking uncomfortable thoughts, and I settled down to nerve myself up to the evening's task.

Coors Road north of I-40 was a long stretch of strip malls and gas stations, with every third address a fast-food joint. Set back from the main road and separated from it by parking lots were a number of bars, some of them strip clubs and most of them seeming to cater to specialized clientele. The parking lot of one was full of young Hispanics, as if they preferred to socialize outside. Another advertised blues night and the people going inside were older and mostly black.

Aces High was actually on a small side street leading off Coors, and at first glance it didn't appear to be open. There was no illuminated sign, no neon, no floods shining on the front of the building. The only light was on a pole over the parking lot. I was wondering if I'd come to the right place when the front door opened and a couple came out, light and loud music spilling out around them.

I pulled into the gravel lot and saw that there were a couple of motorcycles there, a few cars and pickups. Not much of a crowd but it was early yet. On the front door was painted the name of the place along with a skull with playing-card spades for eyes and a joint between its teeth. I pushed it open and went inside.

In a tiny hallway an immense bouncer rose from his chair. His hair and beard were like those of a biblical warrior and he wore a chromed drive chain for a belt. In one hand he held a metal detector of the sort used in airports and, these days, schools.

"Rules of the house, man," he said, gesturing for me to raise my arms. I did so and he ran his device over me expertly. It made its groaning sound when he reached my back pocket. He slid the Asp from my pocket and flicked it open, the telescoping rods snapping into place solidly. He tapped its butt against the wall and it folded back up. He handed it back to me. "Them's nice weapons, but you'll have to leave it in your ride. We don't want to lose our license."

"Okay with me, long as everybody gets the same treatment." I went out and stashed it in my glove box. I'd brought it along only because I suspected that an unarmed man would raise suspicion in a place like this. Back inside the bouncer repeated his procedure, then waved me on through.

Aces High was bigger than it looked outside, with at least two sizable rooms opening off the main one. One room was devoted to pool and another had a dance floor. The main room was for drinking and at one end it had a stripper's stage, currently unoccupied. Loud music blared from a jukebox but since I lost contact with popular music around 1970, I couldn't guess what style it was.

The decor ran to a lot of American flags, guns, presumably deactivated, edged weapons that looked functional, and portraits of American heroes like Washington, Jim Bowie and Wyatt Earp. But dominating everything were huge photo blowups of Nuremberg rallies, panzers in action, SS recruiting posters and Nazi bigwigs, including der Führer himself engaged in a number of poses and activities. Hundreds of Nazi medals and insignia rested behind glass in frames on the walls.

At least, I thought, you couldn't claim these people weren't up front about what they were.

I slid onto a stool at the bar. The bar itself was a huge slab of Lucite with bits of barbed wire, bullets and twisted medals embedded in it like weird fruit in clear Jell-O.

I wasn't especially hungry, but I figured that eating would be better than trying to nurse a beer all night, so I grabbed a menu and studied it. I saw immediately that my new wisdom concerning chile would do me no good in this place. The fare was strictly meat and potatoes, chow of the most Aryan sort. The hefty woman behind the bar took my order and didn't turn a fake-blond hair when I ordered iced tea to go with it.

"Gotta limit my intake," I said apologetically, tapping my chest. "Blood pressure's through the roof these days."

She nodded in sympathy. "Lot of us ain't as young as we used to be, hon. Gotta charge you the cover price, anyway. It's for the entertainment." She nodded her big-haired head toward the stage, which sported a gleaming brass pole.

"When do the ladies go on?" I asked her.

" 'Bout a half hour," she said, pronouncing the last two words as *hay fair,* sure sign of a childhood spent in the southern Appalachians.

The steak and fries I'd ordered turned out to be amazingly good. My friend at the bike shop hadn't been over-praising it out of racial loyalty. I guess there's no rule saying that lowlife racist Nazi scum can't cook.

As I was finishing up my meal and showtime drew near, the place began to fill up. The clientele were by no means all bikers, although the majority had a blue-collar look and they were 100 percent white. There were a few skinheads, some college-boy types and a very few that looked like they had day jobs behind desks and in offices. But most just looked like ordinary working stiffs. The crowd was predominantly male, but there was a sprinkling of couples. I didn't see any women arrive alone.

The lights dimmed slightly as an MC announced the first performer. The girl came onstage amid screeching guitar riffs and thudding bass notes, dressed in boots, black leather G-string and vest. The vest went almost immediately. I ordered an after-dinner beer and turned around on my stool, elbows resting on the bar behind me, blending in with the appreciative audience.

After a few minutes of gyrations the girl shed the G-string and performed a few athletic sex acts with the pole to much applause and enthusiastic hooting. She danced off the stage sweating profusely and was replaced by a slightly more accomplished lady dressed in a skimpy stylization of S&M bondage gear. She was followed by a trio of lap dancers who circulated among the tables. These three retained their G-strings, either because of local law or because they needed some place to stash their tips.

By the end of an hour I'd learned all I wanted to know

about the current state of silicone implants. It made me feel old, because I could remember, as a decidedly under-age high-schooler, sneaking into places on Crenshaw where the ladies still came out fully dressed and made a production of taking it off. They wore tasseled pasties and were pretty much stuck with whatever they'd developed in adolescence. On second thought I decided it wasn't any better back then. I was just younger.

When the set was over the lights came back up but it was still pretty dim, just enough to bring out the lurid reds of the battle banners hanging from the ceiling like scarlet bats. I got up from my bar seat and headed toward the men's room, which opened off the room with the dance floor.

Outside, next to the door was a large cork bulletin board where patrons could post business cards and photos offering cars, trucks, bikes, trailers, boats, hunting dogs and the like for sale. I took my time in the rest room. The Wehrmacht decor was continued inside and even the amazing condom display rated some attention. It was shaping up to be a long evening. I hadn't even started talking to people yet and I was kicking myself for showing up so early. People needed to get properly juiced up to start talking about touchy subjects to casual strangers.

When I came out I scanned the place and saw that all three rooms were packed. That was good for my purposes. It would give me an excuse to sit at tables with a conveniently unoccupied chair and strike up conversations, or listen to the ambient buzz.

As I walked toward the pool room something caught my eye. In a corner, just past the dance floor, two standing men were talking to a group of skinheads in their early twenties seated around a table. One of the men was lanky and dark, the other blond, slender and wearing a linen duster: my two beauties from the chopper shop. Finishing whatever they were saying, the two straightened and began to walk to another table. I didn't think it was a good idea for these two to see me for a second time on the same day. They reeked of the sort of paranoia that makes men reach for their guns the instant they suspect they are being followed or someone is watching them.

I turned away from the room and pretended to study the bulletin board. Then I froze, Mutt and Jeff forgotten, the pounding music suddenly silent in my ears. Nick Switzer was staring at me.

The same mug shots Carson had given me had been reproduced on a flier. Over the pictures was printed, in screaming caps: WANTED: RACE TRAITOR! Below the mug shots were a pair of well-executed drawings done from the photos, but with the addition of the haircut and short beard he had been wearing in the odd photo taken in front of the blood lab. I read the copy below the pictures:

Nicholas "Nick" Switzer is a traitor to the White race, fleeing from racial justice. All who value the future of our White race are called upon to report this traitor upon sighting to appropriate authorities.

To my great relief there was no picture of Sibyl, but the next line read:

Switzer may be traveling with a woman described as follows: White, approximately twenty-four years of age, five feet five inches tall, blond, blue-eyed, speaks with a slight German accent. The woman, name unknown, is a participant in race treason and is wanted as well.

That was Sibyl as in the lab photo as well. But slight German accent? What the hell?

The flier was well printed on slick, glossy paper just

like that used for the "National Guardian." The photo and drawing reproductions were of far higher quality than the ones you see in post offices. The copy was grammatical, too. It looked like a Douglas Tyler production all the way.

"That's a new one on me, too." The words came with a wash of beer breath and I turned to see one of the office-worker types standing beside me, looking at the flier. I had no idea how long I'd been staring at the damned thing. At least, in these surroundings, a slightly spaced-out look wasn't anything to arouse suspicion.

I wanted to take down the flier and stick it in my pocket, but there was no way I could do that without being seen. Maybe, I figured, I could come by tomorrow at opening time when the place was all but deserted. I pretended to study the For Sale ads for a while, then casually turned around.

The blond guy, now seated at a table against a wall, his head flanked by a pair of WWI brass-knuckle trench knives, was studying me. I let my gaze sweep past, not making eye contact, trying to appear just the slightest bit high, knowing that I'd been staring at that flier way too long. I should have looked at it no longer than it took to identify the pictures and read the copy, then strolled away, drawing no attention to myself.

I couldn't see the tall one, and I did not find that comforting. All of a sudden, I was through with this place for the evening. But I didn't want to run. That would confirm whatever suspicions were stirring around behind those washed-out eyes. So I moseyed back to the bar and ordered another beer.

I left the glass where it was and carried the bottle into the pool room. It's much easier to fake drinking from a dark bottle than from a glass. I pretended interest in the pool games and the display of old, bayoneted Mauser rifles on the wall. Whoever was in charge of the music gave the rock a rest for a while and put on some vintage recordings of Nazi marching songs. Glasses thumped on tables in time to the Horst Wessel song *"Die Fahne Hoch,"* quickly followed by *"Heil Hitler Dir," "Heil Deutschland," "Wenn Die SS Und Die SA Afumarschiert"* and, heartbreakingly, a choir of children singing *"Die Jugend Marschiert."* The first song I already knew. I learned the other titles because some guy with a British accent introduced each one.

Except for the children's song, they were sung by choruses of spirited young men, most of whom probably died more than half a century ago on some godforsaken Russian steppe, African desert, deep-frozen Belgian forest, or were squashed like bugs in sinking submarines or worked to death in Siberian mines. I wasn't feeling sorry for them, though. The tunes were absurdly cheerful and they seemed to be having a fine time back then, in the years before the reckoning came.

I dropped the still-full bottle into a trash can and made my way slowly to the front door. The bouncer nodded affably. "C'mon back, now."

"I expect I will," I told him.

The door opened and I walked out into the parking lot. I stepped to one side of the door and let my eyes adjust to the outer dimness before proceeding, a practice I'd been taught in Vietnam and just as practical in the savage jungles of North America in these closing days of the twentieth century.

Coors Road was brightly lighted, its traffic noisy and bumptious, but it was almost a block away. The lot was full of vehicles now, a maze to be negotiated before I reached my battered old heap.

While I waited for my rods or cones or whatever the hell they are to adjust, I thought about the flier. I was pretty sure it hadn't been on the board before I went into the men's room. Surely it would have caught my eye. I now remembered a litter of photos and cards on the floor beneath the flier. They had probably cleared a spot for it and tacked it in place while I'd been in the rest room, putting it at eye level where anyone going by had to see it. There was no reward posted, but maybe serving the race was supposed to be reward enough. Besides, posting a reward was probably in violation of the law. There was neither address nor phone number listed, and who the hell were the "proper authorities," anyway? Presumably, people in the Aryan underground would know how to pass the word. It had all been done to keep everyone anonymous. I doubted there was anything on the flier that could be used in court to prosecute anyone.

So Nick was a "race traitor." In Tyler's publication, that usually meant someone who espoused the causes of nonwhite or Jewish people, or else an Aryan who married or was otherwise intimate with a non-Aryan. I fell into that last category, since my wife had been Vietnamese. The only woman I knew Switzer to be involved with was Sibyl, and I couldn't really picture him as an activist in the civil rights movement or an honorary member of B'nai B'rith.

I could see as clearly as I was going to. No sense stalling. I started across the lot, wishing I'd had the foresight to park closer to the entrance. Instead, I'd parked almost beneath the light. Except for the vehicles the lot was deserted and I'd have felt a lot better if people were arriving or leaving, but no such luck. Not one lousy little drug deal going down. Where are the junkies when you need them?

As I neared the car I sensed movement rather than heard it. At the last second I went around to the passenger's side, jerked the door open, dropped the glove box lid, reached in and grabbed the Asp. By the time I straightened, the man who'd been approaching the driver's side was around the car raising something in his right hand. I slashed out with the Asp and its telescoping segments snapped into place an instant before making solid contact. I was trying for his elbow, got the meaty part of the forearm instead, and made him drop the gun, anyway.

As he squawked I grabbed the collar of the bomber jacket, kicked him behind the knee, slammed him face-first into the front fender as he went down and laid the Asp across his throat, wedging it into the crook of my left elbow while my left hand went to the back of his skull in a sort of reinforced half nelson. This is the infamous "choke hold" with which cops subdue arrestees and occasionally deliver them DOA.

"What you doin' motherfucker?" I shouted. "You been followin' me all day, watchin' me! You think I put up with shit like that?" A Method actor friend had once given me some pointers on how to submerge yourself in a role, and I was imitating every ultraparanoid freak I'd ever busted. The theatrics were for the benefit of my audience, and I knew I had one.

The gun that pressed into the side of my neck felt like a Glock: a cold little circle of steel muzzle surrounded by a square polymer shroud of neutral temperature.

"Let him go, asshole," said an unnervingly composed voice.

Slowly, I released my prize, let the Asp fall, and straightened up. "Who the fuck are you—" That was as far as I got before the tall skinny one came up off his knees, hooked his knuckles onto my belly and jerked a knee into my face as I doubled over. I didn't even have time to get comfortable on the gravel before his boot toe caught me in the side and I felt a rib give amid a wash of hideous pain.

"Motherfucker broke my motherfuckin' arm!" he wailed. "Kill the fucker!" He gave me another kick, this one catching me in the pelvis just over the hip joint. I didn't feel anything break this time. "Shoot him!"

"We need to talk to him first," the other one said. "Keep your voice down." At least somebody was keeping his equanimity.

Each got a hand on me and they pulled me up until I was half-sitting against a fender. I was all but paralyzed, unable to do more than breathe.

"You were studying our wanted poster pretty hard, my friend," Blondie said. His partner was standing behind him, massaging his right forearm, flexing his fingers and wincing.

"What else you put it up for?" I gasped. "You jump everyone who pays attention? There's a reward, right?"

He backhanded me across the face, a big, square ring cutting a gash in my right cheekbone. "Don't be thinking about no reward, man. Be thinking about still breathing two minutes from now." He grasped my collar and shook my head gently. The ring had shifted and I saw that it had covered a small tattoo: the Tyr rune.

"I think maybe it ain't broke," the tall one said. Blondie ignored him.

"We saw you earlier today, at the hog shop." He stroked the uncut side of my face with his gun muzzle, almost caressingly.

"I was asking how to find this place," I told him. "I'm from out of town, heard this was my kind of place. It seemed to be, then you two assholes showed up. And this is the second time today I've seen *you*, so we're even." The tall one kicked me in the side again. It was awkward and lacked full power, but it hurt plenty.

"No, we are very far from even," Blondie insisted. "Why'd you look at the poster so long? That traitor a friend of yours?" Abruptly, he jerked me forward, then slammed me back against the fender. The back of my head hit the metal hard enough to make it flex. At least, I hoped it was the fender bending, not my skull.

"Jesus, man, lighten up!" I pleaded. "He looks like a

guy I saw a few days back." My mind was spinning, try-ing to push back the pain and come up with a plausible story, one that might satisfy them without endangering Sibyl any further, although my concern for her was di-minishing by the second.

"Where?" he said, with what seemed no more than polite interest.

"Little Rock. He was getting gas." I groaned and I wasn't faking it. My stomach was spasming, trying to eject dinner.

"Now we already know you're a real alert guy," Blondie said. "I mean, the way you reacted to seeing us was okay. But just why does the traitor stick in your mind? You must see a lot of people and he ain't real distinctive."

"Wasn't the man," I said, half-choking. "It was the car and the babe."

"Oh, yeah," he crooned, stroking the side of my face, this time with the back of his fingers. It felt even creepier than being stroked by his gun. "Tell me about that. What kind of car?"

"White Grand Am, real clean little vehicle. I always liked 'em."

"All right," Blondie said, sounding like he was ready to unbend just a little bit. "Now let's hear about the woman."

"A real fox," I told him. "Blond, fancy hairdo, big blue eyes. Looked like a model." Here was where they'd prob-ably shoot me, if they had more up-to-date info on Sibyl.

"Was she wearing glasses?"

"I don't remember glasses . . ." I paused for effect. "Wait. Yeah, she had a pair hanging from her neck on one of those chain things. They were sort of resting on top of her tits. Those were worth a look all by them-selves. She was wearing a cashmere sweater, looked real expensive."

"When did you see the man?"

"When he came out of the station. He looked at me like he didn't like me admiring his woman. That was why his face stuck in my memory. I don't like people looking at me like that. I thought about following them, having a word with him somewhere private. But I had to put gas in my car and by the time I was rolling again, they were long gone."

"Doing good so far, my friend," said Blondie. "Which picture did he look like?"

Here was another tricky one. Their contacts might have spotted him recently. But I couldn't afford to hesitate and I played it by instinct. "The mug shots. No beard."

Blondie patted my face again, then stood slowly and stuck his pistol under his belt. "Okay, I'm prepared to believe you. You do seem to be a brother in the cause, after all."

"If you don't want to kill the fucker I will," said Skinny, leveling his piece at my head.

Blondie slapped it down. "Now, now," he said gently. "The chief said to avoid unnecessary complications. We're to be circumspect."

"He's always sayin' shit like that," said Skinny, disappointed. But he put his gun away.

"So is there a reward in this?" I asked.

"Just keep the faith," Blondie said, "and you'll have your place in Valhalla." He sounded sincere.

"You want a reward?" Skinny said. "Here's a reward." He picked up the Asp and smashed it against the side of my left knee, then dropped it in my lap.

It was quite a while before the pain subsided enough for me to do so much as open my eyes. When I had enough energy, I leaned slightly sideways and vomited, almost passing out in the process. That was okay. I'd been feeling sort of guilty about all that cholesterol anyway.

From time to time I heard people going into the bar or

leaving it, saw the wash of headlights as cars came in or left, but nobody noticed me.

After a while I pushed myself to a near-standing position, retrieved my Asp and hobbled around to the driver's side of my car, using my hands more than my one good leg.

Once seated inside, I leaned back and spent some time trying to get my breathing back to near-normal. The pain was excruciating but it was an amazing sensation just being alive. I knew I'd sustained some severe damage, and maybe some permanent injury, especially to my knee. Oh, well, I wasn't planning to enter the Olympics, anyway.

A tougher guy would have just gone back to the motel to suffer in solitude, but I got over that sort of bravado a long time ago. As soon as the trembling subsided and a little strength returned, I started the car and went in search of a hospital. I was grateful that my car had an automatic transmission. I couldn't have worked a clutch to save my life.

Twelve

The hospital was near the University of New Mexico campus, and its emergency room seemed to be the busiest place in town. I've spent a lot of time in ERs, because so many suspects, arrestees, victims and fellow police officers end up in them. Taking statements from people recently shot, stabbed and beaten is one of the least pleasant tasks a cop faces, but it's routine. Worst of all is when you yourself are the one in need of the facility's services.

Not that I was the center of much attention when I went in. The waiting room was crowded with people awaiting treatment and all of them were too wrapped up in their personal plights to spare me much regard. I limped over to the admitting desk, dripping blood on the floor as I did so. The gray-haired woman behind the desk looked up at me and didn't flinch at a sight that would have sent most people running away, screaming. Apparently injuries weren't her line of work because she was primarily interested in my insurance status.

"What do you say I just pay cash?" I asked her, my swelling jaw making it difficult to speak.

"Do you think you can?" My clothes failed to inspire her confidence.

"Look, I don't want to flash my roll. You got some desperate-looking people in here, no telling what might happen. I can cover it, don't worry. I'm not here for a heart transplant."

She didn't crack a smile. "Fill these out." She handed me a clipboard with a stack of forms. From the look of the place I'd have plenty of time to fill everything out before someone took a look at me.

I found a vacant chair made of molded plastic and sat down, a process no less painful than standing up had been. In the chair on one side of me sat a woman who was doubled over with some sort of pain in her midriff. On the other side was a man whose face was a mask of blood from a scalp laceration. I'd barely made a start on my paperwork when the ambulance door banged open and paramedics brought in two accident victims, one of whom sprayed blood from a severed artery they'd been unable to clamp. I was an amateur in the blood-dripping department in this place.

I finished my paperwork and turned it in, then sat back down to wait. People were groaning or crying or sitting stoically silent. Everywhere there were children, most of them with parents who had been unable to find sitters when they had to seek medical help. Some of the kids seemed pretty familiar with the ER.

City and county police kept passing by, some of them looking me over in passing, but none of them intrigued enough to question me. It was just as well, because my prepared story about falling down the stairs probably wouldn't have held up.

Finally a nurse called my name and showed me to a room where, after a decent interval, an incredibly young intern came to look me over. He had me undress and get

161

on the table, then he checked out my injuries and patched up a few lacerations. The rib, it seemed, wasn't worth taping.

"I want to get X rays of your jaw and knee," he said.

"I take it you don't plan to file assault charges."

"It was an accident."

He looked at my hands. "Must have been. There are no signs that you did any fighting back."

"I guess you must be new at this."

He shook his head as he shined a light into my eyes. "Uh-uh. And spare me the Doogie Howser jokes, I'm twenty-six. I just spent half the evening with a pregnant woman who was shot twice in the belly and she's not filing charges, either. Of course, she has sound reasons. She figures a woman shouldn't rat on her husband. Bastard still had the gun sticking out of his back pocket when he brought her in."

"If it'll set your mind at ease, my wife didn't do this."

"Think I give a shit?" He palpated the back of my skull. "You've got a possible fracture here. If so, it should show up on the mandible X ray."

"Two for the price of one. I guess this is my lucky night."

I hobbled to the X-ray lab, then more waiting, then the boy with the M.D. decided I didn't have any permanent damage except maybe some torn cartilage in my knee.

"I guess you can go now," he said happily. "Watch out for those stairs."

"I didn't say anything about stairs," I protested.

"Well, everyone else does. Since you weren't shot or stabbed I don't have to turn you over to the police. Bye-bye. Try not to come back."

His nurse escorted me all the way to the cashier, ready to call security if I should try to bolt. Big chance of that. She left me there and I settled up with the hospital. The cashier didn't seem at all surprised when I paid cash, but all the dealers probably did that, too.

At least the parking lot outside was brightly illuminated. I was getting a bit leery of dark parking lots. For the second time that night somebody was waiting by my car, but right out in plain view this time.

"I have to hand it to you, Gabe," Jasper Holt said, "you are a man who really earns his pay." Tina was just to one side of him, her face as inscrutable as ever behind the glow of her cigarette.

"I was wondering when I'd see you again," I told him. "One of those cops in there tip you off?" I jerked my head back in the direction of the hospital and immediately wished I hadn't. "I got the impression New Mexicans didn't cooperate with Texans."

"Money and mutual favors cut through a lot of state chauvinism. I know you established yourself here in town this morning. We need to talk, Gabe."

"Why should I talk with you?"

"Because I think you might've learned a few things since we talked in Oklahoma City. And I just came by a bit of information you would dearly love to have. Quid pro quo?"

"Quid pro quo," I agreed. "And I need to lie down pretty quick. Let's go back to my motel."

"You want to ride with me? Tina can drive your car back."

"It'll be easier for me to sit down in my Pontiac than climb into your Bronco."

"Fine, but let Tina drive anyway. You look like you're about ready to pass out on me."

I got in and Tina slid into the driver's seat, needing to crank it all the way forward to reach the pedals. She backed out and left the parking lot smoothly, got onto the service road and then onto the interstate without making any of my pains worse. Somewhere she'd learned to drive like an expert.

"What's *quid pro quo* mean?" she asked abruptly. Somehow, I knew she wouldn't have asked Holt.

"It's Latin for 'something for something.' It means we're trading." She nodded, filing away the information. In the skimpy, late-night traffic it took less than ten minutes to get back to the Cactus Inn. Tina helped me out of the car and into my room. Her wiry little body was surprisingly strong. Holt followed moments later.

"Gabe's had a rough night," Holt announced. "Tina, why don't you run along and find us some refreshments, maybe a few aspirin."

"It's three o'clock in the goddamn morning, Jasper; why don't you run along and get it your own self?"

He stared at her coolly. "There's one of those twenty-four-hour superstores about five minutes from here, on the corner of Central and Coors Road."

She glared right back at him until I said, "Tina, Jasper and I won't discuss anything of importance until you're back. And the painkiller the doc gave me won't last long. If that place has a pharmacy, I'd sure like to get this prescription filled."

She didn't break her eye contact as she took the slip of paper from my hand. "Well, since it's you that's askin'." Then she turned and walked out, her spine stiff, but closing the door quietly.

"Holt, I thought you had more sense. That woman looks perfectly capable of trimming your hair right under your chin."

He fumed for a moment longer, then grinned. "Yeah, ain't she a case, though? I guess I wouldn't have her around if she wasn't mean as a four-headed rattlesnake. Just keep in mind she's got permanent PMS and you'll be all right."

"Every man to his own taste." I opened a suitcase and

got out some clean clothes, then hobbled into the bathroom. There I washed up a bit, reconciled myself to my appearance and to the fact that I'd look even worse in the morning. Wearing the loosest, lightest slacks I had and an unbuttoned shirt, I went out into the room and lowered myself onto the bed. I wanted to sleep for a week or so.

A few minutes later Tina returned with drinks, ice, some easy-on-the-stomach snacks and a huge bottle of aspirin. With brisk efficiency she plumped the pillows behind my head, fed me four painkillers, and I washed them down with an iced Coke. In my heightened state of consciousness, common Coca-Cola tasted almost unbearably good.

"You first," Holt said.

"Before I start I want to know one thing: Are you working with the people who jumped me tonight? These other people who're chasing Sibyl and Nick?"

He raised a hand. "I swear to you, Gabe, I have nothing to do with them." Behind him, eyes lowered a bit, Tina nodded. For reasons I couldn't explain, I was more inclined to trust her than I was him.

So I told him what I'd learned about Death Troop Tyr, about my tantalizing glimpse of a dark-haired young woman back in Tucumcari, my quixotic telephone call to Douglas Tyler. I related my suspicions about the deputy who'd been asking about Switzer back East and confirmed Holt's guess about Sibyl's philosophy courses.

He nodded with satisfaction. "Knew it."

"Actually," I told him, "I was concerned that she was getting her brain turned to mush by the existentialists and deconstructionists."

He snorted. "They're just a bunch of French pissants. Back at the start of World War Two the French rolled over for the Germans without a fight. Ever since, they've been trying to prove that nothing means anything anyhow. No philosopher's going to go broke telling Frenchmen that kissing German ass doesn't reflect on their honor."

"Why Nietzsche?"

"He was a great philosopher, but he attracts dickheads. Problem is, he wrote in plain, clear language and he said a lot of things that seem to vindicate antisocial attitudes. He's popular reading among convicts who can read at all. Jailhouse Nietzsche is one of the great baleful influences of our time. They read those passages that praise the criminal as a superior sort of man and they think he's talking about *them!* That poor man has been so unfairly maligned it's pitiful. He deserves better."

With some astonishment I realized that I had just heard, for perhaps the only time in history, Friedrich Nietzsche referred to as "that poor man." I saw that Tina was listening intently, as if this were something important. God knew what sort of education she was receiving at the hands of Jasper Holt.

Holt came out with a handful of mug-shot sheets. "I was pretty sure that we were looking at the handiwork of Jess Marsh back in Memphis and I'm grateful for your confirmation, Gabe. I had these shots of his likely associates sent to me. See if your friends are among them."

It didn't take me long. After my recent experience the faces fairly jumped out at me. Holt smiled and nodded.

"The blond one's a California surfer dude named Scott Bergstrom. He once killed three men for surfing on his beach. Seems the wave riders are real territorial in those parts."

"I've encountered the type. How'd he tie up with Marsh?"

"Can't say. He joined the Aryan hard-ons in the pen while serving his time for manslaughter. Seems his choice of weapon, a fish gaff, ruled out premeditation. The three victims were all armed in one fashion or another and nobody missed them much anyway. He drew twelve and served seven, disappeared on release, jumped parole and is suspected in a number of violent crimes."

"What about the hick?"

"An East Texas shitkicker from the bayou country near Beaumont. Name's Joel Leblanc. Long string of juvenile offenses, did time for assault with intent to kill at Huntsville, suspected of being part of the team that hijacked Marsh's prison bus."

"There may be another one named Martinez." I showed him the copy of the shot Padilla had given me.

"Sort of makes you wonder what Marsh must be like, don't it?" Tina said. "I mean, if he keeps dudes like this in line, he must be the final word in badass." She sounded more intrigued than horrified.

"Your turn," I said to Holt.

"First, Gabe, accept my compliments on a job doggedly pursued. You've accomplished a lot with very little in the way of resources. And your methods, describable only as unorthodox, are effective."

"Screw that. Give me some information I can use. Would it violate the sanctity of bounty hunter-client privilege to tell me who the hell you're working for?"

"It surely would. Let's just say that when Nick tossed his rock into the pond it started some very big ripples going. I'm not real clear on the details myself."

"Then what do you have? I need to get some sleep."

"First, you'll be happy to learn that it was Sibyl you saw back in Tucumcari yesterday. Day before yesterday, actually. You've been putting in some long days."

"Damn! I knew I should've hung around. That's what I get for not trusting my instincts."

"But think of all the experience you'd've missed. Seems they took a break to attend that rodeo."

"They went to a *rodeo*? With you and me and Death Troop Tyr after them?"

Holt chuckled. "Come on, you've dealt with peckerheads like Switzer all your life, Gabe. They're impulsive. They can go along acting real organized, pulling complicated scams just like they were sane, but they have an infantile mentality, easily distracted."

Tina nodded. "I've known plenty like him," she affirmed.

"I take it they're not still in Tucumcari," I said. "After all, you're here. Are they in Albuquerque? If they are, we need to find them quick, with the Tyr guys in town." The prospect of any sort of activity didn't appeal to me a bit.

"Nope. Just before I learned you were in the hospital, a contact of mine in Arizona called me. This afternoon he spotted them in Flagstaff. They've checked into a place called the Canyon Lodge. No car, but it's a hell of a lot better place than this. They're not hurting for money."

It was relief, of a sort. At least they were still alive. "Can you have them picked up, held for a few hours on charges, maybe vagrancy or something?"

" 'fraid not. The local authorities up there don't like me much, for some reason. My friend's keeping an eye on them. I'm heading that way right now. If they're late sleepers, I may just be giving them a wake-up call in the morning." He stood and settled his Stetson.

"Take me with you!" I tried to struggle upright but couldn't even sit.

"Sorry, Gabe. All I agreed to was an exchange of information, and if mine wasn't as entertaining as yours, I think you'll agree that knowing where they are this minute is a hell of a lot more important than knowing where they've been. You're in no shape to travel anywhere and I can't spare the attention to nursemaid you."

He went to the door, paused and turned. "You're a good man, Treloar. On a different job, I'd be more than pleased to work with you. But not this one. My client would never have it. I'll do my best to keep your boss's little girl safe, and she shouldn't be in danger as long as they don't pull a Bonnie and Clyde and come out shooting. Right now, their biggest danger is that Jess Marsh may find them first, so I'd best be on my way. Come along, Tina."

He went out and so did Tina. She paused at the door and looked back at me. "See you" was all she said, then the door shut behind them.

I cursed them and I cursed my own dumbness for ending up in this condition. It was an excruciating task just to reach over and turn out the bedside lamp. I couldn't remember when I had last been in so much pain.

I didn't take long to fall asleep anyway.

When I awoke the sun was all the way up and my body was an explosion of pain. I spent a few seconds dredging up memories of the previous day. Okay, now I had a purpose, something to take my mind off my woes. Somehow, I had to get to Flagstaff.

Slowly, I forced my way out of bed. My jaw hurt so much I couldn't even grit my teeth. My leg kept giving way beneath me, so I had to hop on one leg with a hand against a wall. In the bathroom I dropped a couple of painkillers, managed to get undressed and into the shower. Even the water hurt. Where were those damned endorphins?

Cleaned up, dressed and with a purpose, I felt better. The question was, could I drive the eight hours or so it would take to get to Flagstaff? Could I even drive away from the motel?

I opened the door and there was Tina sitting on the fender of my car, feet propped on the front bumper, smoking a cigarette.

"I was wonderin' if you were gonna make it to the door." She slid off the fender, dropped her cigarette and ground it beneath the pointed, silver toe of her boot.

"Where's Jasper?"

"Gettin' pretty close to Flagstaff, I expect." She brushed past me and picked up my suitcases.

"Why aren't you with him?"

"I'm travelin' with you for a while," she said, brushing past me a second time, setting the suitcases down by the car trunk. She reached out a hand. "Gimme your keys. I'll put these away." I noticed that two more suitcases, undoubtedly hers, stood next to mine.

"I don't recall inviting you."

"Shit, Treloar, you ain't got a chance in hell of drivin' all the way to Flagstaff yourself. Now gimme them keys and get in the car, 'less you want to spend the rest of the day in this fleapit whackin' off like a monkey in the zoo."

I hesitated. "Is Holt—"

"Do you want to get that little bitch back alive, or don't you?"

"Well, hell," I muttered, lurching toward my car, handing her my keys.

"Passenger side!" she snapped. "I'll drive and you can catch up on your sleep."

Obediently, I got in on the unfamiliar side, raked back the seat while she stowed our bags. Had Holt planted her on me? Unlikely, since he was so far ahead of me.

"You and Holt have an argument?" I asked as she slid into the driver's seat, shut the door and started the car all in one movement.

"Why'n't you shut your mouth and get some sleep?" She backed around, pulled onto Central and headed toward the nearest junction with I-40. A few minutes later we had climbed onto the desert high ground to the west of town, and the city was behind us. We were back in the pristine, primeval desert.

I dozed through the morning, waking from time to time to see that we were passing through a series of Indian reservations, all of which just looked like more desert, dotted with occasional shacks, ranch houses and hogans. The really colorful pueblos are off the major highways.

I woke again when Tina stopped for gas in Gallup. While she operated the pump, I made my way to the men's room, astonished to see that I was moving around marginally better than when I got out of bed. When I got back to the car she was firing up another of her cigarettes.

"You pissin' any blood?" she asked, sliding back behind the wheel.

"Not that I noticed."

"My husband got beat up like that a few times when he was drunk, kicked in the ribs real hard. One time he was pissin' blood for a week."

"Sounds rough."

She shrugged. "About the only time I ever got any peace, 'cept for the way he whined about it all the time."

My head was feeling clearer and I couldn't drop back to sleep anymore. "Did Jasper drive straight through all night? Doesn't he ever sleep?"

"He catnaps during the day," she told me. "Usually on the road while I'm driving, like now."

"Do you think he was straight with me about Flagstaff, not sending me off on a false scent while they're really in El Paso or Denver or someplace?"

She shook her head. "Uh-uh. I was sittin' next to him when the call came in on that cellular phone of his. No, Jasper plays games but he don't lie outright 'less he really needs an advantage. And he makes a point of being level with people in his own line of business: police, PIs, mob people, like that. He knows he might have to work with you or your boss again sometime. He's got a net of people that owes him favors all over the country, keeps 'em all in his head. No, he won't lie to you flat out, 'less he really needs an edge on you. That's what he calls a 'professional advantage.' He says a real pro won't hold that against him

171

and can feel free to do the same to him, if they can get away with it, no hard feelings."

"Bounty hunter ethics. I guess it makes sense."

" 'Sides, I think he likes you."

I cocked an eyebrow at her. It hurt. "Why in God's name would he like me?"

She shrugged again. "Jasper's funny that way."

I-40 crossed the New Mexico-Arizona state line in an area of stunning, dreamlike rock formations: immense sandstone cliffs eroded by wind and water into surreal shapes, contoured like melting clay, full of caves and hollows big enough to hold a five-story building and coming right up to the side of the road. The majestic effect is diminished by a horde of cheap, ticky-tacky tourist traps selling bad food and foreign-made junk passing for native.

The land climbs again on the Arizona side of the line, and pretty soon we saw rest areas and roadside stands adorned with drumlike segments of ancient trees turned to colorful stone.

"Do I look like Bogart?" I asked Tina.

"What on earth you talkin' about? You don't look like nothin' 'cept the loser in a hammer fight."

I waved to the scenery outside. "*The Petrified Forest.* It's an old movie, one of Bogart's earliest feature roles, I believe. That's where we are now, Petrified Forest National Park. Bette Davis was in it, too. And what's-his-name, the guy who played Ashley in *Gone With the Wind.* Bogart played a gangster. You can be Bette Davis."

"I don't want to be nobody that's dead. You ain't a movie buff, are you?"

"Not really. It's just a hazard of belonging to my generation. See, we were the first to grow up with TV. The problem was, there were no made-for-TV movies and the studios wouldn't release anything made after 1950 to TV, so the networks and the local stations could only keep running movies made during the thirties and forties. We grew up seeing on television all the movies our parents had seen in the theaters. Only we saw them over and over again, and out of the sequence they were made in. It warped us forever."

"No, it didn't. You ain't gonna live forever."

"You'll never convince boomers of that."

"No kiddin'. We need to get some food into you, Gabe. You're goin' light-headed on me."

Now that she mentioned it, I was feeling a bit punchy. I hoped it didn't mean that some sort of brain damage was making itself felt.

A short while later we reached the town of Holbrook and Tina pulled into the lot of a diner that wasn't, for a blessed change, part of a nationwide chain. She emerged with a couple of substantial lunches and dropped mine into my lap. It was a huge, greasy hamburger with fries and a large strawberry milkshake.

"Now you eat that and don't give me any California crap about it. You need to mend, and a bunch of melon balls and seaweed ain't gonna cut it."

My stomach told me that she had made precisely the right choice. I tied into it and everything was ecstatically delicious. The gooshy softness of it all made it easy to chew and swallow, ultimate comfort food. When I was done I could actually feel energy spreading from my belly to my extremities. I felt ten times better and many years younger.

"By God," I said, finishing up the milkshake, "when you can't trust anything else, you can trust eternal verities like the American hamburger."

"Depends on where you buy 'em," she said, wadding up the greasy paper that littered the car. "You ready to move on?"

"Let's go."

Before long we were up out of the desert and getting

into mountain country, still arid but greener, sparse brush quickly developing into genuine forest with the rapid change of terrain I was getting used to in this part of the world. The air also grew decidedly chilly. Winter arrived early in these parts.

Flagstaff is a medium-sized town, its main drag, like that of Albuquerque, once a part of Route 66. Bypassed by the interstate, it still prospers because of its location. It is set amid beautiful national forest land with a multitude of wilderness areas just a short drive away. It is also the only real town anywhere near the Grand Canyon, less than two hours away by car. Consequently, it is packed with tour buses much of the year.

We were in the off-season, and Flagstaff, while not exactly deserted, was pretty laid-back. All the motels advertised bargain rates and there were cut-rate tours posted everywhere. This area had been hard hit by recent government budget hassles that had closed down the national parks, although temporarily. It was a sort of banana-republic economy, with tourists for bananas.

To save time we asked directions to the Canyon Lodge at the first gas station we came to. It was a little off the main drag, on Highway 180, which leads from Flagstaff to the Grand Canyon. We found it near the northern edge of town, drove close, then parked across the street to consider the latest development.

"Oh, shit," Tina said expressionlessly.

"You took the words right out of my mouth." My burger rush was fading fast. It looked like half the police cars in town were in the big motel's lot. There were county and state cars there as well. All evidence indicated that there had been some excitement earlier in the day.

"Don't see no ambulances," Tina said hopefully.

"They'd be gone by now anyway," I told her. "I'd pull my writer act, but I don't dare try it looking like this."

"That's for damn sure. I'll find out." She began to open the door.

"First," I advised her, "ask some people in the stores on this side of the street, like you're just passing through and curious."

"I know how to do this," she snapped. She went into a drugstore and came out minutes later with a couple of cans of iced tea. Leaning in my window she handed me one.

"A local cop was shot here early this mornin'. Nobody seems to know why, who or whatever. All them cops over there is questionin' everybody at the motel; they been talkin' to 'em this side of the street, too, only nothin' was open that hour 'cept that place down on the corner where they serve breakfast. I'm headin' over there now."

I almost advised her, then stopped myself. "How are you going to play this?"

"There's advantages to comin' from white trash, hon. I'm gonna go over there and ask for a job."

Now there was something I never would have thought up. While she clicked across the street and disappeared into the crowd of official vehicles, I studied the place.

The Canyon Lodge was a far classier establishment than I had been using lately. It was a sprawling, three-story structure, staple-shaped with a big swimming pool in front, the office at one end and at the other a restaurant advertising live entertainment: mariachi night, karaoke night and so forth. Even in the off-season the rates would be pretty high.

Holt had been right. They weren't hurting for money. Either they had whatever they'd ripped off from Tyler and picked up at Jennings's place or they'd used Sibyl's credit card again. Those were the hopeful speculations. The other likelihood was that they'd pulled off a job on the road, and Sibyl might be in even deeper shit than I'd feared.

I wanted to check out the parking lot, but I didn't dare expose my creaky, battered self to the beady eyes of the local constabulary. I knew all too well that there's nothing more trigger-happy in the world than cops right after a fellow officer has been shot.

That raised a further question: Why, under the circumstances, weren't more of them out chasing down the offenders? Either this place was incredibly rich in police vehicles, or else they weren't looking all that hard. That meant they already had the shooter in custody, or else some other circumstance had dulled their sense of urgency.

I didn't see Holt's brown Bronco anywhere, but my view was limited. Tina had left the keys so I set the ignition on accessory and turned on the radio, looking for a local broadcast. In movies, whenever someone does that the requisite broadcast comes on immediately. In real life I couldn't find a damned thing. So I left it tuned to what sounded like a local station and sipped tea, unable as I was to affect events for the moment.

Finally, a news program came on and I turned up the volume. After an urgent story about a brushfire and a few other things in which I had no interest, the very young-sounding, female news reader said: "Flagstaff police have issued no further statement in the nonfatal shooting early this morning at the Canyon Lodge motel of an off-duty police officer." Big deal.

Nonfatal. That sounded promising. *Off-duty* was a bit of a relief as well. It suggested that the guy wasn't part of a police operation aimed at apprehending the pair.

"They ain't hirin'," Tina said as she opened the door and sat.

"Let's not hang around here and look suspicious," I

said. "Let's find someplace where we can get out of the car and talk."

"Right." She started the engine, made a turn and drove us back into the main part of town. In less than five minutes we were sitting on a bench in a little park.

"Did you see Jasper's Bronco?" I asked.

"It ain't there. I expect he's long gone."

"What did you learn?"

She lit up a cigarette. "Name of the cop that was shot's Eugene Wells. He's a county mountie usually patrols in the back country. Seems jurisdictions are a pain in the butt around here, on account of Flagstaff's completely surrounded by national parks, so you got the national park cops all over in addition to the city, county and state. Whatever, he wasn't on duty and wasn't in uniform. It don't look like he was usin' a county car, and I couldn't find out if they'd found his personal car.

"Anyhow, around seven this mornin' people heard a shot—"

"Just one?" I interrupted.

"Just one, and some loud voices. Nobody seen anything, 'cause nobody looked out, for which I don't blame them. I sure as hell don't stick my head out my door when I hear gunfire outside."

"Wise policy. Did anyone see anything at all?"

"Keep in mind I wasn't doin' any interrogatin' myself, just wanderin' around looking dumb and listenin', askin' the hotel people what all the fuss was about. Made sense for me to be doin' it, since I was looking for work there and didn't want to work in any place that was disorderly. To answer your question, I heard that one woman peeked out through her curtains and saw a man and a woman haulin' ass to the parkin' lot. Said she heard a car takin' off but didn't see it."

I had some questions but I wanted to hear everything first. "Go on."

"They had a room on the bottom floor, just past the end of the pool. They was—they were registered under the name of Mr. and Mrs. Patrick Jennings; ain't that cute?"

"I've never figured it out, but sociopaths almost always use the name of someone they know."

"It's because they got no imagination."

"How did you come by this information?"

"I've worked in plenty of motels. It ain't hard to get a look at the register. Anyhow, that's about all."

"All? That was a hell of a productive few minutes you spent back there."

"It wasn't enough. Think I oughta go on back, get a chambermaid's outfit and a housekeepin' cart, maybe get a look into their room?" She might have been suggesting taking in a movie.

"There's nothing there by now. If they left anything, which I doubt, the police have it now. No, we need to do some hard thinking. What the hell happened, and what's our next move?"

"First off, that contact of Jasper's who spotted 'em here? Jasper called him Gene."

I nodded. "I figured that was who it might be. Now, how did it happen?"

"He was keepin' an eye on 'em and he got too close?"

"Possible. A man like Switzer has to have really sensitive paranoid antennae. Maybe they went out a few times during the evening, to eat, or go get ice, maybe take in a show or something. Switzer might have spotted him. A back-country county officer like this guy might not be good at discreet surveillance."

"Or he might've seen 'em comin' out, maybe gettin' an early start on the road, thought he might lose 'em before Jasper got here, so he tried to make 'em go back in the room and wait."

"Maybe he approached them to make a deal," I said.

178

"See if he could get them to sweeten whatever Jasper's paying him."

"He'd need some real balls to cross Jasper, but I've known plenty of stupid cops, so it's possible. I'm wonderin' about the car they took. I'd say they took his, but you'd think in that case they'd've been caught by now. I don't figure they know this country, can't just disappear."

"Right. I haven't seen anything to indicate either of them has any wilderness experience. They wouldn't take to the national forests, and it's awfully easy to be spotted on the major highways."

"Hell, the way them two been actin', they might've just gone up to look at the Grand Canyon."

"It's not out of the question. So, if Wells wasn't in a county car, what was he driving? He was doing something that not only wasn't in the line of duty, but was of questionable legality. Spending his off-duty hours hound-dogging for a bounty hunter might cost him his job."

She looked at me. "You think he might not've been using his own car?"

"That would be the sensible thing to do. He'd use a borrowed one, maybe one impounded by the county, with scavenged plates." I told her about my speculations concerning the number of police vehicles at the motel and the seeming lack of urgency expressed by the news broadcasts. "Let's try this for size: Early in the morning, Wells gets shot. He's county, not city. Maybe the motel staff don't know him and he's not in uniform. He might not be identified until he's at the hospital.

"The cops know he wasn't in an official car so they look for his personal vehicle and find it parked at his home. Now they've got no idea what the suspects are driving, any more than we have. All they've got to go on is maybe they're looking for a man and a woman and no vehicle description or likely direction of flight. By the time they've even figured all this out, Nick and Sibyl are well away from Flagstaff, they've got themselves a new car and it may be untraceable."

"Nick Switzer must've been born lucky," she said, firing up another one. "If Jasper drove straight through from Albuquerque, goin' fast and not stoppin' for anything, he could've been here by ten this mornin', three hours after all the excitement. God knows where he is now."

"Do you have the number to his cellular phone?"

" 'Course I do. Only we ain't on speakin' terms just now."

"I wonder how Wells spotted Nick and Sibyl."

"I imagine he had somebody on the motel staff paid to tip him. It ain't uncommon at all."

"I know how it works. I was a cop once, myself."

"Whoever it was won't say nothin' about it, not if they want to keep their job."

"I think we need to have a few words with the unfortunate Deputy Wells. Want to go and see if he's regained consciousness?"

"Sure. How the hell do you figure to do that?"

"Well, you had no trouble fitting right into that motel."

She looked at me and then, slowly, smiled. It was the first time I had seen her smile, and she had a nice one, maybe all the more so since she practiced it so seldom.

"Well, it's God's own truth you look like you belong in a hospital."

Thirteen

This time I didn't go in by way of the emergency room. Instead I walked, or rather limped, in through the front door, like an outpatient coming in for a checkup. From the parking lot into the lobby was the most walking I'd done all day, and by the time we'd reached the gift shop I thought a crutch might have made a worthwhile investment.

But I had Tina beside me, solicitous of my welfare, the concerned wife making sure her oafish husband didn't injure himself further. She sat me down on a vinyl-surfaced couch next to a guy in a leg cast.

"You just wait right here, honey. I'll see if I can find that doctor we saw last time." She clicked away, then stopped at a hospital directory to scan names and numbers.

"A little early for ski season, isn't it?" the guy next to me said. Apparently this wasn't a high violence area, where injuries like mine were suspect.

I figured the stairs ploy was stale. "Rock climbing," I said. I'd read that rock climbing had become a popular way for baby boomers to recapture their lost youth. A shortcut to premature death does that, for some reason.

He rapped his knuckles on his cast. "Sideswiped pulling onto I-17. Damned tourists."

A few minutes later Tina reappeared. "He's off this way, darlin'." She took an arm and tugged me upright. "Come along, now, and watch your step."

"Is he under guard?" I said when we were in a sparsely populated corridor.

"None I could see, but he ain't goin' no place and they got no reason to think anyone's comin' back to finish the job."

"I was thinking more in terms of someone waiting for him to come around and make a statement."

"I don't believe he's hurt all that bad. He may've talked already."

We got into an elevator with a doctor and a couple of orderlies, then got off on the third floor. "There's a nurse's station here," Tina whispered. "Just walk past like you know what you're doin'."

"If somebody walks in on us," I told her, "we say we were looking for another room, maybe we're in the wrong hospital entirely. They'll believe it. Professionals always think nonprofessionals are dummies."

The door to the room was open. We glanced in, saw a nurse inside doing some sort of nurse thing, and walked on past. A minute later she left and we walked in. Eugene Wells was conscious, and his eyes widened when we entered. He'd been watching a quiz show on the overhead TV, and his limp hand clicked off the remote.

"Jesus, buddy, you look as bad as I do," he croaked. "But I think you got the wrong room."

He looked to be around thirty, with prematurely receding hair. His left shoulder and that side of his chest were shrouded in bandages and he was hooked up to the usual ghastly array of tubes and wires.

"Nope," I told him, lowering myself into a bedside chair. "Not if you got shot by Nick Switzer."

"Who're you?" he said, not sounding too nervous, but then, he had to be feeling pretty wrung out.

"Let's just say I'm a colleague of Jasper Holt."

He closed his eyes. "Jesus. I wish to hell I never heard of Jasper Holt."

"How come?" Tina demanded. "He just wanted you to keep an eye on 'em, not get yourself shot like a jackass. Was you maybe tryin' to shake 'em down? See if you could get a better deal than Jasper was givin' you?" She grabbed a handful of his hair and yanked his head forward, then back sharply. He grimaced in sudden pain and fright.

"Easy there! The man's just been shot!" I was amazed to find myself in the role of good cop.

"You, me and Jasper could all be on our way home now, and we'd all have just what we come for, if it wasn't for this little two-bit shithead." She placed her face within two inches of his. "I don't guess Jasper's come callin' today, since you're still breathin'."

"Hell, I been surrounded by police and reporters until an hour ago. No, I ain't seen Holt. What the hell do you want?" His eyes were wide, but his voice was barely above a whisper.

"We want you to talk to us," she said. "We'll be seein' Jasper pretty soon, so maybe if he's satisfied with what we tell him, he won't come to collect your story personal. That sound agreeable to you?"

"Yeah, I guess so." His eyes shifted toward the door, like he was hoping somebody would come rescue him.

"Did you try to brace them two in their room?" Tina demanded, releasing his hair.

"No, they started coming out just before seven, carrying their bags, like they were leaving, so I went up to them, showed them my badge and my gun and told them to go back inside and sit down. I was going to make them wait for Holt, just like I agreed."

"Sure," Tina said. "That's why you're so scared of talkin' to him. I guess you wasn't just a little bit curious about what they was wanted so bad for?"

His eyes flickered to the door again, to the blank face of the TV screen, anywhere but toward us. "Yeah, I kind of wondered."

"So you told them to open their bags and give you a look," I said. "Is that right, Eugene?"

"What happened?" Tina cooed. "That pretty young lady flash her boobs at you, distract you a little?"

He managed to redden despite his loss of blood.

I sighed. "They weren't even armed, were they, Eugene? They got your gun."

"She looked like such a college-girl type!" he protested, unhappy with the sheer unfairness of it all. Tina almost said something, but I held up a hand and she stopped.

"Describe her."

"Mid-twenties, maybe five-five, dark hair, brown eyes, pretty, kind of refined-looking."

"Did either of them use her name?" I asked.

He looked surprised. "Holt just said the man Switzer was last seen traveling with a woman, name unknown, no description. I asked; she said her name was Bonnie." He looked surprised when we laughed. Then Tina glanced out a window.

"Three county cars just pulled up in the lot."

Wells groaned. "What am I gonna tell the county?"

"Sounds like you have a problem," I said. "We'll have to make this brief. What car were you driving?"

"A Blazer I got three days ago from a guy in Winona that owes me money. I ripped off some plates from the impound lot."

"Have you told anybody yet?"

"Hell, no!"

"Then don't. Did Switzer say anything that might indicate what they were up to, what plans they had?"

"No, just the usual punk spiel. I had the wrong people, they were just tourists, crap like that."

"Time to go," Tina said.

I got up and headed for the door. "You're a lucky man, Eugene," I said.

"Coulda fooled me."

"Nice people like us questioned you instead of Jasper Holt. And Nick Switzer turned out to be a bad shot."

"Piss on that!" I turned at the vehemence in his voice. His eyes flashed through the fog of painkillers. "It was that fucking bitch that grabbed my gun and shot me!"

We walked past the arriving county officials without attracting so much as a glance. They had more important business on their hands: possible corruption inside the county police department. I hoped Wells had the brains to keep his mouth shut and trust in a good lawyer. Not that his recent behavior inspired confidence.

"Where to now?" Tina asked when we were in our car.

"Let's get out of Flagstaff for starters. I doubt if he'll babble, but you never know. We make a pretty distinctive couple, but he's got no idea what we're driving, so we're okay with some distance behind us." I got out the road atlas and studied it. "Let's play a little game."

"What sort of game?"

"Let's get inside Switzer's head and see if we can come up with his next move."

"Sounds like fun, but what makes you so sure it's him callin' the shots." Abruptly, she giggled. "I think I just made a joke. The shots."

"Yeah, I got it. Dear Sibyl is revealing unexpected depths."

"Bein' around the wrong man can change a woman. I've seen it happen."

"Or she may have been just scared and desperate. I saw a lot of cops shot answering domestic disturbance calls. Some woman calls the police because her husband's beating on her, the cops show up and arrest him, then she gets all remorseful, yells, 'You leave my husband alone!', grabs some cop's gun and blows a hole in his kidney. Happens all the time."

"Maybe, but I don't think your little girl rattles easy."

I didn't think so, either. A few miles out of town we pulled into a rest area and studied the map.

"They've got an anonymous car," I said, "and a gun. The smaller roads are going to feel claustrophobic since they aren't familiar with them, so I'm betting they stick to the major highways. I-17 goes south to Phoenix. It's a big city, plenty of room to lose themselves, good connecting highways to the south, east and west."

She looked it over and shook her head. "No, they been headin' west for a reason, and Nick must be feelin' damn near immortal by now." She smiled again and punched a forefinger onto the map. "Las Vegas! A fool like Switzer's gonna head for Vegas like a rocket. Play the tables, tour the town with his trophy girl on his arm. He'd never miss a chance like that."

"But he knows pursuit's close now."

"You think anyone's gonna have an easy time finding them in a place like Vegas?"

"Good point. But what about Sibyl? Everything I've learned about her earlier life says she's cautious, conservative, she plans carefully and avoids risk."

Tina opened her purse and rummaged around in it. I could see a half-dozen cigarette packs, a couple of lighters, lipstick, makeup and compacts, the spines of a couple of Harlequin romances. "She took up with Switzer 'cause she don't like what she was before." She opened a new pack and stuck a fresh butt in her mouth, lit it up, blew smoke. "She's livin' the life she picked now, and she's likin' it just fine."

"Vegas it is, then."

I managed to sleep a bit more, helped along by the painkillers, but around Seligman I woke up and couldn't drop back off. I even got behind the wheel for a while, and the minimal activity seemed to help. While I drove I let Tina look over Sibyl's diaries. I was interested to see what sort of insights she would generate.

"This supposed to be English?" she asked when she got to the later pages.

"She gets a little poetic there."

"My ass. She gets crazy, or tryin' to act crazy, which is worse." She considered it for a while. "This kid wants to be a con artist like Nick, but she's just a cop's college-girl daughter. She needs to believe the people they're screwin' are the real evil ones."

"I was wondering about her take on Switzer. He seems like a psycho Svengali, but I have my doubts. Do you think maybe he's just an ordinary sociopath, and the outlaw demon just a construct of Sibyl's imagination?"

"That ain't how I'd've put it, but I was thinkin' sorta the same thing."

My mind went back to what I'd been thinking about when this all began. "Tina, why do they do it? What makes women with everything going for them take up with worthless scum like Nick Switzer?"

She considered this for a while, then: "You don't know much about women, do you, Treloar?"

"I used to think I did, but I got over it."

"Most men never do. Well, plenty of women find bad men attractive, 'specially when they're young." She looked out the side window at the passing desert landscape. "I did once myself. Still do, sort of. Only thing is, I found out there ain't many."

187

"Not many bad men? I'd think there were way too many."

She shook her head. "Not bad the way women want 'em bad. See, most men that think they're bad ain't. They're just stupid and mean. Like my husband. His name was Cliff. Back when we met I was sixteen and I thought he was the baddest thing around. He'd been to prison and all. It made him seem excitin'.

"We hadn't been married a month before he started beatin' on me. I didn't think too much of it at first, 'cause it wasn't all that different from the way I was raised. It got a lot worse when he took to beatin' me when he was drunk. By that time, I'd figured out that he wasn't really bad, just stupid and mean. He didn't have the guts or the brains to be bad."

I didn't say anything, just let her talk.

"He hung out with friends he thought was bad, but they was just dumb and mean, too. He took to treatin' me like a dog in front of 'em. Pretty soon regular screwin' got tame and he took to usin' me in places where I never gave him permission to. Then one night him and his friends got drunk and high and he let them make use of me, too." She turned to look at me, dry-eyed and composed.

"So when they was gone and he was passed out on the couch snorin', I went into the kitchen and got the bonin' knife, 'bout six-inch blade, kinda narrow. I went out in the livin' room and stuck it in his belly. He stopped snorin' for a second, made some funny sounds up in his nose, then he stopped."

I waited.

"Then he started snorin' again. It looked sort of funny, him layin' on the couch like that, snorin', the handle of that knife wavin' back and forth. Anyway, I just walked out the front door and kept on walkin'. I don't know whether he lived or died, but I don't figure he'll come lookin' for me either way."

I nodded. "Drastic but effective." I wasn't about to become all overmoralistic.

"Yep. Now, when some woman cries at me about how her husband treats her mean, I just tell her go to the hardware and get a decent butcher knife if she don't have one in the kitchen. It's cheaper'n a lawyer, plus you don't got to worry about the bastard stalkin' you afterwards."

"Live and learn," I said.

"Of course, it don't mean you lose your taste for bad men entirely. It just makes you more discriminatin'."

"So how'd you end up with Jasper Holt?"

"Another time," she said, staring back out the window. "I don't want to get too personal."

It was late evening by the time we reached Kingman, Arizona. We could have pushed on to Las Vegas, but we'd put in a long day and figured the lovebirds would be staying there for a while. I wasn't going to be doing any circulating among Kingman's transient population, so we picked a place that was a few cuts above my recent abodes. It even had a pool.

"Rates are pretty good here," Tina said when she came back to the car. "The casinos in Vegas probably kick back 'cause half the people that come to Kingman end up headin' there. That lobby's full of casino fliers."

The room was a little more spacious than the last few, much cleaner with newer paint, carpets and bedding. There was even a remote for the TV. Tina brought in our bags and we settled in for domestic bliss.

"You better take the bed next to the bathroom," she announced.

"I'm going to take a shower, then collapse. Play the TV as loud as you want. I'll never notice."

"Hold it. First thing, you're gonna let me check you out. I don't trust any emergency room to do a permanent job. Believe it or not, I can be a pretty good nurse, when need be. Sit down."

I sat. To my surprise, she took a penlight from her purse, grabbed my chin and shone it first in one eye, then the other. "Open up." I opened my mouth and she checked out the inside. "Any of those back teeth been feelin' loose today?"

"I've been afraid to check." She reached in, grasped a couple of molars and twisted them. "Ow!"

She released them. "They'll be okay. Just stay off the peanut brittle for a few days. Now get your clothes off."

"Now you're going to make me blush."

"Think you got anything I've never seen? Your mama should've told you a man oughta never be ashamed to undress in front of his wife, his doctor or his bounty hunter. Now shuck down."

"I guess now we'll have to get married."

"Damn!" she said when she'd looked me over. "Them two was just reworkin' old territory, wasn't they!"

The ugly new bruises were laid atop a map of old scars, of which I have enough to do a pirate proud. Above my left hip is a mass of chewed-up scar tissue where I'd been shot twice with almost thirty years between woundings. My thighs and buttocks are peppered with shrapnel scars. I have a few other bullet holes here and there, and about four dozen stitches' worth of knife cuts.

"Could've been worse," I told her. "Thank God for GI flak jackets and cop vests."

She frowned at my crotch. "Didn't they kick you in the balls?"

"Nope. I can't imagine why they forgot."

"Men like that can be careless sometimes. Go ahead and get your shower. I'll put some of this disinfectant on you when you're done."

By the time I was out of the shower I was so weak I felt boneless. Tina had turned down the bed and when she was done with her expert ministrations I got under the sheet and was out almost instantly.

I woke to see that perhaps an hour had passed. Tina was in front of the mirror putting the finishing touches on her makeup. She was dressed in a slightly flashier version of her usual attire and her short hair was fluffed out.

"Going out to test the bright lights of Kingman?" I asked.

"Uh-huh. It's part of the job. You never know what kind of information you might pick up. You saw that map. If they was headin' for Vegas, they sure as hell had to come through Kingman. Hell, they could still be here."

"I doubt it. Are you going to contact Holt?"

She turned around. "Anything I do that I don't want you to know about, you ain't gonna know, so don't bother askin'."

"Try not to make too much noise when you come back in." I was off in dreamland again.

When I woke up Tina was sitting on the foot of her bed, watching a twenty-four-hour news channel on the TV. The story was about a terrorist bombing somewhere overseas.

"Learn anything?" I asked her.

She looked over at me. She was wearing an elongated T-shirt that stopped just above her knees and had scrubbed off her makeup, revealing a face that was a tiny bit softer and younger than the one she presented to the world. Her eyes still established uncrossable distance, though.

"It looks like this place is some sort of national center for the down-and-outs. People that cruise the whole West end up here. The ones that lose everything in Vegas come here to scare up a stake to have another try at the tables. The rooms are cheap, hitchin's good, big bunches of bikers cruise through all the time. It's a stop-off point for truckers; there's a whole economy built around just them, the truck stops and bars and so forth."

"Did you pick up any buzz?"

191

"I went into a bar a couple miles from here on Highway 68. Called Chino's, a real scary place, pure outlaw-biker hangout, smelled like a pigsty. I heard in some other places it's where the ex-con ABs hang out."

AB meaning Aryan Brotherhood. I sat up and was surprised to find that I could. "My God, Tina! You shouldn't have gone into a place like that alone!"

"Why? If it'd got rough, a platoon of marines wouldn't've been any help. Anyways, I checked it out, and sure enough there was that wanted poster on the wall."

"Oh, hell. Does that mean my two new buddies from Albuquerque are in town? I really don't feel up to a second meeting."

"I talked around, learned that this one was put up by a pockmarked little spic passin' the word that anyone sees 'em is in for some serious gratitude. I asked how any spic could walk into that place and get back out alive; it turns out he's in town with another dude, and this one's so bad nobody there wants to talk about him. You'd need to see the inside of Chino's to understand what that means."

"Wonderful. Jess Marsh is around, with his power drill and his nails. Did anyone say if they're still in town?"

"They was—were as of the day before yesterday." She turned off the TV, got under her covers and snapped off the light. "You get back to sleep. I'm gonna get a few hours before we head out."

"Has Holt been around?"

"I can't comb the whole town. If Jasper's been here, he's been with his personal contacts, workin' a different level of society than where I've just been."

For a while I lay there, pondering in the dark. It was getting crowded now. When this all began, we were all, pursuers and pursued, strung out over a huge area of the country. Now, heading into the high deserts of the Western badlands, we were getting close together. Entirely too close for my peace of mind.

Fourteen

Taking Highway 93 north from Kingman, you'd never guess that you are heading toward one of the world's most lavish resorts. In fact, you wouldn't think you were headed toward anything except death from heat and thirst. This is where the badlands really get bad. You leave the super-colorful Southwestern desert behind and head into a near-monochromatic landscape of grays, beiges and pale browns, where the highest spots are worn-down ridges listed on the maps as mountain ranges but lacking the grandeur implied by the term.

I'd felt a little better on rising, not quite as sore and stiff, limping a bit less. I took the first shift behind the wheel while Tina studied the material I had on Sibyl, frowning with the effort but determined nonetheless.

Pulling off onto Highway 93 I felt again that odd little wrench at leaving I-40. This time, I felt certain that I wouldn't be returning to that big American artery. We were headed into the high hinterlands where outlaws, by tradition, fled to turn at bay and make their last stands.

The traffic was sparse and I found myself scanning, checking the rearview mirror often, studying every car that came near.

"What do you think they're drivin'?" Tina asked, her attention still on the mass of papers in her lap. Without looking she had caught my anxiety. "The DTT boys, I mean. What do you think they drive?"

"The two I met in Albuquerque were in a blue van, but whether it was their own, borrowed or stolen, I don't know. Psychos are famous for driving vans," I said. "It gives them a sense of comfort to have their little homes along with them as they go. It puts them in control of their immediate environment. Psychos are big on control."

"Not to mention they can grab people, tape them up and have their fun without anybody seein'. Fine way to transport a stiff and dump it. Lots easier than haulin' 'em out of the trunk."

"There's that, too. But we don't know if they're all together. There are at least four of them, so they could be traveling with up to four vehicles. Some could be on motorcycles."

"Maybe," she said, "but I wouldn't figure more than two."

"Why?"

"These boys don't like to be alone much. They're crazy, but they ain't what you'd call solitary. They're used to jail cells and their hangouts. They like to be with their own kind."

"I suspect you're right."

We drove along in silence for a while, the sun climbing in the east, heating the car, giving a hint of what this place would be like in the summer. Finally, Tina set the papers aside.

"This girl," she said and then, uncharacteristically, paused.

"What about her?"

"She's twenty-three years old and she's never been anywhere but school?" She sounded as if she were contemplating some incomprehensible, extraterrestrial life form.

"It's not too uncommon in someone headed into one of the professions. Education can be a long process."

"She's never had a real life at all!"

"Some consider education a part of real life."

She shook her head. "Uh-uh. Classrooms and teachers ain't the real world. And don't tell me workin' in a blood lab's real work, either. Wearin' a white coat and rubber gloves, hell! She probably thought sexual harassment was some college-boy lab assistant feelin' her up at the water fountain. She oughta try bein' a waitress or a chamber-maid in a motel for a year or two."

"Your point being?"

"This is a healthy young woman with her motor idlin'. She's got brains but no sense, education but no experience. She was starvin', Treloar. She was bein' Daddy's good little girl when she wanted to get out there and do all that stuff she saw the babes doin' on the TV. She was datin' dipshit grad students when she wanted to be ruttin' up a storm with the bad studs. She wanted to live on the edge."

"And then she met Nick Switzer."

"Right. He was just what she wanted. Good-lookin', had a great line, probably fucked her cross-eyed the first evenin' they met. And he was a con artist, which was just what she needed."

"You mean he conned her?"

"He didn't need to do that. Oh, maybe he saw what she really wanted and made himself fit the mold, but what I mean is he looked real and he acted bad, but he does what he does by usin' his head. She never pictured herself goin' into a bank gun-first. But pullin' scams on people she'd despise anyway, that's different. You see? She thinks she can be a bad outlaw babe and *still* be the good guy by her own lights."

195

"She was quick enough on the trigger back in Flagstaff."

Tina looked out her window at the dreary landscape slipping by. "She was scared. And I imagine she wanted to impress Nick, show him she's a tough desperado, too."

"I wonder how she felt afterwards?" I mused. "It's easy to fantasize yourself pulling the trigger. It's another thing to do it for real."

"You better hope she didn't like it, 'cause plenty of them do."

Late morning saw us climbing a long, rugged ridge of a craggy spur called the Black Mountains. Once over the crest the road dropped down a long, twisting slope into a deep valley and, there before us, like a mirage conjured up by a parched prospector, was Hoover Dam.

I pulled into the visitors parking area and we got out and gaped at it like a couple of tourists. It was difficult to believe the dam was more than sixty years old, and that people were able to think so big and build so ambitiously in the middle of the worst depression in American history.

We drove across the top of the dam and saw the weird, Deco-style monument on the other side. Two huge, winged colossi sit side by side, looking like something a pharaoh would erect on his border to let the barbarians dwelling beyond know that this is where civilization starts.

Now we were in Nevada, a state that has always reminded me of an artillery range. If it weren't for minerals and gambling, it might not be there at all. Eventually, Las Vegas came into sight, a sprawling city arising from absolutely nothing, as if somebody planted casino seeds and watered them.

"Well, well," Tina said. "So this is the big, wicked city."

"It's a lot more impressive when you come in at night," I assured her. In fact, from a distance, in daytime,

Vegas looks pretty much like most other Sunbelt cities, except for the eccentric shapes of many of the buildings and other structures.

"It's still early," I said. "What do you say we just cruise for a while, get a feel for this place?"

"Suits me. You been here before?"

"Sure, but not in a long time. When I was a kid in L.A., I'd come up here with some friends for a weekend. Later, a couple of times when I was in the army, and then for a few police-related conventions or to pick up a prisoner being extradited by California. But that was years ago. It's changed."

That was an understatement. We drove past a pyramid and sphinx, a giant pirate ship, a circus and high-tech rides like Disney on acid.

"Changed how?" she asked.

"It's hard to say. Vegas was always tacky and sleazy. It's still as tacky as ever, but I miss the sleazy element."

"I ain't sure I catch the distinction."

"This town was built by a gangster as a machine for fleecing suckers. Its purity of purpose was breathtaking. Look at this!" I waved around us, taking in the colorfully garbed entertainers, the carnival appurtenances. "Somebody has taken Bugsy Siegel's monument to greed and turned it into a *theme park*!"

"You gotta change with the times," she said. "People want to gamble, they can go about anyplace these days. Atlantic City's a hell of a lot closer to New York than Vegas. Casino gamblin' in lots of cities, riverboat gamblin'. Hell, even the Indians are gettin' in on it."

"It's the end of a great institution," I lamented. "Somehow 'Las Vegas, fun for the whole family' just doesn't sound right."

"We ain't here to have fun anyways," she reminded me.

So we cruised, checking out the scenery. I was halfheartedly looking for Jasper's Bronco and the Blazer Nick and Sibyl were probably using, but the city was jammed with motor vehicles, and there was nothing really distinctive about these two. ORVs used to be strictly for dwellers in the outback, people who expected to travel off the main roads on rough terrain, who really had a use for a four-wheel drive. A few years ago they became all the rage and now people drive them from home to the office or the mall. Americans have to act out their fantasies, and the car has to fit the role.

I began to notice the people wandering in the streets, going from one casino to another, taking a break from the tables to get something to eat or maybe catch a little sleep in the hotel room. They were dressed in their casino clothes and looked half-high, glassy-eyed, though not necessarily drunk.

"Do you notice something funny about this crowd?" I asked.

"I get what you mean. It's broad daylight, but they look like it's the middle of the night."

"That's it. I think it's the way they make the casinos. There are no clocks inside, no windows looking out, no reference to the outside world at all. They want you to stay there and lose money and never think about anything but what's in front of you, the dice or the wheel or the slots or whatever."

"Like you say, it's a machine."

Eventually we got tired of cruising. "We ain't gonna see them in the daytime. Let's go find ourselves a place to stay and come back after dark."

"You're right. I'm tired, anyway. It's past my nap time."

"Don't get old on me. We may need you to be actin' lively pretty soon."

We found a livable place not far from the center of town that actually had an exercise room. I went there for some slow, cautious, therapeutic workout time, sticking pretty much to stretching exercises, a few gingerly executed sit-ups and other activities suitable to a geriatric ward. Most of my injuries were more painful than damaging, but I was worried about the knee. I might have to do some running soon.

I rejoined Tina in the hotel lounge, where she was playing the slots with a beer on the little table beside her. The stacks of tokens by the beer said that she'd hit a few times.

"Let's eat," I said to her. "It'll be dark soon and the bats will be coming out."

"What do you think?" I asked her as we nibbled sandwiches. "This is actually a pretty big place. Where do you think they'll head?"

"You ask my opinion a lot."

"Is there something wrong with that? If we're going to work together we might as well pool our thoughts. Doesn't Holt ever ask your opinion?"

She leaned forward. "Not often enough, but don't you go tryin' to set me against Jasper. It won't work."

"Agreed," I said hastily.

She sat back. "Okay. Well, since you asked, I don't think they'll be out on the Strip, 'cept maybe early in the evening, to catch a show or something. Hell, since they stopped for a rodeo, why not? But that's too big a territory to cover. I think they'll stay mostly in the center of town, those places along Fremont Street, you know? Where the Golden Nugget is, and that big cowboy sign? Everything's closer together there; there's gonna be more life out on the street, not just inside the casinos. It's the part of town you see in all the movies."

"Right on. Soon as it's dark, let's just go there and hang out."

"Think that knee's up to much walking?"

"Getting better all the time."

199

We were silent for a while, finishing dinner. Finally, she flipped one of her slot machine tokens into the center of my plate.

"Penny for your thoughts."

"I still can't fathom Sibyl. You're probably right about her motivation, but she's not a sociopath like Switzer. She has a sense of the future, of consequences. She has to know how badly this is going to end. Pretty soon she's going to be dead or in prison."

"First off," Tina said, lighting up, "don't go assumin' she ain't just like Switzer. A lot of people go through life actin' just like normal people 'cause they never get the opportunity to find out that they're crazy. Second, what she's looking at maybe ain't all that bad."

"What do you mean?"

"She could get killed, sure, but she's gonna die like the rest of us anyway. Dyin's about the last thing anyone worries about, Treloar. And jail?" She looked at the tip of her cigarette as it marked the passing of time in curling smoke. "If I was to do what she done, I'd be looking at a long stretch of hard time with a bunch of dykes and a matron with an office full of rubber toys. But her?"

"What about her?"

She leaned forward on her elbows, her forearms crossed. "I don't know when was the last time you caught sight of Patty Hearst, but last time I seen her she was in a movie with Kathleen Turner."

"I take your meaning. But Sibyl doesn't have the Hearst family and their fortune behind her."

"Maybe not, but she has plenty. Daddy's a retired cop, owner of an agency with branches in several states. She's got no record, just a squeaky-clean schoolgirl reputation. She'll sit there dabbin' at her eyes with a hankie while her lawyer tells the jury how this poor, innocent little lamb was led astray by that lowlife scumbag, Nick Switzer, who'll be sittin' there lookin' guilty as hell, because that's what he's been all his life."

Now I leaned forward. "Tina, who hired Jasper to track Switzer?"

"Why should I tell you? All you care about's the girl, right? Leave it at that."

I grinned at her. "Jasper won't tell you, either, will he? Is that what you two argued over?"

She glared at me. "I warned you, Treloar."

"The hell with that. I've chased halfway across the North American continent, got the crap beat out of me, and I don't know what the hell's going on! I don't know what Switzer did to piss off the White Front. I don't know why Jasper Holt is after the same people I am. All I've got is a debt to Randall Carson. I'm getting where I'm not all that keen on rescuing his little girl anymore, but I just want to *know*!"

She favored me with a rare smile again. "You're cute when you get mad, Treloar. Yeah, Jasper wouldn't tell me, on account of the man who hired him is someone really, really heavy, and I'm not talkin' some punk-ass Nazi professor. And I got mad 'cause I can handle anything as heavy as Jasper can, but he won't believe it, treats me like he needs to protect me 'cause I'm a woman."

"He's an old-fashioned man. Tina, are we talking mob action here?"

"That's the impression I get. The man don't do business over the phone, wanted a face-to-face, and Jasper wouldn't take me."

"Where was this?"

"In Richmond, a couple weeks back. We drove up from Atlanta for the meet. I was all ready to show my stuff, but Jasper made me wait downstairs in the hotel lounge while he went up to the penthouse." She was still fuming about it.

"Richmond," I said. "Virginia Beach isn't far from Richmond."

"Around a hundred miles, I think. Why?"

"Back in Knoxville, I ran a check of serious crimes in the East during the few days before Nick and Sibyl disappeared. There was a big drug transaction ambushed near Virginia Beach. Right after that, there was a neo-Nazi killing in Charleston."

She nodded. "Uh-huh. You got that printout handy?"

"In my briefcase. Come on. I have a phone call to make, then we can go cruise Fremont Street."

We went back to the room and I dug out the long printout sheet, explained my colored-marker system to Tina and left her studying it while I sat by the phone and dialed Carson.

"Christ, Gabe, I haven't heard from you in three days! Where the hell are you?"

"Vegas. A lot's happened lately and I spent part of the time in the hospital."

He paused and I could hear him take a deep breath. "All right, tell me what's happened."

I gave him a slightly edited version of my latest adventures, leaving out the Flagstaff deputy's assertion that Sibyl had shot him.

"Gabe, are you telling me that you're teamed up with Jasper Holt's partner? Do you just plan to hand Sibyl over to Holt? Are you just beat up or have you gone completely fucking crazy?"

I jerked back from the phone a bit on the last few words. "Well, boss, I'm really not up to much solo driving. Or even much walking."

"Holy shit. Okay, let me tell you a few things. First, Ray Padilla faxed me the info about Marsh and Martinez. I got their records, but they've both disappeared off the face of the earth, neither of them spotted for months."

"That's no surprise."

"About the Nazi stuff in Charleston, four real badass ex-cons were found dead in a rented house in the old part of town—not the tourist part, a low-rent area. From the crime-scene report it was a hell of a battle, and some of the blood on the floor and the walls didn't belong to any of the deceased. It looks like they were seated around the table when the fun started; that's why the Charleston PD thinks it was a falling-out among the Führer's boys."

"Are their Nazi affiliations a matter of record?"

"Three of the four were locals known to belong to militant-right biker clubs. They were all AB in the slammer. But the fourth was the clincher."

"What about him?"

"He wasn't local, a Louisiana boy from Calcasieu Parish named Armand Giffault." He spelled it for me because it was pronounced *Gee-fo*. "You know how hard it is to get a look at an ME's report. I had an op down there pass some heavy persuasion and he faxed me a Xerox of the pertinent pages. Besides the usual gallery of skin art, Giffault had that little arrow tattooed on the third finger of his right hand. He'd been wearing a large ring to cover it. None of the other three had that one."

"Hang on a second, Kit." I scribbled "Calcasieu Parish" on the motel notepad, ripped off the page and held it out to Tina. With my hand over the mouthpiece, I said, "Tina, would you go out to the car and get the road atlas? Find out where this place is in Louisiana." She put down the printout she'd been studying and went out.

"Okay, there's a tie-in, but Nick Switzer's no gunslinger. What did you find out about Deputy Woolford?"

"I was just coming to that. My man there started asking around and was immediately braced by two detectives from Internal Affairs. They called me personally and told me to butt out. Seems there's an investigation going down and they don't want outsiders screwing around. Wouldn't tell me what it was about, naturally."

"It could be ordinary corruption or something. Or it could be they're looking into hate-group infiltration before some reporter gets hold of it."

Tina returned with the atlas folded back to show Louisiana. Her scarlet nail tapped the extreme southwest corner of the state.

"Boss, Calcasieu Parish is right on the Texas state line, just a few miles from Beaumont. My new friend, Joel Leblanc, is from the bayou country near Beaumont."

"The guy who worked you over in Albuquerque? Think they're Cajun cousins?"

"Leblanc doesn't have the Cajun accent, just generic country-boy shitkicker." I took a deep breath. "Okay, boss, just before the Nazi snuff there was a shootout near Virginia Beach involving money and dope. I'm willing to bet if anyone compares slugs and shell casings from both sites they'll come up with a few matches."

"What?" This one made my ear ring.

"Calm down, boss. You know you have to watch your blood pressure. Holt's working for some mob guy in Richmond. Holt recovers people's money, Holt is chasing Switzer, Switzer has the mob guy's money, no tortuous logic required. Just how the hell the Nazis tie into it I have no idea but it looks like our boy pulled one hell of a scam."

There was silence on the other end for a while, then: "We got dead people in three states, we got dope, we got a mob tie-in, we even got a shot-up dipshit deputy in Flagstaff. I don't know how the hell almost two weeks have passed without feds crawling all over this thing. Nobody's made the connections yet, we've got a bunch of state agencies sitting on their evidence, but it can't last long." He paused again. "I'm coming out there, Gabe. I'm taking personal charge and I'm not coming alone."

"Don't do that, boss! You're too personally involved and you're too goddamned old, you said it yourself."

"Gabe, you're hurt, the DTT guys know your face and you're playing pattycake with that untrustworthy bitch. Your brain's not working right. I'm taking you off the case."

"Kit, I've almost got them! They're right here, I know it, and Marsh is close, too, he was in Kingman yesterday. If I just catch sight of Sibyl I'll have her, and Holt and Marsh can fight it out over Switzer."

He breathed heavily for a while. "I'm not waiting to hear from you any three damn days. Twenty-four hours, Gabe, and then I'm out there. I'll start putting my team together right now. I can fight federal indictments, I can hire lawyers. But I want Sibyl back, even if I have to ship her right off to Basutoland or somewhere. And Gabe?"

"Yeah?"

"When you find them, it might be a real good idea if Switzer wasn't to do any testifying later."

"I'll find her, Kit." I hung up and turned to Tina. "My boss doesn't much like the idea of us working together."

"I thought I felt my ears burnin' for a minute there. So Mr. Carson wants to come this way? You know what he's gonna do, don't you? He'll put a bullet in Switzer's head and carry his little girl home and hope nobody ever finds out who she really is."

"The love of a father can be a powerful thing."

"I wouldn't know. How much time he give you?"

"Twenty-four hours, but I wouldn't be surprised if he showed up by morning."

"We best get to work then." She waved the folded printout at me. "Your color codin' system don't mean much, Treloar."

"I didn't know then what I know now. What did you pick up?"

She frowned. "One thing don't make sense. It says there was a bunch of dead men, some money and a lot of dope litterin' the scene. Looks like somebody ambushed a big drug deal goin' down. But why go to all that trouble and leave the dope? Sure, the buy money's substantial, but the street value of the dope's way bigger. That's the way the business works. Why not take the money *and* sell the dope and have it all?"

"Maybe the boosters weren't in the drug scene and didn't want to risk moving the dope. They might've been content with the money."

"How'd they know about the buy if they wasn't in the scene? Who can walk away from that kind of temptation?"

"Good question. Come on, it's dark."

We drove to the center of town through a transformed Vegas.

"No wonder they built that dam," Tina said. "This place sure burns up the electricity."

The surreal profusion of lights was so absurd that you had to see it as the ultimate statement of a mind-set. Like baroque art it overwhelmed the viewer with color and detail. Some sort of aberrant psychology has reached its apogee in Las Vegas. This, if nothing else, would have made Bugsy Siegel proud.

We parked on a side street off Fremont and walked toward the famous avenue. Tina studied my limp critically.

"Think we oughta get you a cane?"

"I'll manage." Actually, it was feeling much better. I hoped it wasn't just the painkillers I was still taking. "I'm not so sure about those heels of yours. What if you have to run?"

"I can move plenty fast if I have to. Besides, I can see farther wearin' these. They boost me up to almost five-two."

It hadn't been dark for long, but Fremont already

looked like Mardi Gras without the costumes and masks. Besides the glassy-eyed gambling addicts in their custom-made coats for holding chips and tokens, there were conventioneers, college boys and packs of old ladies bound for the slots. There were the inevitable hookers in mini-skirts and boots, but the atmosphere lacked the genuine decadence of New Orleans. Vegas was too young for it; there were no long-established bloodlines here. The faces were mostly all-American middle-class, people on vacation, looking for a little fun without any danger.

"I guess it has its own appeal," Tina said as we ambled along, studying faces, "but it'll never beat Beale Street as far as I'm concerned. I wonder if there's any good jazz clubs here?"

"You like jazz?"

"Love it. I gotta meet Clint Eastwood some day. Stud like that, loves jazz, that's a combination I could go for."

I had to laugh. "Hell, he's got fifteen years on me!"

"That's okay. He's got good looks and good taste in music and I never heard he beats up on his women. Money don't hurt, either."

"Anyone else?"

"I like Sean Connery, but I don't know what kind of music he likes." While talking her eyes never stopped moving, studying faces and clothes. "This place is full of plainclothes."

"I noticed." They were working the crowd in pairs, being unobtrusive, not a gun in sight, but every once in a while one of them would raise a walkie-talkie to his mouth and speak a few words. "They'll know all the dips, the scammers, the wanted felons. Tourism is everything in this town. They're going to come down hard on anything that might scare the tourists away."

"You think they'll be on the lookout for Marsh and his friends?"

"I doubt it. If a felon's not likely to show up in Vegas, they won't bother to memorize his face."

It all felt very safe, just a Midwestern hick's idea of naughtiness. "Of course," I noted, "some of these cops may belong to Tyler's police auxiliary. They could be looking for Switzer. Hell, they could be after me by now."

"Do you just need more to worry about? Is worryin' a big thing with you?"

Actually, I was feeling pretty good. My pains were beginning to subside and I felt a little high, like the crowd all around us. I tried to analyze this and came to the conclusion that I had finally OD'd on danger. There was only so much I could worry about and the primitive fear centers in the back of my brain were shutting down.

We cruised the street for three hours, pausing once in a while to sit, have coffee, keep rested and alert. I found that, in a Las Vegas slot machine mill, I could get an amazingly good and amazingly cheap shrimp cocktail at the snack bar. Anything to keep you there, throwing money down that bottomless pit.

Always, we looked for that elusive, dark-haired young woman. I was looking for her so intently that I almost missed the man standing beneath the most famous of the landmarks of old Vegas. My eyes were drawn for the hundredth time that evening to the towering neon cowboy whose constantly beckoning arm has been bringing the suckers in for the better part of a half-century.

Then I saw his near-double standing beneath his neon boots, a young man posed on a providentially vacant patch of sidewalk, wearing a long, Aussie drover's coat and a low-crowned black hat. He thumbed back the brim, grinning, and for the first time I saw Nick Switzer in the flesh. He looked like the happiest man on Fremont Street.

An instant later I saw why the little bit of sidewalk was clear. A few feet in front of Switzer someone was half-crouched, taking his picture. She was waving people aside as they drew near and all I could really see was the back of a colorfully embroidered sheepskin coat.

I felt the smile spreading all over my face like oil. "Look over there under the big cowboy," I said. "There they are. Let's go get them." I was about to step off the curb when Tina jerked my arm.

"Hold still, you fool!" she hissed. Something in her urgent whisper chilled me. "Step back, now. Back away from the street, don't move fast." I did as she said. She got close as if we were cuddling, just another pair of lovers honeymooning in Vegas. "Now look straight across the street from us, just inside the door of that keno place."

"I know how to do it," I said, letting my gaze slip past the doorway, but not missing what was standing there. "Well, shit."

It was Joel Leblanc, of Beaumont, Texas. He wasn't staring at Switzer, but he wasn't letting his gaze get very far away, either. I kept looking along the street. No sign of Bergstrom, but farther down the sidewalk, past the cowboy sign, I spotted a weasely, pock-faced man in a London Fog raincoat. Everybody was dressed for a rainstorm, but the sky looked clear to me.

"Martinez has made the scene," I reported. "About thirty yards past Switzer and Sibyl, same side of the street."

"Then Bergstrom and Marsh ain't far away." Pressed against me with my arm around her shoulders, her tiny, slender body was as solid as a box of bricks, without the slightest trembling. "What the hell're they waiting for? Now's the time to snatch them two."

"The patrollers," I said. "They're all over the street. Marsh's boys will trail them down a side street, back to their motel or whatever. Then they'll grab them."

Sibyl straightened up and slid her camera into a side pocket of her long coat. Switzer wrapped his arm around her and they kissed, then broke apart, smiling like a cou-

209

ple of enraptured consumers in a soft-drink commercial. With their arms around each other's waist they were getting ready to move on when a sudden commotion distracted them.

All over the street, plainclothesmen were jabbering into walkie-talkies. Then, as one man, they all began running up the street, past gaping tourists. Way up there somewhere, I heard sirens wailing.

"Where the hell they goin'?" Tina demanded.

"Somebody's drawing them off. Damn! The snatch is going down right here! Come on!" I began to walk toward the pair who were standing, puzzled expressions on their faces, a little apprehensive but not yet aware that this was all about them.

"Come back here, you fool! You can't do anything for them two except get killed!" She was tugging at my sleeve, but I wasn't paying attention to anything but the woman I'd chased through seven states. People were laughing and pointing, wondering what all the fuss was about, yelling to each other that it was a bank robbery or a terrorist bombing, shrieking at the sheer hilarity of it all.

Leblanc and Martinez were closing in on Switzer and Sibyl, moving with slow deliberation, like pros. They would move fast only in the last few feet. My leg, which had felt pretty good earlier in the evening, suddenly felt as if it were made of lead. My knee throbbed as it had seconds after Leblanc had used my own weapon on it. Come to think of it, I owed him something.

I was behind Leblanc and just to his left when Sibyl looked around and saw him approaching. She said something to Nick and he looked around, saw Leblanc, grabbed Sibyl's arm, half-turned to his left, saw Martinez closing in and paused, stymied. Down the street people screamed as a gray van came barreling through, its windows almost black, the driver invisible as the big vehicle reflected a galaxy of spots and colors. I slipped the Asp from my back pocket.

Leblanc's hand came out from under his bomber jacket holding a big, silver pistol, and in that second I stepped past him, the Asp snapping open, whistling across to smash into the bridge of his nose. He howled, a hand going to his face but keeping hold of his gun this time. I grabbed it by the slide and hit him again, trying for his windpipe but catching the wrist of his face-covering hand instead. The pain was enough to loosen his grip and I wrenched the pistol away as he staggered back, blinded by blood and sudden, unexpected agony. I'd have liked to feed him a few more licks, just for old times' sake, but I had urgent matters pressing.

The van screeched to a halt and the passenger door popped open.

"Sibyl!" I yelled. She looked at me without recognition, her face pale but not terrified. "Come over here! Come with me! It's not you they want!"

Martinez was almost on top of them, but Switzer had already dragged a long-barreled revolver from beneath his Aussie coat. Martinez hauled a short, pump shotgun out of his London Fog. You can conceal a lot of firepower beneath a raincoat. Experience told me that I was holding a military-style Beretta, or maybe a Brazilian Taurus, which is pretty similar. Either one holds enough rounds to keep you shooting far longer than you're likely to survive in a real gunfight.

Scott Bergstrom climbed from the passenger side of the van, but ducked back in when Switzer opened up with his cannon. Martinez was about to cut loose at Nick, holding low to bring him down with a shot to the legs, when he caught sight of me leveling the automatic at his head, swung the huge muzzle toward me, raising it for a killing shot but pulling the trigger too soon. The heavy charge of lead passed by my ear so close that I heard its angry bee-buzz. I hoped it was climbing enough to pass over the heads of the crowd behind me. I hoped to hell Tina wasn't back there.

People were screaming, diving for cover, trampling each other in a blind panic to escape. Nick fired at Martinez, missed, but spoiled his aim once more, and the shotgun roared, only to smash a plate-glass window to glittering fragments. Much as I hated to shoot in that crowd, I lined up on Martinez and began to squeeze off a shot while he pumped in a fresh round, but a crowd of terrified old women piled out of a doorway between us. It takes a lot to get them away from those slots but we had done it.

Then, in the midst of this pandemonium, damned if another unexpected vehicle didn't come plowing in. A big, black, smoke-windowed limo plowed in, horn blaring, scattering people already traumatized by the gunfire. The limo caught the left rear bumper of the van, lifted it and spun it halfway around.

The driver's doors of both vehicles opened. From the van climbed a hulking man dressed in engineer boots, jeans and a coat styled like an army field jacket but made of black leather. His head was constructed of blocky, granite plains, his fair hair buzz-cut. Jess Marsh had at last put in an appearance. In one massive hand was a Smith & Wesson .44 Magnum, a gun much favored by Dirty Harry fantasists. It's way too much gun for ordinary human beings, but for once the wielder didn't look overgunned. Marsh stood there with a sort of monolithic calm, as if he were the immobile center of all this whirling action.

From the limo emerged Jasper Holt, his own pistol already in his hand. The heavy shooters were on the scene and there were going to be dead people all over the place in a second or two.

People were clearing out, leaving us all with a relatively clear field of fire. Great. Just what I always wanted. Nothing to stop us all from blazing away like idiots now. Bergstrom had made it out of the van, his gun out but looking to Marsh for instructions. The operation hadn't gone as planned and he needed orders. Martinez had his shotgun lined up on Switzer, but he was holding his fire and the reason wasn't hard to guess. This was supposed to be a snatch, not a hit. Whatever Switzer had wasn't on him and he wasn't much use to them dead.

"Jess, you know who I am," Holt said.

"Heard of you, Ranger." Marsh didn't take his eyes off Switzer. His gun hung loose at his side, but I knew that was as deceptive as Holt's equally casual attitude. "But that traitor over there is the one I'm interested in. Don't interfere with me."

Switzer was standing with his gun waving from side to side, as if he could keep everyone covered at once. I'd never seen a man in a more hopeless situation, and he looked like he was having the time of his life. Sibyl was standing next to him, bright-eyed, ready to bolt at his signal. The two of them were holding hands like a couple of kids.

It was a great little tableau but it couldn't hold long. Sirens were going off all over town and some of them had to be headed toward us. Then, shockingly, muffled *whumps* started to echo from various points around the city.

"Those are bombs!" I yelled.

"So I noticed," Holt affirmed. "More diversions, Marsh, or are you boys declaring war on established order?"

"Just keeping things lively," Marsh said. "But we are out of time. Are you going to let me have the traitor, or do we dispute this?"

"Can't let you have him, Jess."

They were about to raise their guns when a howling, slobbering, bleeding mass of anger piled into Holt. Joel Leblanc had recovered enough to take unilateral action. Holt clubbed him down with his pistol, knowing as he did it that Leblanc had bought Marsh that crucial split-second, bringing the blood-smeared barrel across anyway. I guess he figured it was worth a try. I wasn't going to interfere. I kept my sights on Martinez, the only one posing an immediate danger to Sibyl. He would try to shoot Nick first, and when he did I planned to put one through his head.

Holt would have died then but Tina was coming across the trunk lid of the limo, took off from it like a damned falcon, her hand dipping to swipe something from the top of her boot, landing on Marsh's back, one hand on his collar, the other wrapped around his neck, holding a glittering strip of silver just beneath his left ear.

Seeing her launch herself at him, I expected him to topple at the impact, but Marsh only swayed slightly, planted on his booted feet like a tree.

"Pretty goddamn good, lady," Marsh acknowledged. "Like to come work for me?"

"I got me a job already." Tina had her legs wrapped around his waist, her silver-heeled boots crossed just above his belt buckle. "Mr. Marsh, you remind me of my husband, and that ain't a good thing. Drop your gun now!"

"I just don't see how I can do that," Marsh said. "Ranger, we have an impasse here."

"And not a counselor in sight," Holt said. "What are we gonna do about this, Jess?"

"Only one way out of a Mexican standoff," I said, my sights steady on Martinez. "We start a new game. Tell London Fog over there to lower his weapon."

"Do as he says," Marsh ordered without hesitation.

The muzzle dropped and I turned toward Nick and

Sibyl. "You two take off. *Now!*" They ran off, still holding hands, actually laughing. What a happy little group we all were. Slowly, I stuck the silver pistol beneath my belt and refolded the Asp.

"Scyld, Gar!" Marsh snapped. "Pick up on Grim. Get him into the van!" Using code names from *Beowulf.* These people were nothing if not consistent. Blondie and Martinez packed away their weapons and dragged the inert Leblanc into the big vehicle.

"You two," Holt said, "get into the limo now."

Slowly, Tina unwound her legs and dropped away from Marsh. She refolded her razor and stuck it back into her boot. The two of us slid into the back of the limo. Then, very slowly, Marsh and Holt backed into their respective vehicles. When Holt shut his door the sudden silence was jolting.

"They could open up on us now," I said.

"Won't do 'em any good unless they have a bazooka," Holt replied. "This thing is armored like a tank." He put it in gear and turned down the nearest side street. That explained how the limo had lifted and spun the hulking van so easily.

"Nice car, Jasper," Tina said, stroking the luxurious upholstery.

"Don't get too attached to it. In an hour it's gonna be a four-by-four cube of scrap metal on its way to a steel mill in Japan."

"This belong to your employer?" I asked.

"Client, not employer. And it can never be traced to him."

"How'd you happen along so conveniently?" I asked him. There were police cars and ambulances streaking everywhere, lights flashing. Fire trucks roared by, howling.

"Happen along? I been all over town, up and down Fremont and the Strip all evenin'. I spotted the two of you hours ago. A limo in Vegas is like a Yellow Cab in New York. Who takes notice?" He patted the dash. "I also been monitorin' police radio traffic. When the excitement started it didn't take me long to figure out what was happenin' and where to go."

"All those casinos," I said, "ATMs everyplace, there's bound to be surveillance cameras on that street."

"It'll be a while before they get a chance to study them," Holt said. "This has been a right lively evenin' even for Vegas." He pulled to a stop. "Here's where you get out, Gabe." He'd stopped next to my car. He must have spotted it earlier in the evening. "If you was well advised, you'd get out of this town right now."

"Great idea," I said. "There's about four roads out of Vegas and there'll be roadblocks on all four."

"Then you better be movin' right smart. Just now they ain't really sure what they're lookin' for and half the tourists in Vegas have just decided to head for home. They can't hold 'em up too long. Bad for business."

"That'll depend on tonight's body count," I said, climbing out.

"I hope it's low," Jasper said. He saw Tina getting out on the other side. "Tina! You get back in here and come along with me."

"Not just yet, Jasper. I'm stayin' with Gabe for a while. You run along, now." She got behind the wheel of my car and I got in beside her.

"Tina," Holt said, exasperation ruining his usual equanimity, "you saw the sort of people we're dealin' with! You can't go up against them with just a cripple like him!" He nodded his Stetson in my direction. "No offense, Gabe."

"Been doin' all right so far," she said, hitting the ignition.

"You get back here!" Holt shouted.

Tina stuck her head out the window as she drove by

the limo. "Fuck off, Jasper!" She rolled up her window. "Damn, that man's annoyin'. Back to the motel?"

"Right. Five minutes there, grab our bags, ten more minutes and we're out of town, going north on 95. We're just out-of-state tourists, scared by all the violence. We've decided it's healthier in Tahoe."

All around us, Las Vegas screamed.

Fifteen

The traffic leading out of town was a bumper-to-bumper crush of cars and tour buses, some taking part in the panic, others right on schedule, because traffic to and from Vegas is a twenty-four-hour business.

"Looks like this is gonna take a while," Tina said.

"At least traffic on 95 north is relatively light," I told her. "It's mostly people heading for Reno and Tahoe and the ski country. I-15 south to L.A. must be a nightmare right now."

"Maybe we should've took it. Might be easier to slip past."

"I don't think so. Jasper was right. We've got to move fast, before they get to analyzing those surveillance tapes. Those things aren't too reliable, but you never know. They could be looking for a small, short-haired woman and a beat-up guy with a limp."

"Speakin' of that . . . ," She rummaged in her purse. "Turn around and I'll see what I can do about them bruises."

We were temporarily stopped and she took advantage of the pause to dab cosmetics on my face. "There," she said, snapping her compact shut. "That oughta do in this light." The light was coming from flares and the flashing lamps atop highway patrol cars. The radio was going crazy. Someone had blown up the big fountain in front of Caesar's Palace, injuring dozens of tourists. Bombs had gone off outside three other casinos, with more injuries, mostly the result of panic-stricken stampedes inside.

Some sort of powerful riot gas had been released in a big keno parlor on Fremont Street, sending scores of patrons to the hospital for treatment. That had been the diversion that had drawn the street patrol away from us.

There was an unconfirmed report of a shootout on Fremont, but police weren't saying anything about it.

"Seems to me they put this little operation together awful fast," Tina observed.

"Those guys probably travel with enough weapons and explosives to fight a war at all times. And, don't forget, they may have a support group right here to help out. Once they had Nick and Sibyl spotted in Vegas, it wouldn't take long to set up their diversion."

"Where do you suppose them—those two are?" The car inched forward as cars and buses passed the roadblock one at a time.

"Maybe three cars ahead. Or three behind. Too bad we can't get out and look without attracting notice."

"You pretty sure they picked this road?"

"It's more likely than 15 south. They didn't buy clothes for L.A. Fifteen north goes to Salt Lake City. I don't know, there's a lot of places they could turn off before Salt Lake. But I have a hunch 95 is their road. But in the meantime, to hell with them. *We've* got to get the hell away from here."

"What's the chances they're just layin' low, stayin' right back there in Vegas, waitin' for the heat to die down?"

"Unlikely they'd try it, not in a city as tightly controlled as Vegas. Maybe in New York, L.A., Chicago—

but Vegas? Uh-uh. They'd want to get away as fast as possible."

Eventually, we crept up to the roadblock. A young patrolman glanced at my license plate before leaning toward the driver's window. Behind him stood a double rank of troopers with shotguns and rifles at the ready. The highway was four-lane at this point, but they were letting traffic through two lanes at a time, with a gauntlet of flanking fire to run if you tried to crash through. It was a conventional setup, and an effective one.

"Driver's license and registration, please."

"You don't think no terrorist is drivin' no piece-of-shit car like this, do you?" Tina said to him, pure trailer trash.

"Now, honey," I said, "the man's just doin' his job. Don't mind her, Officer."

"I'm just kiddin' him, dumplin'."

"I need to look inside your trunk," the trooper said, straight-faced.

"Darlin', you did leave that dynamite at home, ditn you?" She cackled as she got out, keys in hand. "Just kiddin'!" She opened the trunk and the trooper shone his light inside. Then she closed it and got back behind the wheel.

The cop handed back the license and registration. "You can go on." He never cracked a smile. Well, he had a lot on his mind.

Tina negotiated the maze of patrol cars that formed the roadblock and we were on our way.

"Warn me before you pull something like that. I can play the straight man, but I need a little time to get into the role."

"I seen—saw that boy come over all solemn lookin' and shiny in that uniform, I just knew he'd never believe a couple of shit-for-brains hicks could be involved in all this. He wanted us away from him fast as he could get rid of us, before one of us spit tobacco on his shiny shoes."

"Sound psychology," I said.

"Sometimes you gotta read 'em fast and cold. Now, Jess Marsh and his buddies will never make it past there. They all look like they belong on the post office wall, and one of 'em's beat up all to hell—that was a slick move, by the way."

"I'm not so sure. Those guys have all been professional fugitives for years. I suspect they're pretty good at getting around that sort of trap. They could make it out over the mountains on bikes, if they had to."

With traffic backed up at the roadblock, the highway seemed almost empty. After a while the four-lane road narrowed to two. I was getting unutterably tired and told Tina to pull over as soon as she found someplace for us to stay the remainder of the night. A bump in the road called Lathrop Wells sported a few motels and we stopped at the one farthest from the highway.

While Tina checked out the news on the TV I studied the map, trying to figure where our fleeing, latter-day Bonnie and Clyde might be bound.

"We've reached one of the most cheerful spots in the United States," I told her. "Just north of us is the old nuclear testing range where they blew up A-bombs. Nearby features include Skull Mountain and Spectre Mountain. Directly south of us are the Funeral Mountains and just beyond them, fittingly enough, Death Valley."

"Sounds like a fun spot. Now hush." She was sitting crosslegged on her bed, wearing the long T-shirt again. She looked so tiny and fragile I could hardly believe I'd seen her fly through the air, clamp herself on the hulking Jess Marsh and lay a blade to his jugular with the cool aplomb of an Olympic gymnast.

The airwaves were full of the night's strange doings in

221

Vegas. There were no deaths reported as yet but a number of people were in critical condition and there could well be some heavy mortality by morning. Most of the injuries seemed to be caused by trampling, flying glass and inhaling caustic chemicals, but there were some gunshot casualties. The problem was that nobody could figure out whether these were from a putative shootout on Fremont or just the result of a night's ordinary gunplay.

"So far, so good," Tina said.

"Unless someone's just keeping quiet about it," I said, then, "My God, I'm getting just like Switzer."

"That's nice. Might help us catch him. But what the hell do you mean?"

"I mean I'm achieving total paranoia immersion the way a Zen master achieves satori. I can no longer take anything at all at face value without sensing underlying hostility. If I hear a news broadcast pertaining to my situation, I have to suspect that it's been doctored to lull me while the authorities prepare to pounce. If I see a cop or a police car, I have to wonder if the guy in the uniform is one of Tyler's White Front cohorts on the lookout for me."

I pondered this for a moment. "Damn! This must be the way Douglas Tyler feels all the time, with his ranting about the 'controlled media' and the shadow government and endless international conspiracies. I wonder how he stands it? It would drive me crazy. Of course, he *is* crazy. They're *all* crazy. Has it occurred to you that one reason we're floundering around like this is that we're surrounded by crazy people?"

"Lay down and get some rest, Treloar."

She switched to a national news service. Unlike the local station, they were treating it as yet another bizarre story out of Vegas, a sort of Wild West show from America's most colorful city.

"That makes sense," I commented, yawning. "What

else do people expect from the town that gave us crowds of Elvis impersonators?"

"Don't go bad-mouthin' Elvis," she said, switching off the set. She got out the papers and photos and spread them out on the bedspread all around her. She looked them over in a mass, as if, seen that way, they could communicate something new.

"You'd better get some sleep," I said, all but unconscious myself.

"I'll be okay." She lit a cigarette and stared intensely at the papers. "It all keeps coming down to that damn blood lab."

"How's that?" I said muzzily.

"It's the one thing out of place. There's that picture of the two of them in front of it, dressed like doctors, and her wearin' the wig and contacts. They cost plenty, so she had some serious purpose for buyin' them."

"I figured that from the start."

"And this picture's the only place where we see her wearin' 'em, but that's the way she's described in Marsh's wanted poster."

"Right. What about the 'German accent'?"

"That don't make much sense. But that Nazi crap's German, right?"

"You think they were posing as Nazi doctors?"

"Why not? They was sure as hell posin' as something. That clinic does AIDS research. Tyler seems to think pretty highly of AIDS."

"I noticed, but I couldn't figure how they could parlay that into a workable scam."

She put out her cigarette. "Maybe we just ain't thinkin' straight. It might make more sense in the mornin'." She turned out the light, then: "Why'd they take that picture?"

"Maybe to see what they looked like together in those outfits."

"Maybe there's more pictures."

"Blackmail?"

"Why not? Ordinary people use cameras to take snap-shots, remember the family vacation, things like that. For a scammer a camera's a tool. They use 'em for blackmail, or to get something to use for insurance."

It was an intriguing possibility.

"Tina?" I said.

"What?"

"The way you tackled Marsh tonight. That was about the goddamnedest thing I've ever seen. Whatever Holt's paying you isn't nearly enough."

She chuckled. "Actually, I lied. Marsh don't remind me of my husband a bit. Too bad he's so crazy. It's been a long time since I've had my legs around something like that. I could go for him, under different circumstances."

"Now you're making me jealous."

"Don't go all possessive on me!" she snapped. "You'n me ain't even partners. We're just cooperatin', under-stand?"

"You are one damned hard woman to compliment, you know that?"

For once, I woke up before Tina did. She lay on her side in a tight fetal ball, just the top of her head showing above the sheet. The sky outside was a pale gray. I slipped out of bed, splashed some water on my face, pulled on my pants and went outside. We were on the second floor and the door opened onto a balcony that ran the length of the building. I stepped to the waist-high steel railing and leaned on it, watching the desert grow brighter.

I was facing south, toward the highway, and beyond it the Funeral Mountains. Somewhere just on the other side of those was Death Valley, the lowest point in the United States, 282 feet below sea level at one spot. I thought of the Old Ranger, forty-mule teams, borax wag-ons and a haunting bugle call.

Holding onto the top rail, I did some slow, cautious exercises, like those old Chinese men who practice tai chi in the parks. I lowered myself, straightened, found that the knee was coming along nicely. Plenty of twinges but little real loss of function. My sore sides were loosening up, no longer cramping if I turned a little too fast.

It put me in mind of ancient warriors. Maybe they'd had the right idea. It could be that pounding on Joel Leblanc had actually helped my injuries to heal. I made a mental note to check with some New Age back-to-primitive-mysticism expert about this.

For a while I walked up and down the balcony. The morning was uncommonly quiet, except for the sound of an occasional truck passing on the highway. The air was cool, a thin haze coating everything softly. Just before the sun broke over the eastern horizon the colors, limited as they were, came out, about fifty shades of brown. The land looked like corrugated cardboard.

Tina came out onto the balcony, toweling her hair.

"Mornin', Gabe. Ain't this about the ugliest landscape you've ever seen?"

"It gets worse," I assured her.

After I'd showered and shaved, we went to a diner and pondered our next move over coffee.

"Do you think Sibyl knew you?" Tina asked.

"I doubt it. She hasn't seen me since she was a kid, more than ten years ago. That's a much longer time for her than for me. Why?"

"I was just wonderin' what last night's little fun and games looked like through her eyes. Nick's, too. I mean, just how much are them—those two aware of what's happenin', who's chasin' 'em?" Her grammatical self-corrections were getting compulsive.

"Hard to say. As a good con artist, Nick must have meant to make his score and then disappear before the mark figured out he'd been scammed. That's the professional way to operate. But something went wrong. Either the con didn't take the way it should, or somebody tumbled to the scam sooner than expected. Anyway, something happened and he had to split quick. Plus, the mark discovered who Switzer really was."

"I'm with you so far. What about Sibyl? She's got to know her daddy's gonna miss her in a few days, and he owns a whole damned detective agency, has contacts all over the country. She must know her daddy's men are on the lookout for her."

"How about Holt?" I asked her. "Do you think it's likely Switzer recognized him?"

"Maybe. Jasper's the best in the business, and there ain't many in it. Switzer could well know Jasper by reputation and he's not hard to recognize when you see him up close." She shook her head and ground out her cigarette. "I've tried to get him to dress better, get rid of that awful suit and the string tie and that goddamned stupid hat, but he won't have none of it. Says a man needs a trademark if he's to make a proper impression."

"I guess he's done all right with it." The idea of Tina as a fashion advisor didn't bear thinking about. "But Switzer can't be sure just who he's working for. Hell, even we don't know that."

"So last night Nick and Sibyl're doin' the Vegas thing, havin' a wonderful time like they're on their honeymoon, then all of a sudden the street starts to go weird and a bunch of men are closin' in on them. Now, Sibyl's got no way to know who you are, 'less by chance she remembered your face, which ain't in its best shape at the moment.

"They saw right off that not everybody was on the same side. That was pretty plain when you gave it to Leblanc across the face with your little fold-up tire iron. We don't know if they'd recognize the DTT boys, and God knows what they thought when Jasper barreled in like he did. How long do you think that whole little episode lasted?"

"Once the action started, no more than three or four minutes. It just felt a lot longer."

"That's right. Not much time for them to sort things out. I'll bet right now they're sittin' in someplace just like we are, tryin' to figure out what the hell happened last night. And they're plannin' their next move, just like we're tryin' to figure out ours."

"Unless they have a destination."

"There's that. Any ideas?"

"I've been wondering about whatever it was that Nick picked up at Jennings's place just before Jess Marsh showed up there."

"Seems like a lot of people are wonderin' about that very thing."

"He shipped it from his place to Jennings's. Maybe he's done it again."

"You mean maybe he's goin' someplace to pick it up?"

"It seems to fit his mentality. He doesn't want to be caught with it, knows he's on the run, knows he may have to abandon a car, leave luggage someplace. It makes sense to send it on ahead. I'm guessing that it's money, so maybe they took out a stack of bills to pay their way and live it up a little, so they haven't needed to use Sibyl's credit card since Nashville."

"It'd have to be someplace he thinks he won't get caught, can't be traced."

"Maybe he's headed for Hole-in-the-Wall, Butch Cassidy's old hideout."

"Is that a real place?"

"It's real, but I hope it's not where he's going, because it's way the hell up in Wyoming, about a million miles from anywhere."

"That don't stand to reason anyhow. There's such a thing as carryin' this outlaw fantasy stuff too far, even for the likes of Nick Switzer. He may want to play cowboy-and-cowgirl with Sibyl for a while, but he'll want easy access to the bright lights and high livin'."

"I think you're right." I'd been studying the maps again, a seemingly endless task. "I say we keep going north to Reno, see what inspiration is to be had on Highway 95."

"Why Reno?"

"Reno was the big Nevada gambling-and-divorce center before Vegas overwhelmed its business, but it's not really Reno I'm thinking about. Lake Tahoe is just a few miles from Reno. It's pretty, it's a resort and it gets cold early in the year in those mountains."

"Them coats."

"Exactly. And from Tahoe it's maybe three and a half hours to San Francisco. Maybe he's headed to pick up his swag, then go on to disappear in the big city."

"Let's get rollin'."

I hadn't anticipated it, but Highway 95 turned out to be one of America's truly existential thoroughfares. It went on mile after mile through the most god-awful desert landscape imaginable. The low hills and ridges limited the horizon and transmitted no idea of space. It was a landscape straight out of a fifties Big Bug movie, and you expected to see something huge and many-legged heave over the nearest ridge at any moment to devour you and your car.

Everywhere, we passed ghost towns with their deserted buildings and gaunt, skeletal mining machinery long stilled and slowly, slowly rusting in the arid climate. Cars were few and local inhabitants seemingly fewer. Here, as nowhere else on this endless chase, I felt clearly how unbelievably *empty* the American West is. We came this way just long enough to wipe out the Indians, rip some minerals from the ground, then leave. No wonder we were on such a huge, collective guilt trip.

The first hundred miles, we saw odd little clusters of trailers set well back from the road. They usually had signs by the highway identifying them as ranches of one sort or another. Most strangely, some were equipped with landing strips and helipads. When we passed one whose sign was graced with a metal silhouette of a naked woman, Tina slapped the steering wheel.

"I get it! Those are whorehouses!"

"Nevada's famed legal bordellos, huh? Somehow I didn't picture them looking that way." Yet another manifestation of that great American institution, the trailer park.

The road went mind-bogglingly on, a succession of dusty hills, dry lake and river beds, its wildlife tiny and furtive. It seemed devoid of human life, except for the paltry trickle of dwellings that ran along the highway. The settlements were small, few and so widely spaced that here, for once, it really was possible to run out of gas before you reached a station.

"Treloar," Tina said after a long silence, "how'd a schoolboy like you come to be a gung-ho soldier and an L.A. cop and a PI? Not pryin', of course."

"I've wondered the same thing. I suspect that like many of us I was bent by popular culture. Until my second year of high school I lived in a little town in Ohio, in a household that was Catholic and very middle-class."

"That much figures."

"We moved to L.A. when I was sixteen. I finished high school, did a little college, did the usual California-kid things, finally joined the army in sixty-seven."

"Why'd you do a thing like that? Most men was tryin' to stay out of the service back then."

"I wanted to be a cop. MPs got preferential treatment getting into the LAPD academy, got a jump on seniority—there were all kinds of advantages."

"So it was a career move?"

"Partly. But I needed to see if I could take it, if I had what it took to be a tough guy."

"Is this where that popular culture stuff comes in?"

"That's right. We live in a country that values success above all, and success is largely a matter of education, of getting a white-collar position with regular promotions instead of being stuck in a nowhere manufacturing job or something.

"But this is predominantly a blue-collar country, and there's something in us that, whether consciously or unconsciously, despises people who don't work with their hands. If you were a boy raised in the forties and fifties, you knew that you couldn't be a real man if you weren't a worker and a soldier. Every movie John Wayne ever made told us that. I mean, what figure represents America? The cowboy! A glorified working stiff! What other nation chooses an underpaid, exploited proletarian from the agricultural sector as its national hero?"

"So you ran off and joined the army to be a man?" she said, dragging me back on track.

"Yep. MP work in Saigon turned out to be pretty much like police work anywhere else, though it got a little lively in January sixty-eight. That's where I picked up some of those marks you saw. Good practice for L.A., anyway. I got married there, too."

"I was wonderin'. You had that ring on so long you're gonna have to get it cut off pretty soon or you'll get gangrene and your finger'll rot off."

I held up my left hand and contemplated it. After almost thirty years the thin, gold band was deeply sunken into the flesh of my finger. She was right. I'd have to get something done about it.

"Rose died years ago, but I've never been able to take it off, for some reason."

"Sounds like your marriage beat mine all to hell. Why'd you decide to be a cop, of all things?"

"It was another of my unsuitable ambitions. My parents wanted me to be a doctor, lawyer, one of those things, but that wasn't how I pictured myself."

"You wanted to be a hero?"

"It's not at all uncommon among bookish young males. Back then, anyway. I found that out in the army. I ran into other guys like me: Rangers, Navy Seals, a few Green Berets. A lot of them were college dropouts, way overeducated for the enlisted ranks, but drawn to the hairy, adventurous outfits because they'd been raised on the same movies and TV shows I was."

She laughed. "I always knew men were that dumb, but I never met one that came right out and admitted it!"

"It's the great male secret. You want to know why I became a cop? Blame Jack Webb and Broderick Crawford and James Franciscus and all those cop shows back then: *Dragnet, Highway Patrol, Naked City,* I watched them all. Of course, I liked *Dragnet* the best because it was about Los Angeles. After we moved there, I used to drive all over the city, finding the places they mentioned in the shows."

"I guess you liked the work."

"Well, like the army, it wasn't quite as I'd expected, but I found out I was good at it. I learned that one man wasn't about to put a dent in crime in a city the size of L.A., but I also learned there was some satisfaction to be had in just helping to hold the line. I went to night school, earned some commendations, made rank fast." I thought about those young, fear-ridden but heady days. "It was pretty good for a while there." Before Rose died.

"So how high'd you get before they kicked you off the force?"

"You're the soul of tact, Tina. Detective One, in line for a lieutenancy. Did Holt send for a report on me?"

"I don't need to learn everything from Jasper. Hell, I can read the signs, Treloar. You're a boozer. Don't feel bad about it; there's worse things to be and I been some of

---

John Maddox Roberts

them." She drove in silence for a while, blowing smoke out the window from time to time. "So, you got a woman now?"

"Sort of."

She snorted smoke. "What's a sort of woman?"

"Her name's Connie Armijo. She's a detective, too, works for an all-women outfit in L.A.—"

"That'll be McInery Detective Agency, right?"

"Right. Anyway, we worked a case together a while back. It was a strange one, but most of them are. We got pretty close, but we both got scared and backed off some. She's a widow, has teenaged kids. We keep in touch, see each other from time to time—"

"Just a couple of kids afraid of commitment, huh? Well, I can understand her bein' cautious if she's ever seen you act as crazy as you did last night in Vegas."

"Hey, you're the one who walked into Chino's in Kingman, unescorted. I wouldn't—"

"What's that?" she interrupted, silencing me. She was looking straight ahead. In the far distance a black, jeeplike vehicle rolled northward. "That looks like a Blazer to me."

"Get closer, but don't make it obvious." I reached under the seat for my surveillance binoculars. Tina accelerated smoothly. When we were a hundred yards behind the car I could see that it was, indeed, a Blazer. I raised the binoculars, held them in place only long enough to focus and determine that its windows were tinted and it was wearing Arizona plates.

"There two of 'em inside?" Tina asked.

"Can't tell. There must be lots of Blazers with Arizona plates in Nevada."

"What do you think?"

"They're a pretty good bet and we have nothing else. Drop back but keep them in sight."

"That won't be hard. Anyone gets off the main road around here, you can see 'em for miles."

She fell back and we maintained visual contact with the Blazer. Knowing that we'd spotted this vehicle, I watched our back trail even more vigilantly. Bergstrom and Leblanc had seen my car back in Albuquerque. A beat-up old Pontiac with Tennessee plates had to stand out on this stretch of highway.

We kept on that way for another forty or fifty miles. Highway 95 took a dogleg west before turning north again, but the surrounding moonscape remained monotonously the same. The Blazer disappeared over a rise as it had dozens of times, and when we got to the top of the rise it was no longer on the road ahead of us.

"They turned off," Tina said.

"Slow down." I began to raise the binoculars.

"There they are. They went off to the left, about a quarter mile ahead."

"Then drive on past the turnoff if you have to. We can't let them see us turn off, too." Staying behind them on the highway there was no reason for them to suspect that we were tailing them. Where the hell else would another car be? But a car that turned off on the same obscure side road had to be a threat.

"You sure you want to follow 'em? It could be anybody."

"Do you have anything better to do today?"

She shrugged. "Guess not."

The Blazer was still just barely in sight when we came to the side road. Tina drove past, continued for another half mile, then made a U-turn and went back. The sign at the turnoff gave some rural route numbers and said the road led to Salt Peak Ghost Town State Historic Site.

We went along cautiously, taking our time. The road was paved but that was about the extent of its amenities. It lacked center and side lines, there were no livestock fences, no telephone lines or power poles. It climbed into a low range of hills, sere and bleak like everything else we'd seen for the past two hundred miles. It made me wonder about the people of the past century. With the entirety of this beautiful continent at their feet, what in God's name drew them to this high desolation?

"There they go," Tina announced. Far ahead, the Blazer had turned off on another road, leading to the right, entering a fold in the hills. Judging by the plume of dust the ORV raised, this one wasn't paved.

We pulled to a stop where the little road branched off. A sign identified this as the route to the ghost town. Warnings were posted against littering, looting or starting fires.

"You wanna try this?" Tina said dubiously. "Or wait for 'em to come back out? They've got an ORV and we ain't."

"Try it for a way." I had a feeling about that Blazer, and I was sure that if we lost it here we'd never catch up with it again.

"If we get stuck, you get to walk back and find help, bad knee or no bad knee."

Very slowly, Tina turned onto the dirt road and drove on, dead slow. Exerting all her skill, she managed to keep the wheels on the higher parts of the road, straddling the ruts, but every once in a while the bottom scraped and I clenched my teeth, trying to raise the car through willpower, the way a passenger will stomp on a nonexistent brake pedal to stop the car someone else is driving.

Once through the little pass between the hills, we could see the ghost town. It was little more than a double line of dilapidated buildings, one of hundreds of movie-set towns that dot the American West. This one might have been better preserved than most, probably because it attracted so few tourists.

There was no sign of the Blazer.

"We might as well go on," I told Tina.

"We damn well *have* to go on. There's no place between here and there to turn around, and I sure ain't gonna back down all the way to the road." She drove on slowly. This part of the road wasn't as badly rutted as the rest, but she didn't want to raise a dust plume. Within another three minutes, we were among the abandoned buildings.

I scanned the surrounding slopes. No Blazer, no dust plume, no sign of movement whatsoever. It was like driving into a painting.

"You got that gun handy?" Tina asked.

"Yes, but I didn't come all this way to shoot them."

"You don't know for sure it's them, and there's plenty of people in this world'll shoot you for followin' 'em." Sage advice.

"Cruise the town. Take it slow."

"Yeah, we sure as hell wouldn't want to get a speedin' ticket, would we?"

"Why are you in such a bad mood? We might be about to wrap this up."

"I don't like bein' in a blind alley with only one way out."

"There it is." We'd just cruised past an alleyway between a false-fronted store and something that might have once been an office, its wooden sign too weather-beaten and sun-faded for legibility. The Blazer was empty as far as I could see. "Stop here."

"Uh-uh. Let me turn around first." She drove on to a little intersection, managed a Y-turn, then went back.

"You wait here," I said, opening my door.

"He's got a gun and he might be jumpy."

"If it'll make you feel better, here." I laid Leblanc's pistol between the seats. She didn't give me any argument. She also didn't tell me to be careful or any stupid thing like that. She just kept her hands on the wheel and the motor running.

I stepped out and there was a light, crisp breeze blowing. It made lonesome sounds passing through the cracks and open windows of the old, frame buildings. Moving with exaggerated slowness, keeping my hands in sight, I walked over to the Blazer, saw that there was no one inside, saw boot prints in the dust leading to the gaping door of the false-front building. I walked over to it.

"Nick, Sibyl, I'm coming in. I'm unarmed. I'm trying to save your damn lives, so I hope you'll act sensible for once and talk to me. I'm coming in now."

I raised my hands to shoulder height, palms out, and stepped across the threshold. It was much darker inside, a slab of light falling in through the door, long streaks of it streaming through the warped, bare boards of the sides. Swirling dust motes, raised by the breeze, danced and glittered in the irregular light. To my right and left I could just make out two dark forms. One of them stepped close and I was looking at a narrow, weasely, pockmarked face.

"You were right," Jess Marsh said to Juan Martinez. "The bitch's name is Sibyl."

Sixteen

Call your lady friend inside," Marsh instructed. Of all the possibilities that had passed through my mind, this was one that hadn't even made an appearance. It took a few seconds for the shock to register fully. Not only had this not turned out as expected, but I couldn't readily imagine myself in a worse situation.

"Call her!" Martinez urged.

"Forget it, guys. No way is she going to come in here just because I call her."

"Grim, go get her. Move quick, because she sure as hell does."

Martinez darted to the doorway, but he was barely stepping through it when I heard the Pontiac's tires spinning, throwing gravel. There was a shot, no telling whose, then the door of the Blazer slammed as Martinez got behind the wheel. He started it, racked it inexpertly into gear, and drove off, out of the alley.

"This should be interesting," Marsh said. He held the massive .44 limply at his side, but I didn't mistake that for inattention. He could put a bullet through me before I could even start to turn and run. "She's got a head start, but that road is rough and your car is low-slung. I'd put my money on the ORV."

"Maybe so," I told him. "Personally, I'm not a betting man." In the distance I heard more shots, then the sound of both vehicles faded away.

"I need to know a few things about you." Marsh stepped closer. His blue eyes were clear and brilliant. Even in repose he had the springy, alert stance of a professional athlete, or else a man who kept himself almost obsessively fit. "Come over here and sit down." He gestured with the gun barrel. There was a rickety old bench by the wall and I sat on it. By making me sit while he stood he established dominance. It was an old game and I knew how to play it.

"Let's begin with the basics. Who are you?"

"Gabe Treloar." My stomach was churning, but I'd learned voice control long ago and kept my replies steady, but neither sullen nor insolent. There's an art to it.

"And what is your official capacity, if you have one?"

"I work for Carson Investigations, the Knoxville office."

"A PI? I see. And what is your connection with Jasper Holt?"

"None." I saw his neck muscles begin to bunch and added, "We just happen to be chasing the same people." With a man like Jess Marsh you do not hesitate, you do not prevaricate, and you absolutely do not come off as a smartass. I'd known cops like him: expert interrogators, inhumanly efficient at eliciting information from the hardest cases. They were invariably sadists with serious mental problems. Sometimes as a result the evidence they produced wouldn't hold up in court, but that wasn't a difficulty that concerned Jess Marsh.

"And who are you working for?"

"My boss is Randall Carson. The woman Switzer is with is his daughter. We want her back and safe. We don't care about Switzer or what he took from you."

"You don't say. Now what makes you think Switzer took something from me?"

Apparently it was game-playing time. "If you just wanted to kill him, you could've done it last night in Vegas without all the fireworks and overproduction. He has it or knows where it is and you want it."

"That makes sense. What's Jasper Holt's interest?"

"Holt recovers people's money. It's his well-known specialty. I don't know who he's working for; he won't tell me."

"You let me worry about that." Casually, he squatted down until he was resting on his booted heels, forearms hanging over his knees, hands hanging from limp wrists, gun pointed floorward, all his weight on the balls of his feet. He held the pose without effort, his eye level now just slightly below mine.

Jess Marsh's face was lined, but not with worry. It was the face of a man who suffered from neither fear nor doubt. It was the face of a man who knew that what he was doing was exactly, perfectly right. I doubted that his expression changed much when he was driving nails through the flesh and bones of a fellow human being. Then I corrected that thought. Jess Marsh had no fellow human beings.

"Whatever Switzer scammed from your leader," I urged, "I don't care! You and Holt can tangle over that; it means nothing to me."

"You think I have a leader?" he said mildly.

"We're not playing games here, all right? I know who you are, I know who Douglas Tyler is; it's not complicated."

He straightened and walked idly away from me, as if to stretch his legs. I measured the distance to the door, to a paneless window in another room, ran a mental map of the town through my head. Ten years earlier and with two sound knees, I might have tried it. But I didn't really think

I could have made it even then. He was unnervingly confident. He had not the slightest worry that I was going to escape him and it was hard not to share his certainty.

He turned slightly at the rumble of a returning vehicle. I could tell by the sound that it was the Blazer. A minute later it pulled up outside in a cloud of dust and Martinez came in looking both angry and fearful.

"She made it back to the road, man. I couldn't chase her once she got there. We gotta split, I mean . . . " He tapered off and his anger wilted under Marsh's marble-eyed stare, leaving only the fear.

"She's just a woman, Grim, and she's driving an old Pontiac over a goat trail. You couldn't catch her in an ORV?"

"She's got a gun and she's pretty good with it—" Marsh's hand cracked across his face with a sound like a board splitting.

"We don't accept excuses in this organization, Grim. You know that. Don't make it necessary for me to discipline you." He stared Martinez down for a while, then; "Go get my bag. We need to make some plans." Martinez scurried out in a wash of relief and Marsh came back over to me.

"You see how it is?" he asked me earnestly. "He could've come right back at me with how that woman sandbagged me last night, but he didn't dare. That's why some have to be leaders while others follow." He scratched the side of his neck with the big sight on the end of his pistol barrel. "That is a very superior woman you have there." It looked as if he didn't know she was really with Holt. All right, the less he knew for sure, the better. "It's a shame, you know, white people like us fighting when there's a real enemy to deal with."

Martinez returned with a military-type carrying bag, one with lots of side pockets and zippers. Marsh took a long cardboard tube from its top and drew out a rolled map. He spread it on the floor in the spill of light from the door, using his pistol, a heavy pocket knife and a compass to hold it open. Incongruously, he took a pair of rimless, oval-lensed glasses from a breast pocket and slipped the wire hooks over his ears as he settled down to study.

"Cuff the prisoner, Grim," he ordered.

"Maybe better to just kill him, Chief."

"I'll decide that. No rush just now. Do it."

Martinez unzipped a side pocket of the bag, took out a pair of stainless-steel cuffs and walked over to me. "Hands behind you, man." I did as I was told and he clipped them onto my wrists with workmanlike competence. He walked back over to Marsh, dropping the key into his right front pocket.

"This little road," Marsh said, pointing with a pen, "starts down at the south end of town. It goes up over two ranges to the west, then comes out right by Highway 6 near this salt marsh." What he was looking at looked like a topographical survey map, the kind used by the military and the forestry service. It would show every structure and cattle trail for many miles around, and just where had they come up with this at short notice? They were certainly resourceful. "The Blazer ought to make it," he concluded, refolding his glasses and putting them away.

"If it ain't washed out."

Marsh smiled. "Well, that's what we'll just have to find out, won't we?" He gestured to the bag. "Put this stuff back. We'll keep the map out for now." He stood and rolled the map with quick, deft movements, resheathed it in its cardboard tube.

"Time to go," Marsh said to me.

I lurched to my feet and went along willingly. Riding around the desert with a pair of homicidal maniacs wasn't an attractive prospect, but with crucifixion as the likely alternative it seemed like a fine idea.

Getting into the Blazer with my hands cuffed behind

me was an awkward job, but I managed to get into the backseat and Martinez shut the door, then climbed into the front passenger seat. Marsh got behind the wheel, started the Blazer and pulled out of the alley, heading south.

Martinez scanned the nearby hills nervously. "That bitch could be back with help any second."

"Worry is the warrior's adversary," Marsh lectured him. "It's useless, it dulls your edge and it's unworthy." He smiled and shook his head. "Be real, brother. Where's she going to find help? Even if she saw a patrol car on the highway, you think she's going to flag it down? Right now the very last thing anybody wants is official involvement, right, Treloar?"

"We're trying not to bother them," I assured him. "My boss specifically wants his daughter out of this without her ever coming to the attention of the police."

"That's what I figured," Marsh said. "I'm afraid I can't allow him to have her back, though. She's a race traitor, too, and all race traitors are to be put to death, no exceptions."

"Jess," I said, trying to be the soul of reason, "she's not a traitor of any kind. She's just a silly college girl who got taken in by a two-bit scam artist. Let her go."

"Sorry, I can't permit it. You let one get away, and who knows where it'll lead? Once instituted, racial purification has to be carried out with perfect integrity. That's where the old guys back in Germany slipped up. Too many of them were too softhearted."

"I must have missed something in my history classes," I said, unable to believe I was taking part in this conversation.

"Not surprising, since everything you read and everything that's taught and allowed to go on television is controlled by the Jews, who own all the media. But, hell, what I'm talking about you'll find even in the books they sell over the counter." He was really warming to his subject now. He had turned onto a barely visible track at the end of town and we were now climbing slowly into the hills.

"Even Heinrich Himmler himself complained that every German had his pet Jew. Collectively, they were all for getting rid of the Jews, but every one had that beloved teacher, that family doctor, that valued employee they wanted special treatment for. The Jews got special papers to keep working or go on owning their property and, finally, permission to emigrate. Made it absolutely impossible to do a thorough job and look what happened."

"We ain't making that mistake, man," said Martinez.

"So you see," Marsh went on, "I can't let the bitch live. It's the cross for both of them as soon as I get the traitors and some nails together in one place."

I looked around into the back of the Blazer. There were what looked like cased weapons, rope, tools, a set of bolt cutters for getting through fences, but I didn't see any electrical cords sticking out anywhere.

"What you looking at, man?" Martinez demanded.

"The Craftsman or whatever it was you used on Jennings."

"You figured that out, huh?" Marsh said. "Actually, it was a Black and Decker. American-made all the way. That Sears crap, you never know. Makes the job a whole lot easier and more efficient. A masonry bit works best."

Martinez got out a set of binoculars and scanned. "Helicopter over to the north, Chief, cruisin' low."

"That's east," Marsh said patiently. He slowed to a stop, smoothly so as to raise no dust. He took the binoculars and watched the chopper for a few seconds, then handed the glasses back. "It's military. Military bases all over this area. Probably nothing. Like I said, the authorities aren't likely to be a problem out here."

"After the way we blew up Vegas," Martinez countered, "they could have the whole air force looking for us."

"Yeah, Jess, why all the Hollywood fireworks?" I couldn't resist asking. "You were just snatching a couple of yo-yos off the street. You could've just waited for them at their motel or wherever they were staying."

"Oh, we had their room staked out, all right. But the opportunity was just too good. You remember Grenada and Panama?"

"Sure."

"Well, the military never passes up a chance for a good training exercise. That's why half the armed forces of the United States were used to invade Grenada, a job that could have been handled by a couple of platoons of MPs. They hit Panama like Normandy, just to arrest one grease-ball! It looked overdone, but they had a reason. It was good training."

"So we had a little practice in Vegas," Martinez said.

"Practice for what?" They seemed marginally better disposed when they were talking about their little manias.

"Armageddon," Marsh said. "The millennium's just around the corner, brother. When it comes down it'll be race against race, knives out and no quarter. There won't be many left standing when it's over, but the ones who survive will be entirely healthier specimens than you see around you most days. No more mongrels and race-mixers, no more mud people. It won't take long to scour this country. All it takes is will."

"I see." I looked all around and there was nothing to be seen except desolation in all directions. "There's more to the world than this country."

"That's right," Marsh said. "It's going to be interesting. The gooks are going to be the toughest. They're smart and there's a lot of them. But there's a lot of white people out there, too. If America and Germany and Russia hadn't spent the whole century fighting each other, the subhumans wouldn't be causing us so much trouble now."

He seemed to lose interest in talking and concentrated

on negotiating the narrow trail, which sometimes clung precariously to the steep sides of ravines and was all but washed out in spots. Occasional buzzards cruised by overhead, but we never saw another person or another vehicle.

So they'd had Nick and Sibyl's motel room staked out? That would explain how they happened to be driving the Blazer. The lovebirds were, presumably, afoot. Or else they'd found alternate transportation. But if Jess and the other three had been on Fremont Street, who'd been watching their lodgings? This sort of speculation was ruining my nerves. Worry, I decided, was unworthy of an Aryan warrior like Gabe Treloar, who had plenty to worry him right here and now.

Marsh stopped while driving just below a ridge that looked like fifty others we had passed. He got out his map and studied it for a while.

"Grim, the highway should be less than a quarter-mile away, just on the other side of this ridge. Go on up there and see first of all if it's there, and second if there's any suspicious traffic on it."

Martinez took the binoculars and got out of the Blazer. It took him a few minutes to scramble to the top of the ridge, where he got down on his belly and crawled like an infantryman to the crest. There, he slowly raised his head, shading the binoculars with a folded road map to cut glare and prevent a betraying reflection.

"That's right out of the *Soldier's Manual*," I observed.

"Goes back at least to the Apache Wars and probably a hell of a lot further than that. Old techniques are usually good ones. If you want to stay in circulation, it's best not to overlook the details."

"How come you haven't killed me? Not that I'm objecting."

"Curiosity, mostly. I'm not really satisfied that you are what you represent yourself to be. I'd like the opportunity to question you with more time and resources at my disposal."

That sounded ominous, but I'd worry about it when the time came. Every breath right now was a good one.

"Also, I'm reluctant to kill white people who aren't proven traitors. Some of my men are a little too casual about pulling the trigger. I regard every white fighting man as a potential recruit. For a guy who's a little past his prime, you've done pretty good."

"Thanks, I guess. Where are we headed?" Abruptly, he backhanded me, his big knuckles landing right atop the gash made by Bergstrom's ring three days earlier in Albuquerque.

"You're alive on sufferance, Treloar. Be grateful and don't take advantage. That's a trait of Jews and mud people generally—they take advantage of Aryan softheartedness and generosity. I despise all such forms of exploitation. They lead to the tyranny of weakness and that's almost been the death of us already."

I just knew that the very last thing I should ever rely on was the natural, innate softheartedness of murderous lunatics with genocidal ambitions. The unreality of it all was truly dreamlike, but the handcuffs and the pain and the fear kept me thoroughly grounded. This was real and I had to escape, somehow.

Martinez skinned back down the slope. He got back in, dusting his jeans. "The highway's there. I saw a couple of trucks pass, three or four cars, but nothing that looked official."

"Then let's roll," Marsh said. "We've used up most of the day as it is."

He drove down to the end of the ridge, where the path looped around toward the highway. Three hundred yards beyond, at its nearest approach, Marsh drove off the path and onto ground that was a little rougher than the path had been. Then he was up a drainage berm and onto the road, heading west.

"Be dark soon," Martinez observed.

"Good," Marsh said. "Maybe we'll spot a UFO. There's a highway around here somewhere that's supposed to lead the world in UFO sightings." He turned his head slightly to include me in the conversation. "What do you think, Gabe? Are UFOs another manifestation of the approaching millennium?" I couldn't tell if he was serious. It was possible that he possessed a sense of humor, a rarity among ideologues, but Jess Marsh was not your garden-variety fanatic.

"Carl Sagan says they're more a matter of psychology than science. Especially the claims of abduction."

"Was that in *The Cosmic Connection*?" Marsh asked, all affability.

"I don't think so. I read it in an article in *Parade* magazine a while back."

"The press is all owned by Jews," Martinez informed me, glowering.

"Personally," Marsh said, "I believe they're for real. And they're sure to be hostile. Who're we going to call on when they invade? The UN?"

"You think it could happen?" Martinez asked.

Marsh looked at him. "Grim, you're entirely too literal."

Within an hour it was dark and I couldn't get my mind off those bolt cutters in back. They'd make short work of the handcuff chain if I could just get back there, drag them out of the canvas bag they were in, figure out a way to operate them with my hands behind me, and somehow accomplish all this without getting shot. It was something to occupy my mind while I was in the power of two insane ex-cons who wanted to kill everyone who wasn't white and, it seemed, most of the white people, too.

247

"Somewhere around here," Marsh said, slowing and studying the shoulders of the road carefully. Whatever he was looking for, it didn't seem to be a road sign. There were none in sight. After a few minutes he spotted some road mark invisible to me, because he checked to see if any other vehicles were in sight, then pulled onto the shoulder and killed his lights.

"Blindfold time," he said.

Martinez twisted in his seat. "Lean forward." I complied. He had a first aid kit open beside him. He placed gauze compresses over my eyes and secured them with a cloth sling.

"Just a precaution," Marsh said. "I don't think there's a chance in hell you could ever figure out where we're going, but, like I said earlier, you ignore the old techniques at your peril. We'll be meeting with some other people soon. From here on in, only code names are to be used."

"What's your code name?" I asked him. "I never heard it used."

"Grendel."

I was regretting not having paid more attention to the road markers we'd passed. I remembered the last couple of highway signs, but that had been many miles back, and I hadn't kept track of the mile markers. Then I thought: Had there *been* any mile markers? I tried to remember when I had last seen one.

Meanwhile, Marsh was driving off the road, creeping along, whether with his lights on or off I couldn't tell. The Blazer lurched for a while over rough, rutted ground, then the ride smoothed slightly as he pulled onto a road or track about the same quality as the one we'd taken from the ghost town. I couldn't tell much except that we took several turns and, judging by the faint pressure against my spine, we were climbing.

This went on for the better part of an hour. Eventually

we stopped. Marsh turned off the engine and a few minutes passed. Then I heard, very faintly, footsteps approaching from the left.

"You're Grendel?" said a quiet voice.

"Right. And this is Grim." There was silence for a few seconds, during which, I figured, they showed their Tyr tattoos as ID. A faint glow penetrated my blindfold. Someone was shining a flashlight in my face.

"Who's he?"

"A prisoner."

"I don't have orders concerning any prisoners."

"I'll be responsible for him," Marsh said.

"I don't know—"

"You want to dispute it?" Marsh demanded, a psychotic edge to his voice.

There was a moment of hesitation. "I guess not. The others got here a couple of hours ago. They're up at headquarters."

Without reply Marsh started up and drove on. The road was a winding one, and about five minutes later we stopped. A hand pulled my blindfold loose and Marsh was smiling into my face.

"I don't think we need this now."

We were in what appeared to be a box canyon with high cliffs all around. The area was blacked out, but I could see the vague shapes of a couple of buildings that seemed to be draped in something unrecognizable. A man appeared by the driver's door. I could just make out that he was dressed in desert-type camouflage fatigues and had an assault rifle slung over one shoulder.

"I'll show you where to park," he said, stepping out in front of the Blazer with a red-filtered flashlight. Marsh followed him into a tentlike feature where a half-dozen other vehicles were already parked. We got out of the Blazer and I saw that we were beneath a huge, artillery-sized camouflage net. That, I realized, was what draped the buildings as well. From somewhere near I heard the muffled chug of a well-maintained electric power generator.

"Not a bad setup," Marsh said, surveying the area.

"Yeah," I agreed, "it might be effective as long as your enemy doesn't have satellites that can spot a three-day-old heat signature from orbit."

"Put not thy faith in hardware, Gabe. Guts and will are what count. The Gulf War looked good on television, all those pretty rocket strikes. As fireworks displays go, it was hard to beat. But last time I looked, Saddam Hussein was still in office, fat and happy and not noticeably weakened. You know why?"

"Why?" I asked, even though I knew perfectly well.

"Because the U.S. had everything except the will to go in on the ground and finish it. They didn't want the voters to see the ugly, ground-level pictures that would be coming back along with the body bags. It was all an exercise in feelgood, nothing more. If that government isn't willing to get nasty, to let the voters see it with bloody hands, these people will win, satellites or no satellites."

We followed the red light toward one of the buildings and Marsh draped an arm over my shoulders.

"This isn't my personal style, the paramilitary stuff, uniforms and playing soldier, but the movement is a big one. It has room for a variety of styles and attitudes. Some of them are really strange, but the faces are white and we can settle the details after the war."

Two men with shotguns and night-vision goggles stood flanking the door and one of them pulled aside a blackout curtain. We went in and he closed it behind us. Marsh pushed aside the inner curtain and we walked through.

The building seemed to have only a single room and it was the size of a small warehouse. Electric lights hung from overhead beams, along with Coleman gas lanterns as backups. Roof and sides were of corrugated steel. It looked like yet another abandoned mining site.

I spotted a dozen other paramilitary types lounging about, all of them in camouflage fatigues, although several patterns were represented and their boots were even more individualized. All were heavily armed. Three men sat at a table and they didn't rise when we entered. Marsh walked over to them and threw a casual Nazi salute, not the stiff-armed *Sieg heil* variety, more of a not-quite-sloppy palm-forward type, the sort Hitler used to give in parades when his arm got tired.

"Death Troop Tyr," Marsh announced. "I'm Grendel, this is Grim, and the man in cuffs is our prisoner. He'll be with us when we leave."

The man seated in the middle replied with a regulation military salute. "Welcome to the cell. We hear good things about you. But we weren't expecting a prisoner." He looked to be in his middle fifties, gray hair and mustache, tanned and reasonably fit. It's impossible to make army BDUs look anything except sloppy, but his were clean and appeared to be tailored. His grooming was precise. He looked like a mid-level bureaucrat or police official, probably an ex-military officer. I could see the calculation behind his eyes. Sheltering fugitives who were holding a prisoner wasn't just playing soldier. It was abetting kidnapping. The thought didn't seem to stress him much.

"We're on a mission and it called for taking a prisoner. I'll be answerable for him. In the meantime, we need a place to get a few hours' secure rest. Like I said, we're on a mission and we'll be gone by morning."

"Your friends are over there." The commander nodded toward a line of cots that stood along one wall. Bergstrom sat on one; Leblanc lay on another with his face bandaged. Martinez had already joined them.

"Has the traitor been spotted?" Marsh asked.

"None of our people have reported seeing him as of yet," said the man to the commander's right. He was in his forties with curly brown hair and a long mustache. He favored a marine-style cap. "There's no all-points bulletin out on him, so he won't show up over the traffic." He gestured with a cigar toward a small folding table where a fatigue-clad kid, maybe sixteen, sat hunched over a laptop computer. "What we're getting is a lot of fuss over that stunt you pulled in Vegas. Between that and this prisoner of yours," he jabbed the cigar in my direction, "things are getting downright messy."

Marsh favored him with the marble-eyed stare. "It's going to get a lot messier before it's all over, and a lot of us are going to die before the end of it. You've got to show some balls if you want to win a race war."

The man with the cigar flushed. "Chasing down a white boy and his girlfriend don't sound much like a race war to me."

"It's all one war. I'll take whatever steps are necessary to eliminate a traitor."

The commander held up a hand. "Our organizations are in agreement on this. We'll cooperate in anything that serves our cause and doesn't weaken or unduly endanger us. You have your night's refuge. This state has the lowest population density of the lower forty-eight. If the traitor is still around, chances are good that one of our people will spot him before you leave."

"There's a bounty hunter named Jasper Holt dogging me. I encountered him in Vegas and I'd like him off my tail."

The brown-haired man grinned maliciously around his cigar. "I hate to be the one to tell you this, son, but you'll get the Angel of Death off your tail before you lose Jasper Holt."

Marsh turned away. "I guess I'll have to kill him, then."

I followed him to the row of cots. Leblanc had his right wrist and hand in a cast, a mass of bandages plastering his face and head. He groaned a little as he tried to roll onto his side.

"They got a doc here," Bergstrom reported. "He treated him, says he'll probably be okay. The worst was where the Ranger clobbered him upside the head with his pistol. The doc says he'll need a few weeks to rest and heal up."

Leblanc made it onto his side, facing us. "Can't stand. Can't hardly sit up, even. I get dizzy and puke." One blackened eye was swollen completely shut. The other studied me through a narrow slit, full of hatred. "You bring that motherfucker in so I can kill him?"

"Not just yet, and maybe not ever," Marsh said. "I think Gabe here can come to an understanding with us. But we'll take care of you. We should have this mission wrapped up in the next day or so. Then we'll go up north, stay for a while in one of the Identity camps. You'll get plenty of time to rest and recover. They're always generous to wounded heroes of the struggle."

Leblanc rolled onto his back again, groaning, too miserable to care about much, even revenge. "You mean we gotta listen to them crazy preachers yammerin' about how Jesus wasn't a Jew? I'd as soon listen to dogs barkin' up a tree."

"We all must make sacrifices. They may be boring but they're loyal and safe."

"Chief," Bergstrom said, "I'm not so sure about this place. I think some of these guys are cops. That one at the table with the cigar for damn sure is." I could see the source of his unease. Cops and cons weren't known to get along well together.

"Having a common enemy makes for some strange friendships," Marsh said. "And we've all had a lot of experience with police. What's the real difference between them and us? They chose a safer, more secure line of work, that's all. If we're to win this war, they have resources we have to have. Let's defer our differences until later." "You're the chief," Bergstrom said. Martinez nodded and Leblanc just groaned.

"Cuff Gabe to a bunk," Marsh said. "He'll never sleep with his hands behind him like that. I have to confer with our allies. Everybody get some sleep now. We're out of here before first light in the morning; that's part of the deal. They've got a good setup here and we don't want to screw it up for them." He got up and ambled away.

"C'mon, fuckhead," Martinez said. He led me to a bunk and gestured for me to lie down. When I did that he unclipped one wrist and refastened the cuff to a leg of the bunk. "You must be the luckiest fuck in the world. I don't know why you're still alive."

"Charisma?" I asked.

He patted my face. "You need to go out and use the can, let me know and I'll escort you."

I made an immediate decision to stay right where I was, no matter how uncomfortable I got. Some humor had seized Marsh with an impulse to keep me alive. The others would shoot me trying to escape.

I wondered how many safe places they had like this, spread across the nation. How many little paramilitary groups organized on a resistance-style cell system? How many compounds of religious Apocalyptics? It no longer seemed so strange how they could stay at large for such extended periods, although putting up with the company had to be difficult for men as paranoid as these.

And what was this group? I saw no Nazi regalia, and nothing to indicate religious orientation. Maybe they were tax protesters, or Western secessionists, or people worried about immigration or takeover by the New World Order. Maybe they were just middle-class guys who were bored and liked to play soldier in the wilderness. The important thing was that they had some sort of mutual assistance pact with the hardcores.

Eventually, to the murmur of low voices, the clatter of arms and the smell of gun oil, I managed to go to sleep. For almost a whole day, my own aches and pains had faded to the back of my consciousness.

What seemed like seconds later, Marsh kicked the foot of my cot. He continued down the line, kicking the other three.

"Get up and prepare to move out," he said. "The traitor and his bitch have been spotted. We're on our way north."

Seventeen

The desert stars were unbelievably bright overhead as we left the headquarters building. The moon had set, the area was blacked out and, in this place, so far from the light pollution of the cities, you could see the stars in a way that you never see them in a city on the clearest night. The Milky Way poured across the starscape like a pale river. In the middle of the compound Marsh stopped and gazed overhead. Bergstrom and Martinez, guiding the shambling Leblanc between them, looked up as well. Only Leblanc showed no interest.

"We should've been out there by now," Marsh said. "Colonizing the planets, moving on to the other stars. It's the white man's destiny. We made a good start, then we gave up, got sidetracked, lost the will." He shook his head ruefully. "Somebody decided it was more important to see that Israel soaks up American money, and then that Egypt gets a big annual bribe to leave Israel alone. Forget the destiny of white America. It's more important that nigger junkie bitches get paid to breed more snot-nosed little pickaninnies, not to mention providing refuge for Cubans and Mexicans and half the gooks in Asia."

"Breaks my heart, man," Bergstrom commiserated.

"Ah, well, somebody's gotta fix it, and I guess it's up to us. Grim, you drive the Cherokee with Gar in back, where he'll be comfortable. You need to stop to check his injuries or something, beep your horn twice. Scyld, you come with me in the Blazer. Gabe rides with us. Let's roll, brothers."

We crossed the compound to the big camouflage net. Two men were already there in an old army-style jeep. Marsh conferred with them while Bergstrom and Martinez helped Leblanc into the Cherokee, another four-wheel-drive design. Apparently they had ditched the van, which might have been filmed by surveillance cameras and, in any case, could never have negotiated these mountain trails.

"We'll be following the jeep," Marsh informed Bergstrom, as he joined us in the Blazer. "We're not going out the same way we came in. Light discipline all the way. They've got some glow-in-the-dark tape on their back bumper and we've got some on ours for the others to follow."

The jeep started up and crept out from under the net. When it was about fifty feet ahead, Marsh followed. We drove past the old buildings and the jeep disappeared into inky blackness, only an X of glowing tape to indicate that it was there at all. Either the driver was extremely familiar with the path or he was wearing night-vision goggles. They're like the old starlight scopes we used in Vietnam, magnifying any ambient light, such as moonlight or starlight, giving you a green-and-white TV image. The old ones were bulky, but like everything else they've been miniaturized and you can wear them now.

"I wish we had Humvees," Bergstrom groused, "instead of these glorified station wagons."

"They're adequate," Marsh said, "and they're anonymous. Some day soon we won't have to hide, and then we'll be properly equipped."

The sky was just turning gray when we came down out of the hills. The jeep drove into what looked like a tunnel, but in the growing light I saw that we were in a dry wash and overhead was a highway. The jeep stopped and Marsh pulled up beside it.

"This is Highway 359," the man seated next to the driver told him. "Hawthorne is about twenty miles north. Good hunting."

"Serve the race," Marsh said, throwing them a salute as he pulled away. He drove up a fairly steep dirt slope, then onto the highway in the northbound lane. A short while later he pulled into the parking lot of a good-sized convenience store outside Hawthorne. The Blazer stopped well away from the building, and the Cherokee pulled up next to it. Marsh sent Martinez in for coffee and food. He returned a few minutes later with a load of steaming cups and hot sandwiches.

"No highway patrol or local law around," he reported. "I didn't hear no buzz about us or anything much. People just talkin' about the weather and some basketball game last night."

"I'm happy to hear it," Marsh said, "but the level of consciousness of the American public is in a goddamn dismal state. It wouldn't matter if the race war had already started. Most people would still just watch TV and talk about sports and the weather."

"Doesn't it sort of make you wonder why you bother fighting for them?" I commented. Bergstrom aimed a punch and I was already fliching away from it when Marsh stopped him.

"No, the man has a point and it deserves an answer." He turned and faced me, speaking slowly and earnestly. "The white American public has been systematically emasculated and corrupted for the last fifty years. It wasn't all that hard to do. The instrument was the media, especially television. People sit like fucking barnacles in

258

front of the tube and their brains are turned to pudding. They see only the doctored version of the news allowed by the controllers. Israeli atrocities go unreported and unexamined, while any defensive action by the Palestinians becomes a crime against humanity. Not that I have any love for the Palestinians or any other Arabs, they're all just raghead sand niggers, but there ought to be some balance, don't you think?

"The only virtue encouraged by television is passivity. The only ideal it preaches is equality. Compassion is only for aliens, never for your own race brothers. They've been preaching it so long that nobody thinks it's unreasonable that we're supposed to feed starving niggers in Somalia and Haiti while our own cities turn to jungles. Every other nation in the world demands secure borders as a basic right of sovereignty, but the Zionist bloodsuckers who own Congress bawl that even so much as a hurricane fence along the Rio Grande is an insult to our little brown mestizo brothers to the south."

It was all straight from the gospel according to Douglas Tyler, the man who seemed to be able to give a cause to people no other cause would touch with a barge pole. I didn't bother to contradict Marsh. Somehow I sensed that he really wasn't looking for a debate.

"None of this is accidental, Gabe. It was all a part of a plan that got rolling at the turn of the century when the czars and the Hapsburg emperors finally had enough and shoved the Yiddish parasites out of their territories. It was a good thought, but most of them washed up here. They spent the first half of the century getting rich, gaining control of the press, then the radio networks, the banks, everything that would get them control without having to be visible, hold public office. They made sure that we went to war against the one enemy they really feared and supported the Bolsheviks in Russia.

"As soon as that threat was eliminated, it all fell into

their hands; their policies were instituted like a bunch of dominoes falling: integration, welfare, subordination to the UN, everything calculated to make white Americans weak and stupid. By the sixties we were instructed to cheer an Israeli victory like it was won by God personally. By the seventies Rhodesia and South Africa, where white people still ran things, were pariahs.

"And now?" He threw up his hands in frustration. "Most American white kids have no idea who Charles Lindbergh or Henry Ford were, but they worship nigger jocks who brag on television about how many white women they fuck. Then everyone's supposed to cry when they come down with AIDS. Those kids don't know anything about being white except they're supposed to feel guilty about slavery and the poor Indians. Makes me sick." He drifted off into a reverie for a moment, then snapped out of it and pointed at me, his eyes glittering.

"But! There are still a few white people ready to make a stand for themselves. People like the ones we stayed with last night. There are a lot more, all over the country. The white race isn't dead, it's just asleep. It's going to take a few wake-up calls to get the race roused, but we'll have plenty of support when they pry their eyes away from the tube and see what's all around them. When the knives are out, a lot of people are going to realize that they never really liked the greasers and niggers and kikes all that much."

"Was that what Oklahoma City was?" I asked him. "A wake-up call?"

He took a sip of his coffee. "That's damned good coffee. Yeah, it was pretty fucking impressive, but it was badly timed and not well thought out. One blast like that and a whole lot of new security goes into effect. If we're going to be effective, we need to set off fifty like that at once, along with a propaganda barrage to let people know what's really happening. It's going to take work."

"It sounds like this race war is going to kill most of the white people along with the rest."

He nodded. "I'm afraid so. But that will serve to purge a lot of degenerate elements from the race. A small population of high-quality Caucasians is infinitely preferable to any mass of half-white mongrels. And it'll be mostly males we eliminate anyway. Women are passive by nature; they don't need television to make them that way. They follow the alpha male by instinct. When they see the sort of men who bring about the new order, they won't regret the inferior males who had to die for the good of the rest. They'll want to breed the new race. You can rebuild a population fast that way."

I waited while they finished eating. They had a cause, and like a religion it explained everything, gave them a promised land as a reward for their efforts and, best of all, it sanctioned the sort of thing they liked to do anyway, which was kill and terrorize their fellow human beings. They were happy men.

"Scyld, you finished?" Marsh said, licking his fingers.

"Yeah," Bergstrom replied, wadding up greasy paper.

"Then uncuff Gabe and let him eat. But keep your gun on him. We don't want him to give in to any foolish temptations."

Bergstrom did as instructed. I took a long drink of the cooling coffee and followed it with a bite from a ham-and-egg sandwich. It went down well, reminding me of how long it had been since I'd eaten anything. But I felt the way I imagine a condemned man feels eating his last meal: grateful to have anything, but wishing it had been something better, since it was to be the last one.

"Jess," I said as I was finishing up, "please tell me one thing."

"What?" he said noncommittally.

"What the hell did they do? What could a pair of dipsticks like Nick Switzer and Sibyl do to be condemned as race traitors?"

His face turned as hard and bleak as desert stone. "They committed the ultimate sin against the race. They sold us hope. Now shut up." He turned to Bergstrom. "Cuff him."

I stayed silent as we drove on north. The last thing in the world I wanted to do was annoy Jess Marsh. I sensed that he was keeping me by him because, of all things, he was lonely. If his three friends were white and loyal, those were probably their only virtues in his eyes. They were as dumb and uneducated as so many sacks of cement. With me he had someone to talk to, someone who could understand and appreciate his thoughts and feelings.

Unfortunately, he was also crazy and unpredictable. It made him hard to play along with and I sensed that, if he should for a second think I was humoring him, my only hope would be that he would put a bullet through my head before it occurred to him to get out the power drill and the nails.

We continued north for a while, then turned west along a lesser road that was still dignified by identification as a state highway. Then north again on a smaller road, then west again along an even smaller one, still paved but graced by nothing more than a center line. From the time we left Highway 95 we were climbing.

I figured we must be near the California border by now. What we were climbing into was the Sierra Nevada, entering an area of mountainous redwood forest that was as beautiful as that long stretch of southwest Nevada had been ugly. Abruptly, I laughed. Bergstrom whipped around and trained his gun on me.

"I hope you don't think I look funny, man."

"No, it's just that, a while back, I was driving through the Petrified Forest, and now here I am in another Bogart movie."

He looked mystified and offended, but Marsh laughed. *"High Sierra!* That was a good one. Mad Dog Earle was always one of my favorite characters, almost a role model." He caught sight of something up ahead. "There's our viewpoint. I'm going to stop up there. Everyone take the opportunity for piss call. From here on in we'll be operating under strict patrol discipline."

A few second later he pulled into a little parking area with room for five or six cars. The slope above the road was densely wooded, the ground below the trees thick with an accumulation of pine needles. Below, the slope dropped away to reveal a breathtaking view of forested mountainsides and valleys dotted with jewellike lakes. I figured it was entirely possible that Marsh, bored with me, had decided to shoot me here. I certainly couldn't ask for a better last view.

We got out and I stretched as best I could. I turned to Bergstrom, who was just zipping up. "I can't unzip with my hands cuffed like this."

"Then piss in your pants."

"Scyld," Marsh said quietly. Bergstrom looked at him, then stepped behind me. There was a click and one hand was free but his gun was jammed into my spine. That would have been a good opportunity for me had he been alone. It lets you know exactly where the gun is. I might have whipped around, knocking it aside before he could pull the trigger, grabbed his jaw and the back of his head and broken his neck in an instant. It would have been worth a try.

But he wasn't alone. I couldn't have crossed the little lot before Marsh or Martinez put a bullet in me. Even if I'd managed to get hold of Bergstrom's pistol, Marsh and Martinez were standing too far apart for me to shoot them both in time and I couldn't even see Leblanc. Bergstrom cuffed my hands in front and stepped back.

"I ain't taking my eyes off you, man. Go ahead."

I stepped up to the guard rail and unzipped. Peeing was a great relief but I had other things on my mind. The trash barrel near the rail was full of empty film boxes, nothing of any use to me. The slope below was not perfectly sheer, but it was way too steep to run down. I'd be rolling the whole way and I judged I'd be going about a hundred miles an hour before I hit the jagged rocks at the bottom. So much for that. I zipped up and turned and as I did I saw a man walking out of the forest on the other side of the road and when I saw his uniform my heart lurched with sudden hope.

Then he walked to Marsh and began to talk, ignoring the gun Bergstrom held in plain sight. He was wearing a forestry service uniform, complete with Smokey the Bear hat, but he had removed his name tag. Marsh spread his map on the hood of the Blazer and the two of them went over it. After a few minutes of this the park ranger or whatever he was disappeared among the redwoods again, never once looking my way.

"They're about five miles from here," Marsh announced. "They're in a cabin on a little lake, just one road going in. There's a place about half a mile away from the cabin where we can hide the vehicles, then we wait awhile and go in the rest of the way on foot. Any questions?"

"Is it just the two of 'em in there?" Bergstrom wanted to know.

"As far as our local friends here can determine. They arrived sometime yesterday."

"How'd they get out of Vegas?" Martinez asked.

"They probably stole a vehicle. It's what any of us would've done. We don't know that anybody was specifically looking for them or us in all the confusion and we do know how good Switzer is at talking. It looks as if they're driving a brown Bronco now. Our allies are running the plates, but I doubt if it's important. Probably there's some fool sitting at a crap table in Vegas who won't notice his Bronco's gone till next week."

The hair at the back of my neck started to prickle. Brown Bronco? "Did you know they were coming here?" I asked, trying to steer Marsh in a different direction.

"I wasn't asking for your input, Gabe. You aren't one of us yet. Switzer told the other traitor, Jennings, that he was headed for 'a place not far from Tahoe.' Wasn't specific, of course. Scum like that don't even trust each other."

"Why didn't you just come here and wait for them?" I asked.

"Stake out a whole damn mountain range? What if he changed his mind? What if he was lying to Jennings? No, I wanted to catch them as quick as possible and make them talk, then put the nails to them."

"Why did . . . " I got that far before Martinez slugged me.

"Why don't you shut the fuck up? We got important work to do, right, Chief?"

Marsh looked at him a moment, then shrugged. "Put Gabe in with Gar and shackle his feet. Let's roll."

Bergstrom applied the leg irons. These boys went well equipped. Next thing I knew I was lying in the back of the Cherokee and Leblanc was studying me with one bleary, bloodshot eye. I hoped he felt as bad as he looked, because I was going to be alone with him, trussed up and helpless. They'd even run a length of chain through the rim of a spare tire and padlocked it through my leg irons, a variation on the old ball-and-chain to make sure I didn't kick out a window and wiggle off through the woods like a caterpillar.

The vehicles drove out of the little lot and back onto the road. Just a few minutes later we were on a side road and this one, from the sound the wheels made, was surfaced with gravel. Through the side windows and sun roof I saw trees growing right up to the road, their branches interlaced overhead. Then we pulled off the road, onto ground that made no sound beneath the wheels.

Martinez got out and shut the door. I heard the doors of the Blazer open and shut. I tried to struggle to a sitting position.

"What you doin' man?" Leblanc muttered, sounding reflexively hostile.

"Trying to see where we are." Where we were was a tiny clearing. It looked to me as if the vehicles would be invisible to anyone in a car passing by on the road, perhaps a hundred feet away. Marsh, Bergstrom and Martinez had the back of the Blazer open, taking things out. Much of it seemed to be weaponry of one sort or another. They all pocketed walkie-talkies.

"We go up and get 'em now?" Martinez asked, his voice muffled as it came to me through an open front window.

"No," Marsh said. "For now we go up and keep an eye on them. There's only one way out and we don't accost them unless they try to get out."

"Why's that?" Bergstrom asked.

Marsh just glared at him for a few seconds. "Let's go," he said finally.

Then they were gone and I was alone in the back of the Cherokee with Leblanc. He seemed to have subsided into an inert state, possibly unconscious. I considered the possibility that he had a brain hemorrhage and was dying. The prospect brought no tears to my eyes.

I tried to breathe slowly and steadily, through my nose, naturally. I tried some of the calming, heart-slowing meditation exercises California friends had tried to teach me. They had never tried it bound and chained, I was certain. The claustrophobia was beginning to get to me and I could feel the beginnings of panic nibbling away at the edges of my mind.

I had been a prisoner for at least twenty-four hours now, but until this time I had had immediate fears and problems to occupy my mind. I'd had torturing murderers pointing guns at me, my life hanging on their whim, wild schemes of escape to dream up, unexpected paramilitary networks to ponder, and that sort of immediate terror is actually easier to deal with than this uncertainty.

And at least I'd had Jess Marsh for conversation. He was really sort of a fascinating guy, if you could get comfortable with the fact that he was a homicidal sadist living in a racial superman fantasy. I'd known cops who held ideas no less nutty.

But now I was completely helpless, could only move inches in any direction, unable to do anything except wait for them to return, and what sort of mood might they be in then? What made it even worse was that I could see the wild freedom of the forest just a few feet away, beckoning. It was like the torture of Tantalus.

After a while my heart actually did slow down. Maybe I wouldn't have a stroke after all. I looked all around, twisting as well as I was able, looking for resources. Aside from a tire iron there seemed to be no tools in this vehicle, and I couldn't figure any way to use it as a lever.

"The fuck you doin' now?" Leblanc mumbled, sounding even more out of it than before.

"Trying to get comfortable."

"Good fuckin' luck." His head dropped again and he began to snore.

The others had been gone for more than an hour when I thought I heard a rustling outside. A raccoon? A bear? I had a vague memory that raccoons only came out after dark, not that it mattered a whole lot. The rustling got closer. Then my heart jumped, ruining all my meditative effort, when the tailgate jerked open and I was looking along the length of a shiny gun barrel. Back there behind

267

the sights were the hat and the grinning face of Jasper Holt.

"Well, hello, there, Christmas turkey! I see you're well in command of the situation."

"I was making progress," I told him. "I'd've been free in another five minutes."

"Well, what're we gonna do to speed things up? I'm fresh out of hacksaws."

"Bolt cutter in the back of the Blazer, unless they took it to cut a fence."

"No fences in these parts." He disappeared and was back in half a minute with the cutters. They made short work of the chains, although I would be wearing the bracelets and anklets for a while. That was a prospect I could live with, if I could just do it somewhere else.

I was beginning to climb for the back when Leblanc lurched up and tried to grab me. "What the fu—"

Moving coolly, Holt picked up the tire iron and smashed it into the side of his head with a sickening crunch. Leblanc fell back, mouth open, his one good eye rolling up to show only white.

"Christ, Jasper!" I said, sliding out onto the ground. "He was helpless!"

Holt tossed the tire iron on top of Leblanc. "When I was a boy, around ten or so, I was diggin' up fishing worms by the Sabine and all of a sudden there was a big ol' rattler right in front of me. I chopped it clean in two with my shovel. I was real proud of myself and I picked up the front half to take home and show off. Damned if the thing didn't whip right around and bite me. They're never helpless until they're dead, Gabe. Even then you have to watch out for them. Now let's go. And no talking."

I followed him into the woods, a little wobbly at first, but gaining strength and sureness by the second, as the debilitating sense of fear and helplessness faded. I was free, but in a wilderness full of enemies. My earlier humiliation was replaced by an atavistic, killer-ape urge. I wanted a gun and somebody in my sights.

Holt, incongruously, was still dressed in his cowboy boots and brown, Western-style suit, complete with string tie. In spite of this, he moved through the woods surely and easily, as if he was in his natural element. He walked without haste, pausing frequently to look all around and listen. I did the same.

The woods, which had seemed so dense from the road, turned out to be far more open than I had thought. The foliage of the trees met overhead, but the columnlike trunks were widely spaced and there was little undergrowth between them. The foliage shut off the sunlight from reaching lesser growth, I guessed. Beneath our feet the needle mat was soft and fragrant. Best of all, it kept our progress quiet.

We were climbing a slope, though I couldn't see far enough in any direction to guess any more than that. A wind blew through the trees, making them rustle in a way that was somehow different from the sounds made by any other trees I had ever heard. Maybe it was being where I was instead of where I'd been. Whatever, the effect was damn near magical. I felt like one of Tyler's hairy Nordic heroes, tromping through the woods in search of dragons.

That wind was also cold and I wasn't dressed for it, but so what? We toiled up a steep ridge where slabs of sharp-edged stone thrust through the surface in parallel rows, as if it had been turned up by a giant plow. Holt scrambled over these, agile as if he were thirty years younger and fifty pounds lighter. I went after him, my recent injuries not slowing me up excessively. The knee was working pretty well once more, I was pleased to note.

Like Martinez the day before, Jasper stopped at the top of the ridge, removed his hat and slowly raised his eyes above the crest. I bellied down next to him and did the same.

Down the far side of the slope, beside a beautiful little lake, stood a somewhat dilapidated cabin made of logs and roofed with shingles. Smoke drifted lazily from a stovepipe chimney. Even at a distance, I could smell the faint tang of the smoke above the pervasive pine-needle fragrance. Beside it was a familiar brown Bronco.

"Are they in there?" I asked him.

"They are, and they aren't going anywhere right away. What concerns me more is who else is out there."

"There are three of them," I told him. "Jess Marsh, along with Bergstrom and Martinez. I heard Marsh say that they were going to watch the place and wait for a while. I don't know why they aren't going in right away."

"I've got a pretty good idea," Holt said. "They're waiting for someone to show up."

"Reinforcements? What do they need help for? They're armed like a bunch of commandos."

"Not reinforcements, I don't think."

"Then what?"

"Too soon to speculate. Want to go say hello to your boss's little girl and her boyfriend?"

"Lead the way."

We worked our way along the ridge to a narrow ravine that cut through it. Down in the bottom of the ravine, we were concealed from view as we descended the slope.

"I caught up with them in Carson City. They'd hopped on the back of an eighteen-wheeler to get through the roadblock outside Vegas and that was its first stop. A local deputy who owes me a favor spotted them in a used car lot, shopping for cheap transportation. I drove right up and offered 'em a ride."

"My God, half the cops and other public employees in

the Western U.S. are working for you or one of the underground outfits." I told him about last night's militia group and today's forest ranger.

"Shocking state of affairs," he said, pausing to reconnoiter over the edge of the ravine, then coming back to the bottom. "Some doubtless are involved with both. Well, it's highest-bidder time now. We all want something, but you don't have anything to bid with so you've been playing lone wolf on this one. You want the girl, I want the swag and they want their traitor. And something else, it seems."

"What else is there?"

"I'll let them tell you."

We were almost at the level of the cabin now. The ravine cut just behind it, then ended at the lake.

"Is Tina holding them in there?"

"Actually, I was sort of hoping she was still with you, although considering your situation a few minutes ago, I'm just as happy she wasn't."

My head jerked around. "You mean she didn't contact you?"

"Nope. The woman is stubborn, as I suspect you've already noticed. She may be trying to play it alone." He shook his head. "Damn foolishness, but I guess if she wasn't all horns and rattles I never would've taken her on." He saw the look on my face. "Don't worry about her, Gabe. She sure as hell ain't worried about you."

The sun was low already, and when a cloud passed in front of it we made the short dash to the back door of the cabin. Holt yanked the door open and dashed inside with me on his heels.

"Keep clear of the windows," he said.

"Yeah, I learned that one a long time ago."

The cabin had only a single room, and it looked as if nobody had lived in it for some time except local wildlife. It was full of dust and cobwebs and the floor was spattered with bird droppings and the remains of nests that had fallen from the low rafters. One corner held an ice chest and some water jugs. The other held Sibyl and Nick Switzer.

The two of them were neatly cuffed, gagged and bound securely to a pair of solid-looking chairs. Somewhere, somebody was getting rich selling all those chains and shackles. Everybody seemed to be traveling with a ton of the stuff these days.

"I didn't expect to find them gift wrapped," I said. "Mind if I ungag them?"

"Be my guest." He stood well back from and to one side of a front window, scanning the treeline that circled the little lake. He crossed to the pile of gear by the ice chest and dug out a pair of bulky, powerful-looking binoculars while I untied Sibyl's gag. Then I untied Switzer's and I looked at them while they studied me warily. After all this time, all this distance and anticipation, I didn't know what to say to them. Finally, I had a try.

"Sibyl, I don't know if you remember me. My name is Gabe Treloar. Your father and I were in the LAPD together when you were a kid. My wife—"

"I remember you, Mr. Treloar," she said, as calm and self-contained as she looked in those pictures. "Your wife's name was Rose. She was a nice lady. She died a few years ago." Her tone was absolutely noncommittal, utterly devoid of affection or hostility.

"That's right. I'm with your father's agency now."

"I know. He mentioned it when you came to work for him. I take it he sent you after me."

"Hey, man," Switzer broke in. "She was just going along with my scam. It was sort of a class project for her, you understand? Will you tell that big-hat bastard over there that?" He was scared and jittery, but he said it all with the smile and sincerity that are a con man's stock in trade.

"Miss Carson's culpability is of not the slightest interest to me," Holt said. "I've told you that already. You should be figuring out how you're going to convince those people out there."

Switzer's face twisted. "Aw, man! We wouldn't be having this trouble if you hadn't been dogging us. We can work something out, can't we?" He looked at me with pleading, puppy-dog eyes. "Tell him, Gabe. This hardass act isn't necessary, is it?"

"First off," I said, "the DTT guys have had this area in mind since Memphis. Your friend Jennings talked. You know what they did to him?"

"Yeah, we read about it in the paper. It's the breaks, you know? Poor Pat."

"Poor Pat." I turned to Holt. "Jasper, what are we hanging around here for? We could load them up in your Bronco and make a run through the gauntlet down there. I'd be willing to risk it rather than wait for them to come in after dark. They've got serious firepower."

"Can't go just yet. We're waiting on a delivery."

"So you sent it on ahead?" I said to Switzer. "I thought you might do that. Zodiac Air Service again?"

"Yeah," Switzer said. "How'd you know?" He sounded genuinely interested.

"Secrets of the trade. Jasper, a delivery van coming up that road is probably going to get stopped."

"In that event I suppose we'll just have to take decisive action."

I looked at Nick. "Why this place? How did you find it?"

"I did some time in a juvie facility in San Francisco when I was around sixteen. A guy I was in with, name of Alvin Brubaker, told me about it. He was from Carson City; his folks came here for summers back in the sixties. We busted out of the place and hid out here all one winter. It was cold, man. But I liked the place, and it's so isolated. I figured it would be a good address to use."

"How did you know it would be deserted?" I asked him.

He shrugged. "I didn't. But we're both pretty good at making friends with people. I figured if anyone was here we'd just hang around and wait for the delivery. Should be along any time now."

I settled myself on the floor. "I guess we're going to be here for a while," I said. "Okay, Nick, Sibyl, tell me just what it was you pulled. You must be dying to tell someone."

"First off," Nick said, "you gotta understand, it was supposed to come off much cleaner than this."

I nodded. "Sure, some unforseen complications cropped up. I already figured that out."

He shook his head, smiling ruefully, just a charming young scamp. "Man, it was the sweetest con ever! And even a straight arrow like you would've approved, Gabe. These people are . . . "

I held up a hand. "No, Nick, that's Sibyl talking. She thought ripping off the bad guys would be fun and easy on the conscience. You, personally, don't give a damn who you rip off. You'll take a senile old lady's life savings if it looks safe and easy." The woman herself didn't look indignant at my slander of her paramour.

"Don't miss much, do you? Anyway, I'd known some of these guys, they've been around for years, and I never thought much about them. Then I met Sibyl." They smiled at each other, just young folks in love.

"And she told you what a great super-outlaw you were?" I prodded.

"Yeah, but more than that, she showed me that place where she worked! Took me on a tour of the place, and from that minute I knew we could use it—beautiful place, man, high-tech facility, all sorts of equipment looks like it belongs in the space program, refrigerators full of blood samples, the works. I knew we just had to make use of it and we worked up the scam."

"It wasn't difficult," Sibyl said, taking up the story. "Nick knew about these people; we'd discussed them during my interviews. At that time they had just been one among a number of bizarre subcultures inhabiting Nick's world."

"But with possibilities, man, real possibilities!" Nick said. "So we put it together. I know how to run a con, Sibyl knew psychology."

"Their driving motivations are sublimely simple," she said. "Fear, resentment, paranoia. Those are factors to be found in almost everyone's mind, but in them they are coupled to an almost total lack of critical thinking. It came down to finding something that they wanted desperately and wouldn't question too closely because of that very desire to believe."

"Just like selling used cars?" I said.

"There you go, man!" Nick said. "That urge to believe has been the con artist's strongest ally since before fire was invented. We studied up on them and it didn't take long to pinpoint what they desired above all things." He was wiggling around in his chair like a delighted child telling the grown-ups what a good boy he'd been.

"You see," he said, "that lab was doing AIDS research, but it struck me the first time I saw it that you'd have to be a blood scientist yourself to know that. I mean, there were no signs saying, like, 'AIDS research in progress' or something. It was a super-impressive lab, but the people there might have been doing *any* kind of research, as long as it involved blood samples. Tell me, Treloar, have you ever seen the inside of a biological warfare research facility?"

"I confess I haven't."

He grinned. "Well, hardly anybody has! So I became a

mad scientist and the place where Sibyl worked became my secret laboratory."

"You had your own set of keys?" I asked Sibyl.

"Oh, yes. There was no sort of security there. The lab didn't do any work with live HIV, nothing like that. It was strictly blood research parceled out by the CDC in Atlanta."

"So I made contacts and let it be known that I was a fellow traveler of the white underground, doing research that would be of great interest to them, if they had the balls for it." He grinned cockily again. "Wasn't long before I had some feedback, man."

"What was your pitch?"

"We let them know," Sibyl said, "that we were developing a blood-borne disease genetically targeted to kill nonwhites."

I should have tumbled to it much earlier: the blood lab, the Nordic getups they affected, the weird mentality of Tyler's publications. Tina had said that it all came back to that lab.

"And," Nick went on, "we were getting close to a working virus, absolutely guaranteed to kill every black, Asian, Aborigine, Indian, whatever, on the planet."

"People have been so sensitized by AIDS and the other new diseases like Ebola," Sibyl said, "it's surprisingly easy to believe."

"Only one little problem stood in our way," Nick said.

"You needed more money to finish your project," I said.

He nodded. "That's right. Seems we were at the very end of our funding, which, it turns out, dried up when the Zionist-controlled government in Bonn crushed our support cell of loyal Nazis. They ate it up. But of course they wanted to see the lab. We held them off, naturally. Didn't want to seem too eager. But finally we agreed, as long as they accepted our security arrangements. We drove them in two or three at a time, blindfolded. You should have seen the setup we had, man, just slick as hell."

"The building is on a slope," Sibyl said. "It's two-story, but when you drive up to the front it looks like a single-story building. The ground slopes away to the back, where you can get to the lower floor. It has a loading dock and the way into the truck entrance is blocked by a gate."

"So we drove 'em in the back way, took off their blindfolds just as we reached the gate. I'd called in Pat Jennings for backup. We built a fake guard shed, the whole thing put together with hinges so we could fold it up and carry it on a pickup. Got so we could put it up or take it down in less than three minutes."

So that explained the lumber and hinge purchases. Then I remembered the expensive security guard's uniform I'd seen in Jennings's house. "And poor old Pat was the guard?"

"Right. We'd stop and he'd come out with his flashlight and go, 'Good evening, Dr. Gerhard. All secure,' and we'd go in. Once in the lab, you should've seen their eyes bug out. All we needed to do was take down a few signs and hide some notepads. I took 'em all around, explained with a lot of fake-medical gobbledygook about how we had tailored our viruses to attach themselves, for instance, to the gene that controls sickle-cell anemia, some other stuff like that. Hell, I could've said that we'd discovered the secret of eternal youth, they wouldn't've known the difference."

"Except that wasn't what they wanted to hear," Sibyl said. "They wanted a disease to kill nonwhites and that was what we sold them. Jennings created some special software for us. We showed them our computers and ran the program. It looked as if we were tapped into the data system of the Human Genome Project. That's the project that is going to map every last bit of human genetic material."

"I know what it is," I told them.

"We convinced them that we were able to determine, genetically, what made one person African, or Chinese, or whatever," Switzer said, still delighted with the sheer brilliance of it all. "And that we could tailor a fatal disease for each one of them. Of course, Tyler wanted one to target Jews."

"You talked to Tyler personally?"

"Oh, hell yes! He came with the second group, after he'd been assured that we were for real. I told him that the Jew-killing disease would take a little longer since, genetically, Jews were closer to real white people than the others. He didn't like it but I think it was that little bit of disappointment that convinced him to throw in with us. You have to have a feel for that little extra bit of believability if you're going to play the game right."

"And you were his Aryan assistant," I said to Sibyl. "Blond wig, blue contacts, German accent and all. Suppose they'd called you on the accent?"

"I'm fluent in German," she said. "It was so strange—in playing that role, I felt like a real, complete human being for the first time."

"You're just a natural, honey," Nick assured her.

"How much did you ask for?" I asked him.

"We told them that about a million ought to see us through the first stage, get the African-and-Asian killer into circulation, maybe need more later on."

"But you left it up to them to figure out how to get that money?"

"Well, hell yes! It's the American way."

"You didn't know they'd raise it by hijacking a major mob drug buy."

"Well, how the hell *could* I know? It's not like I'm deep in their councils! Those guys are crazy, man! Stark, staring bugfuck! They'll do things no professional heister would ever dream about."

Jasper left the window and rejoined us. "In their own odd way they see themselves as men of virtue. They need to raise money for this laudable project, so they attack drug dealers, another alien evil, to their way of thinking. Why not let one enemy finance their war against another?"

"What Ollie North would call a neat idea," I said.

"Gabe," Holt said. "Come over here with me." I followed him to the window and stood well back in the shadows. He handed me the binoculars. "Looky over there, on the other side of the lake." Following his gaze I could see a car parked there, and men grouped around it.

I raised the heavy glasses to my eyes. They were expensive, with superb optics. The image was highly magnified and incredibly clear. With its small field of view it took me a few seconds to find the car, then to see the men. Marsh was there, along with Martinez and Bergstrom, and two men I didn't recognize. All seemed to defer to a tall, stooped figure whose back was to me. Then he turned and seemed to stare straight into my lenses. He was graying, distinguished, with an ugly-handsome face, like Lincoln's. It was a face I'd seen a good deal of lately, on the inside cover of every issue of the "National Guardian."

"I'll be goddamned!" I said. "If it isn't Douglas Tyler, the Rupert Murdoch of the White Power movement!

Eighteen

I don't get it," I said, lowering the glasses. "Tyler's the idea man, the theorist. He keeps his hands clean, just sits at home and punches his keyboard. What brings him out into the sunshine and fresh air?"

"He's scared," Holt said. "He wants to personally assure that he's going to be safe."

"So it's not just the money and it's not just executing traitors," I said. "What is it, Nick? Pictures? Tapes?"

"Both, actually," he answered. "The lab had a video setup. It wasn't for security, it was for recording experiments and stuff. We just rigged it to record our transactions. Just to be safe, you know?"

"Yeah," I said. "I can see how safe it made you."

"Marsh was bodyguarding him when we brought him in," Sibyl said. "We recorded them both going over the possibilities, the ins and outs of the project. Tyler is fond of statistics, and he has a statistician's obsession with detail: how to dispose of so many corpses, how to take maximum propaganda advantage when the plagues begin, how to steer public opinion against the victims, that sort of thing, all very anal."

"It should bring up some interesting legal points," I

mused. "Is conspiracy to commit genocide a crime when the mechanism is a hoax?"

Holt barked a short laugh. "Are you serious? It works for sting operations every day. Believe me, any prosecutor who craves a few hours of exclusive TV time is gonna come down on these boys like a chicken hawk. Can you imagine what sort of suicidal fool would stand up and defend them? They'll be put away for a thousand years. Prison's a familiar milieu for Jess and his buddies, but I'll bet Mr. Tyler don't relish the idea of being locked up with some of his least favorite minority groups. It won't be quite like Adolf's little nine-month stretch at Landsberg."

"Did they talk over raiding the drug buy?" I asked.

"Not in specific detail," Sibyl said. "Tyler said a million would be a minuscule price to pay for such a glorious result. Marsh told him that he knew where some big money would be moving soon, that he could put together a team to take it, but it would bring on serious heat. Tyler said any sacrifice was justified in the cause." She sounded like an old pro.

"It could be enough," I said. "There were bodies all over the place after the Charleston raid and its aftermath: known associates of Marsh and the others, runic tattoos."

"Drugs and money and dead thugs." Holt snorted. "Nobody's gonna give a damn about that, except, of course, my client and his cohorts. You know what's dancing around in Tyler's head right now? Some federal prosecutor named Goldberg with Judaic vengeance in his eye and the whole might of the international Zionist conspiracy behind him. He's got to get those tapes back and kill these two here." He waved at the bound couple, smiling at them. "I just want the money, Nick, remember that. I'm your friend."

"Nick and I have no friends," Sibyl said with what sounded almost like satisfaction. "Just each other."

"You have a father who's sick with worry about you,"

I said, unable even now to believe that she was as unconcerned as she sounded.

"Is he? Just what is he worried about, Mr. Treloar? Is it my safety? Or is it because I ran away with one of society's rejects? Is he just unable to understand that I could escape, be happy with an outlaw, *as* an outlaw?"

"He knows," I said, "that with Nick you have two prospects. You die young, or you live a long time in prison."

"I'm prepared for that fate," she said. "I'm not Daddy's good little girl anymore. I never was, really. It was how he saw me and it was a comfortable role to play. It got so there were extended periods when I thought that was really me. But Nick took me out of that middle-class existence and showed me the real world, the one beyond good and evil. It's like breathing pure air for the first time. I love my new life, Mr. Treloar, even if it has to be brief."

"What did I tell you?" Holt said. "Too much Nietzsche, too early. It's a bad combination."

She examined him like some lower life form. "Oh. I see you have intellectual pretensions."

He smiled, removed his hat and scratched the side of his head. "What I have, young lady, are intellectual and lifetime *accomplishments,* things you not only lack but are highly unlikely to achieve. If you'd read old Friedrich Wilhelm more carefully, you'd've come across a better fresh-air analogy than yours: 'Those who can breathe the air of my writings know that it is a strong air. One must be made for it. Otherwise, there is no small danger that one may catch cold in it.' "

He put his hat back on. "That's from the preface to *Ecce Homo,* a late work. I guess you never got past *Zarathustra.* You were never made for strong air and you, honey, done caught one god-awful cold."

"And what do you believe in, Mr. Holt?" she asked. "What is the credo of the bounty hunter?"

He grinned. "I believe the one irrefutable constant in the universe is the speed of light. And I believe the only thing really worth having is personal freedom. In America, if you protect rich people's money, you get to do pretty much as you like."

I got up from the floor, my knee working nicely at last, and walked over to the window. The men were still waiting around the car, one or two of them observing the cabin through binoculars. Somebody was setting up a spotting scope. One of them, it appeared to be Marsh, was readying a high-powered rifle with a scope.

"Stay way the hell back from the windows," I warned. "They're preparing a sniper position with a marksman and a spotter. Jasper, do you have your cellular phone handy?"

"Why do you ask?"

"I want to call my boss. He's in Vegas by now, with some hired muscle. If they plan to wait us out, there's a chance he could get up here in time to do us some good. He can hire a helicopter in Vegas, land it right in front of us in a couple of hours."

He shook his head. "Be dark in a couple of hours and no fool's going to land a chopper in these mountains after dark. We have a low cloud cover moving in, if you haven't noticed. It may snow."

"Then they can drive in," I said. "It'll take a little longer, but they could get here in time."

"Nope. Ain't my style to call in reinforcements." He had his revolver out, checking it. It was an old-fashioned six-shooter, nickel plated, with a grip of mellow old ivory.

"Jasper, you were last a Texas Ranger when LBJ was still vice president!"

"Gabe, it's at moments like this that personal style counts the most. No calling in the cavalry. It would attract official attention and neither of us wants that, do we?"

"We're a little beyond such considerations," I said. "Give me the goddamn phone!"

"Loosen up a little, Jasper," Switzer pleaded. "We can always cut a deal with Carson, maybe even with the law." I saw Sybil cut a look at him, not altogether approving. "But nobody can deal with a freak like Jess Marsh. Let him call."

Holt unclipped the phone from his belt and looked at it a moment. Then he dropped it to the floor and stomped on it, the heel of his cowboy boot shattering it to a multitude of fragments.

"Well, hell," I said. "I've never been in the company of so damned much integrity and personal vision. Between the three of you, and Marsh and Tyler, I've lost track of rational thought entirely!"

"And what brings you here, Gabe?" Holt asked.

I thought about that. It wasn't just the job. I'd undertaken this task outside the bounds of my normal work, as a personal favor. "Obligation," I said. "I owe Randall Carson. And my wife liked Sibyl. Sibyl was a lot younger then, of course."

"There you are," Holt said. "Obligation, responsibility, guilt. They're the little hobgoblins that control and direct most people's lives. But don't feel too bad. If you haven't chosen the path of perfect freedom, at least you honor your obligations to the ultimate extreme. It's the sign of a superior man, like the forty-seven loyal *ronin* in the Japanese story."

"My vision doesn't preclude making a goddamn phone call for help."

A sudden, shocking *crack* made me flinch and duck as an old, wall-hung mirror smashed. The sound was followed by the fading rumble of the shot, fired from the other side of the little lake.

"They're not out to kill us just yet," Holt said. "Just lettin' us know that they can."

So we waited for a while, contemplating one another without a whole lot of mutual affection. Even Nick and Sibyl seemed to be alone with their thoughts. Nick's weren't hard to guess. He was already feeling the nails. I didn't have the heart to tell him about the power drill. Sibyl I couldn't figure out at all.

"You people in there!" The voice was deep, slightly distorted by the bullhorn that amplified it. "Come to the window. We promise not to shoot. There is something out here you should see." It was Tyler's voice.

"Yeah, right," I said. I glanced across at Holt. He looked uncharacteristically concerned. "They'll blow our heads off if we look out," I told him. "You and I are just in the way."

"Yep," he said. "That's why Nick's going to look." Keeping low, he went to Switzer and scooted him, chair and all, to a front window.

"You can't do that!" Sibyl protested.

"Whyever not?" Holt said. "Now, Nick, don't you worry. They aren't gonna shoot you because Marsh is determined to crucify you. What do you see?"

"Uh, I can't tell. There's two cars over there, and a couple of guys are holding somebody, looks like a kid. No, not a kid." A smile spread across his face. "Hey! I think it's that woman who jumped on Marsh and put a blade to his throat, back in Vegas!"

"What!" Holt snatched up his binoculars and knelt behind Switzer, aiming the lenses across his shoulder. "Damn! They got Tina!"

"How—" Then it came to me. "Tyler has a network of sympathizers all over the area. Tina drove away in my car. Last night, Marsh must've given those militia crazies her description, along with the car's description and license number. They've been on the lookout for her. We were headed for Tahoe when they bushwhacked me. Maybe that's where some local cell caught her."

"The logistics ain't important," Holt said impatiently. "What counts is they got her and we have to get her back."

"Let me look." I low-crawled to the back of Nick's chair. Holt ducked and passed me the binoculars.

"You two look ridiculous," Sibyl said.

I worked the focus wheel. "Honey, if you're going to live the outlaw life, you'd better be willing to suffer worse indignities than this from time to time."

"Hey, guys," Nick said, sounding dry-mouthed, "I feel awful exposed here."

"Son," Holt observed, "in your position a bullet in the head would be a blessing from heaven."

Tina stood between Martinez and Bergstrom. She wasn't struggling or being otherwise foolish. The binoculars brought her up close enough so I could see the bruise spreading across a cheekbone. Two men were talking to Marsh, apparently the ones who had nabbed Tina. One of them had his forearm bandaged from wrist to elbow. They were standing by my old Pontiac. It was parked next to a new, black Lincoln, and a few seconds later the two men got into the Lincoln and it drove away. I couldn't see the driver, but I could see the two men who had come with Tyler. I informed Holt of this development.

"He wants to restrict this to him and the DTT boys," Holt said.

Marsh took the bullhorn. "Ranger! Our friends ran the plates on that Bronco and we know it's yours. Gabe," he held up a handful of the chains Holt had cut off me, "I also know you pulled a Houdini on us. It was real slick and please accept my compliments. But it was very unwise, and now we have your lady friend."

"They think Tina's with me," I told Holt.

Now Tyler took the bullhorn. "Jasper Holt! I am informed that you are some sort of bounty hunter. I believe we can come to an accommodation. Your concerns are mercenary. Mine might be termed racial. Neither of us has any use for the law or its minions, are we agreed on that?"

I was watching the men behind him. Bergstrom was holding a pistol on Tina. Marsh had gone back to his rifle and Martinez was now holding a stubby submachine gun.

"Keep them talking," I said to Holt. "That rifle's our biggest worry, but it's getting dark and I think I see a few snowflakes blowing around. It's useless to them in the dark."

"What's your pitch, Mr. Tyler?" Holt shouted.

"I see you know who I am. I suppose the traitors have been boasting. I want them, Mr. Holt. And I want certain videotapes, recordings and perhaps photographs in their possession. Those things are not negotiable. The money, of course, is."

"Don't believe him, man!" Switzer said, his voice choked with anxiety. "They're not negotiating anything! They plan to kill us all and keep the money!"

"He knows that perfectly well, Nick," Sibyl admonished. "Don't degrade yourself by begging."

"Baby, you're not the one sitting here tied to a chair with Jess Marsh studying you through a goddamn sniper scope!"

Holt nodded to me and I dragged Switzer's chair away from the window. He smiled sheepishly but she was glowering. Their first lover's spat, I figured.

"Gabe and me need to talk," Holt told them. "Come on out back, Gabe." He started for the rear door.

"You can't leave us here tied up like this!" Switzer said. "It's just the money you want anyway. Let us loose and give me my gun at least!"

"All in good time," Holt said.

"They may have people out in back watching," I said.

"Not likely, the way they been playing this. It's near dark anyway. We'll jump for the ravine. Come along, now."

With that he dashed through the door with me close on his heels. Seconds later we were in the bottom of the ravine.

"So what did you want to talk about that you don't want them to hear?" I asked him.

"Actually, there ain't much to talk about. Here." He reached into the back of his belt and came out with a big, flat .45 automatic, just about identical to the one I had packed around Saigon in 1968. The hammer was cocked, the thumb safety set. "It's got a full clip and one up the spout. Eight shots, that ought to be plenty."

"Plenty for what?"

"We're gonna go down there and get Tina," he said simply.

"Are you crazy? Two of us with outdated pistols against that bunch?"

"There's only four of 'em, and Tyler don't amount to nothin'."

"Great. That leaves three homicidal wackos with enough automatic firepower for a revolution. Nothing doing, Jasper."

Abruptly, shockingly, he reached out and gripped my shoulder hard. "Gabe, you have *got* to help me on this." His eyes pleaded even more urgently than his voice.

Then I understood. "My God, Jasper. You're in love with her!"

"Do you find something objectionable in that, Gabe? You've never been in love?"

"Well, sure, but—I can't believe this! Jasper Holt in love! What a concept!"

"And there ain't a damned thing I can do about it. Now are you gonna help me, goddamnit?"

"If we get killed, they get Sibyl."

"Surely you cannot nurse any lingering affection for that girl!"

I shook my head. "Not now. But if she dies it'll break Randall Carson's heart."

"Hell, it's gonna break his heart when he finds out what she's turned into. And if you're really worried about her, the best thing you can do is go back in there and put a bullet through her head. Otherwise, your only prayer of keeping her safe, and mine of getting Tina back, is both of us go down there and kill those bastards just as fast as we can."

The snow was falling steadily now, but I didn't notice the cold. "All right. But we do this my way."

"What's your way?"

"Come on." I started to climb from the ravine.

"Where you goin'?" But he followed me back to the cabin. Having the upper hand over Jasper Holt was a new experience. He needed me. I was glad that someone did, for a change.

"Don't be deceived by the dark, children," I said as we went back in. "It's high-noon time. Jasper, where's the gun they took off that Arizona cop?"

"Here." He took it from his belt, beneath his coat. He'd been carrying enough iron to draw lightning.

"Is there any ammo left in it? Nick was shooting up a storm in Vegas."

"It uses the same as mine, three-fifty-seven."

"Then load it up. Then turn Sibyl loose."

"What you got in mind?" Holt demanded.

"Just do it." While Holt attended to that I bent and whispered in Switzer's ear. "You don't want her to know what a slimy little piece of shit you are, do you, Nick? Here's your chance to live up to her outlaw fantasy. Just follow my lead. You know how to do it."

"What are you doing?" Sibyl said, no longer quite as self-possessed as she had been.

"I want you to go out that back door and get away

289

from here. Take the ravine and go uphill. Just keep on going. You'll get to civilization eventually. Then call your father's office. Delilah will tell you how to reach him in Vegas. I told Randall I'd get you back to him alive and it looks like this is the only way it's going to happen. Nick's going to help us settle with those people."

"I won't leave Nick!" she insisted.

I prodded his back and he turned to her, grinning. "Sure you can, baby. You just run like he says. Gabe's gonna turn me loose and give me my gun back. We'll fix their butts and I'll join you later on. We lose the bundle this time, but we're still young! We'll go somewhere else and do it again, only better next time. A team like us, how can we go wrong?" I had to hand it to the little bastard, he was playing it out right to the end.

"No more stalling!" Marsh's voice this time. "In three minutes we start cutting pieces off this woman!" It was already too dark and too snowy to see the other side of the little lake.

"Wait!" I bellowed as loud as I could. "We're coming down to talk!"

"Bring the traitors and the goods."

"Okay, let Nick loose." Holt grumbled but did as he was told. When Nick was free and standing, Sibyl rushed, sobbing, into his arms.

"Time's up," I said. "Sibyl, go."

"Run along, honey," Nick told her. He spun her around and nudged her gently toward the door. She looked around, saw his confidently smiling face, sobbed and rushed out.

"Hang on a sec," Nick said. He went to the pile of stuff by the cooler, got his hat and his long Aussie coat and put them on. "All right, I'm ready now. Give me my gun." In two minutes he'd psyched himself into the role. It was something to see.

"Not yet. Drape the cuffs over your wrists like you were still bound." I stuck the extra pistol beneath my belt in back. "You can get this when the fun starts, and try not to put a hole through my back in your eagerness."

"How do you plan to play this?" Holt said as we walked out of the cabin.

"Nick, you stay just behind me to the left. Jasper, you stay just behind him and to the right. Are you as good as people say you are?"

"I'm a fair hand."

"Bergstrom has to go first. He's got a gun to Tina's head. But they think she's my woman so he'll be watching me. As soon as we're close enough, put one through his head. No talk, no negotiating."

"Suits me fine," Holt said.

"What about me?" Nick asked.

"When Jasper shoots, grab your gun and shoot Marsh."

"And you?"

"I'll be shooting Marsh, too."

"Hell, it's that little pockmarked bastard that's got the machinegun!"

"Jess Marsh with a rock worries me more than any number of idiots with machineguns."

I'd been pushed too hard and there were sharp pains radiating from my knee, but the adrenaline overrode all else and I knew I could function for a while longer. But I knew that I wasn't up to anything athletic, no dodging or running. I was going to have to go in standing up and finish the same way, if at all.

The shapes of four men and a small woman became visible through the dimness and falling snow, shockingly close already.

"You got the stuff?" Marsh demanded.

"What stuff?" I said. "Oh, the money and tapes and

stuff? It hasn't been delivered yet. Probably be along to-morrow, I guess."

"Huh? Okay, hold it right there."

But we kept coming. Bergstrom had his pistol to Tina's head, his eyes flashing to me, then to Marsh, then back to me. Tina just watched Holt calmly.

"Hey!" Even as Marsh spoke Jasper drew and fired. I never saw his hand move but the gun roared, Bergstrom's head snapped back and his silver pistol went flying. Tina dropped faster than Bergstrom, flattening as swiftly as if she had been hit with the same bullet.

Marsh raised his massive pistol as I jerked my automatic clear and simultaneously felt the revolver slip from my waistband. Switzer was young and swift, and I knew that he lined up on Marsh first because the muzzle of the big gun swung from me to him and the blast of the .44 came instantaneously with Nick's first shot and the sudden, nervous chatter of the submachinegun. From my peripheral vision I caught Holt standing there, ignoring all the fireworks, pistol at full extension, one-handed in the old way, putting another neat shot through Martinez's forehead. The automatic weapon shut off instantly.

I already had my .45 out, firing as fast as I could. I knew I was hitting but Marsh was still on his feet, still firing, his shots going wilder with repeated jolts to his nervous system. Pistol bullets don't knock people off their feet like you see in movies. Shock and blood loss do the work.

Marsh's gun arm lowered, as if the pistol had suddenly grown heavy. Then he dropped to his knees and he looked at me resentfully.

"Shit, Gabe. We could've been friends. I thought you were a white man." He toppled face-first to the ground and lay there unmoving. Holt, doubtless remembering his childhood rattlesnake, put a final round through the back of his head.

I looked around. Something was missing, then I knew what it was. "Where's Tyler?"

"Over there," Tina said, getting to her feet and brushing off. Tyler lay beside my car, staring up at nothing.

"Jasper, you shoot him?" I asked.

"Wasn't me. Tina, you all right?"

"I guess. How 'bout you?"

"Fine. Martinez must've sprayed him by accident. Excitable little bastard."

I checked myself out. I'd been shot before, and sometimes you don't feel it at first. I turned. "Nick, how about—" He was standing there, the gun hanging at his side, a silly smile on his face. I took the pistol. "Nick, you've been hit. You're going to have to sit down so I can check you out."

"I know," he said. "Two or three times." He turned to Holt.

"Pretty good, Jasper! He had a machinegun and you got him with a pistol. I never would've believed it."

"Yeah, he was missing me real fast. Son, you'd better do what Gabe says." He took one of Nick's arms and I took the other and we lowered him to the ground. Tina peeled away his coat and shirt.

"Jasper, get in Gabe's car and put the headlights on us," Tina ordered. Seconds later we were bathed in light and saw the three thumb-diameter holes in his chest. Taking three big slugs like that and remaining on his feet was a tribute to the power of adrenaline.

With a wailing cry Sibyl rushed into the beam of light, pushed Tina aside and cradled Nick in her arms.

"How fast can we get an ambulance up here?" I asked Holt.

"Forget it," Tina said, digging out her cigarettes and lighter. "That boy's got two, three minutes and you know it. Let him go. Jasper, you get it?"

"Seems delivery's running a little late. We may have to wait a while."

"Great," she said disgustedly. "We'll freeze our butts off."

"Let's go on up to the cabin," he said. "There's plenty of firewood. Gabe?"

"I'll be along shortly," I told them. "You go on." They walked back toward the cabin, Holt's arm draped across her shoulders, hers around his substantial waist.

I walked over to Sibyl. She was saying something to Nick, and his lips were moving, but his eyes were focused on something about half a mile overhead. His face was as pale as the snow falling on it. Then his lips stopped moving.

I squatted by Nick and looked across his corpse at her. She was soaked with his blood and, in the usual, unromantic fashion, his bladder and bowels had voided.

"Well, Sibyl, here's the reality. This is what it looks and smells like."

She glared at me, her eyes red and swollen, hair snarled. "He did it for me, you bastard! He went out and died for me and you and that hired killer don't have a scratch!"

I didn't bother to tell her any different. What would be the use? Hell, maybe he *had* died for her. I'd never fathom his mind or hers. I was more than a little scratched, though.

"I'll go up and get the Bronco," I told her. "We can take him up to the cabin. Can't stay here all night, anyway." She didn't say anything as I turned and limped up toward the cabin. First, though, I turned off my car's headlights. I didn't want a dead battery in the morning.

It was bright and clear, the sky overhead incredibly blue, almost a foot of blinding snow on the ground when the delivery truck came rolling toward the cabin, snow flying from its chain-wrapped tires. Holt and I walked down to meet it and the long-haired guy behind the wheel flashed a bright smile at us.

"Hey, guys! I spent half the day yesterday trying to find this place! Had to give up when it got dark. One of you guys"—he checked his clipboard—"Nicholas Switzer?" He never even glanced toward the four odd humps of snow by the lake.

"That's me," I said, beaming. I signed Nick's name on the sheet and accepted delivery of a bulky package.

"Sorry about the delay, man," the deliveryman said, "but I get 'em all through sooner or later. Neither rain nor storm, snow—whatever."

"No problem," I assured him. "We didn't need it yesterday, anyway."

"Take care, man." He made snow fly again as he backed in a half circle, then drove away in his own twin tracks. Holt and I turned and trudged back up the hill.

"Is there really a million dollars in here?" It was heavy, but it didn't seem *that* heavy.

"There better be," Holt said. "Or pretty near." He looked up the hill, where Tina was loading their things into the back of the Bronco. He beamed at her. "Let it be a lesson to you, Gabe. It's never too late even for a crusty old Ranger to find love. Maybe you oughta give it a try."

"I'll keep it in mind."

When we got to the Bronco, I set the parcel onto the back deck and Holt cut through cardboard and tape with a pocket knife. Inside were nestled stacks of hundred-dollar bills, far more of them than I had ever seen before.

"Can we go now?" Tina said.

"In a minute, honey." Holt fished out an envelope and there was a videocassette inside. He handed it to me. "You want this? I got no use for it."

"I'll take it."

295

"You gonna give it to the feds?" Tina asked. "Seems like they won't be nobody to prosecute."

"No," I said, slipping it into a pocket. "It would just incriminate Sybil."

"Can't have that now, can we?" She ground out her cigarette. "Come on, Jasper. I've seen enough damn trees to last me a lifetime. 'Bye, Gabe. You ain't been as big a jerk as most men I've known."

She even gave me a brief hug. Then Holt took my hand.

"Gabe, it's been a pleasure. You can work alongside me any day. If you ever decide to go into my line of work, I'll be proud to supply you with references."

"Just call my boss, Jasper."

"Soon's we get to a phone. You watch yourself, now." He got into the Bronco and soon it was a dwindling dot in the distance. I waited around for a while, then went back into the cabin. Sibyl looked up at me, dry-eyed now. Nick Switzer's body lay on the floor, wrapped in a tarp from Holt's Bronco.

"What now?" she said dully.

I sat facing her. "I'll tell you what. Your father is going to be here sometime today. While we're waiting, you can make up a story for him, one that makes you seem as innocent as possible. You're good at that. It won't be hard because he'll want to believe it. Nick taught you how it works, right?" I took the cassette from my pocket and showed it to her. She reached for it but I slipped it back in my pocket again.

"I'm keeping this. If you're good, nobody will ever see it."

"What do you mean?"

"I mean," I said, leaning close until she flinched back, "that when you get home, you are going to go back to your job. You are going to finish grad school. You are going to be Daddy's good little girl. You are going to make him very, very proud. Do you understand?"

She held my gaze for a few seconds, then lowered her eyes. She nodded without making a sound.

It was late afternoon when two big, dark all-terrain vehicles rolled up to the cabin. Randall Carson got out of the lead car, followed by two extremely hard-looking pros. Another brace of pros got out of the second car.

Sibyl rushed past me and threw herself into his arms. "Oh, Daddy! Daddy!"

I paused, took a deep breath and went on. When Randall pried himself from Sibyl's arms he grabbed my hand, tears in his eyes.

"My God, Gabe! You look like hell!"

"It's been a rough few days." Had it been just twelve days since Carson had showed up in Knoxville? It seemed like months. I gave him a heavily edited version of recent events, talked only about the money, didn't mention the tape. "I'm still not sure just what Switzer pulled," I told him. "Sibyl's been pretty upset."

"She'll tell me, Gabe. I won't pressure her, after what she's been through. But she'll tell me."

"Yeah. Well, this is a hell of a mess. Her fingerprints are in that cabin, and so are mine. And in that Blazer back down the road. There's another stiff, by the way."

"We'll take care of everything, Gabe," he said. "Torch the cabin, get rid of the vehicles, and you know nobody's gonna look too hard into the deaths of men like these."

"The one named Martinez bagged Tyler by mistake," I said. "In the cabin there's a couple of pistols that got used. Why not arrange things so it looks like they had a falling out and killed each other? Who knows, maybe it'll do White Front some damage."

"That's how we'll do it." He clapped me on the shoulder. "You just take off and leave the rest of it to us. Take some vacation time. God knows you've earned it."

"Okay," I said. "That sounds good. Maybe I'll drive south, look Connie up. Maybe she'll come around if I act nice."

"That's the stuff, Gabe." He patted me on the back and practically shoved me into my car. "Just drive in our tracks down to the main road. It's clear." I shut the door and he leaned down to talk through the window.

"Gabe, I don't know how to thank you for getting my baby back safe. I owe you a big one."

"No, you don't. It was me that owed you. Let's just say we're even now."

A puzzled look crossed his seamed face. "Whatever you say, Gabe."

I started up my beat-up old car, put it into gear and rolled down toward the mountain road, and from there to Highway 50 and to all the long, desperate highways beyond.